THE RUSSIAN DREAMBOOK
OF COLOR AND FLIGHT

Books by Gina Ochsner

The Russian Dreambook of Color and Flight

The Necessary Grace to Fall

People I Wanted to Be

The Russian Dreambook of Color and Flight

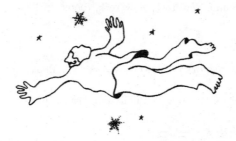

Gina Ochsner

Houghton Mifflin Harcourt

Boston   New York   2010

For information about permission to reproduce selections from this book, write to Permissions, Houghton Mifflin Harcourt Publishing Company, 215 Park Avenue South, New York, New York, 10003.

www.hmhbooks.com

First published in Great Britain in 2009 by Portobello Books Ltd

Library of Congress Cataloging-in-Publication Data is available.

ISBN 978-0-618-56373-9

Printed in the United States of America

DOC 10 9 8 7 6 5 4 3 2 1

For Brian

There is another world, and it is in this one.

— *Paul Elouard*

CHAPTER ONE

Olga

Olga had never been one for numbers, rarely thought in pictures, and couldn't carry a tune to save her soul — had in fact been asked many times to not sing. But as a girl she'd collected languages the same way people collected keys or buttons. At night she dreamt in other languages and she woke in the morning with spoonfuls of those foreign sounds still on her tongue. Her mother, like all mothers did in the '50s, took care to teach Olga to edit her thoughts, to rein in her curiosity so as to keep them from wavering into the dangerous territory of the speculative. But there was no help for it.

'In what language do angels speak?' Olga asked her mother when she was only six. They stood at the river's edge washing laundry. Upriver at the airbase, engineers were testing turbines and across the murky waters at the tank manufacturing plant, loud rumbles shook the ground. It all seemed safe enough to Olga. 'Yiddish,' her mother said without hesitation. But then because the wind had a way of taking voices and putting them in other people's ears, her mother added, 'Please, not another question like that one, not when we are standing in the wide open.'

In those days it was forbidden to bake matzoh, so after prayers, at the time people told stories, Olga's mother put bread out on the east-facing windowsill. The east window some people called the dog window, and so it was for the dogs that Olga thought her mother set the bread. 'No,' her mother said, 'for wisdom.' The bread was an invitation and an appeal to that old woman, who stood on the corner of busy streets, shaking the dust off her skirts. Without her any story would be heard the wrong way, as a jumble of words. 'Listen,' her mother laid her hand on Olga's forehead, the signal for Olga to climb under the covers. Then she told a story, as she did every night, her way of ferrying Olga to sleep.

'One day, in the good times when matzoh still fell from the sky and men lay about up to their elbows in cockroach milk, a few men got a big idea. "Let's build a tower with bricks. Let's build it so tall it pokes a hole in the heavens," they said. "We'll tug on God's ear and make Him explain why — with all our great knowledge — our lives feel meaningless and we are so quickly forgotten."

'This the men of the land said to one another in the single common language that they all knew and shared. Because everybody's sorrow wore the same clothes, knotted and threaded the same way, they all understood what they were working for. But knowing each other so well, never having occasion to misunderstand one another, men in those days were single-minded creatures. They were proud, having forgotten that humility comes with not understanding.'

'And then what?' Olga asked.

'With wind at his fingertips God toppled the tower. It fell into thousands of pieces, and each fallen brick became another heavy language to carry.'

'I don't understand,' Olga said.

'Exactly! The language of man became the language of men, and do you know how many men there are on the land?' Her mother gazed over the top of her glasses at Olga. The answer? Too many to count, and counting lives brought bad luck. At six years of age, already Olga knew this much.

But if all this were meant to discourage Olga from languages, then her mother failed. Miserably. By the time she'd entered the lower grades Olga already had a good working knowledge of written Hebrew – though she made sure to only speak it in whispers, and then only if all the doors and windows were closed. But it was clear to everyone living in their tiny town on the steppe in the way she murmured the positions of stars in Arabic and Greek that Olga was destined for a life in letters.

As a teenager she devoured languages whole the way some people consume entire rounds of cheese, wax rinds and all. 'It'll be heartbreak for you, smart people always suffer at the hands of the stupid, but at least you'll develop your personality, because looks you do not have,' her mother offered by way of encouragement. And her mother was right. Olga was not a great beauty, or even a minor one. But she had a brain in her head. Because of this she was allowed entrance into university where, owing to excessive overcrowding in the dormitories, she shared a room with an Uzbek, a Buryat, a Kumyk, and a Kazakh, each one carrying the smell of wet cotton and cabbage in their hair and dark soil under their fingernails. At night their combined longing for home and the people they'd left behind filled the cramped room in hushed prayers and stinging dreams narrated and translated from one tongue to another. By the end of the first year Olga had picked up their languages and hung them out to dry over the creaking and clanging central heating pipes, which groaned when the early snows fell and sighed all winter long. But in the same way that a great ability can be a terrible curse, the more languages Olga acquired, the more trouble she had articulating her own ideas in any language.

As if knowledge were a deep wound from which she'd spend the rest of her life recovering, everything she had learned at univeristy bit by bit she had begun to forget. Thanks to her many dissertations on linguistics, none of which were approved or published, she had become a permanent invalid, the wisest fool, Ilke – Zvi's mother – said just days before Zvi and Olga's wedding. And yet, by some incredible oversight (had the staffing chief not noticed on her internal passport her line-five classification as Jew? Had the pool of applicants really been so inferior that the local office of such an important newspaper as the *Red Star* found themselves so desperate?), Olga was offered a job at the *Red Star*.

'Oh, take it! Take this job!' Ilke said when Olga delivered

the news all those years ago: she, a Jew with multiple unpublished dissertations, had been hired to translate at what was possibly at that time the most conservative, hard-line, military-propaganda-churning newspaper in the country. 'Take it and don't complain, Olya. What with all this business with Afghanistan and your failed dissertations, you'll not find another job like this one!'

And Ilke was right: nowhere in all of Russia would Olga have encountered a more absurd working arrangement than that of the translation offices of the *Red Star*. For purposes of maintaining mental clarity, Olga had over the years numbered the absurdities.

Absurdity no. 1
Editor-in-Chief Mrosik...

...was rumoured to be lurking about in the building – somewhere – and hard at work. But in the twenty years that Olga had laboured at the *Red Star*, first as an earnest young Soviet of the late seventies, then, after Zvi was called up, as a single mother with a boy to raise, and now as a middle-aged woman (forty-four already!), not once had she ever met Editor-in-Chief Mrosik, whose name appeared in the signature portion of her increasingly meager and rare pay cheques. It was also speculated that when he was either very happy or very unhappy, Editor-in-Chief Mrosik brayed like a donkey, but this, too, Olga had never actually witnessed, though strange trumpeting sometimes did float up through the non-functioning elevator, an old metal cage with a retractable guard arm. Every now and then Olga opened the metal guard and stepped inside the small casket-shaped box, just to see if it might be functioning. As her eyes slowly grew accustomed to the dark, messages scrawled across the walls began to assert themselves: 'This carriage last inspected by #49, 7-OCT-1992,' read one; 'We Can Withstand Anything But Close Scrutiny,' read another. 'Better to Overfart than Underfart Incompletely!' proclaimed another slogan scribbled in orange crayon. But by far the strangest:

Fundamental particle: A particle with no internal substructure. In the standard model the quarks, lepton, photons, muons, W+, W- Bosons are fundamental. All other objects are made from these. It is pointless to ask how.

Olga re-emerged from the non-functioning lift and began the long climb up the steps to the fourth floor. When she reached the translation office, she stood at the threshold, out of breath, her bosom heaving, the straps of her plastic bag – every working woman's purse and briefcase – digging into the flesh of her hands. She was waiting for the jabbing pain behind her ribs to ease into a dull ache. Only then could she start breathing normally. Olga sucked in her stomach and eased her backside onto her metal folding chair stationed behind a small metal desk.

Absurdity no. 2

The desk…

…would be ample, spacious even, if she didn't have to share it with Arkady, who was at this very moment on his hands and knees fumbling with the power cord to the hot plate. For nearly twenty years – Olga sitting on one side and Arkady the other – they had shared bad jokes, flu remedies, family secrets and access to the enormous *Topic Guide*, a bulwark of a book fastened to the centre of the desk by a thick chain. They spent the better part of each day trying not to nudge or bump knees or trample each other's feet. Difficult to do, as Olga, rounded and padded, in every way resembled more and more a matryoshka. Yes, she was fat. And where she had extra padding, Arkady had none. Arkady had the look of a deprived dog, painfully thin, abused by this life and well aware of it. And where Olga had henna-dyed hair, the only colour of dye she could get, Arkady's hair was a dull brick red salted with grey. This hair – curly no less – together with his slightly olive skin tone, was further visual confirmation of Arkady's line-five nationality status of Jew.

The hotplate plugged in and a small kettle balanced on the plate, Arkady – now repositioned behind the desk – passed gas with gusto. For a long time they sat ignoring the robust odour and looking at the large windows that afforded an expansive view of the rolling paper wheels and cutting blades of the newspaper work floor.

'Ach!' Arkady scratched a circular bruise on his forearm that bore the distinct look of a full set of bite marks. He did this, Olga knew, when he was feeling nostalgic and thinking of his wife, who had run off nearly thirty years ago. She woke in the middle of the night and bit Arkady on the arm and in other places unmentionable and then went dashing off – nude – into the forest, where she later contracted rabies and died.

'Oy!' Now Arkady ran his fingers through what remained of his hair.

Olga peered around the *Topic Guide*, a dictionary of military, economic, and ethnic and cultural nomenclature.

'I thought we agreed last week that we wouldn't discuss our family problems,' she said, pushing the Memos that Can't Be Ignored to Arkady's side of the desk. Arkady sniffed and pushed them back. This was part of their daily ritual which over the course of twenty years they had groomed and perfected as a married couple who, so accustomed to one another, had little need to actually speak to one another. The physical arrangement of the office space only reinforced their protracted silences; the super-sized *Topic Guide* created a metre-high barrier between them, while an oversize wire egg basket dangling from the particle board made eye contact almost impossible.

Absurdity no. 3

The wire basket…

…was, according to Arkady, God's way of reminding them to be humble and keep their heads lowered. He said this because by the end of any given day, Olga, in a hurry for the lavs, would stand too quickly and bash her head into the basket at least five times, usually six. For this reason Olga deduced that the basket was Chief Editor Kaminsky's idea of a practical joke. Or perhaps it was the visual representation of a rusty metaphor straining too hard for the literal. The basket, Chief Editor Kaminsky told her all those years ago on her first day of work, had been salvaged from a defunct Kolkoz farm. It was now meant to inspire a sense of nostalgia for all things lost, which included but was not limited to the collective farms and perhaps the memory of the former brilliance of the collective Soviet state. That is to say, a time when the shops had butter and sausage and workers like her had just enough money to buy some of it. Olga could still remember that first day when Chief Editor Kaminsky tapped the basket with his corrector's blue pen. 'This is why *Red Star* workers shouldn't mind working for little or no pay. Sacrifice is the stone that paves the road to glory.' Olga couldn't see the connection between the oversize wire basket and their empty wallets, but Chief Editor Kaminsky seemed untroubled by her confusion. In all honesty, it had been hard enough for her to pay any attention to his words. Everything about Chief Editor Kaminsky's appearance reminded her of an editing sample gone awry. He had two typesetter's bushy insertion marks – sharp mountains – for eyebrows. He was entirely bald except for two long patches of hair – exclamation points – that he tried to subdue with hair dressing. But when he walked the two swatches flopped this way and that. And his eyes! Olga had always believed the tired cliché that the eyes were the window to the soul, an invitation to look and contemplate. But in Chief Editor Kaminsky's mercury-coloured irises, a strange non-reactive colour, Olga could not read a thing.

'Do you see what I mean?' Chief Editor Kaminsky asked, his hands joined behind his back and his pear-shaped body swaying from side to side, his whole body marking the time of his words.

'No. Not at all,' Olga admitted.

Chief Editor Kaminsky smiled. 'You don't understand now,' he rocked on his heels, 'but you will. Later.'

And Olga bobbed her head in assent. It was, perhaps, the longest conversation they'd ever had. And ever since then, each morning, as if by magic, new assignments appeared in the basket which swung, ever so slightly, as if gently pushed by an invisible hand.

The items that found their way to the basket ranged from Letters to the Editor, to soft features like local weather reports and current events (last week she translated the election results of the Magadan Oblast, where a dog had been elected mayor, and from the Amur region, with its sightings of werewolves in nightgowns), to 'work-on-the-left' assignments. The Letters to the Editor, very often discussions of opinions regarding such volatile matters as foreign policy or ethics in time of war, were promptly gathered and trundled off to the women's lavs where they were recycled in a most environmentally sound and utilitarian fashion. That is, they were used for toilet paper. The soft features she and Arkady had permission to translate as transparently as they wished. Harder to handle were the work-on-the-left assignments, which were given, she knew, as a way to generate a little extra money to keep the newspaper afloat in these unbuoyant times. But here again, more absurdity; the translators – that is, Olga and Arkady – never saw a single rouble for all their troubles.

For this reason, when these left-work assignments arrived mysteriously in the egg basket, it was Arkady and Olga's long-established habit to leave them exactly where they lay in the hopes that Editor-in-Chief Mrosik would forget he'd assigned them in the first place. The curled yellowed pages lining the bottom of the basket were, in fact, the text of a children's primer. It had been in the basket for well over a year and Olga knew why: they had been asked to rewrite the history portions so that they more accurately reflected an interpretation of events everyone could more comfortably live with. This, she knew, would involve constant consultation of the massive *Topic Guide*. Every news agency had such a guide, which was really a hernia-inducing dictionary replete with recommendations to the media on how to describe or define various terms. Certain phrases like 'protest demonstrations', 'miners' hunger strike', 'freedom of speech' and 'banking crisis' had no alternate suggestion and therefore were forbidden nomenclature, having been classified as 'Pointless in the context of the editorial mission and policies of a paper such as the *Red Star*.'

Yet in spite of the *Topic Guide*'s conspicuous lapses, they were fortunate, Chief Editor Kaminsky liked to remind them, to have such a guide in the first place.

'How else would we know what to say?' he'd ask with a chuckle. How else would they know, for instance, to rephrase theft of fuel as 'thrift of fuel', Stalin's mass deportations and executions of Jews and Gypsies and other groups of 'rootless cosmopolitans' as 'improving the view', and filtration camps as 'containment resorts'? And without the *Topic Guide*, how else would they know how to navigate words describing the human body, parts and functions – all of which could be for the naturally sensitive Russian embarrassing, indelicate and undignified? How else would they know that urine was water, and blood nothing more than a nutritive fluid? How else would they know to call forced abortions 'necessary interruptions' (though in the case of Gypsy and other women of swarthy complexion, it was called a 'mop-up', the type of which usually resulted in sterilization)? What would they do without these terms tidily rendering innocuous the words that broadcast to the readership the frailties of this life, a reality they were all doing their level best to ignore?

Olga closed her eyes and thrust her hand into the swirl of papers in the basket, feeling for the least offensive one. At last she withdrew a single curled sheet of fax paper.

Nadezhda Radova Vulpin, a chemical engineer
from the Kamchatka region, was charged with

```
disturbing the peace after she slashed part of
the right breast belonging to another woman.
The victim, her sister, Lyuda Radova Vulpin,
retaliated by shearing off a portion of her
older sister's left breast. Back and forth
they went, tit for tat, until both women were
rendered entirely breastless.
```

Fairly painless, as far as translations go, and just the kind of soft feature Chief Editor Kaminsky preferred to run on the front pages so as to dampen the effect of the other bad news. Olga translated the report from Koryak to Russian word by word, only altering the references to body parts while preserving the raw essence of paranoid ethnocentrism: people in the east behaved like animals and should be considered as such. Sadly, in all the offices of the *Red Star* the general feeling was that if it were happening to the people in the east or the south – that is, to the Mongols, the Uzbeks, the Buryats, the Avars, the Chechens, the Laks, the Lezghins, the Kazakhs – then those savages certainly deserved it. Which explains the newspaper's policy of bestowing upon these events an air of the inculpable, the inescapable and thus unavoidable, at all times suggesting that these atrocities had happened to people who in some way asked for it.

Olga dipped her hand into the basket and withdrew another slip of paper. A recent report of anti-Semitism in the oil-rich Nefteyugansk area. Hardly surprising. Olga bit the nib of her pencil and scribbled a draft copy, writing up the incident as a low-grade malaise of ancient origin with a high nationalistic fibre content. The translation completed, Olga rolled the original work order with her rewrite into a tight scroll and slipped it into a bullet-shaped canister that rested in the open mouth of the howling tubes.

Absurdity no. 4
The tubes…

…consisted of a vascular network of transparent pneumatic tubing that snaked the walls then hooked sharply to disappear into the ceiling and floor. The moment either Arkady or Olga finished translating a report they sent both the original and translated version to Chief Editor Kaminsky for verification and approval. But it was hazardous work, retrieving or sending canisters, and Vera, Olga's best friend and senior fact-checker, told Olga about a former translator who had thrust her head in the open canister dock. Her bosom, which was not insubstantial, had been pulled into the dock. It took three men and all their strength to pry the poor woman free. What bothered the woman most was not the indignities to which her body had been subjected, but that she'd lost her brassiere. Even worse, she had been left with bruises in compromising places. And it took some effort on the part of the internal-memo-translation team to render the on-site production trauma sufficiently oblique in writing as to not make the woman the butt of everyone's break-time jokes.

Yes, the tubes were a danger. Olga herself had witnessed the terrifying sucking power of their internal wind and had seen cufflinks and buttons, even the occasional set of dentures, clatter through the pipes, and heard their clacking and rattling against the sides.

She took a breath, held it, then opened the plastic hatch and slid the canister in, one centimetre at a time. The canister trembled, as if it too were afraid. Then it shot up and away through the tubing, through the hole in the office ceiling built specifically for this device. Olga wiggled her fingers, sighed in relief. A good day, all in all, and taking it as a sign, she decided to quit early while she was still ahead.

Through the snow Olga trudged, dimly aware that in faraway places people spoke with purer words of unvarnished meaning. Or maybe not. Maybe at other news agencies in other countries people simply told more palatable lies. And as she rounded the corner and climbed over the remains of the broken stone archway that marked the entrance to the courtyard, she felt despair sliding down her throat, setting up quick residence in her stomach. Language was, after all, just word-shaped stains, simply another way people hide themselves from one another, one more way to evade and obscure the truth.

And then, perched on the roof of their apartment building, was Mircha, a one-armed weathervane leaning into a thin-set snow. 'Truth,' Mircha shook his fist, 'is a whore! And history,' Mircha stopped to point his finger at Olga, 'is giving me indigestion!'

'Mr Aliyev,' Olga said, both a greeting and a dismissal, 'come down from the rooftop. You are drunk.'

'I am fishing,' Mircha pronounced.

Olga surveyed the heap of refuse glistening under a hard drop of frost. Everyone threw their trash out of their windows onto the heap; given the fact that the wind pushed from the east and that the sanitation crews were on perpetual strike, the window-toss method of garbage collection and containment was as efficient as any other. Also, it served as a visual catalogue of items no longer fit for any earthly purpose: rusted cables, engine blocks, even the burnt shell of a PT-76, an amphibious light tank. Balanced on the roof of this tank sat a typewriter minus the strikers and ribbon. And wedged in the typewriter was a fishing rod. Olga pointed to the ungainly pile. 'But your rod is on the heap.'

Mircha leaned over the edge of the roof. 'Where I am going I have no need for such a rod; what I am fishing for requires a much larger hook.'

Olga dismissed Mircha with a single-handed flick of the wrist and began her climb up the stairs to the third floor. At the threshold of the apartment she shared with her son, Yuri, and his semi-permanent girlfriend, Zoya, she stamped her feet and jangled her keys, wordless noise being the best way of alerting them that she was entering.

In the kitchen Yuri sat at the table as he often did these days, swaying slowly from side to side as if in agony. Yuri, Olga knew, was born to suffer and nothing she'd done for him as a child or a man had deterred him from hewing a path through a thicket of sorrow. But she tried to encourage him. She did not pester him about his hobbies, that assortment of fishing flies, wire, paper clips, and goat hair spread across yesterday's copy of the *Red Star* which was in turn spread over the kitchen table. She tried not to mind the fact that Zoya spent much of her time in the kitchen, filing her nails, as she was doing at this very moment.

'Who is making all that noise?' Zoya looked up briefly from her nails.

'Mr Aliyev. On the rooftop again,' Olga said, bending for her jars of schi stacked under the sink. It was extremely rude to point her backside toward Zoya like that, but it was just the kind of mood she was in. Who invited this girl into her apartment? Not Olga, and as the girl had done little to familiarize herself with the kitchen and how to cook or clean in one, she was for Olga simply one more adult-child to care for. Olga emptied the soup into a large pot, slid it onto the ring and waited for it to burn bright red. Now that Sabbath had crept in on the hem of dark, they'd say a prayer, as good Jews should, and eat the soup. And like turning out her pockets by a river, the badness of the days of that week would leave her, if only for a short time. But then the soup heated too quickly in some places, not enough in other. The cabbage despaired in the pot, turning tired and stringy. It was a very bad sign, the soup being life itself. *Cabbage and schi, that's our life.* An old saying she'd learned. She used to know so many more of the sayings, but now they'd flown away from her. And Olga stamped her feet and fumed quietly.

'What the matter, Mother?' Yuri looked up from his fly, which for all the world looked to Olga like a silly wad of ratty hair wrapped around a paper clip.

'Nothing.'

Zoya sniffed mightily in the direction of the pot.

Olga scowled. 'Pay no attention. It's just the soup.'

Yuri swayed on the chair slightly. 'And if it's good...'

'...you don't need anything else in this world or the next,' Olga finished the saying. There. That's what she was trying to remember. Another thing about schi: it's a winter soup. You put it up in summer and let it sour through the autumn. Then in winter, when the stomach turned nostalgic, you ate it, a little at a time, stretching it through the months until May when the first cabbage of the season could be planted. Her mother taught her these things, and told her it was every woman's responsibility to teach at least one other woman how to make it.

But it was so hard to pass on the bits of knowledge, the traditions, to people who did not care to learn them. Olga studied Zoya from the corner of her eye. Yes, the girl was good looking, hair dark as Voronezh soil. But she'd not cultivated in herself any curiosity whatsoever about the past, and little concern for the present. The girl, it seemed, lived entirely for industrial cosmetics. Olga turned back to the pot, quietly muttering her disapproval.

'Why not consult a cookbook?' Zoya tapped a pointed fingernail against the glossy varnish of the wooden table.

Yes, all in all it was a bad day. And now this: opinions. Olga sighed loudly. But Yuri, busy tying flies for an imaginary fishing rod, didn't seem to notice. 'I don't trust cookbooks,' Olga stated.

Zoya started in on another coat of varnish. 'You only say that because you work for a military newspaper. Naturally, then, you are suspicious of all print media.'

Olga clamped her jaw and ground down on the molars. The girl was right. A cookbook was a fantasy, another form of a lie, promising things that could never happen in ordinary kitchens: that an onion sliced a certain way would not weep and neither would the cook who cuts it, that a miracle will boil up from beans if only one remembered to throw off the first three farting waters. But, as any well-seasoned cook knows, the best recipes cannot suffer being placed on permanent record. These recipes, many of them containing guarded family jokes, curses, blessings, and secrets, were never meant to be written, and certainly never meant to be read. This has to be why, Olga deduced, in the steppe culture of displaced Jews, the ultimate insult was to compliment a woman's cooking by asking for a recipe.

The pot boiled over and hissed. 'Too much salt,' Zoya pronounced and Olga shook her head sadly. The second insult was to offer advice in the form of a helpful suggestion. Because soups were like our lives, were like our very selves, they had to be made with a flaw. This is what Olga wished she could teach Zoya. Because only God is perfect and because good Jews like Olga know that until they see God face to face, they can never be perfect, a wise cook deliberately flaws the soup. The imperfection reminds each of them that as they drain that last drop of broth, they take that imperfection – a pinch too much of white pepper, an extra dollop of pickled cabbage, a twinge of the lavender bud – into themselves, a taste on the tongue to remind them that even good things sometimes settle badly.

The simplest of these soups is called the bride's soup, a dish Olga remembered preparing on her wedding day under the watchful eye of Ilke, her soon-to-be mother-in-law. There was Zvi, his best trousers rolled up and the guests standing behind him. Ilke brought in a basin of river water and Olga knelt and washed Zvi's feet. When she'd washed to Ilke's satisfaction, Olga drank the water, drank until she drained even the dirt. For a Jewish wife it has to be this way, taking the dust of the road, of her husband's journey, into herself so that they can carry the road between them. What words? No words, just the dust, the only true element. 'Cry out,' the rabbi canted. 'What shall we cry?' the guests asked. All men are like grass, like the flower that fades. To dust they return. 'It's bitter,' a male guest sang. 'So a kiss to make it sweet,' they all replied. And they kissed. For the first time, Olga with grains of dirt lodged between her molars.

It was just one of the many old steppe traditions that Olga wanted to teach her future daughter-in-law, whoever that might be – but this girl here, dumb as a Tula cookie, simply could not or would not catch on. At this precise moment, for some reason – God only knew why – maybe because her eyes and ears had become well turned for a disaster in progress – Olga looked up. A dark form fell past the kitchen window and landed on the heap with a loud thud.

'Good God!' Yuri jumped from his chair. Olga threw open the window. For a long moment Olga, Yuri and Zoya observed Mircha's broken body, steaming in the snow beside the heap. A disaster all right, and Olga couldn't find the words for it. All the phrases and euphemisms flapped about uselessly, overcoats four sizes too big.

'Go and bring him in,' Olga turned to Yuri at last. 'We'll put him in the bath,' she said, pulling the window closed and drawing the curtain over it.

Having read *The Death of Ivan Ilyich* several times, and being university educated, Olga took Tolstoy quite at his word when he advised keeping death in the living room in order to appreciate life. She just didn't account for Mircha's body bloating so. Normally so small and wiry, it was now at least twice its usual size. And him still missing an arm! It was as if, Olga decided as she poured the last of the three buckets of water over Mircha, that in death God made us larger to give us all a glimpse of how we might become grander in ways we'd never dreamed.

With Yuri's help, Olga repositioned Mircha in the bath. An oddity of the building, this porcelain tub. It had faux gold spigots and claw feet. It was as if the building was so ashamed of its outward appearance, that the building planners, in an attempt to suggest a grandeur of long-gone days, bestowed this strange relic of misplaced opulence. Especially incongruent now, as they had been without running water in the building for over three months.

After towel drying Mircha with a cloth made with no seams or knots, Olga and Yuri dressed him in his military uniform, though already he'd acquired so much gas they could not button the trousers at the waist and they left the service coat open.

Zoya observed their progress from her chair in the kitchen. Occasionally she rose to stir the soup, still simmering on the stove. She pinched her nose. 'Why do we have to lay him out here? He stinks.'

An old and slow-burning irritation flared inside Olga's chest. 'A wife should not have to lay out her husband. We'll do this for Azade and mark my words – she'll thank us for it later.' Olga leaned over Mircha, polished the prized Zhukov medal, brushed the stiff shoulder boards. She made one last adjustment to his collar and then returned to the kitchen for the salt. Olga handed Zoya a small blue bowl filled to the rim with salt. 'Put this on his stomach,' she said.

Zoya brought her hand to her face. 'Oh, no. I'm not touching him.'

Olga sighed. It was the way of these younger girls, she

knew, to turn their noses up at antiquated ideas like duty or compassion. But what are we without our traditions? Olga wanted to ask the girl. Who are we if we will not honour our dead?

Just then Lukeria and her granddaughter, Tanya, pushed through the door. Lukeria wore her second-best dress, the one peppered with the tiny periwinkle- and violet-coloured flowers. She kept her chin tucked to her chest and shuffled towards the bath, ignoring Tanya's attempts to guide her toward a chair. Approaching the tub, Tanya drew the sign of the cross with her forefinger and thumb, and sat in a chair, that tattered notebook pinched between her elbow and her side. A thinker, that one. Given the trouble her own words had been causing her, Olga understood the need to set things down, peg them right and true.

Vitek arrived next, his crow-black hair stiff with shoe polish. He'd slathered thick layers of the blacking on every crease of his leather jacket as well and now that the polish had hardened, Vitek had to walk in a most unnatural way, lest the jacket shatter. Following Vitek was Azade's goat, Koza, and lastly Azade, the widow herself, red in the eyes and looking altogether like a wet newspaper wearing boots. Mircha was no treat to live with – anyone could hear their arguments from the first floor to the fifth, carried through the heating pipes. But Olga understood her tears. Women needed men. What was a woman to do if she fell down some steps and broke her leg? It was only one of the many permutations of fear, that unrelenting contract holding so many unhappy marriages together. Each of them – Olga, Lukeria, and now Azade – had one way or another been left behind. And now Olga knew it was the one thing, this fear, about which they'd never openly talk.

'I'm so very sorry,' Yuri murmured, setting a chair for Azade near the head of the bath. Zoya handed Azade a tissue. Olga brought more chairs in and placed a large chunk of ice in Mircha's outstretched hand. At such occasions it was customary to gather around and think of complimentary things to say about the dead until the ice melted, the signal that they could begin long rounds of toasting.

Five minutes passed, then ten. Drops of water pooled on the floor beneath Mircha's hand, and still no one said a word. The man had loved the bottle. He said strange things. He believed absolutely that all the transcaucasus people – Laks, Avars, Circassians – mountain people at heart – should unite and secede from Russia. Steppe Jews like Olga, who could be more mountainly in their thinking if they tried a little harder, could possibly be grandfathered into the cause. 'Just think – a free state for all of us misfitted types. Free and autonomous. After all, who can deny that Russia has been and will always be a mother to some and a stepmother to others? This is the only solution really, and I can be president. And you, Olga, you can be my secretary.' All this he had said just days before he leapt from the roof.

Olga scooted her chair a little closer to the bath, adjusted a stray strand of Mircha's silver hair. Now just what had changed, what unexpected reconfiguration occurred in his thoughts so that jumping from their roof was the only acceptable solution? When a man loses his dream, he ceases to be a man, he ceases to be alive. Now wasn't it Mircha who said that to her Yuri once? Olga wagged her head back and forth and made her signature sad clucking sounds.

Finally, the last bit of the ice melted. The vodka had grown warm where she'd been holding the bottle next to her body. Olga cleared her throat. 'He was a good man in a tangential way. You could feel that behind the vitriol, the bile, and rage, really he meant well.'

Another long moment of protracted silence, and then Yuri coughed. 'He was in terrible agony,' he said. Yuri touched Mircha's creased forehead, the source of so many of Mircha's agonies.

'He might have jumped sooner,' Vitek stuffed his hands into his coat pockets. 'But at least he did it.'

'He always was one for grand gestures,' Lukeria added.

'A mule among stallions,' Azade whispered.

Olga filled everyone's glasses. 'Well, that's that and God rest him, he's settled now and at peace.' Olga raised her glass and they all swallowed.

'He was never a good-looking man,' Zoya started off.

'But God rest him, he's got both arms and legs now,' Tanya replied, her open notebook balanced on her lap.

'And may he have better boots for longer journeys.' Azade raised her glass.

'And may he teach the angels how to fish the glass sea,' Yuri said, bringing his sleeve to his nose.

And then they grew quiet again, thinking.

'It is just me, or is the stink in here worse than ever?' Lukeria said suddenly.

'The soup!' Olga cried, rushing for the kitchen.

'What I don't understand,' Zoya turned to Yuri, 'is how a Sabbath soup can double for a funeral soup.' Now Zoya turned to Tanya. 'You should write that down in your notebook.'

Vitek leaned toward Tanya. 'Zhirinovsky will save the country. Write that down in your notebook.'

'Please.' Tanya, overwhelmed by the combined odours of Vitek's breath and Mircha's body, waved her hand near her nose. 'There's a man dead here.'

'Zhirinovsky is an idiot. He sleeps with a pogo stick,' Yuri said.

'Please.' Olga returned with the tureen of soup, set it down on the table with a loud thunk. 'There are women here. Jews.'

'Zhirinovsky is a Jew.' Vitek smiled broadly.

'He's a madman,' Zoya said.

'He's inspired,' Vitek said.

'The things people like him call people like us.' Olga looked at Zoya, who looked at Yuri. Olga distributed the bowls, the bright orange ones with the white polka dots.

'Zhids,' Yuri wagged his head from side to side.

'Kikes,' Azade said.

'Dogs,' Tanya whispered.

'Swine,' Lukeria said nostalgically.

'Rodents and murderers,' Vitek sang.

'Well, thank heavens nobody thinks like that anymore,' Yuri said, his voice bright.

At this the room fell silent. Unnaturally silent. Olga saw that Yuri's ears were beetroot red and she knew he was not altogether the child that he so often pretended to be.

'Let's eat,' Olga said and they dragged their chairs to the other side of the room, where she ladled out the soup and they fell to eating in silence. After each mouthful of soup Azade licked the spoon, tucked it into her left boot and pulled a different spoon from her right boot. On this went until Azade had gone through at least twenty spoons and the sheer wonder and excess of it mesmerized Olga, who could not take her eyes off the woman.

'It must be a Gypsy thing,' Lukeria whispered in a voice so loud that everyone could hear her plainly.

'Avar,' Tanya whispered back. 'I think she's Avar or perhaps Lezghin.'

'Well, whatever she is, clearly she's quite mad with grief.' Lukeria paused for a split second and then added as if as an afterthought, 'This soup, it's got a distinct something about it.'

Zoya hooked her chin toward Olga. 'That's because she burned it.'

'In that case,' Lukeria stood slowly and patted her busy print dress into place, 'I won't ask for the recipe.' Lukeria turned to Tanya. 'Let's go. The smell in here is slapping me in the face.'

At that very moment Vitek's pager bleated. 'Big bizness,' he said with a smile, his gold tooth winking. Vitek pushed himself up from the chair with his legs, the whole time keeping his torso straight and level. Still his jacket creaked and complained. He tucked the opened bottle of vodka into his waistband and followed Lukeria and Tanya out the door. The goat trailed at his heels, its thick hooves thudding over the floor.

Azade stood to her feet. She bent over Mircha and looked at him with suspicion. 'Well,' she turned to Olga. 'I better get back to work.' And she shuffled out the door.

Strange, Olga thought as she watched the door fall back into its locks. Strange how they all couldn't help but be ugly at a time when people usually try to offer their best, if only to prove to each other for a short time that they can rise above themselves. It felt strange to recognize that sometimes death did not bring people together, but provided instead one more reason to further the distance between them. It was like digging through her secret stash of socks and boiled sweets only to discover that she'd come up short. That's how she felt: cheated somehow.

And she missed Zvi. Looking at Mircha, dressed in his uniform and stretched over the bath and so still, it was hard not to look at him and think of Zvi. Hard not to wonder what had become of him. She wasn't so lost in her old grief to forget that there were thousands like her in apartment buildings everywhere quietly wondering if their husbands or brothers or sons would miraculously appear. Called out of the dust, from the air, they would somehow be spirited to their doors and they would knock. Weary from their years-long journey they would be faint, tired – but alive. Marvellously alive. Although she knew from her many years at the *Red Star* where she examined so many reports to the contrary that this wouldn't happen, Olga liked to imagine that it could. Without a dream we are dead. Now she remembered, now she knew who said that. Not Mircha, but Zvi. In his service uniform, one of the last things, in fact, that he had said. And the gummy notion that there must be a vital clue in that bit of advice, something essential that she should have decoded by now, something she'd missed that would tell her how better to live, stuck to her like a bathhouse leaf.

Zoya and Yuri had already retired behind their shared privacy curtain, an intricate arrangement of tablecloths and sheets hung over fishing wire. Olga pulled a sheet over Mircha and blew out the candle. In the morning she would think about what to do with his body. But today, she'd had enough trouble. She gathered the bowls and carried them back to the kitchen, where she filled the sink with a little soap and some water from the kettle. It wasn't fair, this life. All these years Azade stuck with a husband she didn't want and Olga longing for Zvi, whom she did want. It was wrong to be bitter, she knew, but a person can't help feeling the way she does. Olga reached for a bowl. It slid from her hand and dashed against the sink, breaking to shards and cutting her palms.

She leaned her elbows over the sink. The tears were there,

she was just that angry and beaten, but on days like these even crying required too much effort. Olga straightened, wrapped her hand in a dishcloth and crossed the darkened room, feeling her way through the strung sheets for her bed. She unbuttoned her sweater and her housedress, and hung them in the tall wardrobe. Lined her slippers carefully at the side of her bed. Then she lay on the mattress and listened to the sounds of her neighbours around her carrying on with their nightly business. Lukeria's heavy breathing rose up through the air vents and from the courtyard she could hear Vitek serenading the moon. Here, inside the apartment from behind the privacy curtains, Zoya and Yuri churned through separate dreams, Zoya murmuring her disapproval, while Yuri called out the names of rivers and the beautiful names of the beautiful fish that swam in them.

Olga's eyes watered. She was lonely. Even in the presence of all these people, all this life, she felt unbearably alone. She passed her hand over her eyes, pinched the bridge of her nose and sighed. Then she felt her blood turn to ice. Perhaps it was a trick of light, her eyes conspiring to organize the dust and grit in the air into strange shapes, but as she stared across the room she swore she was seeing the shape of a man backlit by the light of the moon filtering through the window.

'Zvi?' Olga called as she jumped from her bed, but then he was gone.

CHAPTER TWO

Tanya

There are three secrets at the All-Russia All-Cosmopolitan Museum of Art, Geology and Anthropology. The first is that none of the exhibits are authentic. Not a single gessoed canvas, splotch of oil paint, stick of furniture or beaten metal icon is genuine. Everything inside the museum is a replica. Some of the items are replicas of replicas. That is why, where one might expect stern old women ensconced in wooden chairs and strategically positioned in each exhibit hall, there are none. Why no dehumidifiers, no fans circulating the air in the summer. Why the locking mechanisms on windows and doors have been allowed to gather rust. It is also why the entrance fee is so modest, it explains the second big secret. Out of the six full-time museum employees – Tanya in coat check, old Ludmilla at the ticket counter, Zoya and Yuri as guides – only Head Administrator Chumak, who is, of course, the head administrator, and Daniilov, the caretaker, have been paid in the last three months. This, in turn, explains the third secret, which is a secret not because it's so shocking, but because no one is openly discussing it: the museum toilets. A principal part of the employee benefit package is the free use of the lavs, for as long as they like, as frequently as they like. This explained why Tanya, Yuri, Zoya and perhaps Ludmilla kept working at the museum on Head Administrator Chumak's promise that they would some day (and soon) be paid. The toilets, state of the art and of Finnish design, shone of polished chrome and sleek porcelain. And when you don't live in apartments with running water – Tanya, Zoya and Yuri, and possibly Ludmilla, do not – the importance of the benefits package swells.

Which explains why Tanya patiently put up with her humiliating demotion from the elevated position of museum tour guide to that of basement hat/coat-check attendant. Even so, the All-Russia All-Cosmopolitan Museum was still Tanya's life, the ever-shifting canvas of her love story. And while it was true that the exhibits in the museum disappointed – especially the geological display in the basement which consisted of four rocks, three of which Tanya was fairly certain Head Administrator Chumak supplied himself and which looked suspiciously like Violet Crumble chocolate bars, Tanya found herself unable to stop dreaming of upward movement, both in terms of career advancement and also of her actual geographic position. Which explained why Tanya (though she had been made by Head Administrator Chumak to understand the terrible gravity of minding the claim disks, of minding the wooden racks which contained hats and sweaters and satchels that weighed more than any bag ever should) sat in her fold-out chair, her sky-colour notebook open in her lap.

A whole summer Tanya had sat in this cloakroom, carefully inventorying every rain jacket and umbrella, scarf and satchel, lest she make a mistake. She lovingly itemized and described in great detail their fabrics and textures, even going so far as to describe their owners, their bright chatter in exotic and sometimes ordinary languages. But blame it on boredom. Or maybe it was on account of the dim lighting of the museum's underbelly. But always her gaze drifted to the window that ran high and narrow along the upper portion of the basement wall. Framed inside this long box of light, every moment of every day a dance unfolded bolt by feather, and never the same way twice.

But now summer had gone, the doughy cumulus clouds that rose steadily like good piroshki had drifted away and autumn had brought herring-scaled skies. This very morning they'd had their first hard frost. Outside the narrow basement window the clouds congealed like the winter soups with skins so thick the grandmothers could skate over them. By midday the clouds would take on the look of buckwheat porridge, the mere thought of which always wheeled Tanya back to child-hood, to sitting at the steamer trunk that doubled as her grandmother's kitchen table and TV stand. Every morning before school Tanya bolted down the kasha, fishing with the spoon for the small dollop of butter. That lump of yellow was the sun, the brightest and best part of the bowl, the bit of fat that gave the kasha any flavour whatsoever.

Tanya's stomach grumbled. This soup and kasha stuff, it

wasn't healthy thinking. Not if you were trying to reduce, as Tanya was trying to. All this for a bid to work for Aeroflot, which was hiring flight crew for the riskier southern and eastern routes like the Perm–Krasnodar and Perm–Vladivostok, the same routes younger, better-looking girls with brighter prospects were now giving up. Imagine – trading the dim belly of the museum for the sharp and vertical blues of sky! Imagine – exchanging her sensible shoes for high-heeled pumps and skating on a silver sea of clouds! 'Imagine!' Head Recruiter Aitmotova, a tiny woman with platinum-blonde hair and highly parabolic eyebrows, said a few weeks ago when Tanya meekly eyed the bright glossies and applica-tion form. 'Down-at-heel Aeroflot is renovating its entire fleet.' Head Recruiter Aitmotova shoved an application form into Tanya's hand and plied Tanya with figures, facts and stories of workers repairing cracked wings and faulty electrical circuits. Gone the old colours, gone the bland white bellies and baby-blue wings, for the crisper, brisker blues and oranges. Gone the traditional meal service, which began and ended with a single cup of water and a wet wipe. And gone their old slogan: 'We don't smile, because we're serious about making you happy.'

As Head Recruiter Aitmotova talked and talked, Tanya shifted her weight from one foot to the other. Living as she did so near a newspaper translator, she had learned through the thinness of the walls and the conductive nature of the open heating pipes a few things. Facts. Aeroflot had earned a long and thoroughly established reputation of aviation disaster, planes dropping right and left out of the sky to land in the great boggy flats of Siberia.

Head Recruiter Aitmotova raised her hand slowly and nodded knowingly. 'You are wondering about safety. Everybody does at some point. And I can assure you that even now our very own Aviamotor mechanics are working around the clock to overhaul the old engines. Moreover, engineers have installed black boxes so that if — and this is highly conjectural — a plane should fall, investigators will know why.' Head Recruiter Aitmotova smiled. 'It's progress; you can't stand in the way of it.'

All this the woman had said in a rolling cadence that itself could not be stopped, not by Tanya's quiet doubt, low self-esteem or complete lack of funds. 'Just fill in the application form, dear,' Head Recruiter Aitmotova said, a benediction of practical measures. 'Be focused on your dreams. And lose some weight.'

Dream. She could do that. Staring out the narrow window, Tanya imagined the taste of cloud, swallowing every fluffy hope, consuming and digesting and rising, rising beyond body, beyond reason. Her trouble: she did not yet possess a fully inflatable super-buoyant self-esteem. A theme song would help. Supersonic anti-gravity jump boots. Coiled springs. Wax wings. A flight manual. But she was straying off-topic: a bad habit of hers and the reason why she'd been demoted from guided tours in the first place.

She blamed her sudden deflated status on the oversized painting of Yermak Timofeyevich in the blue room. Who could think straight with that madman foraging across the thick layers of cheap industrial-grade paint? Heavy with winter blues, browns, and flat winter light, Yermak leads a band of Cossacks through a river. They are hacking their way through the line of Tatar defenders. The long creases on his forehead suggest a lifetime of weariness, of hunger, but the look in his eye is of wild joy. All this in spite of the heavy armour he wears – a gift from the mad Tsar. Would he have still worn that armour if he had known that some day its weight would drag him to the bottom of a river? Is he pleased to know that even now on certain days columns of fire shoot out of the river at the very spot his bones are pinned to the riverbed? These were the questions Tanya made the mistake of voicing aloud. And in front of a group of schoolchildren.

This must be why the painting of Yermak was so big, she'd told the children. Yermak was larger than life, daily fighting death in that large river that flowed out the bottom border, as if to show no mere frame could ever contain him. Yes, it was a big painting. Beyond big, the canvas was an immensity. It filled an entire wall in the museum. If it were to fall, if those hooks and cables were to fail, the weight of the painting would surely pull down the wall to the waxed floor. The toppling wall would set off a chain reaction, she speculated aloud, and as each wall fell, room by room, the upper stories would collapse like an accordion folding upon the lower storeys. Yermak would drag down the entire museum all the way to the basement, burying them all.

Naturally, there were complaints. She was demoted. Her embarrassment, colossal. Worse, sitting in the basement next to boxes of rocks and other curiosities put her no closer to Yuri than before, but rather much further away. And this is what hurt her most. She, a girl made of water and air and breath, she a girl who had swallowed cloud and was now more vapour and spirit than girl, was stuck in the underlit bowels of the stagnant museum at the very bottom of the bottom of the ocean of air.

Yuri's voice and that of Zoya's, Tanya's replacement, floated down opposite sets of stairs, Yuri's from the west wing and Zoya's from the east. Even separated, through the acoustic anomalies of the All-Russia All-Cosmopolitan Museum, they managed to find each other, their words falling to the lowest point of the building, settling in the wells of Tanya's ears: Zoya discussing in her bored monotone the icons of Saints Boris and Gleb, while Yuri fielded questions from the purple room where the two pictures of Yermak opening the Siberian interior hung.

'Why does Yermak look so rabid?' The question tumbled down the staircase and fell loudly at Tanya's feet.

'Well,' Yuri coughed politely, 'he was a known river pirate. Ivan the Terrible hired him to go and act crazy in a grand proportion, an ability so natural to Cossacks, it seems a genetic certainty.'

A true interpretation. But risky. It was OK to criticize dead people, but not overly famous ones. Having spent the better part of a summer in the basement, Tanya ought to know. She studied the window, the particulate texture of lowering frost mixed with the grit and pollution. This time of year the rose and lavenders of the grainy air looked like a picture of a famous painting she'd seen in a book somewhere. Viewed up close, there were nothing but dots, hundreds upon hundreds of dots. But seen from a distance, out of the haze of dots a rolling green and a river, and a child and a woman with a red parasol slowly emerged. He must have lived in a very dirty world, that painter. But he found a way, with the point of his paintbrush and unbounded human patience, to render it beautiful. Tanya narrowed her eyes at the grainy block of sky framed in the window. Dots upon dots. She squeezed her eyes closed, then opened them suddenly. Alas, just dots. Tanya sighed. Flipped through her notebook. Took consolation in an old scribble:

Violet in early November, shirring the sightline. Day and night meet in that hue for five minutes. With their barks the dogs in their courtyards measure the lengths of their chains. Outside the city the hills burn with trash fires and the smell of outdoors creeps indoors. This is the smell of the service coat, the one you were wearing when you came home. The patch with your name burned to a crisp and you asked me if I could tell you who you were.

Had she remained more alert she might have detected the sounds of umbrellas scraping the walls as the students from number 37 came bursting through the lower entrance of the museum and filed past the ticket-counter kassa, where phlegmatic Ludmilla slid their tickets under a window. Then she might have heard their stamping and tromping of their many boots and galoshes, the thump of book bags unstrapped and dumped on the long wooden counter that separated her world from theirs.

At the same instant that the children of number 37, in a wave of human noise and coats, pressed against her counter, Yuri's group of tourists – all fifteen of them – descended from the stairs that funnelled past the lavs and deposited them directly in front of Tanya's counter.

'Wake up!' a teacher barked, her brows stitched together in permanent disapproval.

'*Devushka!*' another woman shouted with the too-stern tone of a teacher. Tanya jolted and her notebook slid from her lap to the floor. Strange how with the simple word 'girl!' her body snapped to the posture of primary school, her legs lifting her up and out of the chair, though her ears knew already from the sound of the woman's voice that it was too late – she had already failed.

'Hey!' Two men in suits, regulars who only came to the

museum on account of the chess sets in the mezzanine café, waved their claim disks at her.

'Please!' a woman shepherding two humpbacked pensioners cried. Adding to the bleating of the women was the din of the children, elbowing one another, jockeying for counter space, enthralled at the spectacle of noise.

At the end of the hallway, Head Administrator Chumak materialized, a severe expression gathering on his face, his clip-board pressed to his side – the result being that Tanya, who tended to fluster easily anyway, went completely off the rails, handing the contents of rack 1131 to the holder of disk 1311 and the overcoat with the drooping buttons, 1717, to the bearer of disk 1771. To the businessman went the woman's shawl and to the wilting attendant of the old ladies, the most businesslike worsted wool coat. And on and on until the crush of human bodies, coats and noise dissipated and Tanya was left with Yuri, standing at the foot of the stairs and systematically wringing his hands. Next to him, shifting his substantial weight from his good foot to his leaden prosthetic foot, was Head Admin-istrator Chumak.

Head Administrator Chumak studied her for a long moment. Then he began – *thump–slide, thump–slide* – to climb the stairs. 'Follow me,' he called over his shoulder.

Tanya collected her purse, her notebook, her coat, the packets of sugar she'd taken from the café, everything she'd need and pos-sibly would not be allowed later to retrieve once he'd fired her.

Inside Head Administrator Chumak's office the interior

gloom dampened the attempts of the last light at the windows. Tanya stood at the threshold and waited for Head Administrator Chumak to position himself with dignity behind his desk. He snapped on his desk lamp. From behind the desk loomed a tall soap carving of a frowning Zhilinsky, a painter Tanya had never liked.

'Sit down there, dear.' Head Administrator Chumak's face softened and Tanya noticed for the first time that the splotches dotting his shiny head were, in actual fact, freckles.

Chumak opened her work file. 'I see you've completed university studies and received some medium-high marks.'

'Yes, sir.'

'You have guide licences for several state museums and even a cemetery.'

Head Administrator Chumak nodded at her notebook, still clutched to her side. 'And clearly you've found a way to use your free time. But, I'm afraid it's a black mark for you. Your job performance is not up to standard. Did you know that in one day alone you made seventeen mistakes?'

Tanya glanced at the window and bit her lip. In the newspapers – well, not Olga's *Red Star*, but the others – they were predicting the coldest winter on record. Already geometric patterns of hoar frost latticed Chumak's office window.

Head Administrator Chumak rubbed his hands together and nodded at the miniature rock collection already shrouded in condensation. 'This museum. These exhibits. They are absolutely unique.'

Tanya nodded solemnly. Having fashioned from stretchy foam the entire basement Kuntskamera exhibit and having spent the better part of the previous spring dipping wrinkled paper bags in wet flour paste to make faux-sculptures, no one knew this better than Tanya.

'It's so hard these days to run a museum such as this one funded completely by the kindness of friends and strangers. And employees.' Head Administrator Chumak wagged his head balefully from side to side. 'That's why we all have to work much much harder. That's why I need much much more from you.'

'More?' Tanya croaked.

'But at least we have art and beauty on our side.' Chumak directed his gaze at Tanya. 'At least there are people who still believe in beauty, such as it is. And they are even willing to pay for it, too.'

'What people?'

Head Administrator Chumak opened another work file and withdrew a single sheet of paper. He smiled beatifically. 'Americans of Russian Extraction for the Causes of Beautification. They are coming here. Possibly. Maybe. Yes, here.' Head Administrator Chumak peered at Tanya.

'Why?'

The question pushed Head Administrator Chumak's entire face into a pinch. He reached for his reading glasses and read from an official-looking letter printed on fine linen paper. '"The Americans of Russian Extraction for the Causes of

Beautification are committed to preserving, protecting and promoting art among the people. Specifically we believe in the power of art to motivate, educate and illuminate the human soul. It is a challenge we wish to embrace with a deserving partner museum in Russia."

'Do you understand what this means?'

Tanya suddenly felt as if her teeth had turned to glass. 'Motivate' and 'challenge' were English words having no direct or at least relevant translation into Russian. Certainly Head Administrator Chumak knew that she, given her medium-high marks in school, knew this. 'This means that I should not mix up their coats and claim disks when they come?' Tanya asked carefully.

'Yes,' Head Administrator Chumak drew the word out. 'But there's more. We need to submit a completed application form, which incidentally requires composition-style answers. All we have to do is beat out four – maybe five – other museums for their grant money. But am I worried? No. And why am I so untroubled?'

'I don't know, sir.' There was something about the even cadence gluing his words together, uncannily similar to her own scripted question-answer patter, that made Tanya very uneasy.

Head Administrator Chumak handed Tanya the file. 'Because you, Tatiana Nikolaevna Bobkov, are a girl of enormous substance.' Head Administrator Chumak laced his fingers together and circled one thumb around the other. It was a completely unnerving gesture from a man himself so portly.

'But, sir, I am the hat/coat-check girl. If I'm not fit to lead the tours, how could I be qualified to fill in the application form?'

Head Administrator Chumak's smile broadened. 'That's why I know you can pull this off – you ask the most interesting questions. And if you can manage questions so creatively, I can't wait to see how you'll handle the answers.'

'But...'

Head Administrator Chumak held up his hands. 'I can't ask Daniilov, anyway, he's far too busy cleaning. It's all Ludmilla can do to sit behind the ticket office. Zoya, though artistic in her own fashion, is limited to a discussion of art as it pertains to hair styling. And Yuri, well, he's Yuri. So you see, it has to be you. And if you do a good job, I might even be able to do something about those black marks on your work record. If we get the grant, I could even get your wages caught up. Just think how all of our situations would improve. So be creative,' Head Administrator Chumak finished with a knowing wink, 'but not too creative.' He slid the thick manila envelope across the desk. Then he laced his fingers over his chest, tipped back in his chair and closed his eyes.

Tanya wedged the file into her plastic shopping bag, tiptoed to the door, and stepped into the hallway. Before the door had fallen back into its lock, Head Administrator Chumak was already sound asleep and snoring.

✳

Outside, darkness settled on rooftops, gathered in corners. The sodium streetlamps cast a sullen orange haze in the frost-filled air. Tanya stepped around the potholes and asphalt gashes trembling with antifreeze and hurried toward the bus station, a long stretch of sidewalk that disappeared beneath a shelter of tarps and construction scaffolding. Beneath the makeshift awning, kiosks stretched from one end of the platform to the other selling anything from dried fish to hosiery to pirated CDs. Music blared from competing kiosks and, of course, the veterans, pensioners, lame, drunk, and holy stood at either entrance, their cups, caps, or hands held ready. A veteran, too young to have fought in the Great Patriotic War and too old to have done any time on the Chechen fronts, sat in a wheelchair, his service cap balanced on his one remaining leg. Beside him stood a double-sided wooden advertisement.

Calling all Casanovas! Would you like to have biceps every woman from Moscow to Vladivostok will caress with her appreciative glances? Call now for 3.5 kg weights for arms. Ask for Sergei. Speak loudly: the phone is hard of hearing.

On the reverse side, the advertisement was much more to the point:

Ladies: find your rich western prince here. Hurry.

It was considered uncouth to say so in public, but the highest aspiration for many girls since the Soviet Union dissolved was to find a 'sponsor', the richer the better. But when the services screened the female applicants, they were not looking for girls like her. Like everything else in this world, beauty was a test and Tanya knew with a single glance in a mirror whether she was a pass or fail.

The number 77 arrived with a push of wind. The doors hissed open and Tanya allowed herself to be herded inside with the crush of people and their briefcases, newspapers, umbrellas, and many plastic bags full of kiosk purchases. Ordinarily Yuri and Zoya stood beside her and held hands. But her meeting with Head Administrator Chumak had run her just late enough that instead of Yuri and Zoya, a woman of indeterminate age stood behind her, her bosom jostling against Tanya's back. The woman's perfume, though applied generously, failed to mask her powerful female smell. In front of Tanya stood a short man wearing a winter hat, a cheap knock-off meant to resemble an astrakhan. He kept one arm braced against a metal support and clutched in his other arm a fish wrapped in newspaper, the oil of which dripped onto her shoes.

The bus lurched down the street, careened into turns. With so many people crammed together, the air grew thick and the windows slick with condensation. Tanya squeezed toward a window and rubbed a circle clear with her glove. Travelling silently beside them was a trolleybus. Behind the window panes were the tired figures of people just like Tanya and the fragrant woman behind Tanya and the man in front of Tanya.

But the windows were weeping so thoroughly that the faces of the people in the trolleybus were smears, featureless prototypes of people. Disfigured as they were by glass, water, frost, and darkness, they were like unfinished sculptures recently erased and waiting to be rewritten. Above the trolley in the intricate wire webbing blue sparks popped and flashed and then the trolleybus veered away. The bus bumped along in darkness and hissed to a stop. Once again the press of bodies jostling and jiggling behind and around her propelled Tanya through the open doors to the concrete platform. Then, and only then, did she feel her chest loosen, her breath return.

She always felt as if she'd been given her life back and this sensation made her giddy and generous. Each day she'd see the boy with the burnt face sitting on a folding chair, a black violin case open at his feet. Each day she'd deposit five kopeks into that case lined with the same thin purple velour they used for children's caskets. And each day, she'd turn her horizontal gaze from the bright purple cloth to a vertical gaze of the winter sky where evening folded down one bolt at a time, each one deeper than the next. Though it was unwise to stop on a street at twilight, Tanya allowed herself the briefest of scribbles:

Overhead a Norilsk purple (a purple, incidentally nowhere to be found at the All-Russia All-

Cosmopolitan Museum), a hue that reflects the ice of the uplands, the place you said your grandfather worked to his death. Above those mines the clouds duplicate the gouges of the ice. The clouds mirror the dark patches of water and leads, the dark oily breaks. This map reflected on the belly of cloud is called the ice blink and in it people read above them how the land and water stretches before them. The point of the story, you told me, was that even in the black gut of a nickel mine, where a man knows he will never leave, he can take a walk in the clouds.

Tanya slid her notebook back into her plastic bag. She scurried under the almost-fallen-over archway that marked the opening to the courtyard that fronted the apartment building where she lived. Yellow tape surrounded the building and fringed the courtyard. Though the building had been scheduled for a pull-down years ago, the yellow tape and sagging structural conditions hadn't inspired any of the residents, herself included, to move. Tanya picked her way through the dvor, a decrepit courtyard of broken concrete slabs and tired rose bushes gone to hips. Grass bleached to the colour of an old wooden spoon grew waist high around the jagged slabs. At the far edge of the courtyard loomed the shabby five-storey apartment building, affectionately known as a *Krushchoba*, a Krushchev-inspired slum. Nothing but mice and other small animals inhabited the first floor. Azade, the caretaker of the courtyard, and Vitek, her adult son, occupied a few rooms on the second floor. At the opposite end of the building and three floors up, two windows glowed with light. It was Saturday, still the Sabbath, and Olga's curtains were still drawn. Not to be outdone, Tanya's grandmother, Lukeria, had raised her window shade and set her Vespers candle on the windowsill of their fourth-floor apartment. Only Mircha, before his leap from the roof, had lived on the fifth floor and this because, she knew, it was the furthest he could get from his wife, Azade, and Vitek.

From behind the huge mound of metal scrap and potato peelings came the sound of whispering. Then a pebble flew past Tanya's knee. Tanya picked up a small concrete chunk and lobbed it over the mound, where it landed with a thud against some scrap. No, you couldn't be too careful around the young people these days. Take these kids, for instance, street kids. It was their bad luck that of all the buildings and courtyards they could have chosen to set up residence in, they picked this one where the toilets didn't work, the apartments had no heat and the tenants had no heart. Their bad luck that Vitek, their self-appointed sponsor, was teaching them the multifaceted arts of begging and stealing, drinking and glue-sniffing. And Tanya felt sorry for them. They were like those dog-children from the old stories who needed a mother to call them by the right name. Then they would remember their true selves and how to act like children. She would gladly take care of them – all five of them. If only they would stop throwing rocks.

As if on cue, Vitek unpeeled himself from the shadows. Like the Devil in church, he was uncomfortable in his own skin but tried valiantly to hide the fact. He smiled at Tanya and his gold tooth gleamed.

'I'm sorry about your, well, you know,' Tanya said. It had only been seven days since the wake and it was the orthodox way to refrain from a direct mention of the name of the dead until they'd been gone for a full nine days.

Vitek shrugged and withdrew a vial from his coat pocket. 'Have a gargle?' Marsh Lilac, a cheap perfume with a high alcohol content.

Tanya wrinkled her nose.

Vitek slid the vial back into his coat. 'In that case, I'll come to the point quickly, and incidentally,' Vitek pulled at a greasy forelock, 'I beg your pardon for bringing up the indelicate matter of money.'

Tanya glanced at the city inspector's yellow line of tape. 'You can't collect rent on a condemned building.'

'You aren't supposed to be living in a condemned building.' Vitek shrugged. 'You see the difficult position I'm in.'

'But you live in this building, too. So does your mother.'

'It's a complication, all right.' Vitek smiled.

Lukeria threw open a window. 'Autocracy! Nationality! Orthodoxy!' she shouted, her voice as subtle as a poke in the eye. It was an old saying, something Lukeria liked to shout whenever she saw Tanya talking to anyone she considered suspicious, a saying that marked Lukeria as completely anti-cosmopolitan in her leanings. Which was to say, Lukeria didn't like Jews, Gypsies, Asians, or anyone not personally known to her for less than forty years. Which was to say, living in this building with Yuri and Olga, Jews both, Azade and Mircha, Muslims railed in from the Caucasus, and Vitek, whose facial features hinted at Mongol inclinations, Lukeria was completely friendless.

Vitek rolled his eyes toward the windows and snorted. 'We all have to listen to that, you know.'

Tanya pressed her mouth into a flat line, handed over a crumpled ten-rouble note, and turned for the stairs. The problem with her grandmother was that she sincerely believed that if orthodoxy should ever fall, the world would collapse with it, that it was the secret reservoir of the faithful that had kept the heart of Mother Russia beating during all these troubled years. And according to Lukeria, it was an orthodox sun that shone quietly over their cold land, an orthodox light that provided the necessary illumination to properly see this world by, though most people did not even know it.

But on evenings like these, Tanya wished her grandmother would progress with the times. They were, after all, new Russians, no matter what the red-browns and other reactionaries were saying. All you had to do was look around and you could see times had changed and in ways none of them had ever imagined. Now a hundred grams of cheese cost fifty roubles instead of ten. The rise and fall of inflation could be tracked in the price of chewing gum and chocolates, the morale of the country measured by the price of vodka, which was never more than the price of bread. And where old pensioners like Mircha and her grandmother once could count on a monthly salary, it was now up to the new Russians like Tanya, who made less than the workers at the western-style coffee shops, to look after their own. No wonder her grandmother was so nostalgic for the past.

'Doors!' Lukeria shouted from her perch at the window. It was an orthodox greeting meant to hurry Tanya from the corridor lest the Devil come in on a draught and blow out the candle.

Tanya scuttled into the apartment. She kicked her boots off, and looped her scarf and her plastic bag with Head Administrator Chumak's file over a nail in the wall. Then she folded her coat and carried it to the claw-footed bath where they kept all their necessary clothing.

Lukeria squinted at the dark window. 'Who was the first exile to Siberia?' Tanya shuffled into the kitchen, where she put the kettle on the ring. 'The bell of Tobolsk,' Tanya said. This was the beginning of a long catechism of calls and responses, a test designed to gauge Tanya's appreciation of all things orthodox.

'Seven hundred pounds it weighed when it was cast. Six hundred and eighty after Boris Godunov had it flogged and its clapper ripped out. Exiled to Tobolsk, it sits silent, still forbidden to ring.'

The point of the bell Tanya couldn't quite follow, only that making a lot of noise and suffering for it later seemed an integral part of orthodoxy. The kettle shrieked. Tanya poured hot water over the strainer, aligned cup and saucer, and walked, as carefully as a trained high-wire artist, to where her grandmother brooded. Tanya placed the teacup on top of the steamer trunk that doubled as their supper table, then slid the thin Bible Lukeria liked to use as a coaster under the saucer. This Bible had been given to Tanya by some Baptist minister at the bus station. Because of this, even though the Bible was the verbal icon of Christ, Lukeria announced that it could be used for any domestic purpose except biblical study.

Lukeria slid her chair closer to the tiny fortochka, a small hinged glass pane lodged at the corner of the larger window. It opened separately, a convenience Tanya appreciated, as large-boned girls like her tended to wilt on winter days inside the apartment where the central heating could not be adjusted. Her grandmother, she knew, kept the fortochka cracked open less for Tanya's benefit than for her own: Lukeria sat here to smoke and the open window allowed for convenient eavesdropping on all courtyard conversations. But Lukeria was hard of hearing and the only help available was a toilet-bowl plunger, the bulb of which she'd dismantled and now held to her ear so that she could shamelessly listen in on Olga's Sabbath preparations that wafted up from her downstairs kitchen window, which was also opened a crack. On this night – a gasp from the matches, the lighting of candles, and then the prayer, musical words in a language Tanya did not know.

Tanya tipped her head listening to the plaintive sound of Olga's voice. Lukeria leaned to the window and her features seemed to soften. It may have been the effect of the words. Or maybe it was the way that the yellow orthodox glow of the candlelight made all things more beautiful in the textured bathy haze.

'Jews. They pray well enough.' Lukeria leaned and lit a cigarette from the candle's flame, inhaled deeply. 'Still,' she spoke on the exhale, a long ribbon of blue wafting from her mouth, 'I am sick to death of hearing about their problems. Their persecution. Their obsession with history. If they are so unhappy, they should not be living here. After all, Perm is the heart of orthodoxy. Perm is the bear that carries the orthodox cross on its back, the great white bear that will rise up with a roar.'

'Hmmmmm.' Tanya opened her sky notebook. Most evenings Lukeria's words were easy for Tanya to dismiss. Words of a woman whose world was one of diminished proportion that had collapsed to a single point: this apartment, those suitcases, her trunk full of letters and that newspaper.

'There are, after all, other cities people can live in, these days. Jews don't have to stay here and be persecuted anymore if they don't want to be persecuted.' Lukeria's voice fell to a distant rumble, a hollow knocking that became one and the same with the thuds and pings of the heating pipes.

'Who says they're the only ones on the whole planet who

have suffered? Does anyone ask me what I lived through during that war? I was seven. I watched my mother starve. We ate book binding and wallpaper paste. Does anyone ask me about it?'

Tanya kept her pencil moving over the open page of her notebook. 'No,' Tanya said dully. 'Nobody asks.'

'Who decided some people's suffering was more insufferable than other people's?' Lukeria pushed her chin towards the window pane and the skin of her neck pulled tight. 'It makes me want to choke.'

Instead Lukeria began to cough. And cough. Her face turned violet. Tanya ran for the bottled water kept for such emergencies.

'Do you want me to call Father Vyacheslav?' Tanya held the water to Lukeria's lips.

Lukeria batted it away with surprising strength. 'Him!' she spluttered. 'How can I trust a priest whose beard hasn't even grown in properly?'

'It's not his fault. He's only twenty-one.'

'Exactly.' Lukeria's nickel-coloured eyes bore holes into Tanya's. 'Young people don't know anything anymore. And I don't want him anywhere near me.'

Lukeria stood and Tanya assisted her to the shabby fold-out couch. Divan, Lukeria preferred to call it, a more nostalgic nomenclature suggesting elegance and culture they'd both read about in books but had never actually experienced. To this end, Lukeria had collected fragments of lace and doilies and scattered them like cobwebs over the back and arms of the couch. And now, creak by groan, she slowly lowered herself onto the fold-out.

'You know, Tanyenchka, the real problem of this world is that there are simply too many people living on it.' Lukeria's voice trailed after her like a noxious vapour. 'Why should we all try to get along? What use is that? Where does it say that we should all like, or, God forbid, love one another? Let's say someone annoys me like an old headache, then just answer me this: why should I have to start liking them? Doesn't that strike you as false?' Now Lukeria lay on her left side so as to regain her air.

Tanya tucked a blanket around Lukeria's bony shoulders. These things she said came as a result of seeing and knowing more than a person ought to, of ageing quickly and alone, and with a heightened sense of how little time she had left. All of this, in turn, provoked a terrible need to deliver every scathing remark and cutting observation she'd quietly kept to herself through the years, lest she'd not get another chance.

These things she said, harsh as they sounded in Tanya's ear, were like the old church bells that could be heard every now and then if the wind blew just right; the deep tolling was not a pretty sound, but there was something to the low tones that seemed true and right and somehow beyond question.

Who said to love one another? Well, Jesus. But where was he right now? In heaven, loving everybody and loved by everybody. And here the rest of us were, waiting down below. And what had we been commanded to do while we waited? Love love love. Where were we supposed to go to get this extra love? And what an enormous burden, this business of loving, especially when Tanya had worn herself out loving people who wouldn't or couldn't love her back. Especially when she herself had been given so little, she could ill afford to part with any extra.

Tanya withdrew the application envelope from her plastic purse and returned to her chair at the window. It was hard to read the instructions, what with only one candle to read by and it guttering already. She squinted at the first question.

```
1. If you were stranded on an island and were
allowed to have with you three pieces of art,
which pieces would you choose and why?
```

Tanya blinked. She flipped the paper over in disbelief. This could not possibly be the correct application form. Perhaps this was Head Administrator Chumak's idea of a joke, and yet, there was no mistaking the dead earnest tone in his voice, no questioning how very important it was that she complete this application form, and satisfactorily. Tanya skipped Question One and read the next question.

```
2. Describe what team spirit and cooperation
mean to you.
```

She could read English as well as the next person, but this was not the English she'd learned in books. Tanya shook her head slowly from side to side, her eyes stinging with tears.

CHAPTER THREE

Azade

Because Perm was the fifth coldest city in all of Russia, it was certainly as cold as the Daghestani uplands or North Ossetia, the places where Azade's family had originally come from. Too cold to make a ground burial possible. Especially if you didn't have a backhoe, and Azade did not have a backhoe. Nor did she have a pick, trowel or spade. She had a smallish-sized shovel and this *nyuzhnik*, the Little Necessary, also known as the latrine – small mercies each. If she really wanted to sit down and take a rest she could; she was in custody of the only key and had the broad authority to use as many squares of tissue paper as she might need. Another comfort: mornings like these when the temperature was a near balmy minus fifteen degrees Celsius, the warmer fumes rising up from the latrine made a small dent in the otherwise flat landscape of cold. And here, in her little brown portable Necessary, she had all the time in the world to consider the gravity of her situation – namely, she had a dead husband to bury. A month had passed since Mircha's wake and Azade, a good wife, a respecter of people both dead and alive, was coming off the rails. When somebody died, her father

60

always said the Al-Fatiha over the body. The Sura Al-Fatiha was only seven verses long, but Azade had never been able to learn it by heart. She was, after all, a girl, and unclean. In the mountains girls could pray by memory, but were not allowed to touch the Holy Book.

In the old days, in Vladikavkaz, where her father tended the Muslim graveyard, when somebody died all you had to do was go to the civil registry bureau and before the sun set that very day someone would send a truck around for the body. This the state did, her father explained, because in Vladikavkaz, a town divided between Ossetes – Armenian Christians, Orthodox Russians, Muslims and Jews – it was universally agreed that the worst thing you could do was to leave a body lying about, unburied. And Azade knew this because her father, who had studied mountain history so thoroughly that he received a PhD in the subject, told her how during the mountain wars, the famous Murid warriors would die trying to retrieve a body rather than let it remain above ground.

All this because the unburied were known to visit the living while they slept and bite them all over their bodies or scratch them with their long, claw-like fingernails. It's why, even if she were to travel to Moscow, even if she were to receive a pension so large as to allow such a journey to such an important city, she would not – repeat, not – visit Lenin's tomb. It was craziness – an invitation to disaster – to stuff such a man, paint him with make-up and display him like a puppet under glass. And what has come of it? Nothing but badness. The man still haunted the country, skating with his girl-sized feet into people's dreams, yes, between lovers in their beds. He wasn't biting and scratching, but his memory, and an inexplicable nostalgia for the man, was like yeast, constantly reasserting itself. In conversation. In recycled pedagogy and rusty ideas. In latent bigotries stirred by the crashing economies. Each passing day as Azade stood in the looming shadow of the apartment building, she heard that old ideology, which once was for her family the meaning of their toil and the substance of life, knock from window to wall and wall to window. Oh, yes, she was almost certain Lenin haunted Mircha in his last months. It was the only way she could explain his leap from the rooftop.

Azade stamped her feet and forced the blood to bite in her toes. So put the man to rest, she wanted to tell the world. The man was tired. His words were weary. Bury him, and we will all be better for it, she wanted to tell this new president of the New Federated Russia, whose troubles were really a predictable extension of older troubles that Lenin – for all his greatness and polished thoughts within his shiny head – could not have predicted, let alone prevented. Bury him. No, bury both of them, and quick. That's all she wanted. But it was winter already and she was old. Her joints hurt. The roots of her teeth ached in their sockets. Business at the latrine had fallen off in the sharp cold, the inhabitants of the building preferring to use pots than brave sub-zero temperatures for the courtyard latrine.

This struck Azade as somewhat unfair: she'd never over-charged anyone. She only asked for ten kopeks. Twenty kopeks if the visitor required the use of a socialist textbook or the napkins she pilfered from the pricey western coffee shop. Also she made sure to keep the lid of the commode shut, as the Devil looked for open holes to hide in. This was a service she provided for free. Most days it was lonely work, situated here at the far end of the courtyard under the frozen lime tree, and of course, no one was ever happy to see her, and under no circumstances did anyone touch her hands.

In mornings, if they came, Lukeria would arrive first, supported by her granddaughter Tanya, and a few minutes later Olga would appear. Always they walked with their heads down, their eyes trained on their boots. They were angry. They were broken. Their building had been without sewer service for over four months. They needed her Little Necessary, and this they found an embarrassment. Well, so did Azade. It never seemed right to her to make people pay for what a body natu-rally had to do. But it was a job, and it did have a certain appeal. This job got her out of the apartment. It kept her close to human warble and bustling and their careening stench. And here was a funny thing: when she sat on the cracked seat of the latrine, as, say, a queen on her throne, she was almost content. On her perch she could survey the entire courtyard, seeing without being seen. She could watch the street kids, all five of them, drift from window to window on the second floor where she'd laid out blankets and set out bowls of steaming kasha, and if she could find it, milk. She could keep on eye on her son, Vitek, lounging in the stairwell. And as long as she worked she was eligible for a pension and one doctor's visit per year. At least this is what Vitek, who fancied himself everyone's business advisor, said.

But these expansive feelings of near-contentedness she kept to herself. She'd seen the way the other women in the building looked at her. She knew what they were saying and thinking. For at least two reasons, maybe three, she knew she was considered very bad luck. In the city where she was born people who tended latrines or graveyards were always considered the worst kind of bad luck. The rumour, according to her mother, who knew all the old stories and understood how people thought, was that only jinns – genies – lived or worked in such places. This was why people who work at public restrooms or who keep latrines were never invited to share prayers, were never the guest of unexpected hospitality, as the worst thing that could happen to a devout believer – whatever his brand of religion – was to inadvertently shake hands over the threshold with a jinn. Because jinns, made of fire and air and longing to be more human, will leap into any body they can touch. This was why the faithful hung knotted ropes from their doorways. Why knowledgeable Orthodox Russians arranged fish bones in the shape of a cross over their front and back doors. Why a rabbi blessed the entry way of a home belonging to a Jew anytime a member of the family has used an outdoor latrine or walked past a cemetery. Why Azade's father and mother, good people both of them, were never asked into the homes of their neighbours.

It's why even now, living here in this nearly abandoned apartment building where everyone was almost as poor and as desperate as she, her status was of the lowest sort. No matter what she might say or do, she, regardless of her silver hair – her dignity – plaited and wound around her head and covered by a bright cap, she was and would always be considered a *dikii*, a savage.

This must be why Lukeira spoke to her as if she were a small child, her words over-enunciated and loud, though Azade's hearing and understanding of Russian was nearly perfect. In fact, she felt like Russian was her second skin, though when she wore it, it chafed against the mountain skin underneath. Scratch a Russian and you'll find a Tatar. This is a true saying and one more reason the other women of the building didn't like her: she had wide-set eyes and dark skin and nothing, she knew, could make her more suspect. It didn't matter to them that Azade could write Russian as fine as the next person. It did not matter to them that she could curse in Ossetian and bless in Kumyk, those fibrous languages of mud and straw. Nor was anyone impressed that she knew how to read the moods of her goat, Koza, by observing the movement of his ears. She could speak the language of dogs. She knew what they thought about while they slept, what extraordinary soil their feet ploughed during their dreams. From her mother who taught her to read the Urals, she learned how to gauge sunset by the lengthening of shadowfall, and by the smell of the dust she could tell how many days they'd been without rain. She had learned from her mother, too, who took her to the banya where she worked, that other women did not care about these things. Nobody talked about shadows and rainfall, clouds or mountains. Who looked up to the mountains when the very earth beneath their feet was so unsteady?

'It's this ground,' her mother whispered into her dark hair. 'It's sour. Full of sulphurous gas. And the Kama – pure poison.' That was Perm in those days. A closed city, a red circle on the map. A city of fly ash and coal, salt and tanks, bicycle parts and sighting mechanisms. Smoking hills of mine waste. A city of bad luck.

Just think bad luck and it is sure to find you. That was another jinn saying her own mother told her, and Azade believed it, for around the toppled stone archway strolled her boy Vitek. Boy! – he was almost thirty, and every day he was the biggest heartbreak of her life. Never lifting a finger to help. And here he came, out of breath and reeking of alcohol. And this at eight-thirty in the morning.

'Good news!' Vitek waved a newspaper. 'Given the estimated increase in human population, and hence the increase of human shit, latrine-sitting will be a growth industry.'

'So everything will stink more. That is good news.' Azade swept her twig broom over the tops of Vitek's shoes.

'Yes, but you're forgetting the principles of supply and demand. The price people will pay for the privilege of stinking with privacy will rise.'

'Why?'

'Because it just will. It's so simple, really. Instead of charging ten kopeks, we'll start charging a rouble – maybe even two.'

Vitek jostled the handle of the locked latrine.

'One square or two?' Azade held up the wad of paper.

'Two.'

'Two roubles, then,' Azade said with a smile and Vitek stomped through the frozen courtyard. One by one, the kids left the heap and followed Vitek through the stairwell, where they reappeared on the roof. The oldest child, a ten-year-old girl, made crude gestures, while the next oldest child, a boy with dark red hair, and Vitek dropped their trousers. Jets of urine arced from the roof and froze mid-air, falling to the ground in hard amber drops.

Azade whisked the urine into a pile under Lukeria's window, trudged back to her latrine and sat on the toilet with a loud sigh. Vitek. A disappointment, sure. But it was her fault he turned out the way he did. Vitek's trouble started with her, because his trouble, her trouble, was merely a continuation of older troubles, which all began so long ago it was as if they had no beginning because there was never a time when they didn't already exist. And when Azade thought trouble – her trouble, his trouble – she started with the city of her birth, Ordzhonikidze. Some people called it Dzaudzhikau and on Russian maps it was called Vladikavkaz. In her mind it was a city of changing names, a city of changed people, a city she only knew because other people knew it first. Her father described it so many times she felt like it was she, not her father, who hollowed out the graves for good Muslims with a backhoe. Because he told her in such painstaking detail about his days spent turning the dark earth over – the oily smell of clay and the eyeless fish turning beneath their mantles of mud – she felt certain it was she, not he, who listened to those fish quietly marking the minutes and days of each season. She felt certain that it was she, not he, who carefully notched the graves so that the bodies lay on a burial shelf and so that she could stand in the hole with them, her hands clasped in front of her chest. And it was she who bowed to the heaven and to the earth, and toward the Arab countries where their religion, which nobody in her family had ever pretended to completely understand, had come from. It was she, not her father, who wound the bodies in the white cloth and, after placing the body so that the head faced west, intoned the old burial prayers, words they needed to hear to have a proper send-off.

And because her mother told her about the open bins of cracked coriander, cumin and dried sage, mustard, the stalls of watermelon and cabbage, Azade felt like it had been she, not her mother, who had bartered in the open-air meat market. She who heard the Jewish dogs, who were wiser than the other dogs, bark first at the women with long blue skirts and smart-looking glasses handing out political leaflets. Well, why not? Her mother would say: theirs was still an open city, and as such it was a meeting place, a crossroads in the mountain. Stand at the crossroads and ask what is the good way and follow it. Good mountain advice and in those days the passes were unregulated. Kamyks, Laks, Uzbeks, Georgians, Chechens – even leaflet-distributing Russians – crossed freely from one mountain territory to another. If you were healthy enough for a mountain crossing, nobody stopped you. It was like this through the strange days of the thirties, until that terrible war. Then the city was no longer called Ordzhonikidze, but Dzaudzhikau. Then came soldiers. Security officers. Until then, her mother explained, they had not known they were part of a people's union of soviets. And when her father, a proud man and a fighter at heart, had heard there was a war, he attempted to enlist. Her mother told her this so carefully Azade could see in vivid detail the enrolling officer's amused but weary smile. '*Nyet*,' the officer said, pointing to a sheet of paper tacked to the wall. People of questionable ethnicity – that is, anyone who was not originally from northern Russia – were to serve their country by relocating. The officer explained then that the spot had already been picked out for them. The sudden under-standing that he would be a stranger wherever he went, that he was considered a stranger already in his own town, was almost too much for her father to take.

'What if we refuse to go?' her father had asked, a question so direct it earned him a rifle butt in the stomach. According to that sheet of paper, they were to be allowed to take 500 kilo-grams of their belongings, which, for most families, amounted to a few pots, a blanket, some salt. But everyone was in such a hurry, her mother said, prodded into the cattle cars, packed like animals, they were lucky if they got all their children with them.

All this her mother told her. Every story Azade had ever known she heard first from her mother. Because this is the way it is with words between parents and children. The stories of the adults are given to the children as a gift, as a blessing, as a reminder, as a curse. And when the story jumps from mouth to mouth, skin to skin, it becomes so fluid and malleable as to sustain numerous retellings in innumerable contexts, stretching so much as to allow a daughter to know all that the mother knew, and in this way to thoroughly become her. Because when her mother told these stories, it was as if Azade became her mother, just as when Azade's father told his stories she felt she had become him. And then it was easy to recall how they'd been packed into the cattle cars with an ox who'd had its knees broken. How the children had to stand on the back of the beast lest they be crushed underfoot. How they looked for sky between the carriage seams. The thirst, her mother told her, was unbearable, and those who could, drank their own urine. The babies had no tears to cry with.

For three weeks, no food, no water, everyone pressed together so close they could not squat to relieve themselves and so had to shit all over each other's feet. And when the train stopped in Perm it wasn't until the line workers pushed open the doors of the wagons and offloaded those pressed closest to the doors that they could even tell who was dead and who still alive. 'What are all these darkies doing here?' the railway inspector asked, and that is how they learned, blinking in the shock of sudden light, that there had been a huge mistake. They should have been sent to the Sarozek, the Kazakh desert, but somehow they had ended up at the gateway to Siberia, where nobody wanted them. They'd been deposited here to work the jobs real Russians didn't want to do and to occupy the dwellings of recently relocated families who were – impossibly – even more subversive and less Russian-looking than they. And what did they bring with them? The pain of an empty stomach. And shame.

The officers took turns with the women, her mother even, but not until they'd broken the arms and noses of all the men. The thud of boots. The crack of bones, the muffled cries. With each sound, each push, each tear of fabric, her mother explained how she retreated beneath her skin. Because beneath that skin there was another skin. And beneath that skin was yet another skin. And hiding in the centre of herself where there was nothing, her mother said, only air, a strange alchemy of torment occurred. At the end of her human self and wishing nothing more than for a few moments of flight, misery turned her leaden bones to hollow ones. And then her mother wasn't a woman anymore but a bird. 'This is what you do when something unspeakable happens,' her mother said. 'This is what happens to a girl when something unspeakable is done to her. She turns herself into a bird. This is how she flies away.' And when the men had finished with those women, with her mother, even as the blood dried along the insides of their legs, the women hugged each other and sang an old song:

> *One day I will become a blue dove*
> *And I will sit in the blue grass*
> *Do not rush me, oh stranger,*
> *Do not rush me now.*

A song to numb the senses and dull the dreams. Days passed. Each one another dark bird that rises into a wrinkle and flies away. Her father's nose healed, but now it sat crooked on his face. Her mother, she healed too, in a fashion, the way women do. The song that she sang, it helped as much as any song can, smoothing back old hurt to make way for the new. The stinging hard looks other women gave her in the courtyard as she hung their laundry, the job assignments she could not get, the many kiosk vendors who would not sell to her. It was the same way for her father. The men of the apartment building called him Nose and would not allow him to play chess with them. 'Animals. Godless animals,' her father said. 'Sloppy eaters with foul mouths, most of those men. And their chess moves lack grace.' Azade can remember the indignation her father had felt, her father, who had been proud and devout, prayed seventeen times a day and had the prayer bruise on his forehead to prove it. 'In what way are they better than me?'

For a year her father appealed to authorities, wrote eloquent letters begging for a chance to work in the universities. Then to the factories. Then to the city services to clean windows. But because the factories manufactured military components and because of her father's subversive skin colour, his every request was denied. It didn't matter that he had a PhD and spoke four languages. 'You can clean a latrine in any language,' a clerk, the lowest clerk, at the city office of work affairs told him. Two years later her father died of shame, the thought and smell of shit on his feet and hands never leaving him.

All this her mother told her, in her mountain language that no one else in the building would understand. 'He could not travel beneath his skins to find another skin,' she said. 'He could not trade his highlander skin for a Russian skin.' And Azade understood the lesson in that comment, in the example of her father's frustrated life. Azade set out to be the best kind of Soviet – Russian-speaking and hard-working. Docile and doing nothing to arouse suspicion of being in possession of nationalistic ideas or a simple nostalgia for the past, or – God forbid – a memory of a time when her family had had a place of their own and knew it. Even so, it seemed natural to her in the way that the closed knot of a loop makes all things seem inevitable that she inherited her father's duties and took charge of this little latrine and the courtyard. Natural that a man she did not know or want to know, a Caucasian highlander in an army-issue uniform so new that the creases of his trousers held fast when he walked, saw her in the courtyard. He clasped her hand – still dirty from pulling weeds – in his. He did not ask her, but told her, that they would go the civil registry and be married. 'Where did this crazy man come from?' Her mother pitched the question to the ceiling, to the heavens, and Azade had merely shrugged. And because her father wasn't there to object, her mother, such a progressive Muslim, really, for her day, who had herself longed to wear the long blue skirts and smart-looking glasses, encouraged the match. He wasn't an ethnic Russian and he wasn't Christian, and that's all that mattered. 'Marry him, whatever he is,' her mother advised. 'In this Soviet state, it will be better for you, better for your children.' The civil ceremony took only two minutes. The deputy governor pointed to the place on the paper where they were to sign and gave them a bit of wisdom: 'Life is very difficult. Never forget your parents.'

Azade held open the door of the latrine with her foot and studied the children outside. That's what carried her all these years, the thought of children. But even in that she was cursed with bad luck. Six times, maybe seven, she conceived. But always, always something went wrong. Azade grabbed a bucket and sprinkled salt along the path between the stairwell and the latrine. She counted the children pawing at the heap. The oldest, Big Anna, stood knock-kneed and pawed through the clutter at the base of the heap.

'Up your mother!' Anna hooted at the twin with the transparent veins that swam under his skin. Bad Boris, Azade had called him, and the name had stuck. 'Your mother twice over!' Bad Boris yelled back at the girl.

Good Boris, not to be outdone, hawked a jet of mucus at the base of the glistening heap. 'Your mother like this and that!'

Gleb, the red-haired boy, ran his sleeve under his nose. Eight years old, Azade put him at. 'Your mother up and down and all around.'

'Your mother and seven crosses on her death bed!' cried the littlest child, the girl with the brown skin. She used to have India-black hair, but now it was orange with malnutrition. Five, Azade guessed her age. Maybe six. It was hard to tell just how old, what with all the glue they'd been sniffing. Stunted the growth. Every day she said this to the twin boys with the transparent skin. Seven she was guessing for those two, because they'd each lost their front teeth, and she was pretty sure they fell out the natural way, though there was no denying that Vitek treated them rough and what with all those fumes they inhaled, and their funny lurching walk, they tended to hurt themselves. Five of them. And they might have been hers. It was easy to think this way. Easy to count them and think of all the children she'd lost, every one of them with skins thin and bones soft. She'd lost them and it was her own fault, her own carelessness that caused it – she understood this now. When her mother told her to hang an unbroken, unknotted skein from the door of the latrine, Azade had laughed. She and Mircha had only been married two years and she didn't know then the importance of unbroken thread, didn't really believe that unbroken thread was life.

Only after she lost her children did she remember her

mother's advice. They hadn't grown right and when they came, always months too soon, they slid out into the sheets and once into the toilet bowl, fishlike, and so strange, she could hardly see how they could be human. Fish, they were creatures meant for water, but not for this land. Mircha took them in his hands – yes, in those days he had both his arms still – and wrapped them in milling cloth and buried them the mountain way, red string tied around the bundle, pocketing them in barren ground without a marker, without a reminder, so as not to curse the cotton crop or send their spirits into the trees.

'Not like that, stupid! Like this.' Vitek's voice bounced from wall to wall in the dvor, snapping Azade from her reverie. Vitek shook the boy with the rust-coloured hair and the boy's glasses sailed across the cracked pavement. 'When you rush a tourist, you littler ones should get in front and you,' Vitek pointed to the rust-haired boy and the older girl, 'should stand behind the mark and get your hands in every pocket.'

Azade shuffled toward the children, taking note of their blank stares. 'You're ruining them,' she said, dumping a handful of salt on Vitek's left shoe.

Vitek laughed. 'Oh, Ma – it's all fun and games.'

'These kids need an education, or they'll be good for nothing.' Azade squinted at the kids, who stared back at her with empty eyes.

'I'm giving them an education,' Vitek said.

'No. The kind with books and things.'

Vitek passed his tongue over his gold tooth as he glanced at the *Material Dialectics* textbook Azade kept stowed near the latrine in the event of big bizness.

'Books are only good for wiping your ass with. Besides, what I'm teaching them is better than anything you can find in a book. Not a single one of those books will tell you how to get by in this life.'

'In every equation there is nothing as constant as human cruelty,' Big Anna said.

'See,' Vitek smiled. 'They know everything kids their age should if they want to survive.'

Azade shook her head, mumbled some choice words in Kumyk. He could catch crayfish in winter, her Vitek. He could figure the angles in a circle. But for all this cleverness there was something fundamentally wrong with him. For starters, every time he opened his mouth, he broke her heart just a little more. Not his fault, though. Could he help it that nobody, not even his own mother, had wanted him? It's the only way she could explain how he turned up in their courtyard one morning with lice in his hair and scabies on his skin. At seven years old he was already a confirmed alcoholic, and Azade knew that the street had been his mother and it was his good luck to wander under the archway into their dvor to use her Little Necessary the day he did. And she thanked God for him. It was like the ground had finally returned to her what it had taken. A real child, alive and trailing her like a shadow, and she could not have ignored him even if she had wanted to.

'We can't feed that little runt,' Mircha had said. 'Take him to the orphanage, let the state raise him.' It was the one time she defied Mircha. Mircha had just been sent home from the front, missing an arm. And with only one arm to hit her with, she figured she could care for them both, could stand between them and that, in time, because she loved them both, they would for her sake learn how to love each other.

She should have remembered what mountain women had known for centuries and what her mother tried to teach her: Love made wise people stupid and kind people cruel. And love made the courageous cowardly. This was the only way Azade could explain what happened next. Because the more she cared for Vitek and for Mircha and his weeping stump, the more Mircha drank. And the more Mircha drank the angrier he became. And all that love she thought she had – an ocean of it, the best and purest kind of love – wasn't enough. And beneath her good intentions she was a coward – quiet when she should have made noise. Oh, her mother would have died a second death if she could have seen how her Azade, who had strong arms and the long hair, the source of a highland woman's strength, allowed Mircha with his one arm and fraying hair to push her around. Her mother would have died all over again if she could witness how much of her motherly wisdom Azade had managed to forget. But who really suffered? Why, the boy did, of course. Always it's this way with drinkers and their children. The rage boils out of the body at every chance. And for years Azade had thought that if she kept quiet, silently turning her tears to feathers, Mircha's anger would burn itself out like a match dropped into a deep bucket. But wrath fueled by alcohol never burns out so quickly.

Azade tried for years to figure the alchemy. Maybe it was because of his missing arm. Maybe because he hated his work at the factory. Maybe because there was not enough beer or vodka to make the world beautiful enough. It was so hard to say with Mircha where all the rage came from. All she could attest to was how little it took to incite his fury: a shift in the light, the noise of a bulldozer nuzzling a pile of rubble, the flies buzzing at the window, Vitek mumbling over the chessboard. Azade remembered most of the beatings, but it was with shame she recalled her own cowardice, her complicity. Once she busied herself at the stove simply to steer clear of Mircha, leaving Vitek, lost in thought over a game of chess, to fend for himself. Mircha had pounded his fist on the cardboard box that held the playing board. Up went the chessmen and up went Mircha's fist, catching Vitek on the ear, causing him to fall over and without so much as a whimper curl into the foetal position in preparation for what was coming next. Azade had dragged the kettle over the ring so as to disguise the noise of Mircha punching Vitek with an enthusiasm that went beyond the requirements of punishment meted for purely instructive purposes.

Oh, he liked to hit the boy, kept on hitting him even after he promised Azade he'd stopped. Azade knew it, though Mircha and even Vitek pretended otherwise, violence having forged a secret alliance between them.

But she did manage her quiet revenges. With sour cream a day or two past being bad, with reduced meat from the street market, shiny at the edges where it had started to turn. With an inner guilty joy, Azade would smile with her split lips and Vitek's swollen eyes would shine as they watched Mircha hop from the divan and race for the commode, which in those days still worked. She can remember Mircha gripping the rim of the toilet – *'Waaaaah! Hummmmm!'* – and emptying the contents of his stomach with such a high degree of unswerving perseverance that sometimes Azade almost felt sorry for Mircha.

'Sweetheart,' Mircha would call from the toilet. 'Some water or a snort of vodka. I beg you!' And by the next morning Mircha, broken in body, would turn gentle, so large in his promises, so expansive in his remorse, that Azade could extract almost anything – a bottle of Russian Forest perfume, the alcoholic content of which she knew made a handy supplement should the vodka fail; a trip to the dentist to replace a broken tooth; even the assurance that the beatings would stop.

Azade turned her gaze to the kids. They were almost playing, mock-punching one another, leaping from the heap. The red-haired boy, Gleb, skirled around Vitek, then reached for Vitek's vodka. Vitek pushed the boy to the ground and pinned him with his knee, then brought back his fist. 'Don't!' Azade shouted.

Vitek stood, straightened his leather jacket, smiled, and ran his tongue over his chipped front tooth. With his thumb and forefinger he made a gun, pointed it at her, cocked his thumb and fired.

Azade slumped against the latrine. She had ruined him. She saw that now. She'd indulged him in the strange way mothers, against their better instincts, sometimes do. With a lopsided attentiveness, she had tried to make up for her failures and shortcomings. After Mircha beat the boy, Azade brooded and hovered with aspirins and ice, was careful to keep Vitek out of Mircha's sight for a few days. But she'd not stopped Mircha and told herself it was out of love for her husband, when really it was cowardice. Worse: to make up for Mircha's harsh treatment, she'd spared her son necessary corrections. He'd always been a cheat, a bully, and even a liar. But she'd not punished him. And now he was a grown man, still behaving shamefully. And this was her fault. This was how love, or rather the lie of love, had made her, a well-intentioned mother, raise a perfect monster. A perfectly lovable, fearsome monster.

Koza, her goat, hiked his snout in the air and bleated mournfully. Azade pointed her nose in the same direction. With her true and precise olfactory powers, Azade detected a sharp-edged malevolent odour unlike those that ordinarily swelled out of the latrine. That she could smell anything at all in this cold, which had a way of crimping smell to tight radii, was a testament to the largesse of the odour.

In Mircha's boots, Azade walked the perimeter of the stink. She scattered lime in a rough concentric circle. She counted the neat little piles of human excrement the kids had left. Their droppings were too tidy, too frozen to be responsible for this newer, more aggressive stench. Azade sniffed at the heap, but frost had trapped all the smells of rotting peelings deep inside its throbbing heart. Azade shuffled to the back side of the heap and that's when she saw it: a dark gash in the ground. How it got there and how she could not have noticed it before Azade could not fathom. Azade dropped to her knees, lowered her nose to the trembling gash and took a deep and substantial whiff. Nothing. Just the smell of wet mud, which, if anything, held a round organic scent of soft ooze. Azade straightened and headed for the bank of snow that contained her husband. Yes. Absolutely this was the source of the stink and it was phenomenal. Azade sprayed her lemon-scented fumigant around the bank of snow. But it was as if the odour doubled in strength as if it were swelling with outrage, as if it were indignant that someone as low as she might try to combat it. Azade narrowed her eyes. With her broom she swept at the top layers of snow. It was then that she saw Mircha's boots were unlaced and on backward – not at all the way they had left him. Azade tightened her grip on her broom and headed for the stairs, with each step a chill climbing the rungs of her spine.

The dead never leave us. She knew that. It was a physical law. No, she never went to university, but she didn't need a PhD to understand the law of conservation of mass. A body never completely disappears; it only changes shape or constitution, reasserting itself elsewhere, boiling over, leaking at the edges. And the dead who remain keep themselves frightfully busy. Her own father, for instance, walked backwards with his shoes unlaced, treading up and down these very stairs. He had to do this to reverse the indignities his body and soul had suffered while he had been living those last years in the apartment building and tending the Little Necessary, Azade's mother explained. Azade knew it to be true, for she heard her father's heavy tread on the stairs as he corrected the wrongs committed against him and adjusted the wrongs he himself may have committed. He had to walk backwards through every sorrow, every regret, every wound, in order to leave them properly. It took him seven years to do it, but finally, one afternoon in May when the trees along the wide prospects exhaled a blizzard of cotton, her mother flung open the windows so that, at last, her father, his nose finally straight again and pointing true as a needle on a compass, could fly away.

But with Mircha, one sniff told Azade that things were different. Whatever the rules of the afterlife she and her mother had worked out, they did not seem to apply to him. For there his body was, defrosting down there in the shadows of the courtyard, and yet the smell here in the corridor outside their door – colossal! Azade paused outside the door and checked the knots on her rope, for quick verification. Yes, the knots were all there. Her resolve galvanized, Azade leaned into the door.

'Milii! Sweetheart!' At once Mircha's voice assaulted her. Azade peered into the darkness of the room. There he was, in the corner of the room, sitting in that ridiculous claw-footed bath, wearing a wool sock on his hand and smoking a Turkish cigarette. She had never seen her husband looking so jolly, so alive. So silly.

Azade held her broom aloft as if it were a weapon, or perhaps a talisman, and approached Mircha with caution. The dead, after all, were so unpredictable. But after a moment, her suspicion gave way to curiosity. 'Why did you do it?'

'What?' Mircha's smile loped from one side of his face to the other and she could see that he was drunk.

Azade rolled her eyes to the ceiling. 'Jump.'

Mircha sucked on his cigarette and exhaled a mouthful of rings. 'I was tired of this life and afraid to grow old while living it. I wanted to go with dignity. Not like some of those men shitting themselves to death in their own bed.'

'So then why did you come back?'

Mircha brightened. 'I feel a tremendous urge to express myself in ways I never had before.'

Azade squeezed the neck of her broom. 'Express yourself how?'

Mircha ground his cigarette on his stump then cleared his throat. 'Imagine if you will that I am like a famous prophet risen from the dead. I've come back to rewrite myself, to revise myself. To retell my story with vast scope and with miracle.'

'Is this out of some book you have been reading?'

'I feel this here, in my heart.' Mircha laid a hand over his chest. 'And what I feel I must share.'

'Why?'

'In the fight of cultural and historical ownership of memory one must be vigilant. It's a sacrifice, sure. But one I'm willing to make.'

'I don't understand.'

'I am helping each one of us to revise our personal and collective history. To revise our very lives, as it were,' Mircha said. 'It can be done! I am living proof. With the right attitude and a firm grasp of the Heisenberg uncertainty principle, we can alter anything – especially our concept of the past.'

Azade hung her head. The situation was so much worse than even she had imagined. With the handle of her broom Azade lifted Mircha's trousers and carried them into the kitchen, where she dropped them into a pot. 'The more you talk, the worse it smells in here,' Azade mumbled.

Mircha smiled. 'A little vodka would be convivial. If you don't have any vodka, then apple brandy would be all right.'

Mircha's gaze roamed. 'I see you've rearranged things a bit since I died. Where are my long-play records?'

Azade poured lukewarm water into a teacup and handed the cup to him. 'Vitek snapped them in two over his knee. Also the children played games with them, and the goat ate the rest.'

'My war medals?'

'We sold them.'

'And my best suit? The one with the very fashionable pinstripes?'

'It caught fire, but that was an accident. I think.'

'I had no idea how much you hated me.' Mircha stretched

his hand toward Azade as if to touch her cheek, those scars along her jaw. 'I loved you in my own way, you know.' Mircha let his hand fall to his lap.

Azade rubbed her jaw, remembering how he'd fractured it twice in one year. Love hurt and nobody knew it better than Azade. Like the Devil on a holy day, Mircha's rage knew no bounds. And when he beat her, he acted as if it were his duty, as if he were doing her some kind of favour. As if violence were a necessary tool for acquiring wisdom.

And Azade had learned so much at his hands. It was hard to forget the lesson of a broken jaw or ribs. And never had she been so afraid of anyone as she'd been of Mircha. But now he was so different. Gone the familiar rage. Gone the railing anger. And this new Mircha was so foreign, so odd, she didn't know if she should feel even more frightened or relieved.

Azade backed away from the bath, the broom held out in front of her, just in case Mircha made a sudden move.

But Mircha merely broadened his smile. 'I know what you're thinking. You've given me over for hopeless. But good news. People can change.'

'Maybe. But you're not people, you're dead.' Azade stared into Mircha's eyes that were such a reluctant shade of blue they could pass for metal, and waited for the recognition of this reality to register with him. It was, after all, important for the dead to remember their condition. Otherwise they cultivated ideas, knocked on walls, played silly tricks. Wrote novels.

The dead, Azade knew, had to be dispatched. They had to go quietly to their graves and stay there, lest the earth, unable to stifle all their noise and movement, permanently reject them. And yet, Azade worried that this was precisely what was happening with her husband, who was even now lolling and reeking in their cracked claw-footed bath, singing songs he had learned in a workers' camp.

'My story,' Mircha called from the tub, 'has such potential. If told on the uphill climb of a mountain I would call it a story of Frisk and Wonderment. If told on the downhill trek I might simply call it Momentum. Imagine if you will a boy on his name day shooting guns in the air with his uncles. It's a joyous occasion, this day. The cabbage has been brought in and because this boy brought a mountainside of those buggers in by himself he's considered a man now. His family builds the fire and you know how a Lak fire in Dagestan burns brighter than any other.'

'I've heard, I've heard,' Azade mumbled.

'And they eat their watermelon double-salted the way it should be and live on the top of the mountain where the air is thin and the men are thinner and the wind mixes the days of summer with the days of winter. The peak of a mountain divides a man's shadow, with his past falling to one side and his future to the other.

'In winter the man falls in love with a girl who lives in shadow of the mountain. She nibbles his fingers. He gnaws on her ears. They drink wine from each other's mouths. She has eyes the colour of celery and a voice like a broken road. She is clever as night and beautiful as day and knows how to plait her hair with donkey piss. She's a beauty and the man would give his life for her seven times over. She makes cheese from the milk of her goats and he sells flour, salt and water, things that are weighed and not counted. Are you still listening? Now we get to the good part. The wars the men wage are of the better sort. Everyone comes home a hero and in their absence, instead of cabbage, the hills yield long furrows of arms and legs of perfect proportion, just ripe for the picking.'

Azade grunted. Where the beginning, where the end to this man and his stories?

'You say you've come to tell a better story for each one of us. What is my story, then?' Azade gave Mircha's trousers a final stir in the pot.

Mircha's face fell into a jumble of furrows. 'It's harder for you. You have so much further to go. There's the matter of your family situation, which was somewhat respectable before the forced relocation. But now, of course, your position is so low, of such little consequence. And then, there's the fact of your womanhood. If you were a man, say, you'd have ever so much more potential to rise. It may be uncouth to say it, but it is the reality of revision. And finally, and I think this will be of no surprise to you, there's the matter of your hands. So shameful, really. Will you ever be able to rid yourself of the taint?' Mircha smiled in apology. 'It would be different, of course, if your hands did something of consequence, something that mattered.' Mircha slid into the bath and lost himself in another song.

And it was then that Azade understood what a monumental task lay before her. She understood what he needed. Though he couldn't possibly know it, he'd come back for her. He had returned, or merely remained, not for his healing but for hers. After all, the love of a good woman isn't enough for some men. What Mircha needed now was the back-side of her hand, a push from her broom. In short, she would have to prepare Mircha for his death – again – for clearly the earth, and no doubt heaven as well, could not receive him as he was.

CHAPTER FOUR

Yuri

For as long as he could remember, Yuri had always imagined that he was a fish. Inside his mother's stomach he swam in salt water. And by some accident when he was born, God looked away for a moment. Perhaps to set aright a tilted star, perhaps to paint more speckles and spots on the Dolly Varden trout or stitch more whiskers onto the snout of the sturgeon. Something large or small, miraculous or mundane, and Yuri, who should have been an eel, a lamprey, a dace, was instead a mere boy, flailing and kicking about in his ordinary human skin which he'd never felt, not in all his twenty-one years, quite fit him.

Which is why he went to the rivers and canals whenever he could. To the man-made ponds and the natural. To brackish waters and sweet. Wherever there might be fish or the suggestion of fish. Even the memory of fish was enough for him. So when Azade leaned Mircha's rod against his mother's door the day after the wake, Yuri took it as a sign. Two minutes later, with a satchel stuffed with stale dinner buns, he wheeled his old bike through the courtyard and out to the street.

It wasn't perfect, this bike. It was actually two separate

rejects from the local bike factory, disassembled and recombined to make one working bike. But the parts didn't fit together precisely and somehow he'd reassembled the handlebars out of alignment with the frame. Now the bike tilted to the left and it took a furious effort, powerful strokes with the right leg, to compensate. And with each push from his legs the bike lamented, squeaking such sad complaints that Yuri began to think the bike was the voice of his very own soul, a voice that could only make sound or be heard when under the greatest of outward force.

Then, also, there was the ticking in his head. The sprockets, Zoya maintained, whenever he brought the matter of the incessant noise up with her. But he knew better. The sound was like that of a stuttering oven timer lodged at the base of his cerebellum, which was, come to think of it, not functioning very well and hadn't been, not for a long time. His head, he decided, was a cheap clock that didn't know its own ruin.

Yuri clapped his palm against an ear, as a swimmer forcing out water, then pushed on the pedals. It wouldn't be so bad, this ticking, if it weren't so loud. He had stuffed cotton wool in his ears. He'd fashioned plugs of soft wax. But only two things helped. The first: fishing.

Hardly a surprise. Even before he was called up into the army, before all that business in the south, fishing had been his passion. Fish, Mircha had once told him, formed a connection between the water and air, between our world and theirs. And Yuri preferred their world of water. For water, he had learned long ago, was a far more forgiving medium than air. The water turned light viscous and noise unraveled in muted threads, as if from the edges of a dream. It was the same sensation he could achieve when he wore his father's souvenir helmet, which was the second course of self-therapy. The helmet was a replica, and not even a good replica, of the type of helmet made famous by the cosmonauts. A horizontal crack stretched from one end of the plastic visor to the other. It had no monetary value whatsoever, or certainly Yuri would have sold or traded it by now, but its sentimental value was unbounded as it was the one and only item that had once belonged to his father that Yuri still had.

As a boy he wore that helmet from the moment school let out in afternoons to the moment it began again in mornings. He even wore the helmet the day his father left them to go to the war. He and his mother, along with the entire city, had turned out to watch the motorized rifle unit leave in a line of transports for the Bakharevka base. And while others waved their paper flags, their eyes covered with handkerchiefs, Yuri, his eyes shielded by the plastic visor, trained his gaze on his father. He watched without blinking as they disappeared behind that thick veil of dust.

And he wore the helmet now. All this to return to a world of diminished illumination. A world discerned only through the cracked visor that weakened light to wavering bands. All this to woo water for its own sake. All this to return to a place where that extra inner padding of the helmet pressed against his ears, and all noise dampened to the language of water and Yuri could be, once again, a fish.

Yuri leaned the bike against a frozen birch and stepped cautiously over the shore-fast crusts of river ice. The sound of gunshot thundered through the ice. Yuri dropped to his knees, held his breath, counted the ticking in his head. Not gunfire, just ice compressing. Yuri stretched flat over the ice and peered at the darkness below. They were his brothers and sisters huddled down there, whispering secrets about the rest of them and their clumsy paddling over their glass ceiling. *Tell your dream to a fish and he'll carry it for you.* This was another bit of advice that Mircha once gave him. Yuri cupped his hands to his eyes and squinted at the fish below, his mouth moving silently. His dream: if he couldn't be a fish, then he wanted to spend his every waking moment in the company of fish. He was with Mircha and Vitek ten years ago when he first said this. They'd been ice fishing, a first for Yuri, something he had hoped his father would show him when he returned from the war.

'It's an exercise in patience, what we're doing here,' Mircha said that day. 'Patience is what you get when you divide the number of days you've gone without eating by the temperature outdoors.' Though he was only ten years old at the time and had a poor grasp of integers, by Yuri's reckoning, they were all becoming very patient people.

'Do you know what they're doing down there?' Mircha pointed to the ice, to the fish beneath the sheer layer. The ice was so thick and it was such hard work for Yuri to drill through it with the auger that Yuri had figured the fish simply froze like everything else in wintertime, and had said so.

'No, not frozen,' Mircha explained, helping the hole along by sprinkling vodka at the edges. 'They're just sleeping. And dreaming. Do you know what they're dreaming of?'

Yuri looked at Vitek, who was lobbing small rocks at the power lines. Yuri shook his head no.

'Wings for fins, blue sky for water.' Mircha steered Yuri back to shore. 'You see, fish are just like us. They dream of flight. They look at birds and long for all the same things we do. Do you know what the difference between them and us is?'

'They taste better fried in oil?' Vitek called hopefully.

Mircha glared at Vitek. Then Mircha draped his arm over Yuri's shoulder and spoke in confidential tones. 'The difference is that we — that is, you and I — can do something about our dreams. That's something they don't teach you in school and you won't read it in any book, but it's true all the same.' Mircha said this with a jerk of his shoulder, as if earmarking with his entire body the veracity of his words. 'Yes, fish have dreams, just like you and me. But they've lost their piss and fire. They've forgotten how to fight.'

It was a cold day in March, and windy. Mircha's coat gaped open, wide enough for Yuri to see that Mircha was wearing his beloved T-shirt, 'Make a Splash!' — the one given to him by a portable commode salesman from Canada. Yuri stared at the

T-shirt. He knew that Mircha sincerely believed that it was a man's duty to make his mark in this world. That is, all men should piss in the wilds and the cultivated places, too. The wind whipped up and Mircha's coat sailed out at a crisp ninety degrees. Yuri could not help noticing Mircha's empty sleeve.

Mircha followed Yuri's gaze. 'Over it went. Blown clean off. The captain said he watched it drop four hundred feet or more into the Amu Darya. Ever seen the Amu Darya?'

'No,' Yuri shook his head.

'No,' Vitek called out, lobbing a rock at Yuri's head.

What Yuri wanted to know, what he wanted to ask, was if Mircha in all his comings and goings along the front had ever seen or heard any news of Yuri's father. But even then Yuri understood that you don't interrupt a veteran telling his story. And Mircha's stories, once started, were like the old T-64 tanks that knew only one direction: forward, no matter what the cost.

'Glistening and sharp like the metal of a trap. Like a silver chain and there we were pinned on the road, wounded and dying. Russians and Georgians and even a handful of Lithuanians. And then a sound you don't ever want to hear, Afghan rebels. We heard them baying and calling, "Here we come! The wild Mujahideen, the wild jackals, coming to kill the intruders!"' And then Mircha threw his head back and howled, just like a dog whose ribs wanted to climb out of its throat.

'And then what?' Yuri asked. A small rock whizzed past his ear.

'And then what?' Vitek mimicked in a shrill voice, then threw another rock. Yes, even then Vitek was a bully.

'The Georgians!' Mircha snorted. 'Honestly, they are the world's crappiest fighters. It's no wonder they get their asses kicked so often. All this to say, we tucked our tails between our legs and we ran, those of us who still could. And then a whirlwind of noise filled the air. And what came whistling over the rise?' Mircha leaned towards Yuri as if waiting for the right answer. And when Yuri didn't say anything, Mircha shouted, 'Black Tulips! Those helicopters of death, that's what we were hearing. The sound of the turbine rotors of these big cargo helicopters carrying the bodies of the dead. And something else you should know.' Mircha touched his stump. 'It was the way then to airlift bodies and dump them in the mountain lakes. You can just imagine what it did to those fish – may they all croak!'

Fish. Always the stories ended with fish. Now, as he had done that day, Yuri secured his helmet. It completely obliterated peripheral vision, but some days, that was a true blessing. And people may say what they want about luck and habit and superstition, may laugh at a grown man in a flight helmet, but when it came to fishing, nothing was more important than maintaining rituals, no matter how silly they may seem. This was another bit of wisdom gleaned from Mircha.

Yuri leaned over the sheer ice. The fish were as dark as stones and he loved them for their dodgy and quiet ways. Whatever their secret desires, if it were truly wings for fins, he'd never know. And somehow in Yuri's mind that made fish more noble than man, put them above the petty designs of people like him, standing on frozen ice or on muddy banks, their long shadows looming over them.

They were so splendid, these fish in their shiny coat of armour, impervious to the injustices of the day. And when he thought of them like this, he was almost glad when the wily eel or tricky pike sloughed a hook, freed itself, and swam away triumphant. Almost. Because he needed the food, after all. That was the real reason he and other veterans like him were all standing or crouching over the ice, freezing their hands and feet off. Because fish meant food or fish meant money. A deficit item like fresh fish could bring as much as fifty roubles if the right person arranged it with the right people. Sure Yuri knew about a practice in the West called catch and release. And in his heart he agreed with it completely. But these days his stomach held fewer philosophical inclinations. Besides, people in the West could afford to be more enlightened and environmentally responsible. They ate better over there and had the fat asses to prove it. Which is not to say he didn't believe in being sporting about the whole matter. He used baited hooks. Once he'd tried spinners. Today he was using his mother's ornamental spoon. Never – not even once – had he pulled any of Vitek's low tricks like rubbing slime on his arm and luring the pike or carp to swallow the arm up to the elbow, while punching them between the eyes as hard as he could with his free hand. Even so, Yuri felt a little anxious, couldn't help counting the veterans up and down the ice and wondering if any of them might be police. Nobody had a licence to fish here. Every one of the dark shapes over the ice was in actual fact a poacher. But as long as poachers shared their catch with the right people, life moved along like this river, without a snag, and everybody was happy. Everybody except the fish, that is.

Yuri set the auger, and started drilling.

'You! Prick on a stick! Hey!'

Yuri sat on his heels and squinted. He could not see who was yelling, but assumed they were yelling at him. Yuri pointed to the helmet, waved good-naturedly, and maintained air silence. Then he went back to drilling his hole. After all, as a veteran he had a right to fish here, at Mircha's spot.

'Bugger off, bottom feeder!' Crazy Volodya hollered at him from down river.

The rule of the river dictated that younger vets paid a fishing fee to the oldest and craziest vet. This morning, the oldest and – by far – the craziest vet on the river was Volodya, who lost his legs in the big war. Even without his legs, Volodya could beat Yuri to a pulp any day of his choosing. And Volodya would be well within his rights to do so: Yuri was only twenty-one, had fought in an unpopular war, had come home broken. Not like the old timers, not like Crazy Volodya who had in his day brought down German Junders, had the medals and decorations to prove it. Now Crazy Volodya sat in his wheelchair attended by two muscle-bound vets and fished anywhere he wanted. If you wanted to trade fishing spots with someone or move up or down river or dump bleach into the water or fish with Chinese firecrackers, then you had to work it out with Crazy Volodya. This always involved a complicated negotiation of favours and bribes or, at the very least, a simple beating. That was the hierarchy. And everywhere he went, no matter what he did, Yuri was at the bottom of the ladder.

Yuri packed up his gear and moved to a much less prestigious spot on the ice, close to the bank where plastic bottles and other bits of trash lay frozen in the ice. He leaned on the auger. The bit bucked just as it punched through to water.

'Yu–ri!' A voice, harsh as a crow's, sliced through the morning calm. It was Zoya, there on the bank wearing her most fashionable winter boots. She put her hands on her hips, shifted her weight from one foot to the other and back again. He read in those subtle movements her mood tipping from gorgeous wrath to toxic indignation and back to wrath.

'What are you doing?' she demanded. Even through the flight helmet, he could hear her slow-boiling anger. She was ovulating. He could hear it in her voice. The fuel behind her wrath. How dare he fish when her window of baby-making opportunity was so slim and narrow?

'Ice fishing.'

Zoya tapped her watch, a cheap Raketa, but he knew she considered it extremely fashionable. 'It's Sunday,' she reminded him.

Yuri inhaled deeply, waited for his lungs to burn. 'So, it's Sunday.'

'You're supposed to be at work. At the museum. With me.'

'I am working,' Yuri said. 'I'm fishing.'

Zoya sighed. 'Are you planning to have your head up your ass all your life?'

Yuri thought for a moment. 'No,' he said at last. 'Just through the holidays, I think.'

Zoya threw her hands up into the air. 'You'll lose the only job you're fit for. Nobody else will hire you, you know.'

Yuri hung his head. A muted flash of a tail fin caught his eye. When he looked towards shore a few moments later, Zoya had gone.

Yuri threaded his bait to the hook, a flashy silver chewing-gum wrapper, and bobbed it in the hole.

He supposed it was his good luck that there was a shortage of eligible bachelors. His luck that Zoya needed a place to live. Because, he was beginning to see, he needed a woman. And as his mother had been slow to object, Zoya simply remained, until asking her to go someplace else was almost unthinkable. He just didn't have it in him to make the big decisions by himself. For the most part, this situation, strained as it was at times, didn't seem to offend his mother's sensibilities as long as he and Zoya conducted their trysts at the museum or on the rooftop of the apartment building where his mother didn't have to see or hear them.

And living with Zoya, though an unconventional arrange-ment, sure, seemed natural, logical even given his long-established habit of letting God, fate or other women decide the course his life would take. And it seemed, always, some-body else – his teachers at school, his commanding officers, his friends and girlfriends – wanted to make these decisions for him. So let them, was his motto. Oh sure, every now and then, he'd make a token attempt, like refusing to work in favour of fishing, to suggest the illusion that he was an active partici-pant in his own life. But the truth was he felt grateful and relieved when events or people conspired to take matters into their own hands.

All this to say that when Zoya arrived a few months before at the museum five minutes early and descended to the hat/coat-check corridor, a suitcase in each hand, he did not protest, and was, in fact, secretly glad. But even in that small action, her carrying her suitcases, her broadcasting her intent to live with him, there was trouble. He knew that as Tanya quietly exchanged the suitcases for claim disks, Tanya did not understand what the suitcases meant. By the time they all three left work for crumbling apartment building, Yuri carrying the suitcases, he knew Tanya had figured it out: her gaze never once lifted from the tops of her shoes. As Zoya chattered about this thing and that, delighted and taking delight in even the smallest things as people do when they have found love or convinced themselves that love has found them, Tanya did not say a word. And Yuri had wanted to comfort her somehow, to explain. After all, they had always been such close friends. And Yuri would have just as happily allowed himself to wind up with a girl like Tanya, if only Tanya had made her wishes more clearly known. He wasn't a mind-reader, for heaven's sake.

But somehow he knew saying these things would not make Tanya feel any better. She was a sensitive soul. One look at that overstuffed notebook told him that. And he knew some things people should keep to themselves. He could never tell Zoya, for instance, that they were an item only because Zoya had insisted upon it and his mother hadn't protested. Nor could he ever reveal that another reason he'd gone along with it all was (God help him, it's such a stupid reason, but true) because Zoya's eyes were the same dark shade of purple and blue that spotted the Balık Lake trout. Tanya's eyes were more of a nicotine-stain-coloured brown-yellow like the underside of a Caspian Sea trout of the Kura River. A big-boned fish, the Caspian Sea trout – not his favourite, really. And when a man weighs the benefits of waking up to one face over another for the rest of his life, well, frankly, appearances do make a difference, though he knew it was unwise to say so in the presence of mixed company.

Just then, through the sheer ice, Yuri glimpsed the dark body of a pike. Hope inflated his veins and he felt his blood moving clean and bright. Scavengers and not overly smart, pike will eat anything – even in these temperatures. And they were greedy. Yuri yanked the line and quickly re-baited, this time with a ball of chicken lard, soft from being in his pocket, warmed by his thigh. Further up the line, Yuri tied his mother's tiny souvenir spoon. On the handle was a bright enamel picture of the Matterhorn, a mountain they'd never seen but which inspired the fish to bite. Yuri blew on his hands and dropped the line.

Not two minutes later the rod bowed sharp. Yuri hauled the line and pulled up the pike. It thrashed and twisted, its jaws snapping the air, its eyes consumed with rage. Yuri threw it on the ice and held it there under his knees. With a pocket knife, he made a horizontal slit below the jaw and retrieved his mother's ornamental spoon. He hovered there, waiting for a bellow from upriver. When it didn't come, Yuri tucked the spoon into his boot and the pike into a plastic shopping bag, and he pedalled home as fast as he could, the ticking in his head keeping time with the pedalling of his feet.

As Yuri coasted beneath the arch and into the dvor, Vitek's voice sailed caustic and brisk from behind the scrap heap. Even through the padding of the flight helmet, Vitek's voice was a slap against the ears: 'Queue up, you little creeps!'

Yuri dismounted, wheeled his bike to the lime tree, looped a chain and lock around the trunk and watched the children line up oldest to youngest: a yellow-haired girl, a red-haired boy with cracked glasses, two boys, identical twins with white hair and sallow skin, and a small dark-skinned child, whose sex Yuri could not determine.

'Now when you pick a pocket, you must remember: teamwork! Teamwork is the fuel that allows common people to produce uncommon results.' Vitek waved his arms at the stone archway. 'Now go out there and work as a team.'

The children didn't move.

Vitek picked up a piece of rusted cable and swung it through the air. 'Go on! Get lost!' he shouted, and the children trudged towards the arch.

Vitek stuffed his hands in his pockets and strolled towards Yuri. 'What's in the bag?'

'Pike,' Yuri said, opening the bag and peering inside. Vitek took the bag and bobbed it as if his arm were an imaginary scale. 'Feels like four kilos, maybe even five.'

Yuri handed over the pocket knife and Vitek laid the fish on the stone bench, where he began cutting the pike in two. Well, it was Vitek's way to nose in and take a portion of anything other people had. It was all part of his Mafiya-wannabe protocol. In short, it was Vitek's only goal in life to convince everyone that he had connections and knew things that he didn't and that he should be paid for cultivating his great reservoir of useless knowledge. Always it had been this way, for as long as Yuri could remember. Vitek, the little scabby-kneed apartment bully who grew up to be the big apartment bully claiming equal parts Mongol and Gypsy but establishing himself around the apartments as a full-blooded asshole. Vitek, who liked to wear his cracked leather jacket and slouch in the stairwells and doorways. Even worse, these days Vitek considered himself nouveau intelligentsia because he knew a man who completed computer school and could take a photo of any ordinary woman and superimpose her face over the body of known porn stars. All of which was to say, how people used their know-how left Yuri in a severe state of bafflement.

Yuri observed Vitek sawing and sawing with the knife and making zero progress. No, Vitek wasn't handy. But a few things he did know. That much Yuri had to give him. Though he failed entrance exams to the technical schools and though he'd never seen Vitek with a girl, the way Vitek talked about them convinced Yuri that Vitek was wise beyond his years when it came to matters of business and matters of the gentler sex. And what Vitek didn't know as fact, he valiantly made up for with an unbounded confidence that defied logic. His latest investment, bottled river water which Vitek hailed as having cryogenic properties due to the enormous chemical content, had been a dismal failure. 'It's a free market now. We have to get to the train stations and sell things – anything!' Vitek had urged, and because they had nothing they gave him their vouchers, their savings. Which he'd promptly invested and lost. Yes, Vitek thought he could crush hedgehogs with his bare ass. It was an entertaining image and Yuri closed his eyes, imagining.

'What's so funny?' Vitek puffed his chest out.

'Nothing.'

'Let me tell you something. Fishing is OK, but if you want to make some real money, you should re-enlist.'

Behind them Lukeria's windows crept up. Then out came Lukeria's head, her rubber plunger held to her ear.

'With all your experience, they'd probably promote you right away. Make you an officer. Then you'd really be in the money.'

'I'll think about that.' Yuri slung the bag with his half of the pike in it over his shoulder and climbed the stairs for the rooftop. Call him an idiot, and every day from the third floor Lukeria did, but even Yuri was smart enough to know that the Russian Army would be the death of him.

Yuri climbed the service ladder and pushed open the hatch that opened onto the roof. If he couldn't have water then give him the uncluttered air. Give him the pocked cornices and buckling tarpaper. Give him the rooftop that afforded him the perspective to see the broad expanse of landscape beyond the crumbling fringe of city. Give him the many shades of grey a city could yield, none of them pretty. Because no city lasts for ever. Something breaks the city blocks – in this case, trees, shiny and hard and blacker than city soot. A frozen vein of ice knuckled through them and into the city. It was a contrast hard and sharp on the eye, but somehow soothing to the soul. There was such a thing, even now, as black and white, and that he could still see and recognize the difference meant something to him.

Overhead a plane ripped the sky into halves. Below him in the courtyard Azade emerged from the latrine, a twig broom in hand. Yuri watched her sweep salt over the ice and listened to her muttering. Complaining. About Vitek. There was some-thing wrong with Vitek's head, she grumbled. And she was right, Yuri knew. Since his days in the Mozdok mobile hospital, one thing he'd learned was how to determine whether or not someone had a head problem.

In Yuri's case it was simple. For three weeks he could not see, could not talk, hear or move. It was as if he'd pulled his father's cracked flight helmet on and it had attached to his head completely.

His ears could not bear to hear any more. And within this darkness and silence Yuri was plunged into a loop of nightmarish memory he could not escape: Yuri ploughing through downtown Grozny in the T-90 tank. And what were they ploughing over? The bodies of their own dead and the people standing in the hulks of their apartment buildings. They were ethnic Russians. 'Comrades! Please!' an old man yelled at Yuri, who had the gun barrel leveled at the ground floor of the apartment. Sitting ducks, that's what they all were, the wily Chechens having taken to the hills.

So who were they killing? Yuri asked the targeter. 'Looks like Russians,' he replied. And that was the moment Yuri remembered who he was, that boy who had only wanted to fish, who wanted in that moment to be anything but Russian. And when mortar rounds blew the tank in front of them and gunfire strafed the column of tanks behind them, there was Yuri, miraculously unharmed. Outwardly whole. But inwardly shattered. *Shell shock*, a triage field doctor pronounced – the last thing, in fact, Yuri could remember anybody saying. And then he was strapped in the open cockpit of a Black Tulip, body bags stuffed stem to stern in the small cargo hold behind him, the dark bags the last thing he remembered seeing.

And then the light crept in on tiptoe.

'What can you see?' the doctors asked, wiggling their fingers in front of his eyes.

'Fingers,' Yuri replied. 'And tracers ghosting arcs through the sky.'

'What do you hear?'

'Spookies hosing down the hills,' he'd answered. 'And a metronome.'

The doctor standing to Yuri's left exchanged a glance with the doctor standing to Yuri's right. And then, as the days passed, he began to hear a sound. Just one. Ticking. And he was recovered, the doctors said, but Yuri was not so sure. His head – it was full of problems – even now the broken radios from the heap spat and chattered at him in the too-familiar language of manoeuvres and codes, all of the noise jostling and colliding so that one problem (*Zoya – will she ever be content living in an apartment without a toaster oven?*) merged with another (*Mother – will she ever be happy? Vitek – will he ever stop pestering me?*) and he would give anything to return to that world absent of sound.

Yuri leaned against the thin railing. In the metal he imagined he could feel the vibrations of an aeroplane rumbling overhead. Below him the heap glinted with frost, glistened with hard and hurting objects. And the pile shone and sang and from up here it was not so hard to imagine the allure of a sudden jump.

Yuri cast his fishing wire over the rail and observed its fall and hook around the handle of a Latvian manufactured refrigerator.

'Pssst. Let me give you some advice.'

Yuri whirled on his feet. 'Who's that?'

Yuri watched dumbfounded as a green cockaded service hat crested the service hole. Beneath the hat was the familiar head and face of Mircha. His eyes glittered bright as he hoisted himself up onto the roof, never looking so hale and hearty as now.

Mircha coughed. A polite cough. 'Oh, I like this air. Not as pure as in the uplands, but still, it's good. Smells like snow,' Mircha pointed his nose east and inhaled deeply. The sleeve of Mircha's service coat inflated like a windsock. Mircha looked at the sleeve, then at Yuri. 'Two knots. From the north. Brisk. You know what this air makes me think of?'

Yuri could feel his mouth moving, but he wasn't making a sound, not even a squeak.

'Makes me think of those foil strips they used to drop from planes. Radar jammers. We were all wearing our winter whites and advancing the mountain pass. And silver fell from the clouds, a blizzard of tinsel, shimmering down to the snow.' Mircha looked at the sky then spat over the roof railing. 'Oh, those were confusing times. The good Russian sympathizers and the good ethnic Russians and the good Muslim Soviet citizens hard pressed into a civil faith in civil authorities, all for the common good. Oh, it hurts my liver just thinking of it. Can you imagine the confusion – Laks and Lezghins, and Uzbeks and Ingushetians, and Avars and Kumuks, all of us fighting side by side. We were to defend Soviet interests, which were our interests, we were told. No turning back, Moscow was behind us. So off we went to crush our neighbours. And what were they doing? Singing the zikr and dancing in front of our tanks. Their women and children, too. And goats! Utter chaos, I can tell you.' Mircha rubbed his stump. 'A goat can sing pretty good when it has to.'

Yuri squeezed his eyes shut. 'We laid you out a month ago. Why are you here?'

Mircha smiled a sheepish smile and shrugged. 'That's right. Ask me questions. Go on.'

'Why?'

'Because then I have to answer them.'

'Why?'

Mircha brightened. 'Now you're getting the idea. It's just the way these things work.'

'So, tell me again why you are here.'

'Because I'm not buried. I'm not happy. I'm not happily buried.' Mircha smiled, a lopsided smile. 'At least, I think that's my problem.'

'How's the fishing on the other side?'

Mircha shifted his weight from the bad leg to the good one. 'I don't know,' Mircha sighed. 'I want to fish, but I can't.'

Yuri frowned. 'Why not?'

Mircha hooked his chin towards the edge of the roof. 'Look. What do you see down there?'

Yuri leaned over the concrete barrier. 'There's the heap with the tank and my bike beside the heap.'

'And?' Mircha prodded.

'Snow.'

'Look there at the dark patch next to the heap.'

'Melted snow.'

Mircha groaned. 'Next to the melted snow, what do you see?'

'It looks very muddy from up here.'

Mircha pinched Yuri's neck. 'Look harder.'

Yuri squinted. 'A small trench. A fox hole, but deeper.' Yuri turned to Mircha. 'What's in there?'

Mircha smiled. 'Lost things.'

'Like what?'

Mircha rubbed his stump. 'Arms, maybe. Prosthetic. Pure titanium.'

'You've not been in?'

'No, genius. That's why I'm showing it to you. There's a rule about these things. Living dead people can't go in and dead living people can. Ha! It just kills me!' Mircha leaned over the railing and spat.

'So what do you want me to do?' Yuri rubbed his head. Already he was feeling woozy about this hole business and Mircha who was dead but living. As a Jew, all talk of resurrection made him a little uncomfortable, though he thoroughly longed to believe that the body God had for him after this one expired would not falter and fail him as this one had.

'Get a shovel – a big one. And get busy.'

Mircha stepped away from the ledge then disappeared down the opened roof hatch.

Yuri rubbed his eyes, pulled the flight helmet back on and secured the strap as tight as he could. He took a deep breath, then started down the stairs for his mother's apartment.

'Who's making all that noise upstairs?' Olga called from the kitchen.

Yuri stood in the doorway between the kitchen and the outer room and studied his mother, outlined at the window. 'It's Mircha, Mother. He's on the roof. Again.'

CHAPTER FIVE

Tanya

For the devout Russian orthodox, that tenebrous moment when dark dissolved into day was the very same moment when the knees should touch the floor. This was the moment when the faithful bowed to the red corner, the place in every orthodox home where the family icons and a candle were kept. It was a hard religion for the arthritic and frail, but for as long as Tanya had lived with her grandmother – that is, all of Tanya's life – Lukeria had always been as faithful to these rituals as a barnacle to the bottom of a boat. Every morning Tanya listened to her grand-mother roll carefully off her bed and scuffle through the dark to the kitchen. A soft scraping of the legs of the wooden chair, a quiet grunt, and Tanya knew the woman was up. A clatter of metal, a moment of supreme silence, and then – if she listened very hard – something odd: the sound of a kiss. This morning routine had always seemed a great mystery to Tanya. The only icons Tanya had ever seen were wooden ones displayed in a glass cabinet and that was in a church that had been shut down and then reopened as a museum. Kept as they were under lock and key, there was no possibility of owning these relics. Certainly, no one kissed them.

But then the year Tanya turned thirteen, the bells in a few of the churches were allowed to ring. People were saying the unthinkable and hoping for things they'd never allowed themselves to hope for. At the city university history professors cancelled exams. 'Not to worry,' Tanya saw one of these professors say on TV. 'We believe in the future. It's the past we're not so sure about.' About that same time Lukeria stopped hiding her metal icons behind those shabby pictures of fruit. All this inspired in Tanya a boldness she'd never felt before, and one morning she followed her grandmother into the kitchen, solemnly watched the morning protocol and even ventured a religious question.

'Why do you kiss the icons?'

Lukeria did not look at Tanya, but merely climbed down from the wooden chair as steadily as she had climbed onto it, as if she'd known all along that Tanya had been observing her. 'The kiss is a reminder to hold heaven on the lips,' Lukeria said evenly.

Tanya helped Lukeria scoot the chair back to its proper place. 'Do they kiss back?' Tanya asked.

Lukeria straightened, looked as if she'd been slapped across the face. From that day on, if heaven were at her grandmother's lips, then pure hell was on her tongue. If ever Tanya ventured a question, Lukeria turned surly and short. About her work on the Sverdlovsk line, Lukeria would say very little. Inside that steamer trunk was a wooden box her grandmother had shown

her once – only once – and inside the wooden box – an Honourable Railway Worker Medal. It took her forty years to earn this
medal and was not an easy feat for her, a small woman, and one
of the only women on the tracks working among men.

'Did you sell tickets?' Tanya asked.

'No.'

'Inspect travel documents?' This question produced a dark
look like none she'd ever seen before on her grandmother's face.

'I pulled the traction string that was connected to the
switch at the box. Some trains were sent south, some east
beyond the Urals. And then some were diverted to the spur
that ran to Kutchina.'

Kutchina was a word in Perm like no other. If the Devil had
a nickname it was Kutchina. If there was a hell outside of hell,
it was Kutchina. But being the child that Tanya was, in the
presence of something horrible and secret, she had to ask –
wanted to know – what was in those wagons that barrelled
over the tracks toward Kutchina?

'Freight.'

'Cows?'

'Not cows.'

'Pigs?'

'Not pigs. People.'

'What kind of people?'

'People like you wouldn't believe. Dissidents. People who
talk. Otherwise-minded people. Poets.'

Could this be the answer to the riddle, the answer to the

real question Tanya had wanted to ask: Where was her mother? Where had Marina gone? Had she, too, taken a fatal train ride? Tanya wasn't completely a child anymore, she had started to bleed down below and felt it was time her grandmother told her the things girls like her needed to know.

Lukeria merely nodded to the windows, to the clouds. 'She went to a better place,' she said in a voice as flat and formidable as the steppe in February, as the back of her iron skillet from Magnitogorsk.

Even then, Tanya knew that a better place was anywhere but here. Australia. Canada. Finland. Or maybe the Black Sea – Sochi – where they sold lemon ices. As an Honourable Railway Worker, Tanya's grandmother, Tanya figured, would know all these things. Of course Tanya asked.

'Don't ask the cuckoo in the tree foolish questions,' Lukeria replied, and it was then that Tanya understood her mother's departure had been swift and it had been Tanya's fault. Tanya had been unwanted and there was nothing she could ever do to change that fact. She felt a sadness that no words in the world could name. Yoked with that sadness was the hard and sudden understanding that if she could not be lovable, then she must try to be likeable. And if not likeable, she must at all costs find ways to be useful, malleable, agreeable. If her grandmother loved an invisible God, then Tanya would too. If her grandmother prayed on her knees in the morning, Tanya would pray too. She would learn the protocols and the rituals and recite the prayers, quietly, of course. The stories about the saints and their miraculous visions in the forests, all these things she would treasure in her heart, because these were the grand stories of faith, and her grandmother valued them. And faith, her grandmother said, was cloud, water and air, acted upon by the unseen hand of God. Faith was not about knowing where the path led, but believing the path led somewhere. And when her grandmother talked like that, in a whisper – always a whisper – her words were to Tanya the greatest gift. Her words were beautiful and wise because Tanya knew that they had first come from an old woman, maybe even the great-grandmother Tanya had never met, but who had, nevertheless, whispered them to Lukeria – but only after it had once been whispered to that old woman, and so on and so on. This was how the faithful find God – in repetition of sound and gesture over time. That was tradition and tradition was not some silly ritual or toneless chant, but one woman after another, a mother singing into the ear of her daughter the words and the melody of an ancient unbroken song, which, Tanya was learning, almost always sounded like suffering.

On this morning, Tanya stood at the threshold dividing kitchen from living room. Lukeria had already kissed the icons, something Tanya was still not permitted to do, and now she was reading aloud from one of the many letters she kept locked in the steamer trunk.

Though it is cold and the work is hard winter will not last forever.

This was just one of the many letters Lukeria found on the tracks, tossed from the wagons. Some of the letters even had photos inside, prayer cards, locks of hair. Perhaps they were written by prisoners in transit, men and women desperate to discard anything that might be used against them or their families.

> *Slava has taken ill with a vapour.*
> *I have given him my blanket.*

Or likely as not, they were simply letters in excess, the letters prisoners had written beyond their twice-a-year allowance. Confiscated by the guards, these missives were stowed in the wagons to be pulped and recycled, and somehow they'd found their way into her grandmother's trunk.

> *But do not worry. Some things never change.*
> *The stars shine whether we see them or not.*

Pure poetry, some of these letters. This one anyway. The Yellow Letter, Tanya dubbed it. Folded and refolded so many times it was the suggestion of paper; bends and seams rather than actual wood fibres held it together.

> *I will always love you.*

The kettle screamed. The spell broken, Lukeria stopped

reading, carefully refolded the letter in half and tucked it between her blue bathrobe and the side of the chair.

They had lived together for so long they were like an old married couple, only noticing the other when, like a stitch dropped, a line forgotten, something in the pattern of their routine went askew. This is the only way Tanya could explain why her grandmother would make herself so painfully transparent, reading aloud a love letter that was not written to her, but that she read and reread, claiming it as her own.

Tanya carried the tea to where Lukeria sat in contemplation before the weak light resolving itself to day. A leaden hulking cloud massif, the kind that carries snow, obscured the horizon. Tanya sank into the chair opposite Lukeria and opened her cloud notebook. If she superimposed that horizontal scoring of her grandmother's forehead and the deep crow's feet at the corners of her eyes over her own doughy half-finished face she could translate cloud to image, translate water to woman, and bring her mother back, as long as they two, grandmother and granddaughter, sat at the window.

Today the grey is a hueless hue hovering between light and dark. I want to know you by your eyes, your lashes, your hands, your teeth. Instead you are light dampened by windows, colour with the noise turned low.

'When I was your age,' Lukeria paused to light a cheap Bulgarian cigarette, 'I was prettier than you are now.'

Tanya closed her notebook and made noises of quiet assent in the back of her throat. Like her morning prayers, Lukeria'a cutting remarks were simply another part of her daily routine that she had to complete in order to iron the wrinkles out of the evening. You cannot bless without cursing, her grandmother sincerely believed, and most days, ignoring her grandmother was easy enough to do: as long as the tea and cigarettes held out, her mouth was otherwise occupied. But in that twenty-second lapse, the time it took to stub out a cigarette and light a new one, her tongue moved unhindered.

'Men followed me everywhere I went. But you, Tanyechka! I think all that university knowledge has ruined your chances. You've got no waistline whatsoever. It's as if everything you learned at school went straight to your hips and thighs. I hope you are trying to do something about that. Twenty years old already and you haven't got a man on the horizon. You haven't got a single plan.' Lukeria jabbed her cigarette at Tanya, then collapsed against the chair, exhausted by her own words.

'I have plans.' Tanya calibrated her voice so as not to betray her faltering self-confidence, her very palpable understanding of her many flaws, and the crushing statistical unlikelihood that her dreams would ever materialize.

'What plans?'

Tanya tugged on the hem of her skirt. 'Aeroflot is hiring.'

'Don't get your hopes up. You're lucky to have work at such a fine museum. It took two pairs of galoshes and my entire secret stash of jellied fruit slab to arrange it. Besides, you have unfortunate dentition. I don't say this to be cruel, only to state the obvious as a nudge to the reality of your situation.'

Like an old combine that moves in one direction and at one speed, her grandmother's commentary faithfully ploughed over the same territory, grinding over familiar furrows.

Lukeria fumbled with another cigarette.

Tanya nudged a small box of matches closer to Lukeria's elbow. As she did, her hand jogged the teacup and the contents spilled onto the Bible.

'Shit!' Tanya jumped and dabbed at the mess with the dish-cloth she kept handy for such catastrophes. But already the onion-skin pages of the Bible had swelled like a sponge.

Lukeria narrowed her nickel-coloured eyes, calculating the cost of the loss of tea. 'Shouldn't you be at work?'

Tanya stood, retrieved her notebook, her sweater. Her scarf.

'Another thing. Talk to Chumak.'

Tanya edged towards the door. In her grandmother's rattle-dry voice she could hear the crack and spit of a smouldering fire rekindled.

'Remind him that I knew his mother when she let that dirty pepper-eating Hungarian take her for long walks by the river. Tell him I know things. Tell him you need money for my medi-cine – the expensive one for my lungs.'

Tanya knotted her scarf around her neck – tight – and pulled the door closed.

Love. That's what Tanya was hearing. Behind the quick fury there had to be love. Fire consumes what it loves. That was another orthodox lesson. What Lukeria was doing was for her own good because had Lukeria poured her love unchecked on Tanya, she might have grown bloated and lazy from it. And her still-hungry but overfed heart would split from the excess, and on it would go, Tanya as a mother overindulging her own child. To what end? One little poke in life, one disappointment – major or minor – and her daughter would be done for, unable to cope with heartbreak. Thank heavens that she, now outwardly stout, inwardly anorexic, was so well acclimatized for a life without love. Yes, Tanya decided as she shoved three sticks of chewing gum into her mouth and turned for the bus stand, she'd been so well schooled in the thrifty economy of the heart, she could go months and even years without a single drop of genuine affection.

On the number 77, Tanya worked the gum between her molars. It was a form of exercise, this gum chewing. And she needed it, exercise, in any form. In twenty minutes she'd have to step on the scales for Head Recruiter Aitmotova. The very thought provoked spastic jaw pumping. In front of her a young mother held a baby. The young woman bent her head to her baby, nuzzling the fuzz of the child's hair, her mouth so close to the child's, it looked as if they were breathing each other's warm air. It was so beautiful, so foreign to Tanya that she could not stop staring. 'Stop!' she wanted to warn that mother. Certainly Lukeria would have. Such affection was precisely the kind of waste that infuriated Lukeria, who believed that mothers cuddling and cooing, showering kisses on the heads of newborns, who'd never know the difference, were spending their love carelessly and would too soon run out. Because love, and Tanya knew this for a certain fact, was not as limitless as people in books and movies liked to suggest. Love was like food, like money. It was so rare, so precious, that it had to be accounted for absolutely. This she learned from Lukeria, who knew how to stretch a single chicken through an entire winter, who had spent a lifetime putting up any wayward piece of fruit or vegetable into glass jars that sat on a shelf as a visual reminder of the importance of thrift, the importance of preserving what was authentic and true for a day when it was needed. And as beautiful as this mother and child were, as pure and spontaneous as the woman's love was, Tanya was glad her grandmother wasn't there to see it.

Outside the recruiting office, Tanya spat the wad of gum into a dirty drift of snow, ducked under the door's low overhang, and leaned heavily into the door.

'Sit.' Head Administrator Aitmotova pointed to a tiny three-legged stool positioned beside an oversize scale. 'How many languages do you speak?' She assumed a look of grave interest in Tanya.

'Three, plus I know at least half a dozen universal gestures of varying degrees of vulgarity.'

Head Recruiter Aitmotova scribbled on her clipboard and smiled. 'That's wonderful. Now, drop your coat and step onto the scales, please.'

Tanya held her breath and lifted her arms, as if that might prevent the needle's steady sweeping march across the number dial. Head Recruiter Aitmotova noted the measurement with a click of her tongue and a sigh. 'Big thighs and a big butt aren't big assets with Aeroflot. If you could just lose two stone and about five centimetres off each thigh, your chances would increase dramatically,' she said, offering Tanya several more packs of Juicy Fruit chewing gum. 'It's really quite simple,' she smiled. 'Just don't eat so much. Try following the zero-one-zero plan.'

Tanya slid out of the recruiting office and trudged towards the museum. Eating nothing for breakfast or dinner and relying on a single midday meal was a fine idea, as fine a method of weight loss as any. But not every girl has the willpower to simply stop eating for days on end like Zoya had. And Tanya had never gone in for hawking into toilets. What a waste of good food!

Tanya stood outside the employee entrance to the museum and leaned against a piece of metal twisted in a huge Russian 'R'. It had been donated to the museum in commemoration of the possible resurrection of the Russian rouble. It was modern art. That meant it was OK for Tanya to push her gum into hard rivets along the metal undersides and kick her heels against it to knock the ice loose from her boots.

She pushed through the glass door and waved her badge at

Ludmilla. Tanya's first stop, always, was the basement-floor exhibit of curiosities. Not the tiny storage room where they kept the rocks meant to be representative of the kinds of geological samples one could actually find underneath Perm, but the larger exhibit room with the dark green walls and the torches Tanya had strategically placed to achieve optimal atmospheric effect. This was where they kept the pseudo-Kuntskamera collection, their most popular exhibit with museum-goers. The exhibit consisted of a collection of spontaneously aborted neonates that Peter the Great had obtained from a Dutch doctor. All of the foetuses possessed alarming defects: a third arm, missing legs, no eyes. She and Yuri and Ludmilla had studied the photos of the real exhibit that sat in the Kuntskamera building somewhere in St Petersburg. Then they had lovingly fashioned the babies out of foam, submerged them in jars of orange-flavoured Fanta and artfully draped several of Lukeria's doilies and scarves around the jars – all of which had also been co-opted for the cause. All this in a bid to attract more visitors to the museum.

And it worked. People did come to see the exhibit, out of moribund curiosity, out of boredom, Tanya couldn't say. She herself, for a reason that defied human logic, took comfort looking at them in their glass jars. If she had not known they were meant to be human, she might have considered them beautiful for their excesses and lacks. Especially the boy who had no arms or legs. Having only a head and torso, he was unfinished, as if a seamstress had run out of stuffing and stitched shut his tapered torso. But the real boy, whose picture she'd memorized, had developed enough to grow a short tuft of red hair on his head and wore the sweetest smile on his face. Did his mother love him any less because he was monstrously malformed? Tanya wondered. Or how about the twins, turned toward each other, clasping one another with arms and legs, sharing the same heart and head? Sharing every secret and every thought. Possessing enough between them, what need did they have for this world that would only tear them apart? And yet, did their mother grieve their passing any less? Would not these women have cradled them to the breast and called them perfect? Tanya pressed her fingers to the glass. She knew this much: she would have called them perfect because they'd have been hers.

And if we, each of us still children in our own ways, you missing your father and me having never known a mother, were to have a child it would be whole. Between us, we would be gloriously whole, perfectly completed, giving this child the things we never had or knew. You would teach him to fish and I would explain to her the theology of love unbounded. You could arrange the scales of the trout in intricate patterns that mirror the constella- tions and I would teach her the importance of sorting the greens when making sorrel soup.

Her pencil flying across the page, Tanya almost didn't hear gathering in the stairwell the trademark sounds of Head Administrator Chumak working himself up the steps: *thump–slide, thump–slide, thump–slide*. First his head appeared, brilliant beetroot red, then his thick torso, his legs, and at last, that leaden foot.

'Oh, Tanya! There you are!' Head Administrator Chumak reached the top of the landing. His face burned through the shades of magenta and then as it cooled through the pinks, his freckles slowly reasserted themselves.

'How are you doing with that application form?'

Tanya bit her lip. 'Some of the questions are giving me a little trouble. The one about handshakes, for instance.'

A smile blazed across Chumak's face. 'I love a good handshake, don't you?'

'That's just it. I don't know what a handshake is meant to signify.'

Silence. As thick as calf's liver.

'A handshake signals firm intention, goodwill, and trustworthiness in commercial transactions.'

'Oh.' Tanya rolled her gaze to the ceiling. 'Then I'd say the handshake is most definitely on the wane.'

'Don't write that. An application is an occasion for optimism at all costs,' Chumak said through that blazing smile, but his eyes were steely like flint. 'Any other, er, problems?'

An affectionate pass of her hands over her notebook, a hard swallow. Optimism.

Tanya patted her notebook affectionately and swallowed hard, thinking *optimism*. 'No. Almost finished.'

'Wonderful! Because there is so much at stake, for all of us.' Head Administrator Chumak eyed Tanya's notebook. 'And that's why I believe in you, Tatiana Nikolaevna Bobkov. I believe because you are a little like me – a person of great substance, placed under great pressure, and we all know what that produces!' Another savage grin galloped across Head Administrator Chumak's face.

'Ulcers?' Tanya ventured.

'Ha,' Head Administrator Chumak laughed – a single combustive bark. From his file, he withdrew a fax, a single thin sheet of paper that curled in the air, and began reading.

```
A delegation of the Americans of Russian
Extraction for the Causes of Beautification
will visit the museum that submits the best
application and demonstrates the greatest need
and greatest potential for development. Also
the benefactors wish to observe the museum
workers in their natural environment.
```

Tanya's stomach seized. 'You don't mean…?'

Head Administrator Chumak nodded gravely. 'Precisely. If they come, then they will want to spend a night with you and Zoya and Yuri – in your apartments.'

'But, sir. Our apartments are in no condition to be seen and certainly in no condition to live in.'

Head Director Chumak grimaced. 'Oh, I know. I faxed them most emphatically, but these people are quite determined. They wish to.' Head Administrator Chumak squinted fiercely at the fax: '"Experience first hand how living as you do, amidst the intersection of art and life, defines your artistic aesthetic."' Head Director Chumak winced. 'Apparently this is quite important in their selection process. So it will be up to you to make the apartments habitable.'

Head Administrator Chumak stretched his lips into another flinty smile, then turned and began his long thump and slide back down the stairs.

At the far end of the museum café Zoya and Yuri sat behind a small metal table. To get there Tanya had to skirt around a series of tables pushed together into a long line. A local chess club was practising for a simultaneous chess tournament. Five men brooded over five different chessboards while the other five men roamed from board to board. With each move of a chess piece, Tanya could hear their excited misery and terrible human longings amplified by the strange acoustics of the café: too old for the army, too young to retire, too beat up by life to find a job and keep it, too broke for a bottle.

Zoya blew clouds of cigarette smoke above Yuri's head. Yuri, a metronome out of kilter, tipped his head first to one side, then the other. His colour was off, more sallow than usual.

When Yuri saw Tanya, he hopped up and pulled out a chair for her.

'Are you all right?' Tanya asked Yuri.

Zoya laid a hand across Yuri's forehead, a gesture borrowed from Olga. 'It's just that shell shock again. You know – he hears things.'

'Oh. The ticking,' Tanya suggested.

Yuri's shoulders lifted and fell as he sighed. 'Last night I saw Mircha on the roof.'

'But he's dead,' Tanya said.

'But not buried,' Yuri said.

Tanya bit her lip. 'I wonder what he wants.' Everybody knew the dead only lingered out of spite. Or sometimes a deeply held nostalgia for the tangible provoked their return. A beloved handbag. A pair of shoes.

'We stood together on the roof and he pointed down to our frozen dvor and the scrap heap and to a place beside the heap and that's when I saw something I had never noticed before.'

'What?'

'A black open gouge in the ground. A big dark opening.'

'How did it get there?' Tanya whispered.

'I don't know. But he told me that beneath this world was another world. A bright country of lost things.' Yuri swayed slightly in his chair.

'We live on top of a marsh. Try to be relevant.' Zoya tugged at her hair, which was dyed a brassy brick red.

Yuri's gaze locked on Tanya's. 'You believe me, don't you?'

Tanya blinked. 'Oh, absolutely.'

'Good. Because I need you to ask Daniilov for his shovel.'

'What's wrong with Azade's?'

'No good, Mircha says. It's not big enough.'

'Oh, for God's sake.' Zoya stood and ordered a coffee.

She was, Tanya decided, an impatient woman, lacking in common compassion. She could not suffer any deviation in the conversation. Which was to say, if Zoya were present, all conversation revolved solely around herself. And she was plagued by the artistic temperament. She abhorred all art except her own, found recognition of any other artist or any other unattached female morally reprehensible. Working these days, as she did, in the museum, if Zoya weren't taking a cigarette break or with Yuri, she was extremely miserable. Her only recourse was to dye her hair as often as possible in the most brilliant hues possible. When her hair, brittle and frayed, could not possibly sustain another dye job, she turned her artistic sensibilities upon family and co-workers.

'What are those?' Zoya narrowed her eyes at the manila-colored file.

'Some applications forms.' Tanya rubbed the back of her neck where Zoya had recently burned her with peroxide solution.

'For?'

'Aeroflot.' Tanya's voice was flat and heavy as a grounded Ilyushin.

'Oh.' Zoya's gaze settled on Tanya's hips, measuring her girth. 'Really?'

'Yes,' Tanya slid another piece of gum into her crowded mouth. 'I have to reduce and quite possibly I need to have my teeth looked at before I can begin flight-crew training. But at least I'm on the waiting list. And the recruiter said she'd definitely give me a call. Maybe.'

With another glance, Zoya inventoried Tanya's hair, her nails. 'Well, if you need professional advice regarding hair and make-up, let me know,' Zoya said in a voice meant to be a whisper, but the acoustics in the museum were so highly unique that Tanya knew everyone, even those closeted in the lavs, could hear it all perfectly well.

'And this?' Yuri pointed to Head Administrator Chumak's file.

Tanya laid the folder reverently on the table. 'It's an assignment. For us.'

Zoya opened the folder and began reading. Zoya was smarter than she was, Tanya decided as she watched Zoya. She could read English without moving her lips and she read the entire application form, top to bottom, front to back in less than a minute. It was disgusting.

'Imagine,' Zoya shook her head, but her hair remained absolutely still. 'People in America with extra money and they want to give it away. Incredible. And all we have to do is answer these questions.'

'What do they want to know?' Yuri asked.

Zoya cleared her throat and began reading: '"Describe what 'positive work ethic' means to you. Do you like Americans, and in particular, those of the western variety? Explain what you think team spirit means (please use a separate sheet of paper for your explanation)."'

'This is the strangest application form I've ever heard,' Yuri said.

'It's written by people who appreciate art; you wouldn't understand,' Zoya replied, a sour expression on her face.

'You're right,' Yuri said, his torso listing harder to the right. He turned to Tanya. 'What is "positive work ethic"? Do such words even belong together?'

Tanya shrugged. 'Inscrutable.'

Zoya smoked fiercely. 'Americans are mad for work. It's why they have so much extra money. It's why they feel so positively about working.'

'I would too, if I got paid for it.' Yuri scratched his nose absently. 'But that "team spirit" stuff makes me nervous.'

'Maybe it's like the old idea of the *mir*,' Tanya mused. 'You know – the close kinship of community. Like what we're doing here. We're answering hard questions. Together. This is very Russian. This is very team spirit. We could write this down.'

Zoya licked her lips. 'We could write this down. Team spirit is answering together these three questions: who's to blame, what's to be done about it, and how to divide it all up.' Zoya lit another cigarette. 'This is the very definition of Russian team spirit. And it's easy to answer the first two questions. The blame falls squarely on you, Tanya, if anything goes wrong.

After all, it's not for nothing that Chumak gave the assignment to you. What's to be done about it? Again, Tanya, your problem. How to divide the resources? Now that's where the team work gets interesting.'

Tanya could see in Yuri's eyes that he had his bags packed, was travelling to faraway places, fishing no doubt for the magical pike who would solve their every problem.

'Just imagine,' Zoya sighed happily, spooning sugar into her coffee, 'what we could do with this money.' Zoya looked under her eyelashes at Yuri. 'We could honeymoon like real Europeans. We could have a baby and bring it up *kulturny*, a miniature version of a better us.' She smiled obliquely.

Zoya's desire for a child was so naked and near that Tanya could feel the skin of her face and neck tighten. Always she had considered Zoya to be a little like those cheap bras the Korean woman sold at the end of their street. Fabricated out of whatever materials were on hand, they were transparent and the straps wandered no matter how tightly you cinched them. And this is what bothered her: how very similar she and Zoya really were in substance if not form, in ambition and desire. Tanya glanced at her dreambook. The only difference was that Tanya kept a little quieter about her wishes. That's all.

Zoya, noticing Tanya's brooding silence, turned a vague smile in her direction. 'And Tanya! You could get your teeth fixed or something.'

Yuri spread his quaking hands over the table. 'Yes, well, we haven't got it yet and even if we get the grant, it's not really ours,' he said quietly.

'Of course it's ours. If it comes as a result of our efforts, then most certainly it's ours,' Zoya insisted.

'But Head Administrator Chumak,' Tanya said.

'So he gets a controlling portion, but we'll just make him see. He'll have to understand, because he hasn't paid any of us for nearly four months.'

'Maybe he would finally pay us,' Yuri said.

'Certainly he would pay himself,' Tanya said.

'And Daniilov,' Yuri tipped his head to the right.

'Because he's so handy with the toilets,' Tanya said.

'And because clean toilets are at a premium,' Yuri tipped to the left.

'Which is not in any way to criticize Azade and the latrine,' Tanya said.

'Because, God knows, it's not easy in circumstances like hers,' Yuri said.

'Shut it!' Zoya said, lighting another cigarette. Any playfulness in language, with the exception of verbal abuse, Zoya could not abide. 'First we'll get Chumak to sign a contract for set wages with scheduled raises, say six per cent the first year, twelve per cent the next, and so on and so forth.' Zoya danced her fingernails over the tabletop, figuring on an imaginary calculator.

'What's twelve per cent of nothing?' Yuri asked.

'Try to stay relevant,' Zoya snapped.

'But, really, I don't think it would be wise to let on that we haven't been paid; it makes us sound too desperate,' Tanya said.

'I agree,' said Yuri. 'We should temper our answers with cautious desperation. For instance, we shouldn't tell them that the biggest attractions for us museum workers are the café and the toilets. And if it should come up, we should tell them that we work for sporadic pay because the art exhibits themselves are our reward.'

'In that case we probably shouldn't tell them that we made all the exhibits ourselves,' Tanya said.

'I don't know.' Zoya licked the rim of her coffee cup. 'The inferior quality of the exhibits might work to our advantage. They are proof that we are just that much more deserving of the money.'

'Because then we'd use the grant to buy better art,' Yuri suggested.

'No, we wouldn't.' Zoya rolled her eyes towards the ceiling. 'That's not the point.'

'What's the point?' Yuri asked.

'Money, stupid. We need and want the money.' Zoya dropped her cigarette in her coffee.

Tanya retrieved the application form and stuffed it into the manila file.

'So, as soon as you return the application form we get this grant? Just like that?' asked Zoya.

Tanya could feel her veins deflating. 'No. This is a competition. We have to fight it out.'

'So we have a sporting chance?' Yuri said.

'Well, I don't know,' Tanya said. 'Bratsk is universally agreed upon as the armpit of the world. And they have a museum.'

'And Blagoveshchensk.' Yuri wagged his head sadly. 'Oh, God. If somebody from Blagoveshchensk enters, we're done for. Except for that mummy of an Altai princess drip-drying in their basement, I hear their exhibits are even worse than ours. They are voluminously worthy.'

'It gets worse,' Tanya said. 'Part of the selection process involves a visit from the Americans. They want to observe us. In our natural environment.'

'Oh.' Zoya's eyes glazed.

'Yes.' Tanya nodded her head balefully.

'They can't visit the apartments,' Yuri said. 'There's Mircha holding forth from the rooftop. And then there's that big hole.'

Zoya laid her palm on Yuri's forehead, as if to check for a fever. 'Well.' She stood and brushed invisible crumbs from her skirt. Yuri stood and helped her into her coat. 'I guess it all depends on you, then, Tanya.' Zoya took Yuri's hand in hers, and together they moved towards the mezzanine staircase.

Every man in the café, even those engaged in crucial end-game moves, looked up, fingers suspended in mid-air, while their eyes measured Zoya's legs, her backside. Tanya rolled her eyes heavenward. She took another swallow of air, of cloud. Willed herself towards a more buoyant outlook, and withdrew the application form from the envelope. A simple test and this time, she'd pass. Tanya reviewed the instructions on the cover page of the application form.

```
Please type all answers to questions on sepa-
rate sheets of paper (20 lb rag-linen content)
in 12 pt. font size, leaving one-inch margins
on all sides. No answer should exceed one page in
length. Photos and narrative are encouraged.
```

Twenty-pound rag weight? Tanya pinched the bridge of her nose between her forefinger and thumb. There was a paper shortage in all of Russia. Certain newspaper agencies were offering vouchers and even cash for used paper of any sort. People were even pulping their precious war-time letters and hardbound classics for mere kopeks. The Americans of Russian Extraction for the Causes of Beautification could not possibly know this, and Tanya decided it was prudent not to waste what little paper she did have explaining the shortage. Also, pencils were in short supply. But a Russian can produce a monkey out of a pipe cleaner. That is to say, if anything, she was resourceful. Tanya retrieved an eyebrow pencil from her purse, whittled it between her teeth to a point and considered the question: What is your favourite colour?

Random phrases from past exams, compositions she'd written for university classes she'd never completed immediately trotted to the surface of her memory and Tanya's eyebrow pencil scuttled over her notebook.

When one discusses colour and particularly when one assigns value to colour one must first exercise great care in the naming and distinguishing of one colour from the other. Consider, for example, the vast difference between Ukrainian blue and Prussian blue. Ukrainian blue leans toward the hues of Siberian iris in early May, at skies cooling above the vast steppe, as say in the work of Isaak Levitan (see, for example, the <u>Vladimirka</u>, which is, unfortunately, not at the present moment on exhibit at the All-Russia All-Cosmopolitan). Prussian blue, on the other hand, suggests a darker full-bodied blue that painters in France used to call Berlin blue and painters in Germany used to call Paris blue because it is an unpredictable and risky mixture of hues that tended to crack as it dried.

On the opposite side of the colour wheel, yellow holds an indispensable position in modern art. Levitan found he could not paint the wide open spaces of the steppe without it and had to cut his yellows with iodine. Some painters, like Cézanne, preferred brighter, thicker yellows such as the Indian Yellow made from the urine of dogs force-fed mango leaves. Without a doubt the most important colour to consider when discussing Russian landscape painting is white flake. Get it *into a cut on your finger and you might as well start digging your own grave. However, any Russian painter will tell you it is the queen of colours on the palette if you want to give density and texture to clouds in a Russian sky.*

Utter nonsense, what she was writing. But it sounded arty. And that was what mattered. If there was one thing she had learned while garnering mediocre marks in university, it was how to answer exam questions without really answering them. With the greatest of ease she answered the other questions: Americans of all varieties they absolutely adored. If stranded on an island she would take anything of Chagall's. Always somebody floated free of their cluttered foreground, as if gravity were a force designed for everyone else the artist knew, but not these people he loved in his paintings. Never them.

Ridiculous. Tanya shook her head and stuffed the application form back into its folder.

Outside the museum Tanya walked past the city park, a popular place for newlyweds to stroll with their wedding party, the groom with a blue sash around his chest, the bride carrying a bouquet of silver balloons or carnations. Today a limousine sidled up to the kerb, a wedding doll tied to the grill. As Tanya approached, the limo shot from the kerb, spraying her with muddy ice water while the doll whistled through her painted plastic smile.

'Oh, up yours,' Tanya mumbled, her mood having turned

on a tight hairpin. She was jealous and could admit it. Jealous and angry. Angry that anybody could experience marital bliss or any form of happiness when she couldn't. Angry with herself for being the child that she was, is. Angry that she had so completely fallen for Yuri and allowed herself to imagine that her loving Yuri was all it would take to provoke a similar response from him.

God had given him the artist's eye, but not a steady hand. That's why she was convinced they belonged together, he with his imagination, and she with her vocabulary of colour and cloud. Together they would paint the fish of the world. Which is what she told Yuri in the stairwell one evening. Sentimental, sure, but hers was a clumsy heart that too quickly betrayed her longings. He'd just come back from hospital and was shaky as ever. For one glorious week he allowed her to steady him. And Tanya didn't ask questions, so glad was she that he'd returned, safe and sound in body, if not in spirit. He had not yet met Zoya, and it was a glorious week of possibility, a world without other women or the knowledge of other women, a simple world where two people, friends in life, would become friends in love.

And it had almost happened! Yuri bent his head toward her and with deliberation backed her against the wall. And she thought, at last – it took fifteen years and another war – but at last he was looking beyond that cracked visor and finally seeing her as she was: the upstairs girl who had loved him all her life. And why had she loved him all her life? Because he was like her, missing a parent and feeling the lack. And she had thought that he without his father and she without her mother, leveled equally by their losses, would be perfectly matched. But then of course – of course – Lukeria, whose troubling bladder had always squeezed and pinched at the most inopportune times, chose that precise moment to use the latrine. The door flew open and Lukeria caught them in the near act of kissing. Tanya jumped as if she'd been stung with a jolt of electricity.

'Disgraceful!' Lukeria pronounced with all her former authority of a railway passport controller, accustomed to denying people on sight. Lukeria slammed the door closed. Then she flung open the door again. 'Casting your pearls before swine! You know he's not a real Russian.' Which was her grandmother's way of reminding them all that Jewish blood raced undiluted through his veins and rendered him, to her way of thinking, only slightly more valuable than an ox or a cow, an ox or a cow being more useful and possibly more intelligent.

'Well, he just completed a tour! Certainly he's patriotic for not being a real Russian,' Tanya said.

Lukeria's face flushed beetroot red with rage. 'Just shows how expendable some people really are,' she returned, pulling the door shut.

Tanya and Yuri stood there stunned by Lukeria's words, which were so open, so frank, and so anti-cosmopolitan – that is to say, so anti-Semitic. Never in her life had Tanya doubted that the hand of the Creator shaped the heavens. But having lived every day of her life with Lukeria, Tanya had her doubts about this earth, and specifically about certain people on it.

'She's an old woman, you have to forgive her,' Tanya said finally.

'But not crazy.' Yuri kept his gaze trained on the darkness of the stairwell.

'No, not yet.'

'What, then?'

Tanya shrugged. 'You know how it is. She's just repeating the things she hears. She's traditional.' Another way of saying that Lukeria was conventional, which was to say not even if Tanya and Yuri were the last two humans on the planet would Lukeria approve of such a union.

Yuri squared his shoulders, planted a single kiss on Tanya's forehead. Goodbye, he was saying with that kiss, and then he retreated down the stairway for his mother's apartment.

'Don't let your face get narrow about it,' Lukeria said later, after Vespers prayers and three cigarettes. 'Pearls and swine – it's just something people say.' She thrust her chin forward, pulling her back so straight as to suggest not in all her days as a railway worker, as Tanya's surrogate mother, as a tenant in this crumbling apartment building, had Lukeria ever once adjusted to the idea that she might be wrong.

'Besides, it's bad luck to fall in love with a man who dreams with his shoes on,' she added, another reference to Yuri's Jewish blood, and a warning: he would wander, just wait and see, wandering being the Jewish blessing and curse.

'Enough,' Tanya had said, suddenly wearied of orthodoxy, of nationalism, of being raised so thoroughly Russian, and that had been the end of that. Not long after that Yuri had met Zoya at the museum. And whatever hopes Tanya had for a life with Yuri she kept contained within her cloud notebook.

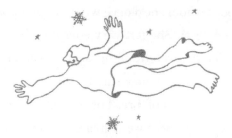

CHAPTER SIX

Olga

Olga's boots punched through the hard crusts of snow as she crossed the square in front of the stout news bureau building. It looked precisely like every other building in a twenty-block radius: glum paperweights holding the pavements and old drifts of snow down.

For three decades only two building designs in all of the Soviet Union had been approved and could be manufactured: tall and ugly or squat and ugly. This lent, according to Zvi, whose work in the military had afforded some opportunity to travel, a mind-numbing sameness to the larger cities. But the buildings had to be made this way to achieve maximum symbolic potential – that is to say, according to old Soviet logic, the bigger the concrete building, the better. Mercifully, the *Red Star* building was of the latter design and so filled up less of the skyline.

An old man sat on a bench in the square and smoked with relish an invisible cigarette. Scraps of newspaper swirled like tufts of hair around his ankles. Though the sun was most definitely not shining, Olga shielded her eyes with a hand and squinted. This man looked uncannily similar to a war hero about whom she'd once written a composition when she was a schoolgirl. She felt very sorry for him now, his head bowed under the weight of his service cap cluttered with its many war medals. A new rule had been passed that no one was to throw scraps of bread or give money to the army pensioners any longer because so many of them had been gathering near the steps of the *Red Star*. Some had even been observed crapping behind the building and now the sanitation crews refused to pick up the turds.

'What's new?' the old man called out in military tones.

'Oh, nothing,' Olga replied mechanically.

'And how is your nothing?'

Olga dug in her plastic bag and gave the man a boiled egg. 'As black as soot.' Olga turned for the building. One look at the man and Olga knew she did not have to tell him anything he didn't already know. It was all there swirling at his feet: how the old pensioners had lost their entire life savings in recent crashes, banking scams and hyperinflation. This Olga and Arkady had dubbed 'elastic economics'. But their job was to shield harsh realities in language so diffuse and vague that the veterans would never know how people like them had edited them out of history books. Her job was to spin the news with stretchy fibrous words of euphemism so that young people like her son, Yuri, and his live-in-girlfriend, Zoya, would never know just how very bleak their situations had really become. Her job was to do all this, and then dispense boiled eggs afterwards.

Olga paused at the lift, contemplated it for its metaphoric value. Then she thrust her head inside. Someone had pasted an advertisement – on the ceiling no less. Quite a gymnastic feat. WILL BUY VOUCHER FOR 10,000R. It was a joke, surely, for someone else had already scribbled beside it some handy advice: Take your voucher, and shove it up your ass. No, this doesn't mean you are BARKING MAD. It just means you're like the rest of us – screwed.

In the office of translation Arkady was already ensconced behind his side of the desk. This was what she liked about him: he was such a hard worker and so rarely did he ever complain. Sometimes he even offered helpful suggestions.

Olga forced her ample backside behind the desk. On the blotter lay a new work order awaiting translation.

```
A prestige apartment building in the Novyye
Lyady district and a tank factory in the
Industrialny district collapsed into a morass
of mud in the early morning hours. In the
Kirovsky district near the Upper Kama, two
female pensioners disappeared into a sink hole
while walking their dogs. Neither the bodies
of the women nor their dogs have been recov-
ered. City officials advise residents to avoid
the out of doors at all costs. If one must
walk about, then he or she should do so in a
state of high alert. If one should find him or
```

herself mud-bound by no means should he or she
thrash about. 'It's best to let nature take
its course,' advises Osip Gregorovich Shudno,
a sink-hole expert with special training in
loon-muck survival strategies and marsh water
recovery. 'But if you can raise your hips into
a horizontal position, then you have a 67%
chance of remaining afloat until help arrives.
Under no circumstances should one drink the
water.'

'Is this a joke?' Olga looked slyly at Arkady. Since his wife left him all those years ago it had become Arkady's habit to tease Olga now and then – his way of flirting, she supposed. If he wasn't dangling exotic facts from far-flung corners of the map, then he sometimes placed on the desk news items Olga suspected came straight out of his inexhaustible imagination.

With his thumb Arkady pushed his glasses higher onto the bridge of his nose. His eyes swam behind his glasses. 'Not a joke, I'm afraid.' Arkady dug into his trousers and withdrew a handkerchief. 'Kaminsky asked me for a translation but I can't do it. Those old ladies. Well, not the ladies, but their dogs, I had grown very fond of.' Arkady honked into his hankie.

Olga reached across the desk and touched Arkady's sleeve. 'I am so very sorry,' she murmured. Arkady sniffed and pulled his chair closed to the window overlooking the production floor. Below them the huge wheels churned the paper rolls in a deafening roar. How could they stand it down there, pummelled by the noise of all those words, none of them quite accurate? Olga wondered. And just what was she to do with this latest bit? When the very earth beneath your feet could not be trusted, what then? Certainly she could not write what she knew to be true: that the ground they lived on had been completely overmined and undersupported. The last time she wrote up a translation a little too truthfully, she'd nearly given Arkady an ulcer. But it was quite by accident.

She'd meant to write up the first attack on Grozny as a sudden climatic shift in the far south. But knowing that her son, a boy in heart and mind, had until just recently himself been out there fighting in this war so few of them cared for and understood far less had incited her instinct for truth, and out it came – colossal and unexpected defeat of the Russian army due to incompetence.

Not a minute later, Chief Editor Kaminsky appeared in the doorway of their tiny office, his eyebrows lowered in a tight band above his nose. 'Very creative work, Olga Semyonovna,' he pronounced, his voice atonal and flat as if the words were produced by something mechanical lodged inside his throat. Olga had cringed. Chief Editor Kaminsky, as every other boss she'd ever worked for, only called a woman by her first name and patronymic when she'd fallen into his extreme disfavour. Olga realized then than too many more transparent flashes of creativity and she'd be given the boot.

Olga pushed aside the report about the sink hole and

reached instead for a work-on-the-left item from the wire basket. This time she withdrew a cocktail menu for an American-style hamburger restaurant. The names of the drinks sent her into an immediate state of flummox. Sex on the Beach. Olga glanced at the *Topic Guide*. Yes, it was a behemoth. But as comprehensive as the *Guide* was, conspicuous gaps had yet to be filled. Because even though glasnost had come and gone, certain things – sex, for instance – were not to be discussed, not even in dictionaries, those safeguards of thought and propriety. Sure you could find colourful graffiti addressing that topic along the walls of every metro station and on any fence. But a word that could be printed, well, that was another matter. The Russian language was great. Greatly expansive. Even so, she could not think of a single decent word, noun or verb, to describe love-making. She considered – briefly – 'Passion on the Sand'. But the word for passion was also the same word for horror and terror, and it didn't seem right to Olga to add to the trauma most women she knew already associated with sex.

The next item on the menu was something called 'Screaming Orgasm', a concoction that featured two forms of alcohol, a juice and fizzy water. An elaborate drink, it sounded like an animal, or perhaps a bodily ailment people in the West suffered from. Olga had heard of this condition – Lyuba in fact-checking claimed to have suffered from it from time to time. But Olga found it altogether suspicious. The deepest physical response one could feel during the act of love was perhaps a great swelling of the heart, a stirring of feeling which one could attribute to passion or to the use of too much cooking grease in one's dinner. All this was to say that Olga had never experienced orgasm and if any woman she knew, except for Lyuba, ever had, certainly they were keeping very quiet about it.

Olga glanced at Arkady, who was at that very moment picking his teeth with the nib of his pencil. They were very good friends, she and Arkady. But he was a man, nonetheless, and asking him for help in this matter was absolutely unthinkable. Also, when Arakdy picked his teeth with his pencil, it meant he was thinking of his most prized possession: a large lump of petrified wood that had been in his family for several generations. If Arkady were ever to sell this wood, he would be a very rich man indeed. At least, that is what Arkady had told Olga about the rare specimen, which he kept wrapped in damp towels in a coat closet.

In desperation, Olga slid out from behind the desk and wandered to the not-so-remote place – that is to say, the toilets, the place where she did all her best work. In the twenty years she'd been at the *Red Star* she'd learned that if she needed to outsource for alternative definitions, her best bet was to park her broad backside on a commode. Because everyone knew that if something were spoken at the toilets, then most certainly it was true.

Absurdity no. 5
The toilets…

…stretched the limits of olfactory tolerance. But, sadly, it was only there, amid the open unapologetic odour of human waste, that Olga could conduct candid discussion, as few women besides herself and Vera could endure the closed quarters with unambitious ventilation for more than thirty seconds or so. Olga pinched her nose with one hand and pushed open the door to the women's toilets with the other. The searing at the back of her throat, this she ignored as she lowered her head and charged for the reprieve of a cracked window, where Vera stood, a mobile phone jammed against her ear, and a cigarette in her hand – smoking being the only way they knew to counter the virulence of a building plagued with desultory plumbing.

Vera was lucky enough to have natural platinum blonde hair, the colour almost every Russian woman dreams of having. And so why Vera insisted on dyeing it dull black, Olga could not figure. Even worse, Vera tended to let the roots grow out so that with her blue-black eye make-up, she really did resemble a skunk. And this observation carried zero connotation of moral judgement. Because with the exception of Arkady, Olga considered Vera her one and only true friend.

Vera tipped her head and switched her phone from one ear to the other. 'Of course it's true. The birth rate has halved in the last ten years and the mortality rates are soaring. Just don't ask for the numbers – it's too depressing.' Vera slid the phone into her purse and lit a cigarette for Olga. Vera had started as junior fact-checker and over the years moved up the ranks, as evidenced by the blaring crimson rings around her ears – the result of the pressure of a phone constantly applied to one side of her head or the other. This was Vera's official explanation, though Olga wondered if her friend's ears hadn't been permanently stained from what she had to listen to. Then, too, Vera had a penchant for collecting naughty jokes and proverbs and altering them so that they tipped from the naughty to the downright obscene. It was the only way that Vera, assaulted by raw data day after day, could maintain her fragile hold on sanity.

Olga smoked her cigarette down to her fingers, then hiked up her skirt and sat cautiously on the rim of the commode. Here, as in all the stalls, the caretaker had exercised his sense of humour. It was rumoured that he had once worked as a copy-editor but had been demoted, though Olga could not see why. FELLOW SYNTACTIC ENGINEERS: PLEASE FLUSH YOUR DANGLING MODIFIERS, he had written on a placard taped above the place where they used to have real toilet paper. ATTENTION OFFICE STAFF: REGARDLESS OF THE QUALITY OF THE WORK PUT FORTH OR THE EFFORT IT REQUIRED – FLUSH! IF RESULTS EXCEED YOUR HIGHEST EXPECTATIONS, PLEASE USE THE BRUSH.

'I'm so stuck,' Olga said. 'I need some of your valuable directive.'

'You want the plunger or some of my vodka?'

'No. Seriously. I need some advice. How would you translate "screaming orgasm" from English to Russian?'

Vera contemplated the lazy ceiling fan. 'Did you know that alcohol has rendered the typical Russian male unable to perform in such a way that would provoke orgasm on the part of the female participant?'

Olga squeezed her eyes closed as she searched her memory for any such recollections of Zvi. But she could not remember Zvi, at least not in that way.

'It's true.' Vera blew a cloud of smoke into the air. 'The average tryst between a Russian man and woman lasts only eleven minutes. Compare that with the Americans, who clock in at eighteen minutes, and the Italians, who average twenty-one.'

Olga knew that as a fact-checker, Vera was in a unique position to verify such claims. Also, Vera had worn out four husbands trying to find one that would satisfy her. But they'd all been drinkers and Vera could not contain her bitterness on the matter.

'Sergei is practically useless. Last night – nine minutes and he was done! And what does he do with himself after? Nothing. He lays about whining, Sergei does. He won't work. He thinks about working. He imagines what work might feel like. This tires him out. Then he drinks himself into a blind stupor. He says it makes him happy. Then I tell him what I know: as long as a bottle of vodka costs less than a kilo of apples and bread is more expensive than beer, he will die of this happiness. You are so lucky, Olya. You married a real *muzhik*.'

Olga shifted on the commode. Sometimes it was painful to sit and listen to Vera. The mildly dissatisfied people she knew rarely recognized how burdensome their conversation was, how discussing their problems only increased the heartache of those who had to listen and so revisit again and again their own loss. And the only thing worse than mildly dissatisfied people were happy people. With all sincerity Olga thanked God that at the present time she did not know anyone who was overly happy, or even slightly happy, and certainly she did not know anyone who was happily in love.

God be praised. Because talking about love, talking about men, only reminded Olga how much about Zvi she had forgotten. Because memory was a strand of hair pulled tight and too easily broken. Because even with her eyes closed, squeezed shut to the uncertain light of the lav, only with great effort could she recall Zvi in his service uniform, his hat perched on his head, his charcoal eyes. And that was it. Olga reached for a Letter to the Editor and scribbled a few lines.

Every day for twenty years on the back of the squares of Very Soft or Pigeon, popular brands of scratchy brown toilet paper, or on the backs of the Letters to the Editor, Olga wrote anything she could remember of Zvi. For twenty years she tried to corral her failing memory and word by word, memory by memory, reclaim her lost husband. But somehow (when she was cramming Hungarian into her ears? When she was

forgetting the family prayers to make room for Nakh conjuga-
tions?) Zvi had inexplicably retreated particle by particle into
the murk. Every day for twenty years she tried to call him back,
detail by detail. For instance, Olga knew that every man wears
a map of skin: sweat creases on the back of the neck or scars
on the knuckles, indelible footnotes of the work done with the
hands. But what signs and markings Zvi's body heralded, Olga
couldn't remember. Only because her notes said so did she
know that he had a star-shaped scar above the right cheek-
bone. In her note she reads how Zvi had an entire constellation
of moles on his back that resembled letters of the Arabic
alphabet, but now she could not recall what words they spelled.
And it was only because the backs of the Letters to the Editors
said so that she knew that Zvi's smile was so wide, it pushed his
ears back. And it bothered her like nothing else that she
couldn't remember his feet or his hands or his knees. If he had
been a dreamer, a loner – the sound of his laugh – it was gone
from her. Only his sneezes trumpeting through the corridor
and rattling plates in the cupboard – that she remembered. But
even then it was with effort, only after consulting her chipped
dishes and stopping to wonder, 'How?'

'Am I right?' Vera's voice pulled Olga back to the bathroom
smoke and stink. 'Should I not insult Sergei mercilessly and
then give him the boot?'

'Absolutely you are in the right.' Olga thrust her notes into
her purse. If a woman asked such a question, it was only because
she knew the answer already and wanted quick confirmation.

But Olga had had about all she could take of sex and husbands. And realizing that she'd get nowhere on the cocktail menu with Vera, she wiped her backside with a Letter to the Editor:

```
To whom it may concern,
I think you should know that it is a well-
established fact the Russian military is
bankrupt and has been for years. Recruits have
gone AWOL in record numbers and Russian
soldiers have given their weapons to Chechen
opposition in exchange for bottles of vodka.
And why not? Under-equipped, underfed, under-
supported, and ill-trained, why should these
boys die in Chechnya? Good God! We sent tanks
into Grozny without giving the tank navigators
a city map!
        (signed General S_____, Mozdok.)
```

By the time Olga slid behind her side of the desk, Arkady's eyebrows had locked in a wrestling match. On the desk in front of him lay the week's inflation index.

'The President is an ass.' Arkady waved a curled transcript.

Olga glanced at the *Topic Guide*. 'I think "donkey" is the preferred nomenclature.'

'OK.' Arkady scratched at his arm. 'Donkey it is. And as such, according to city ordinance prohibiting the use of animals in public, he should stay at home in bed and keep his hangover to himself.'

'Hangover' was a not-so-subtle reference to the President's decision to invade Chechnya, a move prompted by a long round of holiday toasting and reckless dares.

Olga scowled. Yes, Russia was a country manned by drunks. No one knew it more than the fact-checkers and translators at the *Red Star*, but still, even in this age of pseudo-glasnost, there were things you shouldn't say. Now there were unconfirmed rumours that the President might be plagued with a bad heart. To this end, Kaminsky had installed a special cut-and-paste function. Any time the word 'president' appeared in print it was followed by 'could not attend the event because he was labouring over documents'.

Just then the teletype, a squat grey machine stationed beneath the glass window, spluttered to life.

Absurdity no. 6
The teletype…

…was of archival, that is to say antique, quality. Olga held her breath as the large round metal element spun in quick agitation, striking the paper in an exaggerated staccato fashion. Arkady adjusted his glasses and squinted at the transcript unfurling from the yammering maw of the machine. Although office protocol dictated that she and Arkady retrieve and translate as many assignments from the basket as they could, if the teletype went active, then they were to drop those assignments immediately, as something horrific was happening and the public – for their own good – must not at any cost hear about it in its raw and undiluted version.

If these were accounts of the economic catastrophe, such as the week's inflation index, then the assignment fell to Arkady, who could track the manifest rise and fall of the rouble in the cost of chewing gum or the ever-fluctuating price of bread. And Arkady could turn a phrase. A master of commercial euphemism, just the other day Arkady artfully dubbed the fact that for over two years the average monthly pension couldn't buy sausage and butter for a week as 'deficit earning'. The 28 billion roubles of unpaid wages to transportation, construction and agricultural workers he attributed to a common malaise known as 'indefinite delayed payment syndrome' – a condition encapsulated in a saying every Russian worker had known and repeated for decades: 'We pretend to work, they pretend to pay.'

Military reports, on the other hand – estimated numbers of casualties, movements of troops and munitions – fell exclusively to Olga.

Arkady ripped the transcripts from the carriage and squinted fiercely at the type. 'For you,' he said, handing it to Olga.

Olga winced and read the report:

```
After heavy fighting near Chervlenaja, Dolinsk,
Pervomaisk, Petropavlovskaya, 250 troops were
counted as lost.
```

Olga sighed a ponderous sigh. Two hundred and fifty lost might actually mean five hundred dead and far more than that wounded. Russian military organizations, Olga knew, each had different ways of tallying their losses. Only soldiers who actually died on the battlefield were counted as dead. Those who died in transport or various field hospitals did not count. Add to the confusion the fact that each service (defence ministry, internal ministry) had its own hospitals. And even though the actual figures could take months to trickle in, even she could see that during the first half year of the war in Chechnya the Russian Federal Forces suffered greater losses than the Soviet army sustained during ten years of war in Afghanistan. This was a difficult fact to play down. That Russian conscripts like her Yuri gained military experience at the price of their own blood was also a reality that required some delicacy. And from Yuri, who saw it with his own eyes, Olga learned that the bodies of Russian soldiers who died in high-altitude mountain terrain were very often left where they fell. *Kholodets*, they were called, meat in aspic, because if the helicopters designated for carrying human cargo couldn't gain the necessary lift, then those bodies were simply dumped into the mountain lakes.

And now it was Olga's job to whittle the numbers down to acceptable figures. She re-read the report summary and tapped her teeth with her pencil.

Noticing her distress, Arkady plugged in the hotplate then touched her sleeve. 'Round those numbers down and be done with it.'

Exactly what he had said nearly twenty years ago when the first reports from Afghanistan arrived. And in those days, when Olga was young and optimistic that a war could be won, she was only too happy to comply. She purposefully reported inaccurate numbers of casualties, citing figures that did not even remotely correspond to the numbers of actual wounded. This fell not too far afield from the beloved and well-intentioned *vranyo*, a type of fib one told purely for entertainment purposes. In the town where Olga grew up, *vranyo* masters, able to put the best possible spin on any awkward or embarrassing situation, were highly esteemed. And this type of lie was told with the expectation that everyone would immediately recognize the fib for what it was and know not to believe a word. The usual and polite response was to leave the *vranyo* unchallenged and undiscussed, like the discovery of a sudden turd dropped from the sky. The stink was unmistakable, but the custom was to simply step around it without comment and, with a wink, get on with business.

But over the years of reading endless reports of how little had been accomplished in each of these wars and how much lost, Olga had grown more and more uneasy with her work at the *Red Star*. She saw the names of people she knew – neighbours, their sons and brothers. She saw her cousin's name and the name of a boy who had kissed her in the tall grass when her mother wasn't looking. So many names! And how, she'd like to know, do you lie about a name, which is all that was left of some of these people? And how do you decide which names to cross out, when, as her mother taught her long ago, no name should ever be forgotten? It's bad enough to die, but to die and not be mourned? Unthinkable.

Again the teletype spluttered. Arkady and Olga sat listening to it spit and spew. When, at last, the machine fell silent Olga ripped the message from the carriage.

This time, a letter.

```
In days not too long ago the Russian military
was considered the best in the world. It
shames the Russian military, and every Russian
citizen, to be so soundly defeated in our
first assault on Grozny. So completely such an
important city as Grozny. We must act. But we
must have more soldiers.

    To this end we, the undersigned who wish to
preserve Russian honour, urge the President and
the central committee to reinstate compulsory
re-enlistment of former service personnel.
```

'I can't believe what I'm reading.' Olga slid the copy across the desk. Arkady read the report, his lips moving. When he finished he pushed the report across the desk with the end of his pencil, as if he could not bear to actually touch the paper with his finger.

'Burn it with a bright blue flame,' Arkady said, his voice tight as a wound coil.

'As if one humiliating defeat weren't enough, now these military geniuses want to empty every academy and re-recruit every returned vet for a second assault.' Olga squeezed her eyes shut. She thought of Zvi. She considered how lucky she was really, for all her losses, that she still had her son when so many mothers didn't. Then she thought of all those names she could not remember, and all the names of boys she would not be allowed to print.

Olga felt fear taking on an animal quality inside her stomach, moving hard and dark behind her ribs. Loss diminished, loss denied, was still loss. And what purpose did all this loss have if they were not allowed to record it, to remember it properly? What good was their simple sorrow, these raw husks that rattled emptily in their hands? What good when those who perpetuated the loss denied the loss and were later helped along in their denials by people like her? This is what bothered her most: that their generational sorrows were daily diminished. By her. That as a matter of routine, of editorial policy, their suffering had been made meaningless and that she'd helped make it that way – unbearable.

No. Olga shook her head. No. She said it, quietly, then louder, NO. She would not participate. Not anymore. Olga pounded the desk and Arkady's teacup jumped.

'Grozny! Chechnya is full of Groznys! Next it will be Pervomaisk, Arshty, and after that another village, and after that another, and another. Because if you say three attacks, then you are suggesting a fourth, and if you suggest a fourth, most certainly a fifth is implied. And if we say five we may as well admit six or seven. For every village and city in Chechnya is a Grozny.' Olga took a deep breath and glanced at the oversized window. Did she say that aloud? It seemed so, for the pneumatic tubes stopped their howling as if sensing her indiscretion. Arkady passed gas quietly, and then that shrieking from the tubes recommenced.

'This job,' Olga said quietly, 'turns each one of us into liars.'

'So tell the truth.' Arkady scratched savagely at his forearm.

Like putting ashes in a cellar, it might bring badness, but things couldn't possibly get any worse, Olga reasoned. 'It would represent a great triumph over ourselves. That we could openly discuss such things. Don't you think?'

'Not at all the perpetuation of historical sediment to which we have become so accustomed,' Arkady said, all the while scratching savagely at his arm.

Olga's stomach lurched. They could not help reverting to clichés even in moments of high-profundity content. Olga took a breath, held it, and then she started typing: everything she'd read from the generals and the report and the letters to the newspapers, everything she'd heard from Yuri, everything she knew to be true from Vera.

When she was done, Olga rolled the waxy paper into a tight scroll and stuffed it into the canister and secured the hasp. The wind howled through the tubes. She swallowed hard, then slid the canister into the receptacle, holding it there until the next big gust carried it away.

Two minutes passed. Then three. Arkady unplugged the hotplate and Olga sat drinking tea, her eyes fixed on the dull spots of illumination cast by the unambitious banks of overhead lighting hung over the work floor. A great torrent of snorting and braying trumpeted through the pneumatic tubes. And then Chief Editor Kaminsky materialized at the threshold, his usually florid face pale as alabaster. His eyebrows seemed more peaked than usual and his forehead was a jumble of deep furrows. With the demeanour of a man just back from a wake, Chief Editor Kaminsky studied his hands for a moment. 'Oh, Olga Semyonovna. Olga. Olya. You know how Editor-in-Chief Mrosik feels so very passionately about punctuation, how serious he is down to every last comma and full-stop.'

Olga pinched her face into a contortion of concentration.

'And you know how much I like you and you know how rare it is for me to like anyone. As a personal favour to your father I hired you against the advice of my colleagues. Never did any of us imagine how brilliant you were, translating the most difficult military reports and memos and turning them into such pieces of diaphanous gossamer fragility that they've even become suitable for inclusion in children's variety shows. But this latest report of yours' – a measure of starch crept into Chief Editor Kaminsky's voice – 'is rendered so transparently, well, it will give everyone a heart attack! What people want is security and stability. They want to feel good about this new Russia which needs them to feel good about it.'

Olga squinted at Chief Editor Kaminsky's hair standing tall

to attention, pointing the way to the pneumatic tubes, which she now associated with every trouble, real or imagined. Oh, how she wanted to clip those ridiculous strands off his head and knit them into something she could sell: a foot warmer, a tea cosy, a sweater for a dog.

Instead Olga nodded her head with an exuberance she herself did not feel but hoped her body would find convincing enough to believe, if only on a muscular level.

'You are the head of the translation division. The head of the head, the heart and the brains. What will we do if we lose you? We will flounder, that's what we'll do. Flounder and sink and drown. Drown and die. Is that where you want to leave us? Drowning and dying?' Chief Editor Kaminsky wrung his hands. 'Oh, please, I beg you. Nothing like this again, or I'm afraid we'll have to find another department for you – obits, or translating approved recipes from the Ministry of Meat and Dairy, or perhaps something even worse.' Chief Editor Kaminsky's gaze settled on the children's primer for a moment.

Olga bobbed her head meekly as Chief Editor Kaminsky backed out of the office and into the corridor. 'Oh, the tyranny of rock-solid certainties,' he mumbled. 'Oh, help.'

With a trembling hand Arkady set another cup of tea at her elbow. 'I think that went over really well,' Arkady whispered. Together they sat in silence watching the clock. Four fifty-nine. They studied the slow sweep of the second hand and waited for the minute hand to move. Five times the second hand swept the face of the clock before the minute hand finally moved.

Arkady jumped from his seat and bowed gallantly. 'I absolutely applaud and salute your bravery. You are a real woman, Olga Semyonovna. A gem in the rough. A diamond amongst the turds.' Arkady reached for her hand and kissed it.

Only then did Olga notice that her wedding ring had been lost in the tubes.

Outside, the smell of old snow and diesel fumes settled in her mouth. Every swallow brought the taste of rusty coins and grit. It was sad to think what her life had become: churning out sludge, trying in vain to make bad news more palatable. It was hard to keep at it without succumbing to complete self-loathing. Two things sustained her: Olga's fragile hope that there was a heaven for translated words. That somewhere every edited thought and sentiment, every bit of raw truth, was catalogued and preserved, kept safe from the meddling hands of humans. And the second thing: her Yuri.

Miraculously he'd been returned to her from Grozny, unharmed, catapulted clear from the only tank in the column that did not explode. How lucky she was – she did not have to travel hundreds of miles to the train station in Mozdok, where the bodies of Russian soldiers were packed in open railway carriages. But her relief was surprisingly short-lived. What with all these reports coming in over the teletype, who knew what would happen to her boy now? If God would just smile in her direction. If she could be a little more clever, could work a little harder, longer, she might think of a way to save her Yuri, for it was becoming clearer to her each day that Yuri was incapable of saving himself. He would always need a mother, always a woman to look after him, a mother and a wife. If she were very lucky, Yuri would marry a woman who would be both.

In the square a gathering of Red-Browns, hardliners and reactionary communists, young unemployed punks, and old men waved paper flags. Just the type who'd vote for a man like Zhirinovsky, a Jew-hating loudmouth who couldn't wait to orchestrate another world war.

A man wearing a leather jacket with the slogan of a rock band on the back side held up a bullhorn. 'And who will clean up the cities and countryside? Who will settle once and for all the question of foreigners?'

'Zhirinovsky!' the old men and the young men cried.

'And who will erect giant fans and blow all the toxic fumes and pollution from our great country into the pathetic Baltic states?'

'Zhirinovsky!'

Olga ducked her head and concentrated on her feet. Some days the snow crunching beneath her boots and the blast of cold air were the only things that made any sense to her. She passed beneath the stone archway and entered the courtyard. Yuri and Vitek stood next to the heap and sawed at a fish with a butter knife.

'What's the news?' Vitek pointed his nose in her direction.

Olga snorted. 'More than you can bear.' She trained her eyes on the snow and kept charging for the open stairwell, and pretended she could not hear the nonsense spewing out of Vitek's mouth.

'Because, you see, Yuri, you are making no money at the museum. But the Russian army, they pay brilliantly for people like you. Even a child can do the sums.'

'I don't know.' Yuri's voice followed her up the stairs.

'Listen, boy-o. I can't do all the thinking around here. I am whacked as it is, bottling air and selling it as medicinal oxygen. Just the other day I had to beat up an old man who forgot to pay me rent for the privilege of begging on our street. I mean, how much can one person do?'

Olga kicked off her boots and let herself into the apartment. She smelled Zoya before she saw her, the girl's laundry boiled and bubbled in a pot on the stove. And then her voice, plaintive and sharp.

'All the best people have toaster ovens these days,' Zoya said, the trumpet of the phone held tight to her ear.

Olga let her keys fall to the kitchen table with a clatter, but it was no use. Once Zoya got onto the subject of Things She Wanted, it was nearly impossible to derail her. Aiding and abetting the girl's folly was a western magazine, glossy and slick with advertisements for things they could never afford. Where Zoya got the money for the magazine, Olga could not even fathom, though she suspected the Korean-owned kiosk at the end of the street might be to blame for the magazine.

'You know,' Zoya dropped her voice to a mumble. 'If I were to get pregnant, then we'd qualify for a better apartment. Maybe even one with a balcony. What a position of status we would occupy then. And, of course, I would be so much happier if I could hang my laundry outside with a view of more sophisticated trash.'

The smell of the kitchen, the sounds issuing from Zoya's mouth, it was all too much for Olga to bear. She spun on her heels and headed for the stairs, where it was a short climb up the metal ladder that opened onto the roof. The smell might not be much better out of doors than in, but at least she could have the illusion of privacy.

She lit a cigarette. She pulled hard and exhaled a long jet of smoke. By the end of the day, thinking of her responsibilities to the dead wore her out. And more absurdity: she actually envied the women who'd lost their husbands in the war and had the red star on a cupboard shelf to prove it. Better to know what happened than to be stranded amid the rigours of the imagination. Because as long as Olga didn't have Zvi's body, as long as his name didn't appear on any list, she both hoped and despaired. And because hope is stupid and stubborn, Olga couldn't help but conjure him out of the nighttime darkness in the apartment; and by day her eyes couldn't help but parse him from a city of eyebrows, ears and noses.

She blew another cloud of smoke.

'I beg your pardon most sincerely,' a man's voice called from behind the heating stack.

Olga dropped her cigarette. 'Zvi?'

The man coughed politely. 'Not quite.' The man stepped forward and Olga could see that it was not a man, but Mircha. The lights of the TV tower flickered behind his body, which had shape but no substance. She knew she should have found the fact that Mircha was there on the rooftop surprising, or at the very least strange, but strangely, she did not. Nothing – not the purely disastrous, nor the monstrous, nor evidence of the supernatural seemed to move her any more. She might have included the miraculous on this list but it had been such a long time since God had sent a true miracle that she was no longer sure she'd recognize one if she saw it. Certainly what she observed winking at her now was no miracle.

Olga sniffed. 'You have acquired a strange odour.'

Mircha cupped a hand to his ear. 'What's that?'

'You stink.'

Mircha hiked his nose into the air and breathed mightily.

'Why don't you settle down now and go away quietly? We gave you a good wake.'

'I can't go away. These thoughts... these ideas... they torment me.'

'What thoughts? What ideas?'

Mircha withdrew a faded piece of paper from his pocket, pinched a corner and slowly whipped it open with a flourish as a maître d' presented a fine linen napkin, though Olga could see twilight through the creases. 'I am seeing things so much more clearly now that I'm dead. The mysteries – why we suffer, what use sorrow is and the causes of hatred – I see, now that I am dead, how each of us should live this life. You, dear lady, for instance. You are only living half a life.'

'What do you mean?'

'You jump at every squawk from a telephone, thinking it could be your husband. Every scratch at a windowpane, rattle at a door, you tell yourself it could be him. What if your story went like this...' Mircha paused and cleared his throat:

'Once there was and was not a woman who fell in love with words. Each day she gathered eggs from her hens and each egg was another word. But the word had no meaning until it was broken and the contents consumed. The shiny egg, brown and mottled, beautiful in the way things found only in nature are beautiful, of course would be destroyed. The woman buried the eggs in the mud and seven years later...'

'Stop!' Olga held her hands up. 'Please tell me this is not why you are hanging around licking light bulbs. Please tell me there's some better reason why you are here.'

Mircha consulted his notes. 'Your problem is that you lack the courage to see and tell the truth. Your husband is dead – you and I both know it. You are hiding behind your imagination and that flimsy thing people call hope.'

Olga took a breath, held it. 'I see now, Mr Aliyev, why you had such trouble getting up the requisite threesome for a round of drinking. You are frank to a fault.'

Mircha smiled. 'You should try it sometime. They say truth sets people free.'

'It also got them shot or sent by rail to the east. If I'm lucky, and the boss is in a good mood, I'll only lose my job.'

Mircha folded his notes and handed them to Olga. 'Consider this friendly advice, a gift, even. From me to you.' Mircha smiled then retreated into the darkness.

CHAPTER SEVEN

Tanya

Because on Mondays the museum was officially closed, on Sunday afternoons, before locking up, in anticipation of the coming day, Daniilov the caretaker always hung a sign on the entrance: GO AWAY, YOU MORONS. IT'S MONDAY! But every third Monday of the month was designated as a museum work day. This was a purely volunteer venture, which meant for Tanya that her participation was absolutely mandatory. All because she had once taken an art survey course and another in general chemistry and had once read, though never claimed to understand, a translation of Newton's *Opticks*. And because on Mondays the museum was closed, Ludmilla had no reason whatsoever to sit behind the glass ticket office and Zoya and Yuri no reason whatsoever to spew their well-worn exhibit scripts to museum goers. Certainly they were not required to work. 'They have no artistic vision. Not like you do, dear,' Head Administrator Chumak said when she asked why she should have to come in. Then he chuckled as if hers was the most ridiculous question and now she should feel as if his compliment was the greatest of rewards. Almost as great as having the upper floors of the museum to herself.

And here's the strange thing: it was. The resentment she might have felt, would have felt if she were any other girl, vanished the moment she unlocked the back door. Sublimated in a blink at the possibility of the entire museum being a blank canvas, waiting to speak in a language of colour only she could unlock.

Tanya stood before the door, basking in Daniilov's warm welcome. She wiggled the key in the ward of the lock, turned, turned, turned until the tumblers rolled once, twice, three times, and the door yielded with a soft click. She withdrew her key and hurried to the hat/coat check, her footsteps on the dark floor heavy slaps, then echoing as duller softer ones. Hat/coat check was where she kept her artistic supplies, and no, she was not just talking about the dream notebook now. Real supplies. Hidden in a box tucked in a rack. Tanya retrieved the box. She stopped briefly at Chumak's office, just long enough to slide the application form under his door, and then up, up, up the steps she climbed.

On the mezzanine Daniilov dragged the mop listlessly behind him. He had a hangover, always on work days he brought with him a hangover, and the only remedy was to nurse it with cheap apple brandy or vodka, bottles of which stood in readiness beneath a poorly constructed bust of Peter the Great.

'Good morning,' Tanya called.

Daniilov stopped, bent his wiry body in half and clutched his forehead. 'Is it? Is it?' he moaned bitterly.

Tanya opened her supply box and slowly withdrew a bottle of Marsh Lilac and a small tin of boot blacking. Consumed together they could give a man a spectacular intoxication. 'I need to borrow your shovel.'

'What for?'

'Artistic purposes.'

Daniilov eyed the loud first-floor exhibits. 'Burying it, I hope.' He grabbed the perfume, uncapped it, took a swig, and looked at the liquid with fond appreciation. 'The shovel's in the broom closet. Bring it back clean.'

When Tanya had gained the landing to the third and final floor, she set the box in the middle of the room and waited for her breath to return. This was the first step in the creation of art: contemplation. Tanya took a deep breath and held it. All along the walls hung the icons that spelled the story of orthodoxy through the ages. When she looked at the faces of the saints, sombre beneath their weighty halos fitted like tight hoods over their heads, she could see their commitment to calm. For some reason, knowing that others could be calm, even if they were just pictures painted on wood or beaten out of iron, helped her own unsteady heart to settle.

Tanya studied the icon Mother of God, touched Mary's halo, ran her finger lightly over her throbbing heart rimmed in gold. Exposure to the air, the lightest of water, had rusted Mary's heart, but in terms of colour, gold (or in this case, chocolate foil) was a good choice as it advanced on the eye and suggested warmth. This is what she always said to tour groups.

Had said. What she didn't say: If it were true what her grandmother taught her, that God revealed himself through the line
and colour of these icons, then it was through Mary's dark
eyes and dark heart that Tanya thought she could see something of an invisible God. Mary gazed at her child and her
child had his gaze trained on her.

It was as if Mary knew this child would break her heart,
but her eyes said, 'Go ahead, break it a million times anyway,'
because she couldn't imagine her heart designed for any other
purpose. Now that was love – allowing your heart to be bruised
and broken for the sake of your child. It was not the tight-
fisted love a woman gives when she senses her situation may be
far more impermanent than she'd like, in this way sparing her
own heart. Not, say, the frugal love that her grandmother
favoured.

This was the difference between a woman like Mary and a
woman like her grandmother. Mary's heart grew larger
through sorrow, while constant heartache had shrivelled her
grandmother's heart to the size and consistency of the stone
of a cherry. And where her grandmother had once had some
love for Tanya – she had to believe this – and from that love had
tried to instill belief in an orthodox God, now all Lukeria had
was the trappings of faith, the brittle traditions and sayings.
And here was the strange thing, Tanya realized with a jolt.
This faith had been a hair shirt woven by someone else, the
smells of another body of belief running warp and weft. An
awkward fit at first. But this shirt, having rubbed against

her skin for so long, now fastened itself tight to Tanya. So completely had the shirt become her skin that Tanya could not fathom not being orthodox, not loving an orthodox God in all her little orthodox ways. What may have been given to her as a substitute for love had become familiar. And now Lukeria's faith was Tanya's faith, for herself, a faith unfeigned that worked itself through the fingertips, here in this museum, amongst these icons.

Tanya carefully withdrew her supplies: a wooden bowl, a fork, fizzy water, a packet of flour, three eggs. Squares of cardboard with thin wood glued to them. Swatches of cheap fabric. All necessary items in the making of an icon, which, for Tanya, actually started every third Sunday of the month when she glued balsa to cardboard. OK, not balsa, but ice-cream sticks shaved to transparency. Yes, true, this meant on Sundays she ate, on account of her devotion to art, at least eight and sometimes ten ice creams, but that was suffering at the throne of the muse, and because it was the least she could do, Tanya did it.

The wooden sticks having been shaved and glued to cardboard, Tanya then draped scraps of cloth over the sticks. Over all of this she then slathered a gooey layer of primer: a mixture of glue and powdered crushed chalk. OK, not glue, but these eggs and chalk. Depending on whether or not the upper floor had heat that day, it might take two, maybe three hours for this binding mixture to dry. During this time Tanya tried to make herself useful, in accordance with her theology of love. After all, Daniilov, who so often climbed the cork and suffered the dizzying effects afterwards, needed her help. For this reason Tanya cleaned the glass surrounds of the Kuntskamera exhibit and the paltry geology exhibit. She would have skipped the toilets, but nature urged and while she was there, her conscience pinched. Before she knew what she was doing, she was bent over, scrubbing with the brushes, spraying with the sanitizers, aware that if she didn't do it, quite possibly no one else would or could.

When three hours, maybe four, had passed, when the chalk and glue had dried, then Tanya could draw a design incised on the surface with a penknife. Once she had been so bold as to mention in passing to Father Vyacheslav that she might like to learn to paint icons for the church some day. He had assumed a look of umbrage and wagged a finger in the air. Such a stuffy gesture for a man who hadn't quite outgrown the pimples on his face. 'One does not paint icons,' he said. 'One writes an icon. It is an inspired expression affording a glimpse into heaven.' Never was she more aware of this than now, as the knife quavered in her hand. Tanya pulled a sharp breath through her nose, held it. She studied the face of the Mother of God. Then she exhaled, slow and steadily, and let the long lines of her serene sorrow guide her hand.

There. A woman had emerged before her. Then the child. They were not perfect, but they did not have to be. They only had to represent – however crudely – the human form, a receptacle for the God story that was a light so lovely the viewer would gaze in wonder, longing to learn the source of it.

From out of the box Tanya withdrew the rest of her supplies. This was what she came for, for this part of the story. She spread the contents of the box on the floor and blew on her hands. If God is light, then God is colour. This much she had gathered from the Baptist Bible and what she remembered from that lone general chemistry course. Red she loved. In particular, Siberian red, a lead chromate that can be made to dance the scales of colour from lemon yellow to chrome orange to a disturbing blood hue. Also she was fond of oxide viridian, so beloved by Cézanne. So glad she was to see something like these colours in Zoya's arsenal of industrial make-up. And blue. Tanya sighed. One musn't ever rush blue. Certainly one musn't rush blue eye-shadow. Here's the thing: if the world were perfect, if she had money and the shops had supplies, she would buy tempera paints, powdered colours mixed with egg yolk and beer. But the economy being what it was, a mysterious game of constant disappointments, Tanya had learned how to make do with what was available: Zoya's nail varnishes and make-up, Lukeria's tea, shoe polish, chewing gum of assorted colours and flavours, and the occasional beer borrowed for the cause from Daniilov's private stash.

Tanya knelt on the floor and surveyed her landscape of materials. Egg, fork, bowl. She cracked the eggs into the bowl and whisked with vigour. What few people knew was how great a binder egg really was. Egg and beer together would glue the colour fast to the cloth strips. At least, this is what she had read in a pamphlet explaining how the old fathers made icons out in the woods. But this pamphlet was written in Old Slavonic. Quite possibly she didn't understand the recipe fully. But this was the Russian way: substituting at all times one thing for another and calling it good, very good, or at least commendable.

Consider colour, for instance. Tanya mashed the chalk into separate piles. A vegetable broth bouillon cube smashed under her fist into one pile made an earthy brown. The turquoise green oval and boot blacking crushed in the next chalk pile made for a brilliant iridescent blue. With cosmetic brushes she mixed the egg mixtures and chalks, then applied the colours to her canvas. To the Mother of God she gave a brilliant blue veil, the symbol of humility, doleful brown eyes, and pale skin. Ditto for the child, except instead of a veil she left a blank space for a gold nimbus. This required gold foil. Fortunately, Tanya came prepared: inside her coat pocket she kept a candy bar for emergency artistic purposes. Tanya unwrapped the candy bar, carefully flattened the foil, and with the penknife cut a snood of gold to fit around the baby Jesus' head.

The last step, the very last thing, was to seal and fix the colour and the foil with a quick shot of hair spray, which would give the icon the trademark high shine glossy effect commonly associated with lacquered antiquities. Tanya propped the cardboard against a chair leg and sprayed in slow arcs. That done, she rested on her heels, the dreambook open across her lap, and munched the chocolate bar thoughtfully:

Gold was mustard gone fallow in the long fields. Gold was the falling notes of the bells from the church. Gold the sound carried over the river, troubling the water so that things long forgotten at the depths swilled up briefly only to be pulled back under. Gold the flecks in the colour of your eyes. The distance of many miles. 'Where are you now?' I ask. 'What are you remembering? You can tell me. What you say is like a whisper inside a church, it is between us, never to be repeated.' Bells you said. A call to prayer. In Grozny. Where there are good Russians and bad. And wolves and whistles. And ticking.

And then disaster. The blue of the veil weeping. The eyeshadow and beer and glue and flour mixture sliding, sliding. Falling. The flour, egg, beer, cosmetic mixture in all its bright bubbly glory was a blue-green smear and the Mother of God looked like an absinthe-stained impressionistic experiment. The Christ child resembled a sickly watermelon in her arms.

Tanya's eyes burned. Always this was what came of her attempts to think in hues and gradations of saturation; this was what happened when she tried to knuckle an understanding of her own life as it ticked from shade to hue. This was what came of her attempt to depict love in any form, even if it was from stuff as low and humble as wet coloured flour smeared on ice-cream sticks.

✳

Tanya trudged home, pulling the shovel behind her over the
snow. From across the Kama a high series of yodels rose in
the darkness. People believed these were the sounds of wild
dogs crying for their human mothers. The old story said that
wild dogs could be tamed and turned back to their child selves
again if only their mothers would cry out their human names.
It was a good story that bore repeating. In fact she had heard
it many times carried up through the heating pipes of their
building, and with each recitation it became that much more
true.

In front of the apartments the children lobbed ice chunks
at each other and scaled the snow-covered heap with angry
shrieks. With her broad frame Tanya knew she was an irre-
sistible target. If that gaping hole existed as Yuri said it did,
skirting the heap and taking cover inside the latrine was out
of the question. Tanya forged toward the stairwell, keeping a
close eye on the oldest girl, who gripped the neck of an empty
bottle. The girl, Tanya noted, never blinked and Tanya found
this unnerving. It suggested she understood far more than she
should at that age. And then there were the things the children
said and how they said them, each child picking up where the
other left off:

'Blessed are the poor in spirit for theirs is the kingdom of
heaven,' a tiny voice sang out from the stairwell.

'What?' Tanya peered behind the heap and saw the smallest

girl with the black hair crouched over a flattened bottle of kvass.

'Blessed are the meek,' called one of the twins – Good Boris – she was pretty sure of that, because Good Boris always bowed slightly from the waist, an altogether gentlemanly gesture for so young a child.

'For they will inherit the earth,' Bad Boris, standing in front of the heap, replied.

And then from the red-haired boy with the glasses, 'Blessed are those who hunger and thirst for righteousness, for they will be filled.'

'Blessed are the pure in heart, for they will see God,' the oldest girl said, levelling her gaze on Tanya. Always the children talked like this. Tanya didn't know if it was the effect of the glue they liked to sniff, or a manifestation of a preternatural wisdom given sometimes to some children, a wisdom she herself had never possessed.

Tanya squinted at the girl. The thing was, Tanya wanted to like these kids. She wanted to love them as easily as she loved the Kuntskamera boy. But they were so unchildlike, sharing between them a hard feral quality that made them immune to normal human kindness. Even so, Tanya couldn't stop making her attempts. She saw that somebody needed to like them. Tanya understood that they all, and by 'they', she included herself in the count, had quite a lot in common, that they were like her, lost in this world that didn't care for them. Underneath the dirt, buried beneath the layers of soiled clothes, their criminal extracurricular activities, they were children. Tanya walked to the stairwell and held out a piece of chewing gum for the little girl. 'What's your name, anyway?' Tanya asked. Before the girl could answer the other children swarmed around Tanya, pulling the gum from her fingers, pulling her keys and pencils and tissues from her purse.

'Is this all you got?' the oldest girl, Anna, asked.

'Don't you have something better?'

'Like food?' one twin asked.

'Or money?' the other asked, with a measure of indignation.

'What's this, then?' The boy with the glasses found the botched icon. He sniffed at the paint and danced the icon away beyond the heap. The other children kept their hands on Tanya, propelling her to the stairwell, pushing her up the steps. If there was a hole behind the heap, as Yuri had claimed, certainly they weren't about to let her see it, though she noted with dismay that they had made off with the shovel.

Inside their apartment Lukeria, in her best polyester dress, sat at the window as she always did this time of day. A copy of *Pamyat*, 'Remembrance', a reactionary news magazine noted for its anti-cosmopolitan leanings, was spread over her lap and the bulb of the plunger held to her ear. Another ritual. Lukeria was remembering the good days when she sat in the station room for her twenty-minute breaks and sifted through the news brought from the borders: which crops they were railing in, which base metals were going out, which group of undesirables was being relocated. How diminished her horizons

now, collapsed to the four corners of a small window overlooking a dingy courtyard.

On the table Lukeria had laid out a dish called 'Fruit of the
Chicken à la Varit'. Which was to say, boiled eggs. Again.
Tanya let her keys drop on the table.

'Oh, it's you,' Lukeria said, leaning closer to the window.
She frowned and straightened. 'That Yuri,' she circled a finger
at her ear. 'I think he's coming off the rails – even now he's on
the rooftop talking to himself. And then there's the way he
mopes around, looking like he's just seen a ghost.'

'As a matter of fact, he says he's seen Mircha.'

Lukeria shook her head. 'Well, he's always been a little
fragile, mentally, I mean. Take, for example, that space helmet
he wears. At least he's grown into it now. Remember when his
head was a little smaller and the helmet was too heavy for him,
dragging his head towards the ground?'

'I remember.' Tanya edged stoveward where the kettle
waited on the ring.

'Good thing I put a stop to that. What would your life be,
living with a man like that, an expert in the make and model of
other people's bootlaces? You working like a dog so he can find
his feet in this life. He's just the sort to sit on the stove all day,
thinking to hunt up the magical pike that will solve every
problem.' Lukeria wagged her head, a human metronome of
complete disapproval.

'Jews. When life gets rough, they are the first to leave the
country. I know, I watched it happen. They live with their bags

packed in readiness. Why don't they stay and suffer with the rest of us?'

'You keep your suitcases packed,' Tanya observed.

'That's different. Altogether different. But you wouldn't understand.'

No. She doesn't understand, not one bit. And she has tried. She has tried to see beyond the strangeness she was born into and to understand a world of dim light and half-answers. She has tried to understand this woman before her, utterly divided. How is it, for instance, she could sit there with a steamer trunk full of letters, none of them belonging to her? And the buttons! She's seen them, several envelopes of buttons, the dark threads trailing from the eyes. They came from the trousers of the male prisoners. After all, a man can't run if his trousers drop, and only guards wear belts. These buttons were put in envelopes and sent in the mail as messages to families that the prisoner had not run, would never run, would never again wear trousers that required buttons.

Tanya could not fathom how many buttons there might be in envelopes in trunks or boxes or bedside stands or suitcases all over Russia. How many letters. How many such reminders that long outlived the men and women who once lived and ate and dreamed and loved. They turned the soil over with their feet and uttered prayers and wrote letters that were as beautiful as any poem Tanya had ever read.

Lukeria lifted the newspaper, held in front of her like a beacon. 'Americans. They just make me want to spit. First they take all our money, the filthy cheats. Then they take our dignity. Now they want to steal all of our history, too. They suffer from Convenient Amnesia. They think they own the world, doling out their money to whom they see fit, ignoring others who need it far worse.'

'They're not all like that.'

Lukeria smiled a savage smile. 'No?'

Tanya played with the handle of her teacup. 'Some people give money just to give. Because they believe in a cause.'

'What people? What cause?'

'Art-loving people who believe in beauty.' And though it may be unwise, though she'd probably regret it every day of her life for as long as the two of them lived together, Tanya opened her mouth and told Lukeria everything she knew about the Causes of Beautification.

Lukeria shook her head as if this were the funniest joke she'd ever heard. Her bony shoulders quaked with mirth. 'You are such a little fool!' She'd been a beautiful woman once, but when she got into these moods, it was so much harder to see it, even in the forgiving light of the candle. 'Oh, my lungs.' Lukiera batted at the air around her face.

From Olga's apartment below came the sound of soft murmuring, voices drifting up through the heating vents. Tanya withdrew her sky notebook and application form from her plastic bag.

Through the heating vents Tanya could hear Yuri and Zoya. They were in full rut, the metal frame of the bed squeaking and groaning. It was enough to make her want to shove her pencil in an ear.

'There he goes again – talking to a ghost!' Lukeria pronounced.

'That's not a ghost he's with,' Tanya said. 'And they're not talking.'

'Oh.' Lukeria tipped her head and listened. 'Oh,' she said, rolling her gaze to the ceiling.

Tanya squeezed her eyes closed. The problem with clouds was that they so rarely made sounds. So rarely could you count on a cloud to fill your ears with cotton when you needed them to. And then there was the insistent pinchings from her bladder. Tanya made her way to the courtyard where overhead the moon was no thicker than an eyelash. That is to say, the night was dark as a cow's liver. Which is why she did not at first notice Vitek emerging from the latrine. But then he burped and she smelled the sub-grade vodka on his breath, saw his sloppy salute with the open bottle.

Vitek gazed at the windows of the third floor where Yuri and Zoya were still trysting and where Olga was, presumably, sleeping through it. 'Ah, love,' Vitek said with an air of wistfulness.

'Yes.' Tanya ground her molars. 'The walls are thin.'

Vitek smiled. 'The windows, too. Incidentally, I accidentally overheard you talking about that grant thing.'

Tanya pulled at the neck of her sweater. 'That's to remain a secret.'

Vitek shrugged and smiled, pointed to the fortochka. 'Nothing is a secret. Not here.' Though he was spectacularly drunk, his words still maintained a husk of logic. 'Anyway, it occurred to me that you – that is, you museum people, which includes but is not limited to yourself, Zoya, and Yuri – need me.'

Tanya stepped inside the latrine and locked the door. 'Why?'

'For managerial purposes. I can help you.'

'How?' Tanya, now finished with her business, was back outside the latrine.

'I have skills. I have know-how. Connections. I am a businessman. Allow me to demonstrate.' Vitek smiled and held out his open hand. 'You owe two kopeks for use of the latrine.'

Tanya cursed quietly and dug into her pocket for a coin.

'See how easy that was? But seriously, you need a man to arrange entertainment. Big-shot westerners have expectations. They cannot stand to be bored. They must have constant movement and noise. They will want to see the circus, the nightclubs, the discos, the bars, the dancing bears, a ballet – but only if it's a short one – and they will want to see women reaping in the fields with those hook things.'

'You mean a scythe?'

'Precisely! I knew you'd see it my way.' Vitek downed the last of the vodka and pitched the bottle onto the heap, where it bounced and shattered into a melody of breaking glass.

CHAPTER EIGHT

Azade

Though Azade had smelled the upside-down dreams of bats and the warm and weedy dreams of eels, nothing reeked as much as the dreams of humans. This was why angels do not visit us while we sleep — from fear they may carry our stench up their ladders to heaven. And in the same way that a glistening map tells of a snail's night-time journeys, dreams — having all night to gather strength — spill out and follow the dreamer wherever he or she goes, as a wet vapour trailing each step, as oil clinging to the skin. This was why at night Azade kept a tuck of salt under her tongue before careening towards sleep and why she washed her hands so thoroughly and so often as soon as she woke up in the morning. For what people dreamt was not only announced with an overwhelming odour, but also in sweat, tears, and urine, all the body's efforts to slough off what was no longer needed.

And where do people go to get rid of what they don't need? The toilet, of course. Stationed at her post, Azade has detected every souring dream, every curdled nightmare. In Olga's cautious turds, so typical of a woman who has a hard time letting go, Azade smelled Olga's longing for her husband who has long ago left this land and Olga's terrible desire to know precisely where his body lay. Gut the memory and the man. This was the advice Azade kept at the tip of her tongue and she would have said if it were not for Yuri. Every morning at 8.10, his hands still slick from a full night of fishing, Yuri sat on the commode and dumped his aching need for a father, a desire that carried the stagnant aroma of duckweed and stale dinner buns, the scent of a young man unable to leave his childhood. She could detect anxiety coiling deep in Lukeria's bowels and her farts told of her old woman's utter terror at being left alone. Then there was Tanya, embarrassed by her body, sitting in the latrine far longer than she needed to. Always the girl dreamt a translation of her days into the language of clouds, believing that by describing every skyscape she would make her life a beautiful knowable thing. But these days Azade was smelling more gas from the girl. Something was bothering her, something that wouldn't work out tidily in that notebook she always carried. It was as if the girl had swallowed sky and now was bloated with the shapes her longing assumed inside her swelling body.

Azade's odours, on the other hand, and this she readily admitted, were typical – heralding ordinary longings that smelled of her own skin, of woodsmoke, and of soil. Her night-time dreams were to see Mount Kazbek, the holy mountain rising into the purer, thinner air of Vladikavkaz and the foothills driving up the blue mists. She wanted to go to a place where winter stole the days from spring, and the snap of cold forced her breath inside out. She wanted to run her fingers over the silver fur of the kale leaves and to return to a land where there were bees instead of mosquitoes, dizzying heights instead of these low hills, and where the dust was of the cleaner sort. She had heard that chewing a single shiny rhododendron leaf would sustain a body through a hard mountain crossing. She wanted to see if this were true. And did the shadow of the mountain shelter at the same time two countries to the south and one to the east? Another question only her own eyes could answer.

The soles of her feet itched for the hard soil of the marketplace where she could hear fifty languages amid the raucous bellows of camels. For the market where frozen milk was sold and carried as a block, a piece of winter hauled on the back. She wanted to see for herself that there still existed a place where people had the good sense to keep the radishes next to the cinnamon and the lamb near the coffee and where the Korean jostled the Turk and everything that was simple rubbed against the complicated and the beautiful and ugly. She wanted to hear the women working the stalls, the canting and calls. She wanted to see their bright skirts, compassion the needle that sewed the waistband, humility the hem, strength the sleeves and kindness behind every stitch. She would sit and listen to the sound of the bells sewn to the hems of their skirts heralding their every movement. And when the market closed, she wanted to hear them turn the day under their feet, tamping the dust to the road, the bells marking an internal music every woman is born with, but few remember.

Most of all, she wanted to see for herself the graveyard her father had so lovingly cared for and the place he had wanted to be buried. And so sharp were these longings, so pungent the smell of them in her nostrils, that on mornings when the only sound in the dvor was her own breath in her ears and the sweep of her broom, these yearnings for what she had lost mingled with a desire for what she'd never had, and she could no longer distinguish between the two. All of which led her to believe that her dreams were true, shaped either by actual memory or by prophetic vision – how else, Azade asked herself daily, could she dream with such clarity?

How could she feel this nostalgic for a city she'd not seen since she was a child? A question for her father, who knew how to explain anything in four languages. And when she asked, so many years ago that the question itself had faded to a dim echo knocking from wall to wall, *Why? Why did we have to leave?*, he rubbed his forehead, his fingers worrying his faint prayer bruise.

When she was older, sometime after her father had been denied a position with the last school – a local high school known for employing complete dimwits – and before he'd been assigned to work the latrine, he gave her the answer. His answer could have been told in any number of languages, any number of ways, for it was a story he used to tell his students in Vladikavkaz.

'A true fiction,' he said. Always he prefaced the tale this way for his students. True because this story had been proven and lived out so many times, it didn't require the names of actual people or places. The truest stories never do, her father liked to say. And it was a good story because like the finest prayer rugs, it was a braided tale, which meant you could tell it forward or backward or start someplace in the middle, weaving in at all times an understanding of the past rolled against the present, which so very often suggested the future.

But telling stories this way, and listening to them told this way, required a patience most people didn't have. It's why she couldn't get three words out with Vitek before he threw his hands up and shouted, 'Ma, enough!' and stomped to the other side of the dvor, his hands pressed to his ears. So she told the story anyway, to her goat, Koza, because at the sound of her voice he snuffled obediently at the hem of her skirt. She told it to the children because if she gave them honey sticks or sunflower seeds they could be quite good listeners. She told it to the hole in the latrine because if the Devil had crawled in there in the middle of the night the truth of this story would have turned his teeth to rubber and rendered him harmless. She told the story to herself because being so far from her homeland she felt she had forgotten what was important and true. Case in point, ever since her father and then her mother passed on, she'd forgotten how to pray, though, in truth, she'd only known three, maybe four prayers to begin with. Furthermore, a good mountain Muslim could recite family history seven generations back. Her father could tell ten generations' worth. But he died too soon and now Azade could only remember three generations. Having lost the trail of ancestors, having lost the prayers, Azade clung tenaciously to what she did have and hoped that in the mountain tradition her fervour would turn this story into a prayer the way over time soft pitch becomes amber.

There was once a mad prince who wanted to subdue the land as far as it stretched from the frozen marshes of the north to the impassable mountains in the south. But the people from region to region loved their land more than they loved the mad prince and his strange plans. Even after hearing the prince's many promises of a better life in better lands, his royal subjects flatly refused to move. 'This is our home. Here our bones flourish like herbs. Here we buried our grandfathers. Every good memory we have is here. Besides, this is the only land we know how to live on,' the people explained.

But the prince was not deterred. With the brilliance of a mad mind the prince moved the people of the verdant mountains to the infertile plains, the people of the rivers to the ice and the plains people to the hills in an effort to confuse their language, their memory. Though all this movement muddled their language and even their religion, it wasn't enough to completely erase their memory. Because during their forced travels, the people bit their thumbs and wrote their names in their blood on the bark of trees and on stones. And every step they took only imprinted on the bottoms of their feet an indelible map spelling the way back to their ancestral homes.

Infuriated, the prince devised another plan. He sent his royal tailors and seamstresses from village to village, aul to aul, where they skinned each and every royal subject. And then the seamstresses sewed a new skin taken from someone else living far away onto each flayed body. It was an excruciatingly painful process and many people died before the tailors and seamstresses perfected the technique, as some skins were sewn too tight and some too loose. And no amount of sawdust could completely absorb the standing blood.

Men and women wept at the seams – the eyes and the mouth and fingertips, and the bottoms of their feet. But this suited the mad prince. Now his royal subjects could barely move within these skins that chafed their restless souls. The prince then nailed to the very trees that once bore bloody thumbprints royal proclamations assuring his subjects that these sacrifices were socially necessary and completely normal; their pain was of an ordinary type that fell into perfectly tolerable limits.

Still, nothing could account for the terrible itches and longings their bodies beneath their new skins still had for their old skins. And nothing could cure it but to sink their feet with these foreign skins in their own old familiar soils of their walnut orchards or high mountain cabbage rows or the steppes stippled with rapeseed and wormwood. It was a complication the mad prince, in spite of his genius, had not considered: bodies beneath the skin might retain a permanent memory of their homeland.

There was more to the story, but her father explained that it couldn't be told because the other half hadn't been walked out with the feet yet. All of them, displaced into this concrete city of leaden skies, were those royal subjects skinned by the mad prince whose madness passed from ruler to ruler. It was up to her, he said, to live out the second half. Up to her, he said, to remember the family and return them to their ancestral home. Only then could the spell be broken. All those years of hearing her father tell that story to anyone who would listen and even those who wouldn't had made Azade impatient in her muscles. As a girl she knew with a certainty that defied her age that she would do it, she would walk the story backward, walk it to the beginning, to Mount Kazbek where the world began. But she was not a girl anymore. Her father was gone. Her mother, too. The years had ground her down one vertebra at a time. And though she still wanted the mountains, now it was only in her dreams she remembered that old desire. The only way to force clarity of desire was to remember the old pain, the hurt of one skin chafing against the other. The only way to force the memory was to plunge her hands in a pot of boiling water. Like the thin sleeves covering garlic, her own skin curled to paper and peeled. But days later, when her burns began to heal, she scratched and clawed at her skin – a miserable relief, because it only made her skin ache even more.

✳

Azade unlocked her Little Necessary and sat on the commode. Though a fork in a door drives out bad luck and a spoon left out on a step invites it in, the worst thing a person could do was to let a door stand open to the wind. Even so, every morning Azade propped open the plastic door of the latrine. It was the only way to ventilate the virulent odours of all these unfulfilled dreams wafting up around her and fluting the edges of her skirt. And with this plastic door open she could keep a better eye on the children. No matter what the weather, as soon as they heard her stirring, they scrambled to the heap and staked out their spots. The girl Anna maintained a perch on the top of the heap while the younger children, Gleb, and the twins, Good Boris and Bad Boris, and the littlest – dark like Azade – anchored the four corners while they waited.

Every morning went this way, Azade setting out what she thought the children might need, it being the mountain way of greeting the morning with a gift. In Vladikavkaz, her mother said that the Orthodox Russians did this on St Ilya's day, laying out straw and opening their dog doors that swung to the east. And when the dogs gathered, the Russians put out tumblers of vodka – extra tumblers for larger dogs. That was the difference between Orthodox Russians and Mountain Muslims: Russians gave once a year, but Azade's parents and their neighbours, they gave every day, every day a St Ilya's day. And so now, out of habit, out of genuine concern, Azade put

out sweaters, boots, socks – all the things Mircha left behind
when he jumped all those weeks ago.

   And this morning, as she had every morning for the last
several months, she shuffled to the heap and set out bread and
kefir, a sour yogurt drink, so that even if their brains went to
waste, their bodies would not bend with the wilted bones like
those of the street kids who lived entirely on sugar packets
and chewing gum. Still, Azade worried. Their every word and
action seemed to her far too deliberate. They were like ancient
men and women trapped in sad child bodies. Even stranger,
they had never dreamt a single dream – not even one tired
dream shared between them. And when she trained her nose in
their direction she smelled battery acid and the sharp plastic
odour of glue, chemical fumes that spirited the children far
from the world of the more ordinary, palpable dreams.

   Azade rewound her hair and pinned it high atop her head
and watched the children hunker over the food. They ate
mechanically, their gazes trained on Azade. If she were honest
with herself, it bothered her that for all her efforts, not a single
one of them would call her mother, not one of them would
look at her with soft recognition in their eye. Another heartache for her. But she had never been the type to give up easily.
She would mother them anyway.

   'Ma!' Vitek emerged from the stairwell. His hair stuck out
in ninety odd angles. From his stilted gait Azade knew he'd
had a full night of drinking and now even the hair on his head
hurt. Bilious vodka fumes trailed him, knocking a crow from

the rooftop aerial and sending Koza into a paroxysm of sneezing. Vitek bobbed his Adam's apple and spat under the frozen lime tree. Then he withdrew and uncapped a fresh bottle of vodka, immediately downing a quarter of its contents. He was performing a time-honoured therapeutic practice called *pokhmelitsa*, or the 'glass remedy', as drowning a hangover in alcohol was the only way to truly cure oneself. That done, Vitek then dropped his trousers and repositioned himself on the seat.

'Paper!' he cried, thrusting a hand out the open door.

Azade rummaged in her wicker hamper for a suitable text. There was the *Artist's Guide* – a nine-hundred-page instructional tome outlining how and in what poses one was allowed to depict Lenin. Nine hundred pages. Well, some artists needed all the help they could get – at least that's what she'd gathered from the things Tanya and Yuri said about the museum.

'Now!' Vitek barked.

Azade jumped and handed Vitek a copy of the previous day's *Red Star*. Except for the rustling of the newspaper as Vitek turned the pages, it was completely quiet in the latrine. It meant Vitek was constipated with thoughts of high speculative content.

At last he let loose with a low whistle. 'So many things to invest in. Oil, maybe. The war.' Vitek turned the pages in a flurry then opened the plastic door and flung the paper at Azade's feet. 'If only we had a little money. A little money in the right places makes more money.' Vitek winced. 'Then I could buy myself a new liver.'

Azade pinched her nose. 'You're just like your father, you drink too much.'

'And a wise man he was. The one true thing he taught me was that a man can never drink too much.' Vitek rebuckled his trousers and stepped out of the latrine.

Azade sniffed. No, not a healthy smell for a boy his age. His shits smelled like wet rust and his dreams were of the dangerous sort. It would be up to her to save her son from his own greed and folly. Well, it was a mother's duty to lie under her child like a log, her back becoming the smooth road so that her child's feet would not stumble, so that he could walk right over her and straight up into the sky. But on days like these she really feared, despite her best efforts, that Vitek would come to a bad end and for some reason God was punishing her by forcing her to witness it.

Azade nodded at the children, each of them executing wooden pirouettes and curtseys. They reminded her of those carved figures that emerged from the cuckoo clock, their movements accurate, but lacking grace. Azade turned to Vitek. 'These kids – they don't look so good.'

'They're fine. They're just happy.'

'Kids need to play.'

'Oh.' Vitek waved his hand and his rusty fumes swirled up into her nose. 'They play games.'

Azade squinted. As if on cue Big Anna, still in mid-squat, lifted her chin and hollered: 'What's the essential nature of man?' It was a game they sometimes called Dialectical

Materialism and sometimes called philosophy. Either way, Azade really didn't like the sound of it.

'Senseless!' Red-headed Gleb adjusted his glasses.

'Faithless,' Good Boris called out.

'Heartless!' Bad Boris beside him said.

And then from the end of the row the little girl yelled with a gusto that seemed at odds for a mouth so small: 'Ruthless.'

Azade drew her breath between her teeth and turned to Vitek. 'Just be careful, that's all I'm saying.'

'Why?'

'Because when we die God will judge us by how we treat children and animals, calling on them to give an accounting of our behaviour.'

Vitek swung his gaze across the courtyard, to the glittering heap and the children squatting. 'Ma – the way you talk, you could get yourself hurt in the mouth.'

Azade blinked. She wanted to say, 'Shame on you!' – the most potent words in a mother's arsenal – but the words were tied tight to her tongue and Azade realized that she was in actual fact afraid of her own son.

Azade swallowed and aligned her molars. The back teeth couldn't be knocked loose if the jaw was locked tight.

'What you're doing with these kids, it's criminal.' There, she said it.

'They are practising their social graces, nothing wrong with that. Everybody loves a snappy bow and curtsey.'

'Who is everybody?'

'The art-loving Americans who are possibly going to visit us very soon. Possibly.'

So that's what she'd been smelling in Tanya's shit. Foreign visitors, and important ones, too, from the looks of the ferocious bowing and curtseying going on in the courtyard.

Vitek blew on his hands, then tucked them into his armpits and stamped his feet. 'Incidentally, today is rent day,' he said.

'You can't charge me rent. I'm your mother. And you're living in my apartment.'

'Wake up, Ma. This is life – everybody gets screwed every now and then.'

Azade supposed she should take comfort in the small reality that some things, like getting ripped off, you could still count on, that some things hadn't changed. But it was gravel between her teeth: when family treat each other worse than a highway robber. How could she take any real comfort in that?

Vitek's gaze slid over Azade's face and then to her boots where she kept her stash of spoons.

'It costs, you know, to live as freely as we do. But I don't want you thinking I'm not human. I am just as upset with the situation as anybody else. Maybe more. Do I enjoy being forced to do things I prefer not to? Of course there's no joy in it. But life is not about preferences or feelings, and most certainly not about joy.' Vitek ran his tongue over his front teeth. 'And I *am* a human being, no matter what the others may think about me. It isn't as if I don't believe in the enduring human capacity for love and hope, for dignity. It isn't as if I don't secretly want those things. But I'm a realist and I see how things are and understand how things have to be to make it in a world like this one.'

Azade bent and withdrew a silver spoon. In the curved face of the spoon she glimpsed her own image, bowed and beaten.

'I see how things are. You've become a cheap con artist and a crook.' Azade pressed the spoon into the meat of Vitek's palm.

Vitek waved the spoon near her nose, his conscience conveniently unstirred. 'What I'm doing here, it's a small thing. Better I should collect rent than someone else. Do you think someone else would be as friendly about it as me? Let me tell you something.' Vitek leaned closer to Azade. 'In Moscow people are luring the old pensioners out into the woods and killing them. And those bodies lie there under the snow until April thaw when other oldies walking their dogs discover them. Want to know why they're getting killed?'

'No,' Azade shook her head.

'For the keys to their apartments. People are killing each other for space to live in and for the papers to prove they have a right to live there. So tell me I'm a bad man for collecting a little rent, these small tokens of appreciation for the services I provide.'

'Which services are those, exactly?'

Vitek laughed. 'Oh, Ma. I'm keeping you safe from yourself and protecting everybody's interests. And it costs to live with such security.'

'What about them?' Azade hooked her chin towards the children, who were now waltzing with exaggerated slow moves.

'I'm teaching them how the world of bizness works. They're going to clean the courtyard because Americans love clean outdoor places to sit and drink pricey coffee.' Here Vitek tapped the side of his head with a finger. 'I know this because I am a keen observer of human consumption and trends. We will clean the courtyard. We will remove that trash heap with its broad and potent odours. We will steal café chairs and offer pricey teas and coffees and dance in folk costumes at all times and sashay across the concrete.'

Azade held her head between her hands. The more he talked, the stranger he sounded.

'All this to secure the funds which the Americans have very nearly promised me. I mean, us. Incidentally, it would be really grand if you'd service the latrine. The smells are extremely provincial and narrow in focus. Now I'm going upstairs to work out our bizness prospects. And you,' now Vitek addressed the children, 'are all going to be very very quiet and quietly get rid of this trash.' Vitek lumbered toward the stairs, his rusty fumes and the dog following him into the stairwell and up the stairs to the roof, where Azade knew he would spend the rest of the day slowly healing himself with more vodka.

As soon as Vitek was out of sight, Good Boris and Bad Boris, in mid-bow, shuffled over to the mound of snow where Mircha was buried. They peed, their urine burning the letters of their names into the snow. As if that weren't bad enough, Big Anna and Gleb held cigarette lighters to the mound, melting long patches of snow, slowly revealing the rounded shape of Mircha, whose feet now protruded in a completely conspicuous way. As much as Azade loved these kids, she had to admit that possibly they were not quite right.

'Stop that! Stop what you are doing!' Azade shook her broom, but there was no help for it. The twins each had a leg in their hands and were tugging at Mircha's unlaced boots. And then here came the littlest one. She could not speak yet, and always snot dripped from her nose. The girl slipped a hard object into Azade's coat pocket. Azade thrust her hand into the pocket and withdrew a spoon, a prized gold-plated spoon like the ones they used to make only in Tula. Then the boy with the glasses, Gleb, approached. He was covered from head to toe in mud, nothing new there, but in his hand he held a pair of clattering dentures. Not wood or plastic but real Russian Gzhel porcelain, the make and model of which had always been far beyond Azade's financial grasp.

'My, what a fine set of teeth you have.' Azade tried to flatten from her voice all surprise and envy.

The boy studied Azade, his pupils expanding and contracting as he regarded her. He nodded to that soft spot of mud where her foot had first gone under. 'I didn't steal them. They were just sitting there, chattering at me.'

Azade approached the heap, her broom held out in readiness. In the place where her boot had punched through the snow to soft mud, the ground had sunk and opened into a gaping hole. Azade hurried to the latrine and returned with her torch. The children had been digging, that much was clear. They had banked huge mounds of mud beside the heap. And where the hole dropped a metre they'd shored it up with planks. And where the hole turned and tunnelled towards the apartment building they had laid down cardboard and more plywood. She had only to bend over and she could crawl on hands and knees. The tunnel opened into a large cave, the sides of which quaked and pulsed as if the mud were alive.

Azade straightened, squeezed her eyes closed. First Mircha. Now this. She opened her eyes. Azade swept the trembling walls with the beam of her torch. Spoons and spades and shovels, their handles and heads, all glistened in bright silver before her. Azade switched off her torch, but the spoons and spades and shovels winked lovingly at her, catching and casting light from a source she could not determine, but that seemed most certainly to come from somewhere deeper in the hole. Oh, but it was so bad, bad to have spoons lying about. Azade tucked a few into her boots, then hunched her shoulders and peered into the hole. Scattered all about her feet were diamonds and dentures and fabulous pieces of porcelain bridgework, bright and beaming, all there for her, there for the taking. Never had Azade seen anything quite so horrible and wonderful at the same time. Was this heaven offering its bounty for her and her alone? Or was this hell? Was this the devil's purse, the lining of the pocket of him who rode the long-legged camel

backwards through our dreams, knocking loose the fillings
of our teeth?

Azade scrambled out of the hole and into the latrine. She
slammed the lid and sat on the toilet, her whole body trembling. Knowing all that she knew about open spaces and the
dangers of uncovered pots and holes, clearly there was only
one thing to be done: cover the hole, and quick.

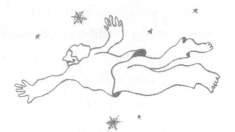

CHAPTER NINE

Yuri

As a swimmer treading water, Yuri paddles in his own blood.

He is perfectly comfortable, his blood being a moderate twenty-three degrees Celsius, and his mother having had the foresight to give him swimming lessons. And he is an idealist, treading without fear, blissfully unaware of the highly symbolic content of this viscous dream. But then – horrors – Mother enters the dream without so much as a knock or a cough. She wears her grey *Red Star* work dress – the one and only dress suitable for wearing out of doors. Around her neck hangs her enormous work typewriter.

Her fingers fly over the keys: `Very Important People Are Disappearing.`

Yuri repeats: `very important people are disappearing.`

The typewriter clacks: `Very Important People Are Treading In Your Blood.`

`Very important people are treading in my blood.` Indeed, they are important. Former gymnasts. Partially (but not wholly) disgraced Secretaries of State. Dignitaries. Diplomats. Security officers. Chess champions. Even the 220-kilo statue of Gogol's nose, rumoured to have been kidnapped by literary extremists, sniffles in a significant manner at the edges of the dream. Everyone nods convivially to one another. Smiles. Yuri nods, smiles. And this is what is so terrifying to him, not the nose or the blood. Never the blood. But how very crowded his dreams have become, how his every move is hampered and cramped. Yuri pulls on his flight helmet, fastens it securely, plants an elbow into the soft middle of a famous cosmonaut.

'How dare you!' The cosmonaut's umbrage knows no limits.

'I beg your pardon astronomically,' Yuri stammers. But the chess masters stretch their faces into shapes of severe disapproval. And then the dream tips toward true nightmare, for here's Mother, her typewriter still clacking away as if possessed:

`Shame on you!`

'Shame on you!' Mother's voice is hard as certainty itself, as the clang of the bell, for now her tongue has turned into a metal clapper. And each word is accompanied by a hard tapping of her fingers, which are not fingers and possibly never had been, but small typewriter hammers striking a page. His mother is justice. Judgement is at her sharp fingertips.

And why not? Mother knows what she knows. She reads the field reports and knows what she thinks her boy did while he was away, called up suddenly into the army. 'Know about it? Everyone at the *Red Star* knows,' Mother says, and the carriage of the typewriter scuttles along. What she is talking about,

Yuri doesn't even need to ask. Always in this nightmare Mother talks about the same thing, her typewriter bearing loud and permanent witness: Badness in Chechnya — *clack*. What Things My Son Did While Being Bad in Bad Chechnya — *clackity clack clack*. The Atrocities. *Clack*. The Constancy of Human Cruelty. *Clack ding. Return.*

He tries to remind her that he is part fish, not all human. But her eyes are flashing hard and bright with fury.

'I know what happened. In Samashk. Raping little girls. Playing field games with the heads of Chechen elders!' And it hurts his four-chambered fish-heart to hear her accuse him — him, her son — of such things. Fish or man, never in his life could or would he do such things. But it's so hard to protest when you are treading in such crowded blood. So hard not to simply let yourself sink under the weight of congealing judgement.

And now the courtyard-dwelling children have jumped in, yes, jumped in up to their waists, their spindly malnourished legs churning his viscous blood to clot.

'Don't listen to her. I did not do those things,' Yuri appeals to the children. They will understand. He is a child, too, more or less. Childlike, anyway. 'The twelve-year-old girls I did not rape. Their grandmothers I did not shoot between their eyes.' Now Yuri pleads with Mother. 'I only opened the tank hatch once during daylight. And then only to ask an old man for directions. And then only to watch as he lobbed a grenade at me.'

'But you saw Atrocious Things happen. You watched the others doing those Things. You said nothing.' Now Mother's mouth is a keyboard, her tongue the element striking the keys. Even worse, she's stepped out of her *Red Star* work dress. The dress, voluminous and capacious as language itself, has sopped up most of Yuri's bad blood. Now, together, mother and son, they stand gazing at one another, naked and ashamed. Never has Yuri been quite so terrified.

'For God's sake, some of us need our sleep!' Zoya's voice rent the nightmare wide open. Her fingernails clawed at the flight helmet. 'If you can't talk quietly in your sleep, as a matter of courtesy you should at least talk about something interesting.' Zoya wrapped herself in the blanket and rolled away from him. 'And if not that,' now her voice, muffled by the blanket, sounded as if it came from a vast and impenetrable distance, 'then do something useful like go fishing.'

Fishing! Such a suggestion.

Yuri hopped out of bed. Down down down the stairs to the courtyard he went, to the place where he'd stowed his bike which appeared to have mysteriously shed yet another essential part, this time a sprocket. Yuri scaled the heap, searching. Up to his armpits in darkness, he could just make out the figure of one of the children. Quite possibly they didn't sleep. Certainly they weren't idle. It was the girl, Big Anna. She'd gathered some of the smaller scraps from the heap: a cracked jump seat from an MTZ-5 – those old tractors from Minsk that rumbled over every lonely field in Soviet films – a shoal of plastic water bottles, and a bike sprocket. It caught and cast the meagre moonlight, shining with such lustre and silvery iridescence that Yuri knew with absolute certainty that it was not his sprocket and could not possibly have been discarded on the heap as rubbish. It was just that fine.

Big Anna dangled the sprocket over her head.

'Wh-where did you get that?' Yuri asked, incredulous.

Big Anna laughed, a liquid sound. 'Ten roubles answers all questions.'

Yuri dug into his hip pocket. He speared the rouble note on the jagged lid of a can of sprats, then watched as the sprocket whistled through the air and landed at his feet.

In record speed Yuri reassembled his bike and pedalled for the river. The more time he spent around people, the more he admired fish.

Ah, fish!

He knew them as well as, if not better than, he knew himself. Men and fish, after all, are more alike than most people know. The body of a fish is three-quarters water. The body of a man is three-quarters water. Man and fish have backbones and skulls housing the brain and the paired sense organs: eyes, ears and olfactory organs. The inner ears of fish, like those of man, detect gravity and motion as well as sound. In both creatures the four-chambered heart lay in a separate cavity at the front of the body. This was why Yuri was almost certain that fish have all the same problems people do.

Having four chambers to harbour their worries, they

understood the need to hide. They had learned to fear the shadow of men. They had seasonal longings that fuelled desperate acts. Consider the instinct to migrate to the sea – so common among trout populations of the Don and Volga where a body of salt water lay nearby. The memory of the sea remained in their mouths and in the gills, which, having learned to breathe in both waters, eventually drove the fish back to the water they worked so hard to leave. Yes, they killed themselves trying to reach the waters of their youth, just as other species of trout killed themselves in their attempts to reach their upriver spawning grounds. Did the trout swimming upstream pass along news to the downriver-travelling trout? Did they grow any wiser for all their troubles? Did they tell the secrets of the men lurking above with sticks and nets, firecrackers and the occasional bottle of bleach in their hands?

Apparently not, Yuri decided as he hid his bike behind a stand of frozen birch. It was each trout for himself. Yuri blew on his hands. The ice was thinning at the edges of the river and in a few weeks it would break and buck with a boom and roar. It was the sound of the Devil coming up for air, driving all the hungry fish before him. And Yuri planned to be right there, rod and net in hand, ready to bring in the hungry pike, one right after another.

Yuri squinted. He could just make out two figures stationed downriver behind a wheelchair. And though Yuri could not see him, he knew that in this chair sat Volodya, taking note of who fished and where.

Yuri uncapped his bottle of vodka. The bottle was the mistress and Yuri understood, had always understood even before his father left, why the old men and the young men on park benches and doorway stoops kissed the neck of the bottle before finishing the last drop. Nothing compared to the love of the bottle – not even the love of a woman. 'Who needs them?' Mircha asked Yuri who, at the time, might have been twelve, or maybe thirteen. 'A man can never make a woman happy and as there are so many of them and so few of us, who's to say we won't wind up with a bad one? But vodka never nags, never complains. Never reminds one of one's moral failings.' Here Mircha gazed over the neck of the bottle to consider Yuri. 'There simply is no such thing as bad vodka. The two words cannot coexist side by side.'

Yuri nodded then, as he did now, and swallowed a mouthful. A man may privately think the vodka is bad (God forbid), after a quick toss back of a hundred grams of poorer-quality stuff. The burn, the wince, the dyspepsia – a body can't argue with that. But never does a man mention it. For vodka must always be praised, regardless of the quality. Vodka is good. Very good. Truly exceptional vodka is excellent. That said, in Yuri's opinion the Rasputin he now held at arm's length was just so-so.

'Bitch!' Yuri spluttered. The gazes of a few vets fishing upriver lifted momentarily, fixing the source of the interruption, then dropped back over their holes. 'Bitch,' Yuri repeated, this time with more tenderness. This affectionate cursing was just one of the many protocols of vodka consumption, which are so firm and reliable that certain birds set their wings by them. And Yuri was as loyal and true to these protocols as a healthy lung was to air. The idea being that in the cosmogony of needed and necessary things, vodka was life. Breath. Hobby. National sport. Every Russian man's first love. The Swedes and Latvians liked to think they knew a thing or two about the stuff, and mention vodka around Polish tourists and they'd immediately arrange their faces into long and superior expressions and their bodies into proprietary postures. But give a bottle to a Russian – that is, give some vodka to a well-trained professional whose body is a finely tuned instrument of consumption – and watch what the stuff is good for.

Yuri took another healthy drink and set to hacking a hole in the ice. The thing was, he imagined now that he was explaining his drinking to all the people in his life who disapproved – that is, Mother, Zoya, Tanya. The thing was, nothing made him feel as good as vodka did. Sure, he was grateful for Zoya's attentions, grateful that there were times she wanted him. But love-making was just a tingle at the base of his spine compared with the way vodka hit the bottom of his stomach and bloomed warm and bright through his chest. And vodka was a practical fisherman's aid, helping him to keep his hands steady and sure.

The ice now opened, Yuri dropped the line, a brass wire attached to a coat hanger. He peered into the black water. Another thing about drinking vodka, about fishing: both activities afforded clarity of thought, a depth of contemplation, a grandiose ability to see subtle connections. Both activities led to the understanding of certain universal truths. For instance, his previous unassailable logic notwithstanding, for all the similarity between man and fish, there were, admittedly, a few differences. Where a man has arms and legs, a fish has fins. Where man wears a singlet of skin, fish wear a shining chain mail of scales. Yuri peered in the hole he'd made, watched the dark water begin greasing to ice. He poured a little vodka into the hole and the ice curled to the edges.

Fish, Yuri knew, had no need for the curative effect of vodka. Where a man has regret, fish have only dreams. Their problems are few. They do not suffer cold sweats or night terrors. They don't worry about employment. They have jobs, sure. Even Yuri knew that. But as they went about it all so quietly, it was as if whatever they did was no work at all. And they don't argue with the clumsy failings of their fellow cohabitants. They don't remind each other of how stupid, how morally bankrupt, how useless they have become to one another.

Likely they were not overly harassed by the females of their species, nor were they bullied about by fish with greater clout. Probably they did not hear ticking inside their heads. In fact, the fish Yuri knew moved about their world with such grace and dignity, flapping their gills in a way that suggested theirs was a world so beautiful, so completely free of complication that they simply could not fathom an end to it. Which explained their umbrage, the baleful looks they cast when hooked.

The line went taught. Yuri yanked the line and hauled up his catch, visor-level for inspection: a pike, and ornery, judging by its vicious snapping and thrashes in the air.

'You! Spaceman!' Volodya's bellows knocked from bank to bank, tree to tree.

Yuri dropped the fish on top of his plastic bag and pounded on the flight helmet with an open palm and scoped the fog.

Volodya's entourage emerged from the darkness, material-izing grain by grain until Yuri could discern with definite clarity the two vets, each of whom had a hand on one of the chair grips, and each of whom now appeared taller somehow, broader of shoulder. Volodya sat straight as a plank in his chair, his service cap low over his forehead. Volodya had lost his legs just below the hips and with his service trousers tucked tight under his stumps it appeared that the front wheels of the chair were his feet. And now the vets had set the brakes so that those wheels rested on top of Yuri's feet.

'What are you doing here?' Volodya asked.

Yuri looked at the pike on the bag. 'I'm fishing.'

Yuri glanced at the vet standing to the left of the chair and took in his service coat with the many badges, confirming what he already suspected: here was a man honoured several times over for doing serious harm in Georgia. Yuri squinted at the vet on the right. This one had received even more badges for his service in Bosnia. In the hierarchy of the feeding chain, Yuri, who had received no medals, no honours, no badges for kicking anybody's ass anywhere, would be lucky to make off with the fins and tail of his pike.

'You know the rule,' the vet on the left said quietly.

'Whose river do you think this is?' the vet on the right asked.

'His?' Yuri pointed to Volodya.

'So whose fish is that you're holding?' the vet on the left asked.

'His?' Yuri lifted his visor, pointed to Volodya.

'The kid is not as stupid as he looks,' the vet on the left said to the vet on the right as they took off their coats and draped them over the grips of Volodya's chair.

'Gentlemen, please!' Yuri pulled off the flight helmet and attempted the cavalier pose of one who has considered the possibility of getting beaten within a centimetre of his life and found it not a bit troubling.

'This pike is so small, of such insignificance, but absolutely I was going to bring it to you anyway.' Yuri looked at the pike resting stone still on the plastic bag. 'I just haven't had time to bash it properly on the head.'

Mention an itch. No sooner were the words out than the vets rolled up their sleeves.

'Cheer up, boy-o.' Volodya flashed Yuri a munificent smile as the Bosnian vet retrieved the pike. 'This is the price of living. And you're lucky.' Volodya glanced at Yuri's legs, marvellously whole and intact.

Then pain: a pounding punctuated with sharp interjections.

A dash, dash. Boxer's blows to the face. Oh Mother. A comma, a semi-colon, a reprieve and then ellipses. All the pieces of punctuation brilliantly effected by the closed fist, the knee to the groin. Yes, he was getting the message. He was, merciful God in heaven, learning the lesson loud and clear. Oh Mother. Full-stop.

When he came to, a quick inventory. Afternoon glare achingly white. His flight helmet, check. His rod, check. Pain scale was six and holding. He hadn't made out too badly, all things considered. And Volodya was right: Yuri was lucky. This time they'd only given him a warning beating. Yuri pulled on his helmet (Oh, Mother!), retrieved his bike and pedalled slowly towards the museum. Beyond the city the sky had cracked open for the afternoon, allowing a thin verge of throbbing light to spread into a low welt of frost and pollution. Yuri turned his head and trained his gaze on the front tyre. The ticking in his head – still there – and afternoons like these, even the sky hurt him.

He wheeled his bike through the back door of the museum. This door no one ever bothered to lock because, with the exception of the toilet paper that Caretaker Daniilov stocked on Tuesdays, there was nothing to steal. Which said something about the art hanging on the walls. The art! Oh, God, it hurt. Yuri moaned and steadied himself on a faux statue of Venus. Someone had taken a healthy bite out of Venus' left buttock – not hard to do, as the statue been fashioned from foam.

In the beginning it bothered him, this art. If he had any

pride, any shame, any artistic integrity he would denounce this museum as a cheap fraud, ridiculous in its pretensions. But the sad fact was that even if he were to shout it from the rooftops, no one, not a soul, would care. Even sadder, after a few weeks of working in the museum, Yuri stopped caring, too. After all, a job was a job. And he needed a job. Catching the occasional pike or carp, deficit items each, wasn't enough and even though Russia was a new country, it still went better with men who made some attempt to work than with those who outwardly loafed.

Yuri let the visor fall and felt his way towards the hat/coat-check counter. This corridor he'd never liked. Even in the interior gloom of low wattage lighting, the art was still offensive. The pseudo-Kuntskamera exhibit turned his stomach. Never mind that he had actually helped fashion the foetuses out of yellow foam. In the main, Yuri was a big fan of babies everywhere, but these were not babies. These were circus freaks, and not even real circus freaks at that. And yet, the babies paled in comparison to the painting boldly displayed next to the bathrooms. A reproduction of an eighteenth-century painting divided into twelve squares, each square depicting deaths of beloved apostles. Yuri flipped up the visor and squinted at the apostles meeting their reward, in this case horrible deaths by dismemberment, boiling, crucifixions, stonings. And the expression on their faces was so serene, of such solemn patience, as if the loss of their life was of no great importance, that Yuri couldn't help looking at them. Couldn't help looking at them and counting twelve more reasons why he could never be a Christian.

And then came sound, noise of a museum in the afternoon. Shoes and umbrellas, galoshes, clicks and thuds, thumps, the noise of children moving in groups, and then the distinct sound of Tanya behind the check counter: clomp clomp clomp. Even when wearing her most fashionable pair of shoes her tread was of the heaviest sort. And there she was, her full face round and close and peering through the darkened visor at him.

'Oh, Yuri,' Tanya flipped up the flight visor, 'what have you done to yourself?'

'I went fishing and I got into some trouble.' Yuri sat cautiously in Tanya's fold-down metal chair.

Tanya bit her lip. 'We're going to have to clean you up. Take off that silly helmet.'

'I can't.'

Tanya sighed.

Together, he pushing, she pulling, they worked the yoke of the helmet over Yuri's head, painful centimetre by painful centimetre. In the relative warmth of the museum basement Yuri felt the blood moving behind his skin, felt his face swelling and the cuts opening.

Tanya licked her finger and smoothed Yuri's eyebrow. The pain, definitely a seven now. Why does a woman's touch hurt as often as not? And then their words. Mother, for instance, some months ago speaking on the subject of Tanya, who was so close now he could kiss her if his lips weren't split and bleeding: 'Please do not disgrace yourself by falling in love with a Gentile. She's nice, but she's not one of us. If you marry her your grandmother Ilke will torment us in our dreams.'

No, Tanya really didn't have a chance with him. It wasn't right to let her believe that she ever would, either. And yet… and yet no denying the small pleasure he felt at this very moment. Tanya chewing her gum close to his ear, cooing over him, grooming him, giving him soft womanly advice he in no way planned to heed.

'You might fish elsewhere, you know.' Tanya licked at a paper tissue and dabbed at a gash on the side of his face.

Yuri winced. He could feel the tissue cling to the cut. 'But it's my spot. I earned it.' It was further evidence of his self-loathing, a plague that he could only ascribe to having grown up without a father and to that hazy generational curse of growing up a Jew in Russia.

Tanya stepped back to examine her work. 'You can't take schoolchildren on tours looking like this. And we can't let Head Administrator Chumak see you, either. Let's get that helmet back on.' Tanya shoved the helmet over Yuri's head.

And just in time, too. *Thump–slide. Thump.*

Yuri crawled under the counter.

'Oh, Tanya! News! Big news!' Wedged as he was beneath the long hat/coat-check counter, Yuri could not see Head Administrator Chumak. But he could see the effect Head Administrator Chumak's words had on Tanya. Her hands shook and her knees literally knocked, setting the dimples on her rump in an uproar. No, for all her efforts, that cigarette and chewing gum diet wasn't helping her much. But she was kind, and though kindness didn't get girls like her very far, it ought to, Yuri decided. She deserved much better than what the bowels of the museum afforded.

'The Americans are coming! It's officially confirmed. They are buying their airline tickets even as we speak!'

'They're coming,' Tanya repeated, with what sounded to Yuri like disbelief and horror.

'In three weeks.'

'Three weeks. That's wonderful news, sir.'

'Wonderful? Wonderful?' Head Administrator Chumak's voice rolled through the corridor. 'This is better than wonderful. Do you know what this means?'

'No, sir.'

'If we get this grant I will buy a fence. I will buy my wife a car. And driving gloves. At last she will be happy and stop pecking at me. But of course, of course, there's so much to do in the meantime. This is such a delicate operation and there's so much...' Head Administrator Chumak peered over the counter. 'What is that unsightly protrusion? That cannot be a hat.'

'No, sir. It's Yuri. He is not feeling well.'

Yuri unfolded his body and straightened for Head Administrator Chumak's inspection.

Head Administrator Chumak's smile faded and his liver

spots darkened. 'Well, young man, if you weren't feeling well, you shouldn't have come here. We have been charged with the honourable task of preserving and presenting fine art. It won't do to look like a bleeding tomato wearing a mushroom for a hat.'

'Preserving and protecting art is, of course, of vast importance and I have the utmost respect for art in all its configurations and manifestations – high, low and everywhere in between.' Yuri glanced at Venus' half-chewed ass.

Head Administrator Chumak turned to Tanya. 'What's he saying?'

'He says he's leaving this very moment.'

Outside the museum, the light had fallen to hips and knees. A three o'clock dusk, and the basement windowpanes reflected a lavender wash and the streetlights dispatched sullen arcs of hazy orange.

Yuri tied his rod to the frame of his bike and wheeled it through the narrow path shovelled through the snow. Winter was a dangerous time because the cold forced people closer together than nature intended. Not that Yuri didn't love his fellow man, but last week alone he'd been mugged twice on the same day. This very morning he'd nearly lost his sprocket and he'd most certainly lost his entire pike and five-eighths of his remaining pride. What next? Yuri wondered as he walked his bike around a corner, and then immediately wished he hadn't.

At the sound of his steps, two men leaning against a

doorway straightened and approached Yuri. They had a sleek and sporty air to them Yuri had learned to recognize as Mafiya. Probably they had been like him once, vets of an unpopular military action, but unlike him, they had the broad shoulders of wrestlers or near-champion boxers. And unlike Yuri, they wore slick tracksuit trousers with long stripes up the leg and expensive sports shoes, the hallmarks of eager recruits who understood that violence was necessary for their career advancement. And cruelty was inexpensive entertainment. Experience had taught Yuri that the only hope for a guy like him was to stick himself to shadow and disappear. Or walk straight up to them, and get it over with. Yuri lifted his visor and smiled. He knew they were considering his suspicious features, the unusual length of his face, his jaw. His blaring cuts and bruises that advertised his victim status.

Yuri unstrapped the rod and tucked it behind his trouser leg. 'Please fellows, take the bike. It may not look like much, but part by part, it is of extreme value.'

'Bargaining already?' the leader, a tall man in an Adidas sports jacket said.

Yuri sighed. 'Please, fellows. I don't wish to be hit in the face. Or the knees either.'

'Life is full of hard decisions, isn't it?' Adidas ran his tongue over his gold tooth.

Where it started – with his ribs – he could recall, but where it ended, how many blows to the back and kidneys, Yuri lost count. That they'd found his fishing rod was not in doubt: he heard it whistle through air and land some distance away in the snow. Then came the pounding of fists. His head felt like a big empty box hit with a stick, but never the same way twice. The important thing was not to beg for mercy, or they'd kill him. Also, it was important not to appeal for help to any passersby. A street beating in Russia was purely a spectator sport. Possibly the next Olympic event. In no circumstances would anyone help out his fellow brother being thrashed within a micrometre of his life. That being said, when Yuri spotted Mircha, materializing from behind a lamp post, Yuri could not help himself: 'Do something.' Penny whistles between his cracked teeth.

'Me?' Mircha mouthed, thumping his own chest with a thumb.

His attackers took Yuri's words as a sign. That is, they fell to beating him even harder. Yuri lay still as a fish beneath ice. Because a man who doesn't moan, doesn't complain, must be dead.

At last, when they'd got their wind up, they quit. Yuri heard the ticking of his bike as they wheeled it around the corner and then Mircha reappeared, steam rising from his hands.

Mircha cradled Yuri's head in his lap, withdrew a bottle of vodka and administered the remedy, a capful at a time, into Yuri's mouth.

With a splutter, Yuri revived.

'Where is your backbone?' Steam rose from Mircha's palms. 'I've been studying you at the river, at the museum, here on the street. Everybody walks all over you, even the women! You have to stand up for yourself, fight like a man. Right now, it's like you're only half a man. Maybe only a quarter.'

Yuri held his head in his hands. 'Look at you. You can't even fix a lottery or steal a windscreen wiper. Or scare away street thugs. All you can do is talk. And write.'

'OK. So, OK. I can see that you're bitter. We'll talk more when you've assumed the correct emotional posture. But honestly, Yuri. How can anyone have any respect for a man who doesn't act like a man?'

'I don't know.' Yuri touched his face cautiously. The nose, still there. The ears, there. Front teeth, chipped but there. A side tooth, definitely missing. 'What is a man, anyway?' Yuri swallowed a mouthful of blood.

'Nonsense. You're supposed to shout – no, no – to protest: "I'm a man!" Whatever that is.'

'Sure,' Yuri patted his legs, arms. Intact. Pain level seven and rising.

Mircha looked at his hands, the steam curling skyward. 'I see that I have quite a lot to write. When men don't know what it means to be a man. When they forget how to fight, what it means to live with honour. The importance of kicking ass. Keeping promises. By the way, I'm anxious about that titanium arm. Did you dig out the hole like I asked you to?'

Yuri blinked. 'I've had sightings of a shovel, but whenever the slender neck is almost in my grasp, the damn thing disappears.'

Mircha slapped the back of Yuri's head with the palm of his hand. 'This is the fate of a prophet – to be abused at the hands of my disciples. To dispense wisdom that people, and by people I mean you, disregard. It's quite a sad and sorry state.' Mircha handed Yuri the flight helmet, then retreated into the lowering frost.

At the courtyard Yuri sat on the bench and packed ice around his nose. The twins were out and in high spirits. They took turns harassing Zhytka, Vitek's dog, first patting and then pinching it. The dog, confused, alternated between wagging his tail and whining happily, then hurting. Happy, hurting. The dog understood the dualities of life, the hardship and inherent humiliations and contradictions of existence. Good Boris tickled the dog's stomach. Bad Boris lit a red-tipped match and fed it to him.

Yuri pulled the metal bench behind the heap. Though dusk had yielded to true darkness, he could see that the hole had grown much larger, longer and deeper. He lit a match. A placard in neat script read 'WHO HATH MADE FOOLISH THE WISDOM OF THIS WORLD?' and a trail of sunflower seeds teetered at the hole's edge. Quite obviously the children lived down there. Yuri peered inside the hole and spied a pile of shoes and galoshes of all sizes and umbrellas in varying states of decline tucked to one side. He dropped his line, dragged it carefully through a channel of wet mud.

'Five roubles if you want to fish here,' a child's voice sang from the rooftop.

Vitek joined Yuri on the bench, his palm held in readiness. Without a word, Yuri handed over the five-rouble note. Yuri could see that Vitek had stuffed more padding into the shoulders of his leather coat. Despite this effort, Vitek had acquired a strange two-dimensional look to his body. But then, given the day's events, his swelling face, it was quite possible that Yuri had lost sight in one eye.

Vitek scrutinized Yuri. 'Boy-o. Do you look beat.' Vitek ran his tongue over his gold teeth. Security, those teeth. It was fashionable for street businessmen to cap their teeth in as much gold as they could afford. It would buy a good funeral some day, provide for nonexistent heirs. Give the doctor something to dance about. But just now, the way they caught the moonlight so peculiarly, it only made Yuri's aching head hurt a little more. 'Listen. I can help you.' Vitek opened a fresh bottle of Crowbar. 'We're a team, you and I.'

Yuri quelled the urge to shudder. In actual fact, Vitek was the kind of guy who could crawl up a man's ass without using soap. Even so, vodka-drinking protocol dictated that one must never refuse it, regardless of its source. 'We are?' Yuri took the bottle and swallowed long.

'We are the men of the building, after all.' Vitek studied Yuri's shrinking posture, the stove-in chest, the sagging shoulders, the flight helmet resting against his ankles. 'Well, I'm the man, anyway. And with some work, you will have manly moments. Just consider how manly you'll feel in the hull of a tank sighting down the enemy.'

'How manly?'

'Very,' Vitek assured him with another pass of his tongue over his teeth.

'And consider how manly you will feel bringing home a tank gunner's wages.'

'How manly?'

'Extraordinarily manly. A successful operation gets each soldier three million roubles. Knocking out an enemy firing position would get you three million more. Knock out a tank and get a voucher for another three million.'

'What if I die?'

Vitek's smile broadened. 'Fabulous news! You'd get 130 million roubles.'

Yuri took another healthy drink, wiggled his line. 'Where do you come by your vast reservoir of information?'

Vitek held up the latest issue of the *Red Star* and smiled a smile as shiny as an oil slick.

'I don't know.' Yuri shook his aching head slowly from side to side. 'What do we need to go down there for? Give me another reason.'

'I can give you millions of reasons. There's millions of litres of oil down there. And if that doesn't make a man rich, then I don't know what does.'

'What about the Far East? We've got so much oil in Nefteyugansk, we could swim in it for years and never come up for air.' Yuri stood and tucked his helmet under his arm. 'I just don't see.'

'Oh, you don't see? Well, that makes everything all right, then, doesn't it?' Vitek's voice was pure acid.

Yuri blinked in surprise.

Vitek draped an arm around Yuri's shoulder. 'Here's where the dog has teeth.' Now Vitek was all honey, his boyhood best friend again. 'How old are you?'

'Twenty-one.'

'How many arms have you got?'

'Two.'

'Legs?'

'Two.'

Vitek smiled. 'Here's the thing. You being so gloriously whole, you'll likely be called up anyway. So why not beat the crowd to the punch? Voluntary re-uppers get paid more.'

'I'll think about it,' Yuri said, pulling in the line.

Vitek strolled toward the stairwell. 'Think, but not too hard.'

Dangling from the line was a small silvery-coloured fish. All bone, no flesh. This fish, he had heard, lived at the bottom of the world. It measured time by turning quietly in the mud, but nobody believed that this fish really existed. And here it was, gasping for air at the end of his line. Yuri carefully pulled the hook out and threw the fish back into the hole, which looked all the world to him now like a huge wound, dark and weeping.

Yuri trudged up the stairs. The noise of the pounding of drums in his head was terrific. The noise outside his head was colossal. For here was Zoya's voice falling like a sledgehammer from the windows. 'Plums! Plums!' She believed eating fruit out of season would increase her chances of conceiving. Ditto for eating liquored cherries that came in fancy boxes. Did it matter to her that these were deficit items, and therefore nearly impossible to find in the shops, even if they did have the money to buy such items?

'Cherries!' Zoya yelled and pulled the windowpane closed.

Apparently not.

Yuri pushed open the door to the apartment and stood on the threshold, scanning the apartment. Mother not in sight. The little Latvian TV in the kitchen spluttered and cracked, and in between the static Yuri detected the sound of women greatly vexed, speaking rapidly and without pause. It was the Spanish soap opera Zoya loved to watch, *The Rich Also Cry*.

Yuri walked to the kitchen, sat heavily in the chair and worked the helmet over his head painful centimetre by painful centimetre. 'I ran into some trouble today.' Yuri set the flight helmet on the table with a loud thunk. 'I got beat. Twice. And I lost my bike, and a tooth. But then a miracle, of a sort. There is a hole behind the heap. It is quite large and possibly growing. And I don't care if you believe me or not. I dropped my line in and caught a small silver fish. It smelled bad so I threw it back.'

'Inconsequential,' Zoya sighed and continued thumbing through a western magazine. 'All the best people have toaster ovens these days. And dryers.' Zoya shifted in her chair to contemplate her laundry in full bloom over the gills of the radiator. 'And babies. Every one of my friends has a baby. Even Galya from number thirteen. In fact she has two. You remember Galya – the girl with the pickle nose?'

'Having babies is not a competition. It's not some kind of measure of success. I mean, any idiot can have a baby.'

Zoya turned her shining wistful eyes on him. 'I know, isn't it wonderful? More good news.' Zoya withdrew a thermometer from her purse and waved it in the air. 'I took my temperature, and today is the right day.'

Yuri swallowed and tasted blood. Not the kind of talk that inspired phenomenal feats of gymnastic love-making.

Zoya raked her fingers through her vermilion hair. 'I think your mother is having a nervous breakdown. She's been talking to herself in the kitchen. A baby would be a good thing. She could take care of it and have someone to talk to. A baby would elevate our deflated social position.'

'Don't joke about a baby.'

'Who's joking?' Zoya stood on tiptoes and licked his eyebrows.

'We cannot raise a baby here. We have nothing to give a baby.'

'We have the grant.' Zoya bit his ear.

'We don't have the grant. Not yet.' Yuri placed a hand on each of Zoya's shoulders. 'We have five glue-sniffers living in the courtyard nobody cares for.'

'I will not live as if I am dead already.' Zoya clutched Yuri's hand and pulled him through the maze of laundry lines and sheets to their cot. 'I want life, a life of my own. In my hands. At my breast.' Zoya pulled her dress over her head. 'You don't know what that means to a woman.' Zoya pushed Yuri to the cot and pulled off his shoes. 'Unbuckle your belt,' she said.

'I think I may have a bruised rib.'

'Take off that belt and let's take a look.' Zoya smiled.

And Yuri did. The socks, they came off without a complaint and the pants flew off the ends of his feet as a silly dance step that ended in a low kick under the cot. And then it was all systems go. His face? His jaw? Hurting? Hell, yes. But again, the value of vodka be praised, the pain had dulled to a heavy weight, had dulled his hands and his face so that he could even endure the attentions of a bitter woman turned sweet. Somehow he would get through it. Zoya would see to that, Zoya shrieking his name as if it might mean something to her: 'Yur–I! Yur–I!' How manly does this make him feel? Ver–y, ver–y.

'OK, then.' Zoya rolled off Yuri and reached for the thermometer. 'I feel better now.'

Yuri rubbed his jaw.

'I'm glad we talked this matter through so thoroughly. Now we understand one another.' Zoya hung her stockings and dress over a laundry line.

'Absolutely.'

'Because, Yuri, this business in Chechnya – everyone knows it'll be over in no time. We have nothing to lose and everything to gain.'

'That's what everyone said about Afghanistan.'

Zoya clicked her tongue and looked askance at Yuri. 'That was just practice, a drill. This time it will go better. The Russian Army will put those mangy rebels in their place and fast.'

With each word the liquid ticks grew louder and the throb in his jaw and cheekbones more insistent. 'Could we talk about something else? Please?' Yuri reached for the bottle of Crowbar.

Zoya pulled on her nightgown, a thick and matronly garment. 'Did you know that the Yenisei is so contaminated that it doesn't even freeze anymore?'

'I thought it was just the Ob and the Lena that didn't freeze anymore.'

'Yes, and then there's the nickel poisoning in the Arctic. The reindeer herds have dropped like flies.'

'We're lucky, I suppose, by comparison. We're still alive,' Yuri said.

'Yes, but can you really call this living?' Zoya circled her hand at the wrist, indicating their cot, the sheets hanging from the line. 'I want things.'

From TV came the melodramatic swell of sentimental music. Yuri glanced at his flight helmet. The ticking, it was back. 'We have things.' Yuri looked at Zoya. 'We have each other.'

Zoya wrinkled her nose. 'I don't want to guide tours in a dusty museum for ever. I want a life of my own.' Without warning, she began to cry, softly at first and then, taking her cue from the TV programme, her cries swelled to sobs and then to full-scale wails, her shoulders shaking, her mascara coursing in black rivulets over her cheeks. It was such a grand, mysterious, and sudden show of utter despair that Yuri didn't know how or even if he should try to console Zoya. It was a weeping that defied consolation, sounds he'd heard Mother make, and before she died, Grandmother Ruzya, but in all cases he, a boy then, had dismissed their cries as a peculiarity of the female of the species. And because in all cases after such jags his mother had worn a determined smile on her face, maintaining a posture of complete cheerfulness, she'd made it easy for Yuri to believe that what he'd heard, those cries, were slips, mistakes, unintended lapses that he was not to take seriously.

Yuri waited until Zoya's sobs quieted before offering her squares of Azade's prestige tissue. 'Now, now,' Yuri patted Zoya's shoulder cautiously. Zoya honked and snuffled, then tucked her knees to her chest and promptly fell asleep, her breath whistling through her red and swollen nose the only indication that just five minutes before she'd suffered a major emotional moment.

That was the other thing about women and tears. Once they'd cried them out, they usually felt heaps better. Not so with men. Men took all their sorrows and complaints and insults and added them to the already mountainous pile of shit they carried around. It would be easier if men were allowed the occasional crying jag too, but the last time Yuri had succumbed to that kind of emotional freedom (in the yard of School Number 13) he had paid for it dearly. It was unmanly to wear your sorrows on your sleeve, Vitek said all those years ago in the schoolyard, and even then, Vitek had a way of driving a lesson home.

Yuri spied the bottle of Crowbar on the windowsill. An opened bottle of vodka must be finished. That was another rule. He poured a shot into a teacup, dipped a handkerchief into the liquid and dabbed at his cuts. Vodka was healing, was the silvery light of the moon in a bottle, was the tears he and every other vet he knew would cry if they thought they could get away with it. Yuri tipped the downed bottle on its side. Fallen soldier — that's what you called a dead bottle. And then you waited for the last drops to collect on the glass, and drank those down too, the final salute.

A rattle at the door and then Mother came into the apartment. Yuri listened to her find her way through the dark to the divan that folded out into a bed. He listened to her hang her coat over a line and her purse and scarf on a nail. He listened to the slide of her shoes stowed in the cupboard. He counted the ticks in his head and at thirty he heard the sniffling, Mother crying in the dark. She couldn't help it, he knew. She brought her work home with her, in her purse, under her arms, carried it word for word in her head, and now in the quiet of a darkened apartment with nothing but the hours, she was parsing through each and every phrase and sentence.

Yuri rearranged his body along the narrow mattress,

willing sleep to drag him to darkness. Zoya mumbled. Angry words about electric beaters and their bright silver dashers. Because it is universally true that people dream what they want, dream what they can't have, he knew she was dreaming of a fleet of them, shiny as steelhead and moving away from her, to spawn upriver. Mother was breathing deep and evenly now. He imagined the she dreamt of manna on the tongue, of living on the bread of faithful speech.

Yuri curled his body around Zoya's. But the ticks, the throbs, they were a hook snagged in his cheek. A convenient image. The very thought of which inspired more thoughts of hooks and flies he longed to tie. Which took him to the world of fish. To rivers in the south. To ancient seas and seabeds, to the grandfather sturgeon who lived in the Caspian Sea.

To find him, Yuri knows he has to row as far as he can against a storm. His arms churn at the oars but his boat – where he found it, he doesn't know, only that he's in it now and it's sprung a leak – makes no gain against the wind and water. It's like this in the dream world, working against your own weight and getting nowhere. But Yuri can't quit. He must have this fish. And then he remembers the rule: Cry three times into the sea, and the old codger will swim to the surface. There are many reasons for this, the first being that the fish is old, and therefore lonely and longing to sharpen his wits. But longing is such a terrible thing. For this fish, sure, but also for anyone who has wanted to catch it, for Yuri, for Zoya.

Now they're both in the boat, knocking elbows and knees,

because desperation puts people in tight quarters. Especially in dreams. And they are hungry, Yuri and Zoya. And because hunger makes its own argument, they determine that no matter what the fish promises them, they will not let it go should they catch it. And so Yuri rows into the storm and cries three times and when the sturgeon swims up to the surface, he plucks it from the water with a net. Then Yuri rows furiously towards the shore, ignoring the sweet words of the sturgeon, who is promising them the moon for a mirror and the stars to salt their front steps.

As they make shore the sturgeon promises them wisdom for their suffering, joy for their sorrow. 'Wisdom won't fill my stomach,' Yuri says to the fish. 'And joy won't quench my thirst,' says Zoya. But she lifts the fish from the net, pats its sides, holds it to her chest and cradles it as if it were a child. The scales are thin gold coins and the fish smells like salt and air and clouds and mud. 'Gold,' Zoya inhales, 'this must be what gold smells like, and the slick sides, this must be what a new life feels like.'

The sturgeon, out of the water and held tight to Zoya's bosom, pants hard, its magnificent sides heaving like a small dog's, its eyes reproachful, so full of fury to have been taken from the world it knew and so unceremoniously brought to this one. Because it is a dream – his dream – Yuri knows this is what the fish is thinking. But held so close to Zoya's face, Yuri also knows that the sturgeon can read in her empty eyes how much she wants heaven and earth, sky and water, and everything in between them. And the fish can divine Yuri's future and knows there is no help for him.

'Let me go,' the fish says. 'I can't help you.'

But Zoya clutches the sturgeon even harder. It flaps helplessly and Yuri, watching and dreaming, both in his own body and beside it looking on, watches the fish struggle. He thinks how interesting and strange it is that such a magnificent creature as the golden sturgeon in his last moments looks less like a fish and more like a bird taking to the sky. Then, with a jolt and a terrific thrash of its tail, the golden sturgeon stops breathing.

Beside him, Zoya's voice thundered in the dark. 'You are dreaming – again. Knock it off!'

CHAPTER TEN

Tanya

The trouble began with the changing weather. It was the fault of all this water sleeting the one and only window in the entire basement of the All-Russia Museum that Tanya careened toward a lethargic contemplation of the sky, the rain falling from the sky. Neither white nor black, it wasn't even grey. Valueless. Odd that something so ordinary and important as water dropping from the sky carried no colour. So unlike the virulent hues her grandmother remembered in the days when the mines and smelters to the south released their char and glow and ash into the air. Tanya nibbled on the end of her pencil.

In evening the sky, you said, this sky you loved and hated, burned magenta. The ash separated into belted colours of hurt and glory, then quieted to a smoulder of brake dust and chaff. In evenings, while you slept, you rose buoyant in your dreams. With your hollow bones and skin of paper you flew, like a crane, like a kite. I listened to you breathe, to your rattles, knocks and whistles. I

stood below your dreaming, holding a string around
your ankle, reading the sky through your skin, that
parchment of those letters you and I have memo-
rized all these years together. I listened to you
snore, to your snores muscling through you, the
only sound making any sense.

Tanya rubbed her eyes. Another mistake. Because as she did, the sudden urge for sleep overtook her. And as she watched the colourless liquid sheeting over the colourless glass, her eyelids fluttered. She rested her chin (so heavy now she couldn't lift it even if she wanted to) on her ample chest. And then she was up and flying. And where Tanya's fold-out chair had formerly been earthbound, held fast by the sagging metal seat, now it soared, the legs spread as steel pinioned wings piercing the bright heavens. As always, Ludmilla, inside her glass ticket office, encouraged Tanya's flight with powerful snores of her own that first rattled the glass and then fluted the arms of the many coats and sweaters. And this was how, in the cuffs and sleeves of the flapping coats and sweaters, the old woman's snores began as the sound of saws and burrs and slowly became the low rumbling of the Ilyushin. Then the museum whirled below Tanya, a colour wheel of beige and yellow spiraling away, growing snore by snore more distant.

Her course: upward and eastward. East where all manner of madness roamed freely, but nobody minded. East where the vermilion beets and cow parsley breathed quietly in loamy black soil. East where the tongues of the bells rang out the hours in iron tones and people called it beautiful. East where people still remembered how to behave like people.

But what's this disturbing the relative calm of her dream? Tanya pulled a deep breath through her nose and verified: Americans. Not only that, but Americans with artistic inclinations. Stowed neatly in the overhead bins, their leather baggage exuded the brown suede odours of the upper classes. Beneath the bins three women sat side by side, smiling. Their dentition so bright it dazzled and spun Tanya's thoughts. The women have such mighty teeth – white as flake, white as the finest grade of Cremnitz, a white of a calculating quality. And then, from a vast distance, Zoya's voice unspooled: 'I myself have always preferred silver to gold, which is so heavy.'

Heavy. Heavy as lead pigment in the tube. In the hand, in the blood. The mere thought of the word ushered instant panic. The cabin alarm bleated with mechanical insistence. She'd slap the alarm with her palm, if only she could reach it. But her hips, far too wide to allow for easy passage in these narrow Aeroflot aisles, will not allow her to move. That was to say, she was stuck. Wedged tighter than ten sprats and all their cousins in a tin. The truth (how it hurts) was that she had not lost the weight. Not a single kilo. More bad news: the oxygen piped through the cabin was not of the therapeutic sort. Not dense enough to support her massive high-altitude dreams. And now the plane was crashing. Falling fast toward a flat land of cold hard silver where there were no shadows to receive them. The horror – unimaginable. Nowhere in their travel correspondence, in their many faxes with Head Administrator Chumak, did these women come across mentions of in-flight free fall. They could flap their arms, could beat madly at the air, but it would do no good. The engines had failed, the rumbling gone quiet.

The women gnash their teeth and rend their clothing. They break their fingernails while punching the crew-call buttons on the consoles above their heads. They brace for impact. They are beyond the reach of Tanya's stocky arms, her silly tray of coffees and sugar. Nor does it buoy their spirits to observe the beautiful well-stitched baggage huddling at the lip of an open cargo door. To make matters worse, the luggage has conspired to appropriate the only parachute. And why not? This luggage, built to last, will outlive them all, just as their warranty tags proclaim. But how confusing all this will be to the cows below, who, turning their slow gaze upward, will see geometrically shaped versions of themselves tumbling down down down.

'Up! Up! Wake up!' A voice, really a shriek, sharp and sure, pulled Tanya down to her chair anchored now behind the hat/coat-check counter. 'He's coming!' Ludmilla from the ticket office called.

Tanya forced open her eyes. Yes, Head Administrator Chumak was coming. She could hear him labouring down the stairs and the sound of his uncooperative foot lagging: *thump*, *THUMPITY*, *slide*. But he was making good time and as he cleared the stairs the syncopation of his gait quickened. And in that slight skipping triple beat of Head Administrator Chumak's weighted step, Tanya detected the giddy excitement of a man kicking at the threshold of a long-awaited dream. For never in her two years of working at the museum had Tanya heard her boss move with such speed or purpose.

At last he gained the counter.

'Big news,' Head Administrator Chumak gasped. He leaned on his elbows, waiting for his breath to catch up with him. 'They're here, my dear girl, they're here!'

'Who?' Tanya stood and straightened her skirt.

'The Americans of Russian Extraction for the Causes of Beautification! They're here. Well, not here, as in right here.' The heel of Head Administrator Chumak's leaden foot fell with a final thump. 'But they are certainly very nearly here.'

'How near?'

Head Administrator Chumak glanced at his watch. 'They'll be arriving at the airport first thing in the morning, or possibly in the afternoon. It depends. But you, Tatiana Nikolaevna Bobkov,' Head Administrator Chumak's voice swelled with the calibrated mirth of fine-tuned optimism, 'you will be the friendly face of the museum, there to greet them the moment their feet touch the ground.'

Tanya squeezed her throat. 'Oh.'

'Yes, I thought you'd be pleased. And I know you will take good care of our distinguished guests and cultivate in them an appreciation for this museum, for this staff, for this city. I trust you completely. It's a big job, I know, but believe me, you have my hearty endorsement.'

Tanya gulped. Despite her nightmare from moments ago, never had she really believed that their museum would be in the running. Certainly she didn't think the Americans would actually come. When people from the West make promises to visit, her grandmother had assured her all these years, they most certainly do not mean it.

'When they arrive, while you are getting them settled into their lodgings, Daniilov and I will clean the museum like men possessed.' Head Administrator Chumak tipped his head slightly. 'Well, Daniilov will clean, anyway.'

'Lodgings?' Tanya croaked.

'Yes. They're staying with you, remember?'

'But, seriously, wouldn't it be much better if they went to a four-star hotel or something?'

Head Administrator Chumak handed Tanya the file fat with travel itineraries and grinned ferociously. 'Off you go then!'

'But sir, what about transportation? Am I to hire a microvan or perhaps a car?'

'Cars!' Head Administrator Chumak clapped his hands. 'I myself have been thinking of a Zhiguli, or perhaps something German. Of course one must factor in the cost of petrol, spare parts, but still.' Head Administrator Chumak sighed an expansive sigh, smiled at the ceiling.

'My wife has her eye on a pair of leather driving gloves. Imported from Austria.' Head Administrator Chumak snapped his gaze on Tanya. 'Well, don't just stand there like a historical monument. Get moving!' He patted her backside in a manner far too firm to suggest genuine affection.

Tanya pulled on her coat, tucked her colour notebook under her arm and hurried for the metro. The boy with the open violin case blew her kisses, but she was too distracted to contemplate purple and the lining of the boy's violin case. Now she was on a mission. The Americans were coming. With many questions and probing eyes and theories and advice, the Americans were coming. With ultra-white teeth of perfect proportion and baggage stuffed and overstuffed, thrice stuffed with hair dryers and razors equipped with the wrong adapters. With highlighted dictionaries and travel guides. Tourists, not travellers, they will have no intention of blending in, of being inconspicuous. Of travelling lightly or quietly or with subtlety. They will arrive bringing with them their many expectations. Their good intentions. Their endless curiosity. Their needs and unspoken longings to experience things. What things? Tanya knows the list: ambiance, ice cubes in cold drinks, the assurances of quality medical care should the need arise. Private transportation. Extra pillows on their beds. Clean drinking water. Hot water for bathing. Prestige toilet paper for wiping the backside. A serenade by moonlight and girls dancing in folk costume. Black caviar, not red. Cream for their coffee. The moon and stars. They will ask without understanding how impossible their requests are to fill. They will not know how deep and thoroughly devasting the recent crop failures and economic crashes have been, how turbulent the transition from command to market economy. Nor would it be wise for her to point it out. They will want to believe that they are making a sound investment in the future of art, that their dollars will be put to good use, that this is a sure thing.

Tanya sighed and allowed the wind whistling along the streets to propel her over the platform, past the under-stocked kiosks and the vendors shut up tight inside there like walnuts in shells. Several of the kiosks had signs posted to their windows: WE ARE OUT OF EVERYTHING. BY EVERYTHING WE MEAN ALL CONSUMPTIBLES AND EVEN NON-CONSUMPTIBLES — SO DON'T EVEN ASK. WE ARE MOST ESPECIALLY OUT OF BEER AND VODKA. A group of boys in long-sleeved shirts and not a coat between them kicked a ball around in the slushy mud. They were waiting in line anyway. Winter was tipping slowly towards spring and they were taking advantage of the longer light. Tanya knew this feeling — a quiet madness that pulses through the blood and bypasses the brain entirely. When you live in darkness six months of a year, you can't help it. Noticing, that is. The light. And the trees. Naked to the skin only a week ago, now they were studded from trunk to tip with hard yellow buds. In a few weeks they'd explode with green and the whole world would drift into longer light and quieter tempers, into patience.

But right now the ground had warmed to mud. Every side street, every footpath was a dangerous morass. The snow-melt lining each path was a sharp landscape of lost items: the silver spines of an umbrella jutted like oversized needles from an invisible pincushion, a ladies' evening shoe, the heel ground in but the shank jutting viciously from the mud. Tanya skirted the debris and picked up her pace. The heels of her boots issued obscene noises with her every step. And it seemed to her that the street itself was complaining, groaning – she imagined – under her weight. Worse, the kiosk at the end of their street, 'Everything You Covet and Can't Have', that sold women's stockings, chewing gum and vodka – had disappeared altogether. It was not an omen that inspired confidence.

With effort, Tanya lifted her feet from the melting slush and mud and ducked under the stone archway of the court-yard. But it was the same story here too: mud and more mud. The only good thing about this mud was that it was familiar mud and she knew from hard lessons during other thaws just where she should and shouldn't step.

The children picked at the heap with their bare hands, scooped banana skins and orange rinds, empty tins of sprats and tats into small wheelbarrows. Blood oozed from matching open sores on the knees of the Good and Bad Borises. They were working hard, she could see, to improve the ambiance of the courtyard. When they filled their wheelbarrows with refuse, they pushed the load through the mud, past the broken archway and out onto the street where they deposited the trash onto the roadway. Red-haired Gleb blew snot out of his nose with a single blasting honk of mucus. Tanya felt her stomach rolling over.

'Swine!' the oldest girl called.

'Cow!' the littlest girl joined in.

A reference to her bovine eyes or her portly bearing? Hard to tell, and Tanya tucked her chin to her chest and kept ploughing towards the stairwell. *Love, heart. Start loving, you useless lonely muscle.* And then a rock whistled through the air.

Who said suffer the little children? A stone, big as a plum from the feel of it, pummelled Tanya's backside. Christ said suffer the little children and so she's suffering. He said to love them, too, and so she commanded herself to love, but the rocks, God almighty, had grown teeth and were biting at her now. No chance she'd get past that heap without losing an eye. And that older girl had developed quite an arm. Clearly the children blamed her for adding to their workload, though how they had known before she did that the Americans were arriving was beyond her. Tanya's bowels, knotted with worry, roiled and turned. She shielded her head with her cloud notebook and retreated to the safety of the latrine. And not a moment too soon.

CHAPTER ELEVEN

Olga

In the women's bathroom Olga sat solidly on the commode and fought the urge to fall into a dead sleep. For five hours she'd worked like a maniac. The wire basket, emptied of translation tasks that she had completed the day before, had once again mysteriously filled to capacity and beyond in the middle of the night. And with tidings of the strangest events.

```
Manufacture of penguins at a plush toy factory
in the Trans-Dneister surpassed all production
records to date. In commemoration of this
achievement, new currency will be minted,
replacing the old currency which was minted
last July.

The explosion at Tomsk-7 chemical separation
plant is believed to be responsible for
regular sightings of Our Lady of Kursk in the
low bank of emission clouds.
```

And the strangest, news from their own city.

```
100 barrels of Georgian white wine from
Tbilisi have been hijacked from the train
station and held for ransom.
```

Why she was being asked to translate such matters, and in the *Red Star*, a military newspaper of conservative leanings, was beyond Olga's comprehension. She rapped her knuckles against the corrugated metal that divided the bathroom stall she occupied from the one where Vera sat. Olga guessed from the unbroken plume of smoke curling into the air that Vera had nodded off again, this time with a lit cigarette in hand.

Olga knocked louder, and began reading the sinkhole report. 'I don't think this life could get any more bizarre,' she concluded. 'Do you suppose we will survive any of this?'

'Oh, cheer up, Olga.' The cigarette hissed as Vera dropped it into the toilet bowl. A small flask of nail polish remover appeared beneath the partition. 'Things aren't so bad. According to a recent World Values Survey, Ukrainians have it, or think they have it, worse than us. Only forty-eight per cent of Ukrainians say they are happy as compared with fifty-one per cent of Russians.'

'That is a comfort,' Olga conceded.

'On the other hand, ninety-seven per cent of Icelanders claim to have attained true bliss.'

Olga sipped at the vial, then slid it back under the metal

divider and thought for a moment. 'It must be on account of their warm summers and natural hot water springs. Also, they haven't gone to war in decades. Russia, on the other hand, has a war of some sort going on at all times.'

'You'd think with all this practice, we'd be better at it,' Vera mused. 'Of course, we did win the Great Patriotic War. But since then there's been Afghanistan, Georgia, Bosnia, Georgia again, and then this business in Chechnya. Our problems in the south, such an embarrassment. The atrocities! Russians setting fire to houses with women and children inside.'

Olga wagged her head slowly from side to side. It never ceased to amaze her what the human animal was capable of. What great acts of generosity and cruelty. And how a human could harbour the inclination for both within the same heart! She wished she could say it was beyond her. But it wasn't, because she felt it, too: compassion and rage, love and hate. Even good people could – and did – commit acts of cruelty. Even people like Olga. How many times had she wished Afghanistan and everyone in it would simply fall off the map?

'I cannot reconcile myself to it,' Olga said at last.

'To what?'

'This job. This work. What we do here. What we see and hear and what we pass on and how we pass it. What about truth?'

Vera snorted. 'Truth doesn't bother me. It's the incontro-vertible insistence of certain facts that wakes me up in the middle of the night. Did you know that in the twentieth century, thirty to fifty million Soviets died as a result of war?'

'No,' Olga said dully.

'Well then maybe you already knew that Mafiya-related economic activity accounts for forty per cent of the total economy?'

'So we are more economically healthy than we know?'

'Healthier than what's good for us,' Vera said, lighting another cigarette. 'But get this – every two out of three male workers is drunk on the job. The third worker is hungover.'

'Sad.' Olga clucked her tongue.

'Sad, nothing. Joint Military Generals set a draft goal of 140,000 for this fall.'

'This war is not over then, is it?'

'Good Lord, no. We've only just begun to kill each other off!'

'I worry about my Yuri,' Olga whispered.

'And well you should! Statistically he has a one in three chance of reintegrating in a useful manner into society. Let's not forget the number of vets who've committed suicide. Not an insignificant figure, by the way.'

Olga shook her head. 'I'll tell you, it makes one wonder just what humans are made of. We're not human, that's what I think. We're dogs or maybe worse.'

'Why would you say that?'

'Because,' Olga crouched over the bowl and carefully wiped her backside with strips of the previous day's copy of the *Red*

Star, 'dogs only behave the way they do to survive. They are beyond malice.'

Vera laughed. 'Let me tell you what the city engineers have known for years and dare not say. In a decade the dogs will rule the cities. They outnumber us now three to one. They'll eat every last one of us for sport. Don't talk to me about malice.'

Vera tapped the temperamental trigger of the commode. Olga stood and did the same. Together they listened to the plumbing labour – a slow-moving sound, and Olga imagined that Fact itself, the visceral substantiation of every ugly reality they'd just discussed, had clogged the pipes. At last, with a loud gulp, the bowls emptied.

'Well, that's that.' Vera stood at the sink and wiggled her fingers under a trickle of murky water.

'I suppose,' Olga said, and watched Vera exit the bathroom. Olga stood at the sink and scrubbed her hands vigorously. Her hands red from her efforts, she at last gave up. In twenty-odd years of using the *Red Star* lav, she'd noticed that no amount of washing could keep the lavatory reek from following her into the corridor.

Inside the narrow glass office Arkady sat behind the desk and raked his fingernails ferociously over the mottled skin of his left arm. What Olga had all this time thought were bite marks made by his ersatz wife, she realized with a jolt was in actual fact a service tattoo. She eyed the pneumatic tubes warily and slid into her folding chair. The tubes hissed like a tyre leaking pressure and Olga was trying hard to ignore this sound

– that and the way blood and dark ink bled from the corners of Arkady's tattoo.

Arkady lifted his nose and sniffed prodigiously in her direction. 'Is that a new scent you are wearing?' he asked.

'No,' Olga said.

Arkady sniffed again. 'All the same, you wear it very well.'

He was flirting with her, again. It occurred to her how very lonely Arkady must be, how very alone he was with only this desk and that enormous *Topic Guide* and his tea to keep him company, his pencils with the bite marks. Olga looked past Arkady to the darkened glass. 'Do you think often of your wife?' Olga ventured.

'Who?' Arkady squinted.

'The woman you married. Can you recall her?'

'Only all too well! I'm trying to surpress the memories. Such teeth – like shrivelled olive pits. Why do you ask?' Arkady blinked rapidly behind his glasses.

Olga turned her gaze to the dim panes. 'The thing is, I can't at all recollect my Zvi.'

'Who's that?'

'My husband. I can't remember him. Not a bit. This is cause for dilemma. Am I missing him properly if I can't recollect him fully?'

Just then the grey teletype in the corner spat and spluttered. For several minutes the machine spewed a torrent of paper out of its yammering maw. And then, just as suddenly as it started up, it fell quiet again. Arkady looked at the machine and then at Olga. The plastic tubes whistled a grim melody. Neither of them made a move towards the machine.

Chief Editor Kaminsky materialized in the open doorway. His gaze shifted to the teletype, then to Olga. Standing as he was so close to the tube hatch, his pale blue tie and the two strands of his comb-over slowly lifted toward that source of immense suction power. To Olga's way of thinking, it lent to Chief Editor Kaminsky the look of a human windsock. Or perhaps a kite. And she observed again how very much his eyebrows resembled the typesetter's steep-pitched insert symbol and how opaque the lenses of his glasses were, so that even though she was close enough to him to smell the tomato and pickled herring he'd had for lunch, she could not see his eyes.

'How are things?' Chief Editor Kaminsky asked.

'Normal,' Olga said. 'I think.'

Chief Editor Kaminsky aimed a meaningful glance at the machine, then looked at Olga. 'Olga, to tell you the truth, I'm getting concerned. You look pale, and then again, sometimes quite flushed. You look as if you've lost a great deal of weight, or possibly gained. Clearly you are a walking manifestation of internal and external contradiction.' With both his hands, Chief Editor Kaminsky slapped at the errant strands of hair and held them tight to his head. His hands otherwise engaged, there was nothing he could do about that dull blue tie pulling him slowly towards the tube hatch. 'Probably there's not a thing in the world I can do to help, but I feel compelled to offer my assistance anyway.'

Olga glanced at the report still lodged in the teletype. It, too, flapped in the direction of the mighty tube system.

'Is it trouble at home?' Chief Editor Kaminsky leaned towards Olga.

Olga extricated herself from her chair and stood. She tapped her forehead. 'My body is in an uproar. I can't sleep at night. I'm seeing strange things at the apartment building, stranger than usual. And I'm smelling things, too.'

'Go on, go on,' Chief Editor Kaminsky murmured.

'I am forgetting things and,' Olga paused and glanced at Arkady, 'sometimes, I am terribly afraid that my semi-truthful rendering of fact will carry disastrous consequences.'

'Olga, Olga.' Chief Editor Kaminsky draped his arm over her shoulder. 'You are investing far too much thought into your work. You aren't being paid to think about the deep meanings of words and draw profound connections between them. Your job, more or less, is to cast upon facts and figures the penumbric shadow of neutrality and normality so that nothing, not a word, not a thought nor an idea unduly shocks the eye of the reader. Always remember that the written word is fact in itself. Especially when it is written with confidence!'

Olga nodded. It was a simple enough sounding procedure in theory. In practice she wanted desperately to chew off her hands. She wished she had five sets of hands so that she could chew off each and every pair. Chief Editor Kaminsky shifted more of his weight onto his arm and leaned into Olga.

'Always remember, the Russian language and, therefore,

print media itself, abhors a vacuum. Your job is to keep filling the blanks with vague substitutes, to euphemize anything that carries a disturbing tone. The trick is to make sure your deft substitutions don't lack in subtlety. Here's where your gift for humour is so necessary. See?'

'But sir, truth is a transcendent value; it matters what we say and how we say it.'

Chief Editor Kaminsky paled slightly. It may have been her imagination, but it seemed to Olga that the howling from the tubes grew higher pitched. And most certainly Chief Editor Kaminsky's arm had grown heavier, its weight now driving her heels into the floor.

'Good God, woman. You know that and I know that. But that doesn't mean you have to go about repeating it! After all, we have our readership to think of.' At this, Chief Editor Kaminsky cupped his free hand under Olga's elbow and gave a panicked squeeze.

'Right, then!' Chief Editor Kaminsky spun on his heels. He glided through the open door and down the hallway, the whole way his tie whipping over his shoulder and fluttering towards the open mouth of the tube hatch.

'Everyone knows that paid fools are no better than the ones we get for free,' Arkady said. He rose, ripped the paper from the teletype, scanned it briefly and handed it to Olga.

Olga read the report quickly. Then she started back at the top and re-read slowly, her eyes drinking in line by line her every worst fear confirmed: name after name of the dead and the missing. Her heart pounded in her ears, her eyes watered and blurred. There were over a hundred names. And in the report conclusion even worse news. The President was calling for unilateral draft with no exemptions or exceptions, a request that had been enthusiastically passed in the Duma.

Olga sank into her chair. What to do? Forget rendering the facts harmless by means of deft and draughty euphemism. This was her boy they were talking about. Her boy who would be sent out in a ground infantry unit. Her boy who would be sent back in an open rail carriage stuffed with bodies. Olga laid her forearms on the desk and cradled her head in her hands.

'What shall I do?' Olga turned to Arkady.

Arkady speared the report with his pencil and examined it at arm's length for several minutes. At last he cleared his throat. 'You've suggested now and again that your son may be a bit of an, er, how shall I say? Idiot? Did you mean that in the literal or euphemistic sense?' he asked cautiously.

'Well,' Olga bit her lip. Yuri was more of a *balbess*, a dunder-head, which, as far as she knew, didn't carry a definite clinical classification, though perhaps it ought to. But her Yuri – an idiot? She could say yes. Her situation – his situation – was that desperate. But it wouldn't be true. And wasn't she the one who held forth her internal appeal for the truth made external? For telling a truth so pure it could not be heightened or dampened by people like her? Or was this one of those rare moments in a mother's life where she would and should break every rule for her children?

'He is an idiot in his own fashion,' she said at last, the sound of her voice in her ears foreign and strained.

'But do you have any proof of it? Anything in particular that is strange or crazy?'

'He fishes from the rooftop.'

'Does he catch anything?' Arkady sounded genuinely interested.

Olga shook her head. 'No, but he wears a souvenir cosmonaut's helmet day and night.'

'Yes, I knew about that,' Arkady said. 'Sadly, a lot of young people are dressing in odd ways. We need something more definitive. Something hugely idiotic – in writing, say. A silly love poem or poorly constructed joke?'

Olga squeezed her eyes shut, thinking. The tubes whistled and the sound was slightly obscene, like a low wolf call. 'Of course!' She opened her eyes. 'Mircha!'

'Who?'

'The Manifesto!' Olga dug through her plastic bag and withdrew Mircha's semi-transparent papers. Carefully, so that the shaky writing would not crumble at her feet, she began to read aloud:

Today a boy explains to his father how feathers on a chicken grow. Today a man looks over his shoulder and says 'nothing is impossible.'

'Ah,' Arkady muttered.

'Wait. There's more,' Olga continued to read:

Today a woman washing shirts in a bucket of bleach watches the skin from the tips of her fingers disappear.' Enough,' she says. Today an old man with a violin breaks his bow and says' now.' Today I rattle every door handle of the city looking for the one still warm from the touch of my lover's hand and I say,' I will never stop looking.'

Arkady's eyes brightened. 'It has a nice poetic odour of sentimentality. And absolutely no meaning. None. Only an idiot could write this.'

Olga nodded sombrely.

'I know people who know people. People who know idiocy when they see it. People who can do things to care for such idiots.'

Olga clutched the Manifesto. 'Things? What things? You don't mean an institution?'

'Lord no! Those places are reserved for the truly handicapped – Gypsies and Grades One and Two Idiots, for instance. But Grade Three idiocy is another matter entirely. A Grade Three Idiot is eligible for food and medicine coupons and could ride the metro for free. Yes, the benefits of being an imbecile are too numerous to count.'

Olga glanced at the tube. 'But the draft.'

Arkady scratched at his arm. 'That is just it: Grade Three

Idiots can't be drafted. Most certainly arranging for the necessary documentation, that is, the Grade Three Idiot ID card, will take a little time and money, but we've nothing to lose.'

'Money?' Olga whispered. 'But I don't have any money. None of us do.'

Arkady shifted his weight from foot to foot, slowly, but with deliberation as if he were wrestling with something inside himself. At last he stood still, closed his eyes and spoke in a breathless monotone.

'I will sell my near-priceless petrified log. On the Internet. To the highest bidder.'

'No,' Olga gasped. 'You can't! It is all you have, this highly collectible item that has been in your family for generations.'

After a long moment Arkady opened his eyes. 'I've decided. My mind is made up.' He nodded to the Manifesto. 'Desperate times call for great sacrifices. Besides, something isn't priceless if someone will pay money for it. And if your son is the idiot I think he may be...'

Olga clamped her teeth and handed over the Manifesto. Still, she could not help thinking again of the lie in which she was participating. Was her son really an idiot? There was no denying he had been altered by the war, but then that was true of any veteran of the Russian army who survived a tour of duty. He was childish. A shirker. He would lie about on a stove and gather cobwebs if he could, but that was no more idiotic than anything else other people did. And the fact was just this: he was her son, flesh of her flesh, bone of her bone. If she allowed Yuri to be drafted he would die a certain death. If not at the hands of the enemy than certainly at the hands of the other veteran soldiers who had no patience for combat-shy recruits, even those who rotated in voluntarily. Olga studied Arkady, who even now was drafting the letters to the appropriate people on behalf of her Yuri, and on company time! They were doing something to save her boy. So why didn't she feel any better?

She ran her fingers over the report curling over the desk. All these boys, these other mothers' sons. She couldn't do a thing, not one thing to save them. She looked at the report again, the water in her eyes brimming. Sometimes only tears restore the heart's equilibrium. Her mother used to say that. Her mother also used to say that the sun would stop rising if we forgot the names of our dead. This was why her mother made her memorize the names of the dead from her village. This was why every night in the darkness of her corner of the apartment, in that dim space between wakefulness and sleep, Olga added the names she read here in this office to that growing lexicon of the dead. And at night she stitched those names to an old melody every mourner knows. Each night, the same song, only each night it took just a little longer to sing it, this song built of names. Every name became a musical phrase, and every phrase was a life that had ended and shouldn't have, and Olga wanted to remember every single one.

Olga's fingers tapped the keyboard. Name after name, she saw these boys, every one of them a boy from her town, the

boy who sat behind her at school, the boy who tied her shoelaces together and cried later when she wouldn't forgive him.
The boy with the stutter, the boy with the girlish lips, the boy
whose father jumped from the bridge. All these boys and more,
she set down in print. Gone her subtle sense of humour that
turned the edges of an atrocity-in-progress into a general's
folly, easily forgiven. Gone her desire to dampen. Loss divided
was still loss, after all. She would tell what she knew, and more.
She would say with as much certainty as she dare and more
everything she'd kept hidden. God – she had to believe because
the prophet Isaiah declared it – would write their names on the
palms of His hands. But she would type their names on this
report.

```
Vladimir Gregarovich Aitmotov
Alexander Andreyevich Akimoff
Vyacheslav Stepanovich Aliev
Boris Vladiromich Anichov
```

She had no idea there could be so many names. And still, she
kept typing. What would happen to her next she didn't much
care. She had lied to save her son. There was nothing honourable in that. And these boys on her list, they were beyond
saving. But at least they might be remembered.

Twenty minutes passed. Thirty. Olga kept typing. At first,
the pneumatic tubes whistled merrily as if nothing important,
nothing any different than usual, were happening at the scuffed

metal desk. But as the minutes ticked by, thirty, then forty, a low growl boiled up through the pipes. By the time Olga finished with the last of the names, all two hundred and sixteen of them, the growl had risen into a full howl, like that of an animal in great pain. She pulled the last sheet of paper from the typewriter carriage. She scanned the pages and rolled them, placing them carefully into the canister. As if it could read her translation, the tube howled an octave higher.

Olga lifted the hatch. A secondary, and her favourite, definition of the word 'translate' was to convey to heaven without death. Olga eyed the canister and wiggled her fingers at the hatch. It could happen, should happen. The world was just that strange. She squeezed her eyes closed, thrust the canister into the tube. With a jerk at her hands, the canister whizzed through the tubing and disappeared, leaving Olga stuck and dangling at the hatch. The wind rushing through the pipe tugged at her shirt sleeve, pulled savagely at her arm, all the while a loud shrieking coursing through the piping. Arkady stared in bewilderment at the tube and Olga, held fast as a fish on a hook. Only two words came to her.

'Help me.'

CHAPTER TWELVE

Azade

After a week of hard rain, the suggestion of sun, especially spring sun, lured everyone but Lukeria out of their apartments and into the courtyard. Vitek lounged in a cracked plastic chair and barked at the children. Big Anna, Good Boris, Bad Boris, and Gleb, the red-haired boy with the glasses, barked back, shouting obscenities at anything that moved. The littlest girl had disappeared. No amount of crooning at the heap or at the lip of the hole (the hole! Oh how she hated it!) coaxed her out and Azade had to consider the possibility that the girl had gone underground to live there permanently or perhaps had gone to live in the sewers. Or perhaps the other children had driven her off. Street kids were like that. They had maintained a hierarchy, like dog packs. Also, the boys preferred now to lift their legs when they peed.

Yuri lay on the stone bench. Zoya sat in the stairwell, the trumpet of a phone pinched between her shoulder and the side of her face while she painted her fingernails. Yes, she was a talent, that girl. And she knew how to talk. 'Really?' Even now her voice filled the stairwell, spilled into the courtyard. 'Because if Lara would consider knocking twenty roubles off the microwave, I'd colour her hair and throw in a manicure.'

Even Mircha was out, in both body and spirit. Though the mud had thawed and Azade had been digging with her little shovel for three days, she'd still not properly deposited Mircha's body into the ground. But it wasn't her fault. The spring thaw was not cooperating with her in the least. The entire courtyard was a boggy morass of mud. The heap of trash and metal scrap listed dangerously towards the ever-widening chasm, but wouldn't quite topple in. The mud seemed deliberately contrary, possessing a stubborn, sullen, petty will-fulness she could only consider Soviet in nature; every attempt to move the mud around with that shovel she'd borrowed from Yuri came to nothing.

She had, however, located a copy of the Qur'an (stashed at the bottom of the heap, of all places!) and had memorized the Al-Fatiha. She'd bowed to the east, to the west – in all direc-tions, actually, as she did not have a compass and could not say for certain in which direction Mecca lay. All this she'd done to dispatch her husband and put him both bodily and in spirit to rest. But still he lurked in doorways and behind windows, the steam from his palms fogging the panes. Worse, she noticed that at night he crept about the courtyard, silently returning all the garbage the children had removed during the day, re-building the heap to its former glistening putrid dimensions. She would have tried to stop him, would have shouted from her window, but she didn't want to wake the children. And, too, there was such a dogged gait to his shuffling, such determination in his carrying the rusted cables, the prosthetic leg, and even the cracked Moskvich engine from the street all the way into the courtyard, that she knew there was no point in objecting. For all his talk of revision, Mircha seemed determined to repeat the meaningless tasks as if it was repetition itself that held value.

But at the moment it was Tanya that Azade was worried about. Two hours she'd been in the latrine and making the strangest noises. When two hours turned to three, Azade knocked cautiously on the plastic door.

'Are you all right?'

Tanya's arm emerged slowly from between the plastic jamb and the door. 'Extra paper,' she whispered. 'Please.'

Azade handed over the roll and sniffed mightily in her direction. 'You should have told us about the foreigners sooner. I could have cleaned a little more.' Azade leaned on her broom.

Lukeria threw open her window. 'What foreigners?'

Tanya emerged from the latrine, her hem muddy from where it had grazed the plastic floor. 'Art-loving Americans of Russian Extraction with money are coming to the museum tomorrow,' Tanya explained, and it seemed to Azade that the very idea had wearied the girl already. Azade could smell exhaustion, the kind that comes from inside the bones and from the roots of the hair and follows a woman to her bed and back.

Olga, having become so adept at tiptoeing in the presence of potentially bad news, appeared at the latrine. 'What's so bad about that?'

Lukeria planted her elbows on the sill of the opened window. 'I like Americans. They have nice luggage. Strong zips and good solid stitching.'

'They want to spend the night and live like real Russians, here in this apartment building,' she said with a deep and profound sigh. And in her long exhalation, Azade's keen nose deciphered the true and multi-faceted nature of Tanya's predicament, which Azade understood was, collectively, their predicament.

'Oh.' Olga's face blanched to the colour of split almonds. 'Disaster.'

Azade took a liberal sniff of the courtyard air. She could detect Tanya's flagging optimism, and behind it, a whiff of reality. Their chances were not good. Only with monumental orchestration between all the factious residents of their apartment building would they manage a solid wall of goodwill and unbrooked good manners. Or at least a lack of bad manners. And even then they would likely fail.

'We must construct the Russia of their expectations,' Tanya said in a solemn tone.

'Definitely then, I will hang out my best laundry,' Zoya announced.

'We can work together and do this.' Tanya pitched her voice towards the heap and the old woman's window, her voice warbling on the last words. 'After all, we've come a long way from the days when we'd spit into each other's tea water and salt each other's food mercilessly.'

'Speak for yourself!' Lukeria leaned over her elbows.

Tanya consulted her tattered notebook. 'For starters, no more visits to this latrine. We've got to save room for the Americans. Everyone knows that their turds are the biggest in the world.'

Tanya glanced at the heap, at the hole behind the heap. The hole was now a chasm of profound dimension. The children had erected a water-resistant tarp over the opening and installed a ladder. How they had managed it was beyond Azade's comprehension, for she herself each evening did her very best to fill the hole and keep it covered with metal sheeting.

'We have to cover that hole. Someone will fall in. And we must get rid of that stinking heap. It implies all the wrong things about us.' Tanya turned to Vitek. 'Weren't you supposed to handle this?'

'I have. I mean, the kids are. Every day.' Vitek swept his arm through the air. 'Can't you see the difference?'

Tanya squinted at the heap. 'No.'

'I don't understand,' Vitek said. 'I've personally supervised their daily heap hauling. I've watched them dump the rubbish on the street.' He ran his fingers through his hair in rapid succession. It was a gesture Azade knew he had borrowed from a character on a daytime television soap opera that he liked to watch. The character was a Mafiya thug who was always killing the wrong people and then had to kill some more people to make up for it. For some reason Vitek found this an admirable trait.

Vitek shoved his hands in his pockets. 'So, OK. It's a joke somebody's playing on me. I get it. But you'll be happy to know I've got a full evening of entertainment lined up for our visitors.'

Olga groaned quietly.

'First we'll arrange to have a car pick them up and take them to Lapyushka for drinks and whatever.'

'Isn't that a gentlemen's club?' Zoya asked, looking up from her fingernails.

Vitek grinned. 'And then I know a Gypsy guy who's got a dancing bear. For the right money, he'll lend it to us. They'll love it. Trust me. And then after that, we'll go to the pigeon races. All the best people follow the races.'

Azade narrowed her eyes. She saw now Vitek's true problem. Which, she admitted, again, started with her. She was like the woman who, mistaking an agate for an egg, swallowed a stone. The next morning she opened her legs and out slid that same stone. Only it had grown in the night, had acquired the shape and properties of a stone boy. It had agate-coloured eyes, small pebbles in its ears. And in place of a heart, more stone. She was that woman always mistaking one thing for another. So why was she so dismayed when her boy lived up to the story that seemed to have been told specifically about him?

'Capitalism is brushing its teeth,' Mircha bellowed. 'The dollar is on the march, but we shall overcome. The rouble will stabilize, we shall secure all that's been lost! Our history belongs to us, but only if we are willing to reclaim it!'

'Hear, hear!' Lukeria shrieked.

Everyone except Vitek looked to the rooftop. Azade could sense more than see that Tanya was biting her lip, probably drawing blood. It would not do to let him weave about on the rooftop broadcasting his ignorance as loudly as possible.

'Come down here. We need to talk,' Azade called to the rooftop.

'Is that you love? My pigeon? My sweet paw?' Mircha disappeared for a moment then re-emerged at the stairwell, his eyes too bright to inspire trust. He was drunk. Again. How he managed it, Azade could not imagine.

Azade pinched her nose. The stink. Really, it was hard to work around and no amount of Russian Forest perfume sprayed fore and aft head to toe had helped.

'You really smell bad. You need to wash yourself. With real soap.'

'That hurts. Right here in my heart,' Mircha said. 'But I forgive you. You see, I'm a better person now that I'm dead.' Mircha smiled a wobbly smile. 'I want to set things right. I want to make everything up to you.' He shuffled toward her, his arm outstretched, his lips puckered for a sloppy kiss.

Azade sidestepped Mircha. 'Listen. You heard the girl. People with money are coming to visit. If you really want to do something that matters, you'll settle down and be quiet. No more big ideas from the rooftop. And stop hauling all that crap back into the courtyard.'

'That is not crap. Those items are of inestimable value. They represent every good thing of our former country. Those rusting items are our national treasures, our identity, our cultural historical identity. Just look at them!'

Azade surveyed the glistening heap. There was that cracked Moskvich motor, several pairs of crutches, a pirated copy of *Rambo*, clocks that ticked out of time, rusted scythes, ripped flags belonging to the southern republics – items of high symbolic content and laden with nostalgic overtones, even she could see that. But still.

'You have no country anymore. The villages we grew up in have been bombed out for years, razed to the ground. Only a few old-timers still speak our languages. It's pointless, what you are doing.' Azade folded her arms across her chest.

Mircha thumped his chest with his fist. 'For the first time, I have purpose, I know what it is I am about. Why should I settle down and be quiet when I feel this good? Even my stump feels good!' Mircha swayed slightly as he took a few steps towards Azade. His boots were too big now for him and he had to slide them across the concrete, the laces trailing as afterthoughts.

'You'll ruin everything in spite of yourself. You can't stay. It's not natural,' Azade said, making a last attempt at reason. The problem with the dead was that they lived to unfix what others had fixed, to undo what others were trying to do. The dead untied knots. They climbed staircases the wrong way and, in so doing, turned time backwards on a clock. Shout 'Stop!' to a dead man and he keeps moving. Shout 'Listen!' and he will merely point to his ears filled with words fibrous as cotton and round as pebbles.

Never in her life had she wanted much. Never had she been able to do much. But hope had whittled her desire to a sharp slender point, shaved it to a mere sliver. And now she knew what she wanted and, more importantly, was ready to cast that sliver in the direction where it would do the most good. She would have to get rid of him once and for all.

As if he could read her mind, Mircha gave Azade a bitter look and drew himself to his full height. The blue vein alongside his neck stood to attention. Mircha assumed his posture of rage, clenched his hand into a fist. Azade understood the momentum of instinct and emotion, how easy it was for a man like Mircha to work himself in a blink from feeling hurt to feeling pure rage. Even now he towered over Azade, his brow drawn into a scowl. The muscles in his jaw pumped mightily. 'I won't go,' he said.

Azade leaned on her shovel. Who was it who told her that a woman's strength lies in her hair and her hands? Her fingers moving independently of thought tugged the long darning needle out of the bun fastened to the top of her head. A thick rope of hair tumbled past her shoulder and her fingers combed through it.

'You can't hurt me anymore,' Azade said, unwinding the braid. Now she knew, now she remembered. The words of her mother from a lifetime ago tumbled in her ear, clear as a chiming of a bell in thin air from across a high mountain lake: the hair is the strength, and the needle holds the hair. Break the needle and be strong. It was, after all, the only message the dead could really understand: the complete irreparable quality of a strong thing broken. The only way to dispatch a deathless body, her mother proposed all those years ago, therefore, was to snap a needle between the teeth. All these years of biting her tongue had made her teeth hard, and they had been waiting for such a moment as this.

Azade put the needle in her mouth.

Mircha's eyes widened. 'What are you doing? Lapushka, please don't,' he begged.

Azade bit the needle and felt it break.

Mircha staggered towards the stone bench. 'I never!' he gasped, clutching his stomach.

'I know,' Azade said, and she heard sadness in her voice. It surprised her that she could feel sadness for her husband at such a moment, and yet she did. For he was shrinking. Not quickly, but steadily. And she could see him in a way she never had before. Literally. She could see the interior of his body. She saw his heart, a sickly thing, smaller than an early swede, dark as the eye of a rhododendron. What would have happened if as a boy that heart had been fed properly? Would it have swollen, like a root that drinks oil, and filled whatever space it was given? Would that heart have grown so that a boy like Mircha would have grown into a man who could feel the things he ought to have felt?

Mircha fumed quietly and attempted to squeeze his hand into a fist.

Azade stood and folded his hand, now only slighter bigger

than her own, against his chest. 'You can't hurt me,' she said. 'I won't let you.'

Mircha turned for the stairwell. With effort he began the long climb, this time his body facing the right way up, and Azade did not offer to help him. It was not over yet, this business with Mircha. He still had his mouth, after all. He was broken, but not beaten. Azade reached for her shovel. Still, there were things she could do to hasten his departure. The Americans were coming. It would not do to have Mircha stinking up the courtyard with his revisions. Azade leaned against the shovel and turned a sliver of earth. Would it make a difference whether or not the hole was exactly six feet and whether she cut an angled shelf as her father always had when he dug holes? Really she didn't know. It was one more thing on a long list she would like to ask God when she saw him. There were so many forms and rituals, codes of dress and rules for fasting, for standing up and sitting down, and then, of course, all the extra rules for women. If she were to see God face to face, if such a thing for a woman like her were possible, Azade wondered would she hide her hands when she saw Him? Would God think them unclean, given all that her hands had done?

CHAPTER THIRTEEN

Yuri

So tired he was of women. The worrying and wishing kind, the nervous and shouting kind. Yuri scaled the heap, green and wet with rotting banana skins and rinds. Angry women, they were everywhere. Talking, accusing, bullying, demanding, and never in a congenial tone. They blared like tone-deaf trumpets. This new Russia, it was really the old Russia. The only difference was there were more women now than ever and they were more vocal about the causes and sources of their unhappiness. And they were so much quicker to lay blame. Take Zoya – plagued with sudden rages and terrible desires. For babies, no less. He knew, dim-witted as he was, that he would never make her happy. Babies would not fill her empty heart. There she was now in the stair-well, her phone at her ear as she meticulously turned her coat inside out so as to reduce the wear. She'd crawl out of her own skin and hang it wrong side out too, if she could. Her voice tumbled into the courtyard and shattered into pieces: '*I want… I want…*'

The sound was a steady blow to the head: thump and pound. *Want.* Electric toaster ovens. Upholstered ottomans in split leather. Brocade and velvet. Window treatments and stays. All of this wanting like the stone of a cherry rattling inside his head, against his teeth, hurting him in a steady unstoppable way.

Then there was his mother, home from another day of work. Through the kitchen window he could see her beating her frustrations into a lump of dough. Each blow to the soft mound was another lamentation for a lost memory. And this punctuated by sounds from the third-floor window. Lukeria making the same demands: '*Who? What?*'

No denying it, no matter what people said on TV, in newspapers, no amount of deliberate cheer could hide the fact that people everywhere were miserable. Especially the men.

The only remedy was his space helmet. In the foam lining he could smell his father. But always somebody wanted to disturb him. When he was a boy it was his mother who cautioned him, saying things. 'Don't wear that helmet so much. It will make you feverish. It will cramp the natural growth of your brain.' This she'd say while tapping on the visor. Then she'd pull off the helmet, lay her hand on his forehead, feeling for a temperature. The worst thing that could happen – not stunted brain growth, but a temperature. Every day at school in the city the very second a child crossed the threshold a school nurse shoved a thermometer into the kid's mouth. Why? Because a kid with a temperature was contagious. And a contagious kid was sent away with his mother. And a mother with a kid in tow could not clock in, and if his mother didn't clock in, she would lose a day's wages. Disaster. Which explains why more than once while on the way to Day Care Centre Number 137, his head burning, his eyes bugging out, off came the helmet and into the mouth went clumps of snow or chips of ice. Anything to fool that thermometer.

Yuri pulled on the helmet, stretched out on the stone bench, and sighed.

At the opposite end of the courtyard, in the one and only patch of mud completely thawed, stood Azade, a shovel resting on her shoulder. Behind her green bullet-shaped buds studded the limbs of the lime tree fore and aft. Above him the clouds converged overhead in the oddest of shapes. They were men and women kissing. Yuri closed his eyes for a moment, then opened them. Now the men and women had drifted so far apart, men westward, women eastward, no hint whatsoever remained that only moments before they were inextricably intertwined. Yuri blinked. In fact, there was no suggestion of the metaphoric in the sky whatsoever. The clouds were simply clouds gathering and stretching, and nothing more.

Yuri closed his eyes.

Tap. Tap. Tap.

'Mother, I feel fine. Not hot, not in the slightest,' he mumbled.

Tap. Tap.

Yuri opened his eyes. Mircha. On the bench. Sitting next to him and squeezing Yuri's shoulder. Hard.

'Brilliant!' Mircha said. 'What you were just muttering, that bit about women. Brilliant. I agree with you entirely. The world is far too full of women and not one of them is happy. It's beyond me, really it is.'

Yuri sat up and squinted at Mircha. He seemed different somehow. More unsteady. At a loss for breath.

'But your problem is that you don't know what it means to be a man.'

'Why is that, I wonder?' Yuri squinted at Mircha. He seemed smaller, shrunken inside his service coat.

'Russia is a country of boys coddled by their mamas and henpecked by their wives. Look at you, for example. Living with your ma and on the brink of marriage to a devil on ten ball bearings.'

'Well, what's the solution, then?'

Mircha raised his hand, closed it into a fist. 'A man shows a woman who's the boss.'

Yuri turned his hands over in his lap and studied his palms. He closed his hands into fists, opened then closed them again. Was there anything more beautiful than the architecture of a man's hands?

Mircha snorted. 'But you know, women do have their worth. They are more resilient, women. Built with twenty or more little motors inside of them, when life poses an insurmountable problem, they simply gear to another motor, turn their hands to another task, as it were. But men, they have just one big motor. All their self-worth is in the strength and power of that one motor. And once that motor is snuffed, men – they're finished. Because we only know one way.'

'Why are you telling me this?' Yuri squinted at Mircha.

'I have thoughts, insights, as it were. And no one to share them with. Now that I am dead I can see how better the rest of you should all live.'

Yuri watched Vitek emerge from behind the heap, the children in tow. 'You could tell him these things. He is your son, after all.'

Mircha worked his mouth in a circle and spat. 'Believe me, I've tried. Messages on mirrors, in dust, waking dreams, sleeping dreams. It's a lost cause. He can't hear a thing I have to say. He never could.'

Vitek approached the bench. He stretched his arms and inhaled deeply. 'The sun is shining. The birds are singing.' Vitek's chest swelled. 'It's enough to make you shit!' Vitek punched Yuri convivially in the arm. *Thump.*

Yuri rubbed his shoulder. 'That hurt.'

'Listen, the wind is whispering. Let's have a drink.' Vitek sat next to Yuri and uncapped a bottle. 'We're a team, you and I.'

'Who?' Yuri tipped his head.

'Who?' Lukeria hooted.

'Do you want to get out of this shit hole? D'you?' Vitek's dark face loomed in front of his visor.

I want...

'You want to make everyone happy, and by everyone I mean yours truly. Don't you?'

Yuri nodded and smiled obliquely.

'That's my boy.' Vitek smiled and withdrew a bottle from his coat.

'That's my boy,' Mircha echoed and hung his arm around Yuri's neck.

'So here's what you're going to do.' Vitek uncapped the bottle and took a generous swallow. 'Tomorrow you're going to get to the museum, early, and get washed. Use soap. And then go and see Kochubey.'

Yuri lifted the visor. 'Who's Kochubey?'

'The recruiter, stupid. Go and see him. At the old-new Caucasian bakery. Tell him I sent you.'

Yuri nodded. Uncomfortable it was, with a dead man's arm draped over his one shoulder, a semi-blind and semi-deaf man's arm draped over the other. He couldn't decide which arm bothered him most, Mircha's or Vitek's.

'Maybe you'll get lucky and get a cushy assignment. Mine-sweeping or something.' Vitek dug an index finger into first one nostril, then the other, then examined his fingernails. 'You have no idea how much a mine-sweeper makes.'

'What's the average life expectancy?'

Vitek wiped his fingernails against his trousers. 'Incon-sequential. What matters is that we each of us have only one life to expend, so we each of us must make it count.'

Meanwhile Mircha kept talking. 'I really did want to be a good father. But nobody told me how.' Mircha leaned forward and poked Vitek with his crutch. 'So I am sorry, son!'

Vitek slapped his ear as if plagued by a pesky gnat. 'Be sure to take a pack of Marlboros. It's all Kochubey will smoke.'

'I was a terrible father. My father was a horrible father and his father before him. It has been a long and honoured family tradition. Our rage, our cruelty, and you must appreciate the importance of tradition, overrated as it may be. Which is not to say I am exonerated. Certainly not! So, I'm sorry – a hundred times sorry.'

'Speak for yourself! I am sorry for nothing!' Lukeria's voice wobbled from the heights.

'Crazy old harpy. Who does she think she's yelling at?' Vitek stared at Lukeria shaking her fist from her open window.

'Your father.' Yuri pointed to Mircha. 'He's here. Sitting next to me. Talking to me. Just as you are.'

'OK, OK. I know when a joke's being played on me,' Vitek frowned. 'Fun and games. I have a sense of humour, too. Ha! Just don't forget to get your ass over to Kochubey's tomorrow.'

'Yes,' Mircha echoed. 'Don't forget. This is just the kind of thing we men live for – to die gloriously in battle.'

Yuri pulled the helmet back over his head and the noise of the courtyard instantly went under water. It was fear that kept fish swimming. Instinct told a fish what to do, where to go. But for the right bait any creature will ignore instinct. At least this is what his commander told them in Stavropol, or maybe it was Beslan. This is why it was necessary to crawl on hips and elbows through the snow, crawling toward the heart of another village where they would kill people, some of them Russian. They were learning to replace their fear, their natural instincts to flee, which were just other names for common cowardice. All this the commander said while thrusting a knife upward into the torso of a cardboard man as he demonstrated how easy, how vulnerable the human body really is.

But a man is not a fish. A man is a thinking creature, a creature who can reason with and beyond pure instinct. His instinct? Easy. To survive. Isn't that what everybody wanted? But why should his survival come at the expense of someone else's? There were other ways to make money. He could sell a kidney. He could yodel on a street corner. He could keep out of Tanya's way so that she could get that grant thing. He could fish.

CHAPTER FOURTEEN

Tanya

When she says the first line of the Lord's Prayer, *Our Father, existing pure in heaven,* she thinks of the old story of Chestnut Grey, the mighty horse who flies through the air unhindered, powered by the great gusts of steam from his nose. Of fathers she knows very little, but of the sky, so much more. At the approach of Chestnut Grey, the clouds buck and pearl, then cool to the colour of birch bent by ice. The colour of God's pockets turned inside out. It was the only story Lukeria ever read to her as a girl and for this reason Tanya has invested in the tale great symbolic value. What that symbolism is, Tanya can't really say, though as she hurried for the bus she fingered her cloud notebook and imagined she was that horse: large and powerful, enlisted to aid others who cannot help themselves. She is the work horse necessary to further the plot, though it has not escaped her notice that in the old story once the peasant and princess unite, Chestnut Grey spends most of his time eating apples and making the wishes of others come true.

Much better to be the steam. Far better to be the cloud. Much better to be exactly who she was, a girl in love with sky, swallowing every cloud and telling herself she was satisfied, her empty stomach full. Tanya pulled at her short skirt and clung for dear life to the black strap dangling from the carriage ceiling. The air inside the bus was dense and weepy like boiled chicken bones. Her eye make-up, which Zoya had generously applied, was already rising to a sweat on her skin. A twinge against her calves and behind her knees confirmed that new ladders had climbed up her fishnet stockings, the most stylish hosiery she owned. Despite her zero-one-zero diet, she'd not lost a single kilo of weight, and in fact, she seemed thicker than ever. To make matters worse, the American art-lovers had arrived at the airport and she was late for the meet and greet. Naturally.

Inside the arrivals lobby it was a job finding the Americans. A load of Germans and Australians from the Lufthansa flight burst through the lobby and spilled out onto the pavement, where they haggled with the taxi drivers. A pointless prospect, Tanya wanted to tell them. Most of the drivers were Armenian, and such fierce negotiators that God didn't even haggle with them. Another plane, a TU-204 from Tashkent, brought a load of Koreans and Uzbeks, the women wearing bright coats and trousers and wrapped in scarves. It took a while for Tanya to separate out east from west in the lobby, but finally, when there was only herself and three other women, the same women she'd noticed waiting through the waves of human arrivals, a terrible knowing gathered across her features. These were her Americans. And so odd looking they were!

All three wore trousers. Well, not trousers, not the kind
with buttons, anyway. Trousers with zips. She knew it was the
style in the States for women to look like men, but these three
had pushed the style to limits. They wore their hair cropped
shorter than Tanya had ever seen on a woman. And the colour,
at least on the two older women, was not grey, but silver.
Bright silver. In Tanya's experience only the poorest of the
grandmothers wore her age in her hair. But from the way in
which the two women ensconced themselves within a ring of
luggage – sturdy leather suitcases with stout clasps – Tanya
knew they weren't poor. Nor were they comfortable being
in this lobby in such close proximity to so many others who
were. Twice the oldest of the two, a small but sturdy-looking
woman, touched her necklace and watch, as if to verify that
her valuables were still on her. Standing a few paces away, as
if to distance herself from her companions, the tallest of the
women, a girl really, looked at travel glossies. She stood at least
six feet tall, six three if one took into account her spiky hair.
Her hair! Clearly an experimental work in progress. Short,
purple-black and well articulated. A good deal of hair spray
and egg whites had clearly gone into this risible project.

Tanya hurried towards the women as fast as her high heels
would allow and stretched her lips over her faulty teeth. She
did not want them to see her crooked dentition, not yet,
anyway, and also, she was making a valiant attempt at inhab-
iting the future of the handshake in her very walk – that is,
embodying the very metaphor she imagined they wanted to

see. Artistic firm intention and goodwill, style and grace at a gallop over wide open spaces. Hard to do in high heels. But she was determined. 'Good morning. You must be the Americans of Russian Extraction for the Causes of Beautification. I am so very glad to meet you.' Tanya thrust her hand towards the oldest woman with the shortest, sharpest hair.

The woman took a step forward, her eyes measuring Tanya. In her long gaze, Tanya detected a windswept quality that she wanted very much to believe spoke of the woman's ability – or even better, desire – to see potential in the openness of an empty canvas. Or, at least, the ability to look past Tanya's flimsy attire and see potential in a sub-standard museum. Or in her attempt at the graceful galloping handshake.

'Justine Barker,' the woman said at last. She gripped Tanya's hand and pumped it strong and hard. 'I'm the eldest Barker and this is my daughter Livia, and over there,' Mrs Barker hooked her chin toward the girl, 'is my granddaughter, McKayla.'

'Ah.' Tanya nodded at each of the women. Grandmother, mother, daughter. A matryoshka in reverse, with the grand-daughter being the largest, the empty shell, and the capable mother easily fitting inside her large daughter, and the grand-mother a snug fit inside the mother.

The grandmother looked at her watch and shook her head. 'We're on a schedule. Perhaps you'll take us directly to the museum now?'

Tanya smiled wide. Then she remembered her teeth and adjusted her face.

'Of course.' She gestured toward the open door and the women moved through it, leaving Tanya, in a skirt far too short for the task, to manage all five pieces of their luggage.

Outside the airport a light rain began to fall. The women stood on the walkway, their umbrellas held in such a way as to ensure maximal harm to passersby. Meanwhile, Tanya attempted to flag a ride. Though it was a short distance from the airport to the museum, the rain made for hard competition. The Aeroflot flight crews in their smart uniforms and heels had no problem stopping cars. Tanya jutted her hip out a few extra spine-wrenching millimetres and wiggled her fingers in desperation. When she had all but given up, a maroon Sputnik lunged for the kerb.

'This doesn't look like a typical taxi,' the grandmother observed as they piled in the backseat, the grandmother and mother flanking either side of Tanya and the girl with her moose legs sitting in the front passenger seat.

'In Russia every car is a taxi,' Tanya explained, the whole time pulling savagely at her skirt.

The driver turned to the backseat and grinned. Then he touched his finger to the wooden icon of St George wedged in the open ashtray. 'For good luck,' he said in English to the girl. Then he ground the gear and the car charged over the roadside potholes. Though Tanya had heard that shock absorbers were standard issue on most modern cars, they seemed conspicuously absent on this one. Three times the girl's spikes brushed the roof of the car and each time the girl's mother's face took on a deeper shade of grey-green.

Only the grandmother seemed to take interest in the city, her wide and roving gaze taking in every broken window, every pile of rubbish floating in slush, each veteran begging on the corner: all the signs of a developed country unable to recover from the shock of a sudden free-market economy.

After they passed the third tanker – this one full of spoiled milk, judging from the rank odour – the grandmother pinched her nose.

'Why doesn't someone move that truck?'

'It's cheaper to let it sit and spoil. Petrol prices are astronomically high,' Tanya explained. 'So, until we get fuel, we go without.'

'Oh I get it. So that's why there's the war in Chechnya, for oil?' The girl in the front seat turned her head slightly to address Tanya.

Tanya gulped at the air, swallowing invisible cloud. It felt wrong to contradict her visitors and possible benefactors, and yet she was not in the habit of drawing such connections. At last Tanya settled for diplomacy, and pressed her palm hard against her sternum and shrugged.

'Commerce stalled for lack of fuel. That's a crying shame,' the grandmother broke in. 'This would never happen in America. In America if people want something, they get it. And at decent prices, too.'

'You don't mean war?' Tanya couldn't help asking.

The grandmother looked at Tanya as if she were in sudden

breach of good manners, or perhaps incredibly stupid. 'No dear, milk.'

'Though some of us choose not to drink it,' the girl added.

At this, the car lurched to a halt in front of the All-Russia Museum.

The driver hopped out. He followed the women down the steps to the museum ticket entrance, leaving Tanya, again, with the luggage. A suitcase under each arm and in each hand, and a carry-on slung around her neck, she just managed to squeeze through the basement door, past Ludmilla coughing behind the glass ticket office, and to the hat/coat-check counter. And then the awkward moment: what to pay the driver. Tanya dashed to the ticket office and retrieved a roll of tickets – a lifetime of visits to the museum – and from her own purse she withdrew a bottle of apple brandy and a pack of cigarettes.

The driver pocketed the items without a word, as if he'd expected all along to be shorted. But as he pushed open the door to leave, he stopped, fixed his gaze on Tanya and opened his mouth. A tirade of obscenity spewed forth – curse stacked upon curse. Add to this the fact that the man was a multilingual curser, swearing fluidly in German, Russian and even English. Having exhausted his supply of invectives, the driver at last left for his car.

The mother turned to Tanya. 'Does everyone here talk like that?'

Tanya pulled their luggage behind the counter and piled it on to shelves.

'The execution of obscenity is, for many Russians, a form of art in itself,' she improvised. 'Some say this is what makes our language so mighty.'

'Interesting.' The grandmother reproportioned her smile to express a measure of appreciation. The granddaughter adjusted her hair. Clearly, if Tanya was to cultivate in these women an understanding of the mystery of the Russian soul as expressed in art, as evidenced in this very museum, she had to get them upstairs. And fast.

'Shall we?' Tanya attempted a smile of utter serenity and pointed to the stairs where she spied Head Administrator Chumak looming. Apparently he'd been there all along, sound-lessly observing her all these minutes.

'Ladies!' Head Administrator Chumak bellowed. 'How wonderful, how completely fabulous that you are here at last!'

The women climbed the stairs and surrounded Head Administrator Chumak. The eldest Barker – Ernestine? Clarine? Tanya would never remember, she knew this already – thrust her hand toward Chumak. A case of unfortunate timing, for Chumak was in mid-execution of a deep-waisted bow. The woman's hand glanced of Chumak's shiny pate and she brought her hand to her chest as if she'd been touched by electricity.

The mother brought her hands to her face and sneezed. And sneezed. 'Such dust!' she exclaimed between sneezes.

Head Administrator Chumak, too, was temporarily over-come. Apparently Daniilov had finally run a cloth over the many faux marble statues and now ten years' worth of museum dust cluttered the air. Head Administrator Chumak produced a white handkerchief from his pocket and secured it to his face.

'I like to think of it as ambiance,' he said between sneezes. 'Some people say that the Russian soul doesn't exist. But when I look around at this spectacular museum, my nose tells me there is spirit in excess.' Here Head Administrator Chumak began another low bow.

Tanya pointed towards another set of stairs and the women began climbing. 'The top floor is, in my opinion, the best place to begin. All of history east and west hangs on the walls which are,' here Tanya paused on the landing to catch her breath, 'just that much closer to the heavens and thus, God himself.'

'So you've got religious art here?' The mother paused on the landing.

'All art is religious, but yes,' Tanya continued the climb and tried hard to focus, 'some art, the subject matter, say, is more so than others.' At the top of the stairs Tanya gestured towards a second-rate reproduction. 'Take, for instance, this diptych of the brothers and saints, Boris and Gleb.'

'What did they do?' the girl asked, shoving a stick of chewing gum into her mouth.

Fully prepared and willing to launch with the approved and earnest explanation, Tanya's mouth opened. Closed. Then opened. 'Nothing, really,' Tanya said. 'Sometimes in Russia that is all it takes to become famous, though it helps if you die a miserable death.'

'They were martyred then?' the mother asked.

'Oh, yes. But they maintained their blissful countenance through it all.'

'How exhausting,' the girl said.

Tanya gestured towards the opposite wall, populated by more martyrs. And that was all it took, that sweeping gesture with her arm, and her mouth went round and open, flowing with the well-oiled speech she'd memorized for just this occasion.

'Why do we start our discussion of the third-floor exhibit with the east wall?' Tanya asked. And because she never allowed more than a hair width's pause before answering her rhetorical questions, the words kept tumbling: 'We start our discussion of the third-floor exhibit with the east wall because Orthodoxy began in the east, where the sun rises and all things begin.' She pointed to the ninth-century fresco of Saints Cyril and Methodius. 'And who are these saints and why are they important? These saints are the beloved brothers Cyril and Methodius. The genius brothers are important because they brought Byzantine Orthodoxy to the Slavs and bridled the wild Slavonic tongue to a written alphabet. Also, they were formidable chess players and mathematicians.'

The girl scowled at the genius saints. They were not the best examples of Tanya's finest work: the linseed oil egg binding hadn't quite taken hold, which gave the brothers an oily look to them.

'And now we turn our attention to the west wall, which is reserved for fading things, for boundaries of place and time, which are continually rewritten, and for man. Why? Because even men such as those shown in these portraits – kings and princes and warriors – are only temporarily on this earth, a mere illusory shadow of spiritual events.' Tanya's voice took on a round and draughty quality she'd learned to imitate by listening to so many lectures delivered by art history scholars. And like those scholars, if her listeners showed any signs of distress or confusion, she would not stop or slow down, but merely charge ahead, forward at all costs. 'Notice the oil reproduction of Prince Vladimir, whose father, Svyatoslav, kicked down the gates of the mysterious Volga Khazars. Why did he kick down those gates? Because the Khazars were Jews who had acquired more power than was good for them and so Svyatoslav had to defeat them. Afterwards, the Khazars disappeared so thoroughly, they took their graveyards with them. Not a trace of their dead, their strange-shaped currency, or even their language remained.'

At this point Tanya resurfaced just long enough to gather her air before plunging back into her script.

'Pardon me,' the mother touched Tanya's elbow, 'but I have a question.'

Tanya shook off the moist hand. A discussion of Russian Orthodoxy was like the Trans-Sib freight line – you don't stop it on a sneeze.

'After Svyatoslav died, his successor, Prince Vladimir,

considered accepting Judaism as the state religion, but rejected it. Why did he reject Judaism? Because he had observed how scattered throughout the world Jews had become. He contemplated adopting Islam, but rejected that, too. Why did he reject Islam? Because Prince Vladimir knew that no Russian man could ever be happy without alcohol. Then he remembered Cyril and Methodius. He admired them for being men whose intellect sharpened their faith and their ability to drink wine and solve difficult maths problems. He recalled, too, their reverence of icons, which were known to produce miracles on the battlefield. And this was the deciding point for Vladimir. He believed in miracles almost as much as he loved playing chess and drinking vodka. So Orthodoxy it was, and a very good choice, too. Just think,' Tanya leaned forward, her finger outstretched in a gesture she'd borrowed from Lukeria, 'what would have happened a hundred years later to the men of Novgorod under attack by the Suzdalites if the priest had not carried the icon Our Lady of the Sign into battle. The outnumbered and ill-equipped inhabitants of Novgorod would have been slaughtered. When the first arrows flew across the battlefield, one of them struck the icon, lodging into Mary's eye. The priest, leaving the arrow as it was, lifted the icon high overhead. The men of Suzdal took one look at that image of Mary, bleeding from her eye, and were blinded, down to the last man.'

Tanya noted that the women had a trapped look about them, the daughter's gaze lifting to the illuminated exit sign.

'The cross is mightier than the sword, is that what you're

saying?' the grandmother asked, peering at the icon.

Tanya, still mindful of her teeth, smiled carefully. 'Exactly. Not only are holy relics potent salves, but when used properly, powerful weapons as well.'

'Do you believe miracles can happen – even today?' the mother asked, her wet eyes searching Tanya's.

'Oh, yes. Each of these icons is a miracle,' Tanya breathed, squaring her shoulders to the icons. Because here's the strange thing: she meant exactly what she said. When she stood there among the faux icons she herself had lovingly crafted out of gutter flashing and chewing gum, she did not see the silver halos she'd fashioned from the wrapper of the many chocolate bars she'd eaten. Nor did she see the used toothpicks that radiated in all directions from baby Jesus' head which spoke of his sharp radiance. When she stood here she saw the icons as they were intended to be perceived – masterful copies of the copies shown in her art books and duplicated on her assortment of museum postcards. And looking at these icons and paintings with this hope-infused vision, they were not cheap, amateurish attempts, but the real thing. Like the subjects they depicted, these items were made of humble stock but in all ways suggested the divine.

The grandmother squinted, touched her finger to the gold frame. 'Is this cardboard?'

Tanya grimaced. 'Cardboard of the highest quality. The Director knows a man who knows a manufacturer of high-end cardboard picture frames.'

The mother tapped a fingernail at the glorious cloud of effervescence backing Our Lady of the Sign. 'And this?'

'Tobacco stains.'

'And this?' The girl leaned toward a mosaic made entirely of chewing gum.

'I wouldn't touch that one,' Tanya warned.

The third-floor tour complete, Tanya escorted the women to the second floor, where she extolled the virtues of each shabby exhibit, including the rooms full of pseudo antiquities and indigenous art, comprised chiefly of faded wooden spoons, and then to the mezzanine where a four-metre iron Yermak loomed in chain mail. Yermak was the last in a long line of busts and partial busts, and because this replica was intact – except for his axe, which went missing sometime last year – Tanya felt expansive. If only she could explain why Yermak, though a Cossack and therefore a savage, was so wonderful and terrible and terribly important, hacking hip and thigh through other more savage savages to extend Russia's borders, then she would have accomplished something, however small. And so she talked, as expansively as possible, until the women could take no more.

The grandmother folded her arms across her small chest. 'Such hard and cruel people,' she said, her voice conveying admiration or nostalgia, Tanya could not say for sure which.

Tanya stretched her upper lip across her upper teeth, carefully, carefully. 'History is not carried in the smile, but in the teeth.'

'What does that mean, exactly?' the mother asked.

'To be frank, I am not completely certain. But it is a statement that frequently appears in the history exams,' Tanya conceded.

Inside the museum café Tanya stood at the counter and paid for their lunch order: pelmyeni, pirogi, small bowls of borscht. She felt proud of herself that she had resisted the urge to load the tray with tumblers of vodka and sweets – a typical breakfast for those far too young to quit working and too old to give a serious thought to their figure. Tanya carried the trays to a table where the women waited.

'Try the pelmyeni,' Tanya said. 'They're quite good, even by museum standards.'

'What is it?' The mother reached for one and took a bite.

'They're like dumplings with meat, and the pirogi is like a meat pie, usually with ham and with onions.'

The girl eyed the plate. 'This world is a cruel one for animals.'

'She won't eat meat,' the mother said.

Or anything else, for that matter. For nothing on the trays – not even the borscht, which was primarily a winter root vegetable dish, nor the horseradish-tongue-mayonnaise salad – met with the girl's approval.

'Vegans don't eat any product that is derived from an animal,' the girl explained wearily.

The mother reached for another pelmyeni. 'Also she's developed an allergic reaction to those things.'

'Ah,' Tanya nodded.

The grandmother swallowed a spoonful of borscht. 'But you may have noticed that she wears make-up.'

The girl rolled her eyes. 'That's different.' She stood and with one hand slid the waistband of her jeans past a hip. 'My body is my art.'

Tanya blinked. And what a canvas! A winged horse, not at all unlike the Chestnut Grey, spanned the small of her back, the strong wings unfurling over her hip and the hooves dipping into the dark crevice of her rump. The girl hiked her jeans over her hips, turned and bent at the waist. Her shirt gaped open and between her breasts, for everyone to see, a red rose. All in all the horse and rose looked pretty good now, but Tanya had to wonder how well the wings would hold up, how long that short stem rose would grow over the next twenty years. Skin, by and large, made a poor medium, the tensile capacity being woefully comprised when a woman hits her forties and sometimes, Tanya sighed, much sooner.

Finally, the girl sat down.

'She's always making a spectacle of herself,' the grandmother said through a fierce smile.

'What about you?' The mother sipped at her tea. 'You must be some kind of artist or something – you know so much about the exhibits. And there's that very interesting notebook you carry with you.'

Tanya's face burned. She gratefully accepted the mother's query as a way to salvage the lunch break.

She could say she wanted to write pliant phrases that hummed bright and vibrant; to do with words what the masters did with colour and placement, painting a dot of red next to a dot of blue and in this way allowing the viewer's gaze to turn the eyes of the angels violet. There were the clouds, her dreams of flight. And then, of course, she wanted to be everywhere Yuri was. But these were not the things she could say aloud, not what people want to hear about even when they assure you that they do.

Tanya rubbed her hand over the colour notebook and smiled bashfully. 'Colour is life. It's how we bend light into laughs. And also shades of weeping.' She could feel her own face burning, could not bear to bring her gaze to the woman's and settled instead on turning to the girl's untouched food.

'I couldn't possibly eat this,' the girl said, pushing the bowls in front of Tanya. The potential waste. That's what provoked her instantaneous steady rhythm between spoon and bowl. And then her thoughts – they were not arty at all, not focused. Too fascinated she was by the intricacies of motherhood and daughterhood. It was all so foreign to her and yet within elbow's reach, jostling against her, played out across the table top. Tanya's furry eyebrows beaded into tight concentration. The parries and barbs between grandmother and granddaughter, the quick looks of irritation, the silent nudge of the salt and pepper packets across the table. Is this what it meant to love and be loved, or at least to care about one another? Oh, how Tanya wished she could know. How she wanted to ask this mother whose wide open cornflower gaze suggested the best of all Tanya had read and wanted to believe to be true about wide open Western benevolence. Tanya's stomach seized and rolled. Oh, how desire is so terrible when it is served up before you and you are so terribly hungry. She reached for another bowl of borscht.

'My, dear. Are you all right?' Now the mother had her moist hand on Tanya's wrist. Tanya felt her face going to fire again. But there was something comforting in that warm hand on her arm; she didn't want the mother – Livia? Lidia? – to withdraw her touch, so motherly, so genuine the urgent concern signalled in the pressure of her hand.

Tanya brought a paper napkin to her mouth. 'Fine,' she mumbled behind the greasy veil of paper. The girl and the grandmother had averted their gazes, startled and embarrassed by Tanya's hunger exposed.

Tanya gathered her notebook. Her museum senses fully engaged, her script galloping at full speed, she stood and brushed greasy crumbs from her lap.

'Perhaps you'd like to see the basement now. It contains the hat/coat-check room as you know, and then, of course, our famous Permian rock exhibit. Then there's the last exhibit, a real crowd-pleaser and my personal favourite.' Tanya smiled wide, wider, until the tall girl could not bear her faulty Slavic dentition any longer. Numbly the women followed her through the corridor and down the narrow staircase to the basement where Ludmilla sat coughing.

Tanya held a finger to her lips. 'Peter the Great was great for many reasons: his love of starting and finishing wars, building up the fleet and opening new ports. But he also possessed a boundless curiosity for the sciences and in his lifetime he amassed marvellous collections of animals, insects, flora and fauna. One of his oddest collections is now housed in the Kuntskamera building in St Petersburg and people travel hundreds of miles just to see it. Unfortunately, we could in no way obtain the original collection, and therefore we worked very hard to recreate specimen by specimen a reproduction of the famous Kuntskamera collection.' Tanya tiptoed into the darkened room and switched on the torches. Then she gestured as elegantly as she knew towards the glowing orange liquid exhibit.

The women circled the exhibit slowly. Tanya knew that she wasn't the only one who looked at these interrupted bodies and tried to complete them: a week's worth of fingerprints spanned the glass. In the wood veneer schoolchildren had traced their names in the dust. Their own names, or the names they would have given these foetuses had they been real, had they lived, Tanya did not know.

Tanya leaned her forehead against the glass and peered at two tiny bodies, the one climbing over the back of the other, and not a head to share between them. They were beautiful in their excess, beautiful in their lack. They were a good idea split in the middle and gone wrong. And Tanya couldn't help feeling that warm maternal swell behind her chest. Not cloud, this time, but love, the genuine article.

'Horrible.' The girl turned her back to the exhibit.

'They're absolutely monstrous,' the grandmother breathed. Her jaw hung slack in astonishment. 'Why in the world would anyone collect them?'

Tanya's stomach bunched and dropped. With effort she forced the words. 'For instructive purposes, I think.'

'But what on earth could be learned from collecting deformed foetuses and displaying them in glass jars?' The grandmother's repulsion knew no bounds.

'It's so sad,' the mother said.

'They're not real,' Tanya said. 'Just stretchy foam replicas.'

'I'm going to be sick,' the girl mumbled.

'The toilets!' Tanya's heart leapt within her chest. 'You must visit our toilets, then. They are of superior design. They're Finnish and absolutely stunning.'

'I think we've seen enough,' the grandmother said.

CHAPTER FIFTEEN

Olga

'Olga Semyonovna!' Chief Editor Kaminsky barked from the open door of the *Red Star* translation office. His face was flushed but the lobes of his ears looked pale as puffball mushrooms. The two major strands of his hair stood at attention. 'Good news. I'm not going to fire you on account of that most unusual report – you know the one I'm talking about.' Here, Chief Editor Kaminsky attempted to rein in his hair, pressing the dark strands against the crown of his head. 'Bad news is, I have to let you go anyway. It seems the press has run out of ink.' Behind the sound of his words the tubes howled and shrieked. 'Yes, it's a complete mystery – even to those of us who know things – but that is the position we are in. And because I in no way want to appear capricious or feckless I'm letting you go, too, Arkady.' Chief Editor Kaminsky handed over the termination slips, small as postage stamps and completely devoid of ink. 'Believe me when I say I will write the most glowing of recommendations for both of you should you seek employment with another newspaper.'

Olga drifted to the windows, spread her hands over the smoky glass. Arkady stood at the desk, looking at Olga. Below her the print drums slowly turned. Editor-in-Chief Mrosik's braying, steady as the honk of a swishy Mafiya sedan in panic mode, rattled the window. Behind them the wind howled through the pneumatic tubes. Olga's wedding ring was somewhere whizzing through these tubes. Also a glass eye belonging to that copy-editor they were under no circumstances to mention by name. And yet, hearing these noises, the sounds of her world as she knew it falling about her ears, made the fleeting trumpet blasts of Editor-in-Chief Mrosik, the quick exit of Chief Editor Kaminsky, strangely comforting.

'What next?' Olga's breath fogged the window.

Arkady smiled. 'We go.'

'Perhaps you could show us something of the city. A monument or something,' the grandmother suggested. They stood outside the museum. Head Administrator Chumak's shiny pate appeared from behind his office window. Tanya could almost hear him clasping and unclasping his hands.

'After all, we are as interested in the museum environs as we are in the museum,' the mother said, attempting to interject bright tones into her words.

The spikes of the girl's hair had started to droop. The sky turned wet and wobbled. The cottonwoods, oh how Tanya hated them, exhaled their white fluff. It was called Stalin's snow, but she preferred to think of it as the Devil's dandruff.

If she had a match, she'd set it all on fire. Instead she sneezed. The grandmother groped for a tissue.

'I could show you a war cemetery,' Tanya said between sneezes. 'It's quite green this time of year and very popular with newlyweds.'

A central concrete walkway divided the cemetery into two halves and low cement jetties rising from the grass separated one massive plot from another. The dead were buried in groups of hundreds and large stone slabs in front of each plot noted the year and month each group had died. Except for the stone slabs standing no higher than Tanya's knee, there were no other markers. Just the stand of birch which had gone from their characteristic whips and tails to tiny new leaves of a shade of green Tanya could only call hesitant. And, of course, the grass. Long, wide swathes of it, verdant and lush, vibrantly alive as only grass fed by the dead can ever become.

Orchestral music blared from speakers strategically located in the linden trees. This prevented serious discussion unless it was carried at a shout. Tanya scrambled for her notebook. An inopportune moment, perhaps, but surely a little scribble here, a little scribble there could do no harm.

The bones of your grandfather, the one who worked in the silver mine and survived only to die of black lung and the bones of my great grandmother who was taken in the middle of the night for singing seditious songs about saints, perhaps they are buried together somewhere in a grave like this one. Perhaps in a deep warren of mud they found each other. Perhaps it is they who breathe and tell the grass to grow in such sharp hues to remind us that we are the temporal ones. We are the ghosts fading.

'How does one locate any one individual within this mass group?' the mother shouted at Tanya.

'One doesn't.' Tanya shouted back, slipping the notebook into her plastic bag.

'In the States,' the grandmother shouted, grave severity amplifying every word, 'each serviceman gets his own cross. A white one.'

'Well, not always – not at every cemetery,' now the girl piped up.

'You mean, they can get other colours if they want?' Tanya asked.

The grandmother opened her mouth as if to reply. She then seemed to think better of it and clamped her mouth shut.

Outside the memorial entrance they had to compete with a bridal entourage for a ride. They had no chance whatsoever, as the groom was well stocked with spirits and even some hard currency. Just when Tanya had all but given up a microvan careened toward them and the driver, a middle-aged man with a munificent smile of all gold teeth, urged them in, even going so far as to help with their luggage.

Once settled into the seat next to Tanya, the girl touched Tanya's elbow. 'Weren't there prison camps in this area?'

'McKayla has visited several concentration camps as part of her graduate thesis studies,' her mother explained. 'She is a student of atrocity, suffering, and other chaos.'

'She can't get enough of it,' the grandmother observed dryly.

Tanya felt the girl stiffen. 'Suffering – if beautifully done – is an art form.'

'If suffering is what you want to see, then Russia is full of it,' Tanya said carefully.

'But what about the camps? There were camps,' the girl persisted.

In the rear-view mirror Tanya saw the driver's eyes boring a hole in her forehead.

'There are still stories of such places,' Tanya whispered. 'Of course people don't like to talk, don't like to remember. Historical memory is not necessarily a blessing.'

'But it is your birthright,' the girl said, squaring her shoulders.

The driver ground the gears and the car rounded the corner to her street. Tanya's thoughts were a whirl. Acid rose to the back of her mouth. This girl sitting beside her – what a confusion, what a piece of chaos, what a strange contradiction she was. The babies, or rather, the foam replicas of the babies, whose lives had simply been foreshortened but were now remembered and loved by everyone who saw them, repulsed her utterly. But she couldn't wait to get out to Perm-36 where she would no doubt touch the fences where prisoners were routinely lined up and shot. This girl would fold her so-tall body into an isolation cell to see what such torture felt like for a mere twenty seconds and she'd look at the glass display case of bones and hair, shoes and glasses – the things that outlasted the men and women who'd died so horribly in a place that was nothing short of hell on earth. She would do this, and if not here in Perm, then somewhere else, Tanya was certain of it, because she felt entitled by distant heritage to some portion of collective suffering, as if suffering were something one could lay claim to and collect. As if this kind of suffering were something one should wish to remember.

The microvan suddenly lurched for the kerb. The driver hopped out as if his shoes were on fire. He opened the hood of the car and inspected the engine. There wasn't a thing in the world wrong with it, Tanya knew. He was simply feigning a breakdown so that he could affect a miraculous repair at the sight of a few extra roubles.

'What's wrong?' the grandmother asked.

'A small paper shortage,' Tanya said, climbing out. She fished in her purse and retrieved all the items she'd co-opted in the event of such an emergency: one of Zoya's bottles of nail-varnish remover, a vial of Russian Forest perfume, one of Daniilov's beloved wrenches. But the driver shook his fist and cursed bitterly at her anyway. They'd run out of petrol, really and truly, and nothing short of fuel falling from the sky would console him now. From a box beneath the dash, he withdrew three bottles of vodka and a garden hose, currency he'd co-opted in the event of such an emergency, and stood in the street, waving the bottles at passing cars.

'What now?' the mother asked.

'We walk,' Tanya said.

'But our bags,' the girl said.

Tanya hefted a bag onto her shoulder. 'They'll have to walk, too.'

Outside the news building the pigeons lifted from the trees. The skins of the lime trees had thawed and the sun shone hori-zontally just as it should this time of year. Whatever disaster was brewing inside the *Red Star* offices, it had not stalled the cautious approach of a new season. Olga trudged through the muddy square behind Arkady, who slowed every now and then to offer her his arm. When they reached the metal bench, Olga brushed aside some trash and sank down gratefully. Though sitting on metal benches, according to Vera, put the ovaries in jeopardy, Olga was long past the age of caring about such things. And sitting, she'd learned from her years at the *Red Star*, made a shaky situation more stable, dropping nearly any disaster to a more manageable altitude.

Arkady lowered himself carefully beside Olga. 'Thank God!' he sighed. 'I hated that job.'

Olga started. 'I thought you liked that job!'

'I hated every minute of it. The only reason I have stayed on this long is because of you. Because, Olga Semyonovna, I have always liked you.'

Olga stared mutely at Arkady.

'In fact,' Arkady continued, 'from the first day I saw you, I loved you. All these years I have pried myself out of bed and trudged to work only because I knew you would be there. That we would talk, however briefly. That we would drink a little tea, however lukewarm, together.'

'I had no idea, no idea whatsoever,' Olga muttered, her numb gaze trained on Arkady's shoes.

'You possess a rare and noble soul and though I cannot offer you much, you have my heart, if you want it, and of course, my unfailing admiration.'

'Why?'

Arkady blinked rapidly. 'Because of the nature of our work and the quintessential nature of who we, Jews, are – lovers of words and seekers of wisdom. We have suffered alongside each other and, therefore, we understand each other.'

As he was speaking something liquid shifted behind Olga's ribs, something anciently familiar, light and heavy at the same time. Olga jolted upright on the bench for sheer shock of it. Could she really be feeling the first giddy rushes of the possibility of love? And for such a man as Arkady? And Olga could not help allowing herself to smile. 'It's quite a lot to consider. All at once, that is,' Olga managed at last.

Arkady rose to his feet and laid his gloved hand over hers. 'That is all I ask. Consider it. Incidentally, this is for you.' Arkady withdrew an envelope from his coat pocket, then pulled his coat collar around his neck and walked across the square.

Olga watched him go. Then she looked at the envelope, considering just what might be inside. At last she opened it. Inside was an official-looking letter and attached to the letter an official-looking card. The idiot card.

At the edge of the square Arkady had stopped to look at her sitting there on the bench, the letter opened on her lap, the card in her hand. They observed each other from across the square. Olga tipped her head, considering Arkady. That word *consider* tied her eyebrows in a knot. Built from the Latin root *siderus*, the word rested on two meanings. Just like the old parables in which two images lie next to each other and forced meaning from the ground between them, this word demanded that she reconcile two seemingly unlike meanings from the common core: 'to observe the stars'. But the other meaning: 'desire'. The very thought of the word was enough to make the ovaries jump – and her on a cold metal bench!

Olga lifted her hand in a wave. Arkady raised his arm, then turned and trudged on. Olga hopped to her feet, slid the card between her bra and breast, and hurried for home. All these years she'd looked at Arkady as a friend, durable as the desk they shared, faithful but unimaginative as an oar to a lock. The idea that Arkady could provide, for her and her son, in such a significant and tangible way was such a surprise to Olga, who had learned over the years to expect so little from people, especially those who meant well. The idea that Arkady could surprise her, and that she might like this, that she could feel something for him and on such a hairpin turn, made her wonder what else about Arkady – about herself – she had miscalculated.

CHAPTER SIXTEEN

Azade

Azade leaned on her shovel and squinted at the festering heap. A real puzzle there, Mircha. Not at all following the rules of the old stories. She'd broken him with the needle. And in his body she could see that he was diminished. He clung to a rusted pogo stick anchored in the heap, looking very much like a human accordion bent by the wind. But his mouth! It still moved. And his voice carried all too well.

'Capitalism is brushing its teeth! Global corporate domination is on the march!' Mircha hooted towards the stairwell where Zoya emerged wearing a strapless dress with a bra that wasn't, as was the fashion. She stomped across the marshy courtyard to the latrine, where she rattled the handle.

Azade could smell the thermometer warming in the girl's pocket, the biting odour of mercury, and her quick irritation, which, as all things do, worked its complement through the bowels. Which is why Azade did not need to ask to know that Zoya would require ten squares of paper, at the very least.

Azade unlocked the door and held it open for Zoya.

Mircha cupped his hand to his mouth and hooted in their

direction. 'Behold, we stand at the crossroads. I speak to you as a prophet! The Japanese are stealing our icebergs and auctioning them on the Internet!'

Azade tipped her head, considering the largesse Mircha had acquired in death. Bodily he was smaller, dwarfed inside his service coat, but the sheer verbage issuing from his mouth and the stink of it – their little courtyard filled as it was with the heap – could barely contain it all.

'A story! A story! This one I think you will like.' Mircha balanced on the top of the pile. 'Actually it's several stories bleeding into one, a popular architecture, and none of the stories really finishes, but that just proves the best stories are like life, completely unresolved.'

After a few moments Zoya emerged from the latrine. She shielded her eyes and gazed at the heap.

'God, what a nuisance,' she said, dropping fifty kopeks into Azade's collection tray with one hand and pinching her nose with the other. 'If he doesn't shut up, he'll ruin what little chance we have for the grant.'

Yuri stretched his body over the bench and listened to the clouds. They spoke to him in familiar voices. Correction. They spoke in a familiar voice. Just one. Mircha's. Yuri opened an eye.

Mircha sat on the heap and made music with empty tins of sprats. 'Fish are birds without wings!'

Yuri smiled at the noise. Who would have thought the man had done so much thinking in his as-yet short afterlife! And it was all so very profound!

'Yu–ri!' Zoya's voice rang out shrill and sharp, breaking his name into jagged halves. Yuri raised himself onto an elbow and listened to the sound of Zoya's shoes punching angry holes in the soft mud. Punch–squish, punch–squish. Heel–toe. Heel–toe. How she managed that full-throttle approach, complete with her trademark hip thrust and wearing those shoes in this mud – and all without a single break in her stride – it was enough to send him reeling. And then there she was, bench-side and not a bit out of breath. Under the May slant light her hair cast a metallic borscht-coloured sheen. Yuri winced.

Mircha flung his arm at Zoya. 'The Mongolians are bottling ordinary air and peddling it as medicinal oxygen!'

Zoya pointed her chin towards Mircha. 'Some people just don't know when to quit.'

'Oh, I don't know.' Yuri inhaled deeply. 'Even a fool can have a moment of primal wisdom.'

Zoya sat next to Yuri. 'But he doesn't make any sense.'

'Few prophets do. At least he's keeping all his clothes on.'

'Speaking of which,' Zoya said, whipping out her thermometer from her open purse. 'Look! I am ovulating. Right now.' Zoya hooked her finger between a shirt button and pulled. 'As in this moment exactly.' Now she had a hand on his knee. Who was this vixen with the sharp tongue and radiating hair, pulling on his shirt, yanking at his belt buckle?

Tick.

Yuri blinked.

Heapside, Mircha bellowed: 'Be a man! Fulfill your calling!'

Tick. Yuri blinked again. Yes, the ticking was back. Distinct as ever. 'Now? This moment exactly?'

'Yes!' Zoya and Mircha cried in unison.

Tick.

Yuri held his hands up, as if in protest. Or maybe surrender. 'But the art-loving Americans are coming.'

'Yes. I know. They want to see how real Russians live.' Zoya smiled and slid her hand along Yuri's thigh.

He swallowed. His voice shook. 'But the timing is so delicate and the need for social graces so severe. I mean, honestly, how would it look?'

Zoya leaned and licked first one eyebrow and then the other. Yuri felt his chest tighten, his heart gallop. 'Who cares?' Zoya unhitched his belt and pulled him towards the darkened stairwell where his muscles seemed to move of their own volition.

Off went the belt. Down came the trousers. And then they were doing what two young people do when they are in love, or at least amiable towards the idea of togetherness even if it has nothing to do with love. And then: horrors. Malfunction. Negative lift. Complete and absolute system failure.

With a snort Zoya pushed Yuri. 'You really are worthless, you know.' Zoya sidled her dress over her hips.

'I'm sorry.' Yuri tried steadying his hands over his knees. 'I just can't. Something's wrong, I don't know what. It might be that ticking.'

'Your problem is that you think too much. Or maybe not enough. Either way, you better pull your head out of your ass and soon!'

Yuri stood and yanked his trousers waistward. His face contorted with shame and more thinking. Yuri pulled on his space helmet. What did she mean, he did not think enough or possibly too much?

At the edge of the courtyard Tanya hesitated. Her every instinct told her to turn back now before it was too late. To herd the women to the city's only three-star hotel, where an earnest brass band and recently laundered bed sheets awaited them.

'Well,' the grandmother prompted.

Tanya cleared her throat. 'I suppose there are a few, er, things, I should mention.'

'Things? What things?' the mother asked, craning her neck.

The girl gazed over the top of Tanya's head for an unobstructed view of the portable latrine and Azade ferociously sweeping at the mud in front of it. Olga sat on the bench and contemplated the latest issue of the *Red Star*, the pages of which were utterly blank.

Lukeria leaned out her open window and shouted in English, 'Hey! American ladies! Are your suitcases made from real leather? Or are they Chinese imitations?'

The grandmother looked at the mother and the mother looked at Tanya.

'She says things. She is very ill,' Tanya whispered.

'Watch out for those conniving Jews!' Lukeria hooted. 'They engineered the revolution, you know.'

The girl turned to Tanya. 'Which revolution is she talking about?'

Tanya sighed. 'All of them, I think.'

The mother touched Tanya's elbow. 'Why don't you take her to the hospital?'

'Unthinkable.' Tanya shook her head. 'She'd never make it. One has to be extraordinarily healthy to survive a stay in a Russian hospital.'

The women gazed at the windows. Tanya couldn't decide if they were merely baffled or in a state of extreme consternation. But as they'd passed the latrine, Tanya decided to keep them moving through the courtyard. A good plan. And it would have worked, too, if only the women didn't have the Western lolling gaze so perfectly honed. For with every step they took, Tanya could see that they were taking in detail after detail, absurdity stacked upon absurdity. No matter where they looked, they saw something Tanya knew fell outside the realm of what they had hoped to see. True to her word, Zoya had hung the best of her laundry: her sheer nightgowns and tights.

Then there was Yuri sitting on an overturned bucket beside the gaping hole, a fishing rod in his hand, his whole face tortured by thought.

Though the sun was not bright, the girl shaded her eyes with a hand and squinted ferociously. 'What is the matter with him?'

'He's fishing,' Tanya said.

'He looks like he is in great pain,' the grandmother remarked.

'He is a thinker,' Tanya explained.

'He is, in fact, sick in the head,' Zoya called from the stairwell, 'if not in body.'

'He is an idiot,' Olga said.

'Is that a fact?' Now the grandmother squinted at Yuri.

'Oh, yes.' Olga laid a palm solemnly across her bosom.

At this the grandmother exchanged a significant look with the mother.

'I know what you must think,' Olga said. 'But I have to face facts. Facts are the building blocks of larger truth. And what is truth but a tall tower casting a very long shadow? And what is shadow but a terrible darkness for some but a restful shade for others?'

Vitek unpeeled himself from the side of the building and strolled towards the women. 'This is what comes of applying oneself to the rigours of metaphor.' His voice acquired a well-lubricated quality and his English flowed smooth as motor oil. 'It makes people ask absurd questions.'

'Yes, but is that normal?' the mother asked.

'It's extremely normal. Better than that, it's as Russian as birch bark shoes, I assure you,' Tanya said.

'I assure you,' Vitek mocked gently.

'Right.' Tanya wiped her hands along her skirt. 'It's been a long day packed full of, er, sights. Let's see the rooms now.'

She steered the women towards the stairwell. It looked as if they might follow, too, the grandmother double-timing it behind Tanya, the mother behind the grandmother, and the long-legged daughter behind her mother. At the rear, Yuri had dropped his rod and shouldered up their many bags. But then the grandmother stopped short. Mother collided with grandmother, daughter against mother, Olga into the winged rump of the girl and Yuri into Olga. All of whom were overtaken by the baggage, which flew, as fate or luck would have it, to the foot of the heap.

'What is that?' The grandmother wrinkled her nose and pointed to the heap.

'We don't have regular sanitation service. Therefore, it is customary for us to throw our rubbish out the window.'

'Is that what I'm smelling?' The girl pinched her nose.

Just then the twins, Good Boris and Bad Boris, emerged from the open chasm. They circled the luggage, their heads lowered, their teeth bared. Good Boris unzipped his trousers and peed on the mother's leather suitcase. Or quite possibly it was the grandmother's suitcase. It was hard for Tanya to say with certainty. She was far too distracted by the twins' teeth, which were definitely longer and sharper today than they were yesterday.

'Do they bite?' the girl asked.

'No, but they throw rocks and metal scrap pretty well,' Tanya conceded.

'Whose children are these?' The mother turned to Olga.

'Nobody's. That is, to date, no one has claimed them,' Olga said.

'They are community property,' Vitek added. 'The future of our great country.'

The twins straightened and Good Boris adjusted his zip. Bad Boris bent from the waist in a stiff half-bow.

The grandmother walked purposefully towards the children. Though she didn't speak a word of Russian, her posture conveyed with a clarity that needed no interpretation her firm intention; she would transcend any barrier – hygienic, linguistic, or otherwise. Her mission: this child. Not the one that had micturated upon her fine luggage. But this one, still bowing.

'Come here, child.' The grandmother bent and held her hand out as if coaxing a dog. 'Someone ought to be taking care of you.'

Bad Boris's gaze darted from one woman to the next. 'It is in the shape of the Lord God's emptiness that we are made,' Bad Boris said in perfect English, his pure tenor voice rising high as notes taking flight in a tall cathedral.

Just then Big Anna emerged from the hole, a bullhorn held

to her mouth. 'Queue up, you creeps! Buy your trinkets and authentic Siberian souvenirs here!'

'Pay no attention to her.' Tanya stepped between the women and the heap and the chasm and the girl, but the women moved towards Big Anna, pulled by a force Tanya could not name nor fathom nor stop.

The mother placed her warm hand on Tanya's wrist. Again with that warm and comforting gesture. 'Please tell me, dear girl, that these children don't live in that hole.'

'Why not?' Vitek smiled. 'It's prime real estate. Very spacious. Growing more so with every passing second. And the things these little shits are unearthing! Just yesterday I found a full set of dentures. Beautiful. You should really take a look.'

'Since when do these kids speak English? And with such grammatical precision?' Olga addressed no one in particular.

Now grandmother, mother and daughter all stood precariously at the edge of the chasm, each of them peering into the darkness.

'I can't see a thing. What's down there?' The girl craned her neck.

'Everything you covet!' the children screamed in unison. From their pockets they produced war medals and tiny metal icons, the kind soldiers going into battle wore around their necks, striped navy shirts, and the hats and stoles made of prized sable fur — not those made of soggy rabbit fur that smell of damp forests.

'Down there is everything elemental. Smokeless fire. Fear.' Azade walked the perimeter of the chasm. She lifted her nose and sniffed at the air with grave suspicion.

'I'll tell you what's down there. It's an old story. As old as east and west,' Olga said. 'It's a story about mud because that's where every story begins and every story ends. Beauty for ashes, the oil of joy for mourning, the garment of praise for the spirit of heaviness. Because mud is like love, constantly asserting itself. One day God awoke from troubling dreams and realized that He was lonely. He had mud in his beard and mud under his fingernails. And that's when He got an idea. Out of the mud He made man.'

'To the rooms!' Tanya cried, sweeping her arm in the general direction of the stairwell. If she could get them out of the courtyard, away from the chaos, then she could show them their lives behind closed doors, the lives as she wished them to be, as she wished them to see – the kettle whistling on the hotplate, the postcards from beautiful places on their walls, the claw-footed baths.

The mother straightened suddenly and waved her hand in the air as if conducting an orchestra. 'Such a punchy odour,' she observed. 'There must be a septic tank nearby.'

Vitek leaned in the direction of the hole and sniffed mightily as if his nostrils were as sensitive as a canary to coal gas. Tanya closed her eyes and inhaled deeply. And then she prayed. To her heavenly father. *Dear God, if you love me even just a little bit, make him go away.* When she opened her eyes it was just as she expected, things could not get any worse: Mircha stood beside the hole and was reading from a ream of papers tucked into an old philological textbook, the kind of material Azade normally doled out for use in the latrine. As Mircha finished with each page, he peeled it from the binding and let it fall, as a petal from a blowsy flower.

Mircha licked a finger, peeled another sheet from the stack and levelled his gaze on Tanya. 'The best story, by far, is yours, dear girl. A heartbreaker, too, a real three-hankie affair, five if you are easily moved. Imagine a girl haunted by her mother. The mother was water and her daughter was air. Even though the two were elementally composed of the same matter, at all times they were fundamentally separate.'

'Don't listen to him,' Azade said to Tanya. 'A fool will say anything.'

'What the girl knows about her mother could fill a thimble,' Mircha continued, completely ignoring Azade's hex-eye glares. 'What she can remember weighs less than a cobweb. Only this: pink rushes of blood behind her mother's fingernails, the soft warm hands and the skin that smelled of woodsmoke.'

'The smell!' The grandmother fanned the air around her nose. 'It's getting worse.'

Tanya hands shook. 'We better keep moving,' she said between clenched teeth.

'Don't you want to know where your mother is?' Mircha pitched his voice towards Tanya. 'Don't you want to know how your story tangles up with hers? I'll bet she's down in this hole with every other unanswered question. Don't you want to know how to live this life abundantly?'

'Enough!' Azade approached the bench with her shovel in hand. 'What makes you think you can tell any of us how better to live?'

'What's she saying?' The mother turned to Tanya for a translation.

'Is she talking to us?' The girl seemed moved, at last, to curiosity.

'What is that woman doing?' Now the grandmother gripped Tanya's arm. 'Why is she waving that shovel around?'

'It's hard to say.' Tanya heard her own voice coiling tight, tight.

'Well, let's reason together.' Mircha tucked his sheaf of papers into his waistband and withdrew a plastic vial of nail-varnish remover. 'You've tried your old housewives' tricks before and not one of them has worked. That's always been your problem, failure to accept complete reality. You see, you can't really make me go away because it's not part of the story. You need me. I am the conflict, the plot complication. I am utterly necessary.' Mircha took a healthy drink.

Azade gripped the shovel handle. 'Let me tell you a story of weight and spectacle. Some people call it the Invention of Zero but I call it the Immeasurable Importance of Wising up to Oneself. One summer all the cucumbers in a man's field went bad. The leaves on the man's prized Persian Ironwood turned black as ravens and then, one day, grew wings and flew, carrying off his ancestral stories and history beyond the four points of a map. He had counted all that could be counted – buckets, stars, wives, feet, lakes, words and devils – and still came up empty. There was nothing to fill that yawning expanse, and so he ate a cabbage, the last one on the last hill of his property.'

The grandmother tugged on Tanya's sleeve. 'Is that woman mad? Is there something we should do to help her?'

'Is there another staircase we can use to get to our rooms?' the mother asked.

All this English and Russian flying willy-nilly from window to broken concrete, mud chasm to heap. The noise and commerce and questions and stories – subversive and malicious – knocking knee to hip to ear. It was enough to throw Tanya into a full spin.

Sensing her suffering, the girl, an expert on the subject, touched Tanya's elbow. 'What's that lady talking about? Tell us.'

Tanya turned to the girl. 'You asked for this,' she said balefully. And then she translated word for word Azade's story.

'The cabbage spoiled inside of him. It curdled his blood and even his very thoughts to the point that even if he wanted to think good, he thought ill, even if he wanted to do right, he did wrong. Everything he touched became contaminated. On shearing day, a time of rejoicing, he shut himself in his house because otherwise the pregnant ewes lost their lambs and the horns of the rams withered on their heads. If the man went fishing, the fish swam sideways and in spring would forget the rivers of their youth. Meanwhile that cabbage in his stomach continued to grow, as if it had a mind and will of its own. Old women teased him mercilessly, for he looked like a woman carrying a terrible burden. The man became weary with this souring weight that pulled his sinew from bone, joint from socket, pulled his body towards the ground. You may be wondering what this man ever did to deserve such luck, and the answer is not so simple. Because the man was like a jinn, or maybe something worse. More air than earth, he was a man in search of new skin to inhabit, new stories to wear. This was why he felt so empty, this was why everything he touched became cursed. But he was not without some charm. He could still talk up the requisite threesome for a round of drinking. And he had a knack for telling stories.'

'This is the strangest story I've ever heard,' the mother mumbled to no one in particular.

Mircha brightened. 'I like this man. But the story – what a mess! It has no complication. No dramatic rise. No denouement. Terrible,' he pronounced, bringing the vial of nail-varnish remover to his lips.

And here Tanya paused. For Azade, now a mere metre away from Mircha, had raised the shovel high. 'Every story, good or bad, must have an end,' Azade said, and swung the blade down hard across his shoulders. Mircha doubled over.

Azade brought the shovel down again and again, breaking bones with every blow. And Mircha, with each blow, sunk a little deeper into the mud. But his mouth worked as well as ever as he registered each hit with a bitter complaint: 'My knees! My shoulder! My back!'

'Why is she doing that?' the grandmother asked.

'She's thrashing the mud. Very routine part of spring cleaning. It brings good luck,' Olga explained.

'Is this normal?' the mother asked.

'Very,' Olga replied. 'We each of us are like olives. Only when we are beaten, trammelled, and utterly crushed do we yield up what is essential and what is the best in us.'

Mircha flailed. 'A story is an arrow, dear girl. It always flies true and once it is spoken it can't be taken back! Tanyechka! Ask me what your future holds. I might tell you!'

Azade handed Tanya the shovel. 'There's on old mountain saying: the man is the head but the woman is the neck.'

Tanya gripped the handle. Her rage, white hot and boiling, the rage she fed with chewing gum and self-loathing, had not evaporated into cloud or into nothing as she had hoped. It was still there, in her arms, her hands. She did not hate this man with his overachieving mouth. She had never allowed herself to hate anyone. Passive by nature, she lacked the energy for pure hatred. But she hated his words, each one a stinging nettle. How dare he taunt her with her knowledge of Marina, her mother, the one subject everyone in the courtyard knew they were never to discuss? How dare he ruin this one chance with the Americans and their no-strings-attached money? Tanya lifted the shovel, so light now in her steady hands it seemed to rise in the air of its own accord. And then it arced, level and straight, and connected with a solid crunch against Mircha's shoulder. The bad one. Mircha yelped. Tanya swung again, this time against the backs of his knees.

'She should have done this a long time ago,' Olga whispered in a confidential tone to the grandmother.

The girl turned to Vitek. 'What is going on here?'

Vitek circled a finger at his ear. 'Beats me. But listen.' Now Vitek had his arm draped over the girl's shoulder. 'You're cute and I'm lonely. Let's you and me go to a club I know run by some very close personal friends of mine. We'll waltz on champagne, we'll feed dancing bears, eat reindeer meat and caviar. We'll...'

'You are utterly repulsive in every way.' The girl shrugged out of Vitek's loose embrace and charged for the bench where Zoya sat, her colour wheel of hair dyes fanned over the stone.

Finally, Tanya threw the shovel at the mud. She rested her hands on her hips, her chest heaving. Mircha lay broken and silent on the surface.

The grandmother consulted her watch. 'If we hurry, we might make the evening train to Ekaterinburg.'

'You're leaving?' Tanya asked in despair.

'You're going east?' Azade and Olga asked in unison.

'Oh, don't go there,' Tanya begged.

'The wolves,' Olga said.

'The thinly veiled malevolence,' Vitek called out.

'The tasteless art,' Zoya chimed.

'The wild savages,' Lukeria hooted. 'Jews, and Russians of Asian Aspect.'

'Give us another chance,' Tanya begged.

'Give! Give!' the children shrieked.

'Clearly we've come at a bad time.' The grandmother gripped the suitcase handles. 'And we have so many other museums to see.'

CHAPTER SEVENTEEN

The Americans of Russian Extraction for the Causes of Beautification stood on the kerb, leaning towards the traffic, their shoulders brushing against one another. Beside them, their baggage reflected their tired and threadbare state. A latch had been damaged in transit, the teeth of a zip pulled from its track, and mud spackled the broad sides. A light rain began to fall, pulling down the sky in particles of thick-grained pollution. The rain and grit had overwhelmed the willpower of the girl's high-altitude hair and it hung sullenly in her eyes. This she seemed to take as a personal slight.

Tanya stood a few paces down traffic, wiggling her fingers, as if they were a lure on a line. A last, she flagged a ride, this time a battered blue Lada. Not all of their luggage fit in the trunk and several pieces had to be tied to the roof rack. But some good news: there was just enough room in the backseat for mother and grandmother and, if she didn't breathe too boldly, for Tanya. In the front seats, plenty of room for the girl and her long legs and, of course, for the driver, a young man who beamed munificently at the girl.

The women rode in silence. The driver engaged the

windscreen wipers, an outrageous luxury for such a car, and together they watched the wipers smear the sky across the screen. Tanya was grateful for the wipers' rhythmic whine, for the squeaks piercing the steamy silence between herself and these women whose disappointment was as thick and palpable as the grit spread across the windscreen.

They had wanted to see a museum that resembled those on postcards, a museum like the Hermitage with perhaps a miniature golden carriage and maybe even a Fabergé egg. They wanted wide rolling rivers and green fields, or maybe yellow ones of mustard or wheat, sunshine and violins. They had wanted, Tanya realized, to see a Russia that existed only in dreams their grandmothers dreamed and perhaps had never existed at any time – ever. Well, in paintings, perhaps. What they had been shown far and away went beyond the neatly contained disrepair that they had hoped to remedy within the four walls of the All-Russia All-Cosmopolitan Museum of Art, Geology and Anthropology.

'You must understand our position. You must grasp how difficult, how very awkward this is,' the grandmother said. 'But we must give where it feels good to give – where and how it feels right to us. That is the privilege of practising micromanaged middle-class benevolence,' she continued. 'And it's always been my contention that money is only as worthwhile and as useful as its recipient.'

'I understand,' Tanya muttered.

'I'm not sure that you do,' the grandmother continued. 'It

isn't that the exhibitions, the staging and lighting, the overall presentation and the concept behind them are inferior and unsalvageable, but it is *what* is exhibited inside your museum that falls so very short of the mark. Exhibits replicating Matisse's work, or Kandinsky or even Chagall – well, that would be acceptable, in your case, laudable. But you must understand, a savage display of humans preserved in glass jars – that's grotesquerie, not art.'

'We are enterprising, absolutely. We put our hearts into our art,' Tanya said dully.

'Your gum and cosmetics, too,' the girl observed.

'It isn't that we don't find the human body palatable.' The mother carefully splayed her fingers over the fabric of her pant suit stretched tight across her knees. 'It's just that some forms are more palatable than others.'

'So, it must be clear, even to you, that when we speak of art and its upkeep, the preservation of the artistic aesthetic, we – that is, you museum people and us – are speaking of something entirely different.'

'And then we must consider what kind of people you are,' the grandmother continued.

'The savage way in which you live and call normal.' The girl aimed her athletic knees in the direction of a gutted trolley that now blocked the road.

Tanya's hands lay limp in her lap. She could say that at least they had TV. They had Turkish tobacco. They had their collective grand and shameful past they shared in every bowl of soup they ate. They had each other. They were living life as well as they knew how. It may not be rich, this way of living, but it was honest, much more so than any exhibition she could show them. At last, Tanya opened her mouth. 'Whether we are savage or civilized, I can't say. But we are authentic, this much I know.'

'We can see how grim the palette of your situation is. It isn't as if we haven't eyes in our heads,' the grandmother said.

'Or hearts in our chests,' the mother chimed. 'We want to help. That's why we've come.'

'So, we still have a chance – is that what you're saying?' Tanya hated the pleading sound her voice had acquired, how very much like Mircha begging in the mud she sounded.

The grandmother's jaw set in a way all too familiar, in a way that transcended linguistic boundaries. 'We'll send a letter announcing our decision.'

The mother patted Tanya's knee. 'We'll write.'

At this, a supreme silence fell inside the car.

At the train station Tanya and the driver lugged the baggage up the many steps to the platforms. The eastern-bound train sat ready on the tracks. Beside the carriages the sturdy blue-skirted conductresses inspected tickets and stood by, watching passengers struggle with their bags. When the conductress overseeing the sleeper car saw Tanya, saw the oversized luggage, she frowned. It did not look good for the luggage. It did not look good for Tanya, who would have to explain to the American women why it was necessary to buy extra tickets for the luggage. But Tanya needn't have worried; the women stood together on the platform, blissfully unconcerned what troubles their largesse would cause.

'Here, whatever the fare is for ourselves and our luggage, this should take care of it.' The grandmother pressed several bills into Tanya's hand. Too many bills. 'Whatever is left over, give to those poor kids living in that hole.'

Tanya whirled sharply on her heel, grateful for a quick dismissal. Grateful for quick generosity. Angry that a woman who had so much could not have given more. She purchased the tickets and pocketed the change. As she turned for the women she was again reminded of how very much like wooden dolls they were – outwardly lacquered and brittle, inwardly hollow and unfinished somehow. But whereas before, at the airport, they stood so as to occupy as much space as possible, now they huddled together in such a harmonious closeness that Tanya was jealous. Then she felt ashamed of her jealousy. And then, as quickly as it had come, the envy left, leaving only the sooty taste of pure defeat in her mouth. All of which sent her mind reeling back towards the fibrous grey colour of a cloud overstretched. The colour of a shrug. An echo bouncing from corner to corner inside a very large church. The texture of a shadow in early May. The things people remember and will never forget for as long as they live.

She would have written all this down, but the cloud note-book was nowhere to be found. A good thing, really, or she might have missed seeing the grandmother's slight nod, or maybe it was the mother's exhale, an instinctual cue signalling movement. The women linked arms, a completely Russian thing to do, so Russian, so familiar that Tanya almost missed the inky blue wings on the girl's hips unfurling. Pegasus trembled, lifted, took flight, and carried the women up, up, up the carriage steps and through the narrow aisle to their Class K sleeping berth, which, as luck or fate would have it, faced the platform where Tanya still stood, waiting. They looked at each other through the window. It seemed right to Tanya to say goodbye then, though she couldn't imagine quite how to say it without sounding angry, wearied by their visit, or worse, relieved to see them go.

Finally the grandmother slid down the window.

'I can see that you are disappointed, and I don't blame you, dear girl. You are a victim of circumstances. We don't think any less of you than we did before.'

'You could try again in two years. Perhaps with changes in the museum and, er, elsewhere, you'd have a stronger chance,' said the mother, warmth and hope curling the ends of her words.

'I don't believe in chance or luck. Not anymore.' Tanya wagged her head balefully from side to side. 'I've been told that this is a great lack in my repertoire of social conversation and quite possibly an indicator of moral and imaginative failings as well.'

The grandmother squinted at Tanya. 'How old are you?'

'Twenty-four.'

'Oh.' Her voice dampened. 'You have plenty of time for moral failure, dear.'

The train jolted, then slowly began to glide away. Tanya lifted her hand in a limp wave, but the women had already turned their faces eastward towards the tracks. In the set of the grandmother's jaw Tanya could see the recalibration of her charitable vigilance narrowing on new sights. In the mother's face Tanya saw exhaustion. In the girl's face, soft as dough still rising, and fringed now with fallen hair, Tanya could not read a thing.

The mother Tanya would miss, her motherly hand on hers. She would miss her open honest eyes, would miss a woman calling her 'dear' and meaning it. But Tanya could read how already in their bodies, in their forward gazes, they had moved on and she knew they could not see her there on the platform, standing on tiptoe, craning her head in their direction, and holding the sky by the handle of her umbrella.

Not far from the lime tree, Yuri lay half-dozing in his mother's claw-footed bath. The lead of his fishing line drifted over the watery skin of the enormous mud swamp that had overtaken the courtyard. The rain had stopped. The clouds, pushed hard by God's invisible hand, hovered now over the Kama River where the rain, tap dancing on the water, would bring out the fish. If only he had a little motivation, he might be there, now, fishing. Instead, Yuri watched Vitek emerge from a bank of smoke within the darkened stairwell. He observed how the kids squatting heapside were also watching Vitek's approach. The canine manner with which they licked their lips put Yuri's teeth on edge.

Vitek paused at the latrine, jostled the latch, then urinated at the base of the lime tree, not more than three metres from Azade's feet. Beside her sat Yuri's own mother, Olga, her gaze resolutely trained on the building which seemed to Yuri not to be sinking so much as it was pushing dark mud from the depth to the light, dredging from an unseen world. Displacement. A principle of physical science, but also of history, love, time and of anything else elemental and elementally tied to physical existence.

Vitek shoved his hands in his pockets. 'Where are the Americans?'

'Gone,' Azade said.

Lukeria coughed and coughed, her chest bent to her knees. 'They were getting on my nerves,' she managed at last.

'I liked the girl,' Vitek said. 'A little snooty, funny hair, but still.'

'What about their money?' Zoya exited the stairwell with a field chair tucked under her arm and a halo of magnesium red toxicity framing her head. Yes, her passions had been stirred and now she would sit and paint her nails with the angriest varnish she could find.

'Gone,' Yuri sang out.

'Who wanted their greasy hard-currency dollars anyway?' Olga asked.

'We did,' Zoya said, unfolding the chair.

Vitek withdrew a bottle of vodka from his waistband. As he drank, he grimaced as if he were taking in an ocean of pain one swallow at a time. When he'd had enough, he strolled towards Yuri and handed him the bottle.

'Drink,' Vitek said.

Yuri drank. Did he swallow a bomb? Or was it a stopwatch he was hearing? Because with that drink came that ticking again, this time from the pit of his stomach.

'I talked to Kochubey this morning. He said you never showed up.' Vitek's body threw a long shadow over Yuri. 'Survival demands that the individual sacrifice his sense of self for the communal group to which he belongs.' Vitek retrieved the bottle. 'I could drain this bottle in a single swallow, if I wanted to. Right now. But that would be selfish. Therefore, I abandon my selfish inclination and consider the group at large. The benefits of this action are manifold.' Vitek took another long drink.

'What benefits are those?' Yuri squinted at Vitek.

Vitek smiled. 'Who's talking here, me or you?'

'You.'

'So, OK. You'd rather not do certain things. I understand. But survival demands that at times we do things that are contrary to our wishes or liking.' Vitek handed back the bottle.

Yuri drank silently.

'Do you see what I'm getting at?' Vitek's voice held an edge.

Yuri blinked. It was so hard to think around all the noise within and without.

'What?'

'You should have gone to see Kochubey when I told you to.' As he spoke, Vitek's gold-capped teeth caught the last of the afternoon light.

Yuri took another drink from the bottle. 'I'm not going.'

'What?'

'I'm not going to see Kochubey. I'm not going to re-up. I don't care how much money I could get.'

Vitek's smile vanished. 'Maybe you should think about what you're saying. It's the hasty word that gets a man into trouble.'

'I have thought about it.' Yuri squinted at the kids approaching now on hands and knees. They had a mangy rabid look about them. In school, which one? Number 130? Yuri had learned from his science instructor that the human mouth is the source of all contagion. One bite, a wayward finger caught between overambitious canines, say, and your whole hand would be infected with bacteria. The hand would swell until the fingers split. You could even die from it.

'This isn't about you. This is about the group.' Vitek nodded at Zoya in the field chair. 'Let's face facts. Your net worth is limited to certain profit-producing enterprises. Fishing isn't one of them. The least, the very least you can do for your mother, for your beautiful girlfriend, for everyone in any way associated with you is to go and fight. Now. For Mother Russia.'

Tick. 'But I could die.'

Zoya blew on her slick fingernails. 'You would die a hero. Wouldn't it be wonderful?' Her smile, a kind of ovation, a glorious but terminal shining just before the open door shut.

Vitek winked at Yuri. 'You see, she understands sacrifice.'

Tick.

'Maybe,' Yuri conceded. Certainly she understood leanness of affection. Also she knew how to catch crayfish in winter. That is to say, she was clever. She recognized the appalling shortage of age-appropriate men who were intact in the essential ways a man must be in order to start and maintain a family. Hey, he may be an idiot, but he wasn't a fool. Hers was a practical love forced from necessity and desperation. But, Yuri wondered as he took another drink, was that real love or merely pragmatism wearing an affectionate face? Yuri sat up in the bath and reached for his helmet.

'This is the only way, Spaceboy.' Vitek helped Yuri out of the bath, then pressed his forehead to Yuri's.

'I've racked my brains thinking it through. I even almost managed to have one of your kidneys harvested – for the greater good, of course – but there were certain equipment shortages to consider. So believe me when I say this war is the only way to realize your full potential.'

It may have been his imagination, but whereas the building once had five storeys, Yuri could now only count four. The unoccupied ground floor had disappeared entirely. Yuri tipped his head, recounted. Yes, it was gone. Sunk, he decided, under the weight of its many contradictions. And then there were the kids, bless them. Hunkered behind Vitek and looking long of tooth.

Yuri pulled free from Vitek's arm. 'I told you. I'm not going. I don't want to come home in a zinc coffin with a red star.'

Vitek paled. 'Listen, you stupid zhid. Who do you think you are? Who gives a shit what you want? I'm in up to my ass with Kochubey. You have to go. I'll kill you myself if you don't.'

Yuri smiled. A man condemned twice has nothing to lose. If he goes and fights, he will die. If he stays behind, he'll be killed. Should he escape imminent death, he will certainly die at some later date. Everyone does. Yuri straightened, utterly liberated by the existence of so much possibility. How free he felt! Inwardly he soared, though outwardly he was falling down down down under the pounding of Vitek's hard fists.

'For God's sake!'

Yuri lifted his head. It was Mircha calling out, Mircha still giving advice from his dark warren of mud, Mircha bleating willfully like a broken alarm clock. 'Be a man!'

Be a man. Isn't that what he wanted, all along? To know who he was and how to be? A man who knows the value of his own life. A man who will defend that life. His muscles remembered what his mind could not. Yuri pushed himself to his knees, pushed himself to his feet, the whole time keeping his back to Vitek, dear Vitek, who'd always been a slack-jaw mouth breather. One kick, a sloppy donkey kick, and Vitek went down. And that was the signal the kids had been waiting for. As Vitek fell, they bore down, tightening the ring of their circle. It was every man for himself, and Yuri – call him a coward and he would gladly agree – fled for the nearest bath.

CHAPTER EIGHTEEN

By late afternoon, the sun was a low-wattage bulb hung from a short string, sinking into a purple bank of clouds. Lukeria, Azade and Olga sat side by side on the waiting bench and gazed at the oversized pieces of luggage resting in Lukeria's claw-footed bath. There were four baths in the courtyard now, all four of them filled with suitcases, books, glass jars of pickled cabbage, and iron pots. Koza, never happier, stood by a tub and gnawed at the handles of Olga's ancient valise.

The apartment building had sunk, or perhaps the mud had risen. It was hard to say, for the heap was gone now, and with it, Mircha. Like the wooden figurehead jutting from the prow of a doomed vessel, he disappeared first by feet, then hips, and torso, and finally, the mud folded over his lone arm reaching for the sky. He was at last put to rest, but not altogether quiet, for Olga and Azade and even Lukeria could hear the soft burring of his snores.

Which in no way competed with Vitek's loud yelps. Good and Bad Boris had pinned Vitek against the lime tree. With deft and quick movements, Big Anna tied him fast to the trunk while the red-haired boy swabbed iodine circles on Vitek's abdomen. Where the boy found the iodine and how he knew precisely where the vital, harvestable organs were located, Azade could not even begin to guess.

The women listened to Vitek cajoling, bargaining with the children as the building lost another floor and their horizon gained another five or six metres.

'Maybe we should do something,' Olga suggested at last.

'For thirty years, I've smelled the future in his shit,' Azade said. 'They won't hurt him. At least not badly. They're having far too much fun tormenting him. Besides,' she said, exhaling. 'I am tired of helping a boy on whom all help is lost.' Azade's chin trembled. And then her shoulders caved.

Olga linked her arm through Azade's. 'There is some good in him. Somewhere.'

'If so, those kids will find it. Eventually,' Lukeria observed.

Azade wiped at her eyes with her handkerchief. 'Nobody knows sorrow but the mother of a son.'

Lukeria shook her head from side to side. 'At least you have your son. He is here. That is some comfort. What do I have?'

Olga brightened. 'Your suitcases. Your maps and railway schedules...'

'Nostalgia is a bitter taste in the mouth.' Lukeria waved her hand towards the mud. 'I pushed those suitcases into the hole.' Lukeria squinted at the chasm as if seeing it for the first time, as if she'd just realized the finality of what she'd done. A loose rumble grew in her chest, a phlegmatic sound that immediately gave way to a spate of coughing. With each cough her body curled another several centimetres. When she recovered her breath, her mouth was a flat line. 'I've felt autumn in the legs, winter in my blood, and now spring is in my lungs. I am ready for the next place.'

Olga nodded in agreement. 'None of us are getting any younger.'

'Which is not to say that I am unafraid,' Lukeria said.

'We are all afraid.' Azade scanned the horizon. When the end of the world comes, it will first burst at the seams. It will swallow what is no longer needed, leaving a landscape of water and mud, this much Azade knew. Sirens from an ambulance wailed from several street blocks away. In the newly opened horizon she spied a stand of birch she'd never before known existed. Beside the trees the old church of St Seraphim squatted in the mud. For many years the church had been used as a Komsomol meeting hall, and then, later, as a petting zoo. All that was visible now was the rounded dome, cracked like the shell of an enormous egg. The gold cross strung tight with guy wires on the dome still held, but whether it would make it through the night was anyone's guess. Somewhere to the north was the last standing Gulag tower and it, too, would sink to the mud and nobody would miss it.

Olga observed Yuri, still in the bath and half-heartedly casting and recasting in an attempt to snag a ladies' evening shoe. From the looks of the ferocious shank, she guessed it to be one of Zoya's. 'The worst has happened. It can only get better from here,' Olga said.

Lukeria's head wobbled over her knees. 'We live in a fallen world. As in collapsed. This world is a miserable place and it is only becoming more miserable.'

'The outward, visible world is miserable. I'll give you that,' Olga said. 'But there is an ocean of buoyancy in the unseen places of the human heart.'

Lukeria craned her head. 'What the hell are you talking about?'

'I am in love,' Olga stated.

'Olga Semyonovna!' Lukeria spluttered.

'I never smelled it on you – not even once!' Azade blinked rapidly.

'I myself just discovered it. Today, as a matter of fact.'

'This man, he's not rich,' Lukeria said.

'Heavens, no!' Olga laughed. 'But he is clever. He has managed to obtain an idiot card in the third degree for Yuri.' Olga withdrew the card from her bosom.

'That is no small thing,' Azade said, her emotions again roiling like water in a pot over the ring. Every joy carries a shadow of a former sorrow. Sure, she was glad for Olga, for Yuri, that was the joy; the shadow, her loud and angry Vitek, bound to the lime tree and not a bit wiser for it. She could boil rice in her own tears, for all her weeping, but it would do no good.

'What about you? What will you do?' Olga ventured.

Azade raised her gaze to the listing radio tower and studied it for a long moment. 'The latrine is gone, my husband, gone, my son,' Azade wagged her head. 'I think I will go to the mountains. To Mount Kazbek. I have always wanted to breathe that air.'

'Look unto the rock whence ye are hewn,' Olga said.

'That's very nice,' Azade said. 'Did you compose that just now?'

'No. The prophet did. Isaiah.'

'He's got some talent.'

Lukeria rested her head on her knees. 'What about work?'

Azade kept her gaze at the skyline. 'You may not have ever guessed, to look at my hands, but there was a time when I could really cook. Soups, in the main.'

'Soups!' Olga exclaimed.

Azade pointed her chin towards Olga. 'As a matter of fact, I have been meaning to ask you. For months now. About your soup – you know, the one you made for the wake.'

Olga lowered her head. 'A family recipe. I don't know why it burned.'

Azade nodded towards the building. 'I thought it was wonderful. I have never tasted such a soup.'

'It could have been a trouble with the heating ring, they are so temperamental in these buildings,' Lukeria offered.

The two women glanced at Lukeria and quickly looked away. It was as if those coughing fits had broken the woman's back, and her customary ill-will had been broken as well. Now they weren't quite sure how take her sudden and small gestures of goodness.

'And then it could be the recipe itself,' Olga said. 'After all, certain soups cannot suffer a change of continent. Not even a change of city. For instance, Gypsy salt is not the same as Jewish salt.'

Azade smiled. 'And a cabbage grown in the mountains tastes different from a cabbage grown in the flats.'

Olga nodded her head. 'Exactly! And the seasoning, you may as well know, comes from the cook's tears.'

'But if you cry too much or too often, the soup cannot bear it. This is why God sets a limit to one's sorrow, lest it become too bitter to serve to others,' Azade said.

'I have no idea what the two of you are talking about, but it's making me hungry,' Lukeria said.

Azade scoped the courtyard. Three baths, still there. One goat. Two pots. Several jars of cabbage.

As if reading her mind, Olga recited her ingredients list. 'You must throw everything in the pot and hold nothing back: shoelaces, potatoes, moss, boot blacking, vodka.'

'We don't have much,' Azade said. 'But we have those things.' Azade leaned forward and pulled at her boots. 'And we have plenty of spoons.'

Tanya took her time walking home from the train station. She would have to face Chumak, his starchy disappointment, his shiny forehead glowing pink, then burning red like the bulb of a thermometer. She practised different apologies, variations of the same theme, really. Nothing in this world was as sure and stable as anyone had once thought or hoped. She could say this. It would be true. Tanya surveyed the street. If all these wooden kiosks painted in the Byzantine colours of gold and cerulean blue and verdant greens of larch forests, if these hinged huts of colour and wax and lipstick and smoked herrings pounded flat as an onion skin could slide off the pavement into wide flats of a deep and bottomless black, then what made her think the museum wouldn't be halved, then quartered, then completely taken by the mud, their best exhibits gone? Even the bright blue and orange Aeroflot recruiting office was not immune to sudden shifts. As she walked past the headquarters, Tanya peered through the small windows. Where she would have expected to see Head Recruiter Aitmotova dusting glossy brochures with a handkerchief, Tanya saw instead that a man and a woman, both of them wearing blue tracksuits and new trainers, had taken over the office. Open Aeroflot application forms littered the floor and a few caught in the updraught swirled like bits of paper inside a glass globe. The man caught a piece of paper as it whirled by and he wiped his nose on it. A single display shelf held three open relief boxes full of individually wrapped sugar-iced fruit slab from the UK, a jar of red peppers bearing the label 'Good', a can of flake coffee stretched with powdered milk, and three rolls of Very Soft, the most highly sought-after toilet paper in all of Russia. The prices had been marked in black wax on a white placard and when she made out the prices of items, Tanya jumped back as if she'd been stung by a wasp. Only criminals could become successful business people. Tanya understood that ordinary people like her would never fare well in a world like this one.

Tanya pulled her scarf tighter around her head and walked even slower than before, her shoulders collapsed under the weight of her iron-clad dreams. And then, too, it was really important to mind where she stepped – the mud was just that aggressive. With each step it tugged at her boots and she had to fight, pulling and thrashing to shake free. Never in her memory of spring thaws had the ground been this greedy. She rounded the corner of her street where bulges of mud pushed over the kerbs and up against ground-floor windows. The stone archway had crumbled. In the courtyard the situation had rapidly deteriorated. Only the top floor of the building remained visible above the mudline. On the roof, which was so low now that she could see every passing change on the wet canvas of sky, the heating stack and TV tower leaned at an unnatural angle. It was hard to look at the building and not think of sinking disasters: the *Titanic*, the *Komsomolets*, the *Karluk*.

Adding to the devastation was her grandmother packed tight between Olga and Azade on the bench. When they saw her, Azade and Olga did their best to make room for her, wedging their bodies into Lukeria, whose gaze was fixed on the widening hole and the bright, hard country deep within.

Tanya perched her backside on the open space of bench and

listened to Azade and Olga discussing vegetables – namely, the prowess of the parsnip over the turnip when boiled side by side in a pot. Four claw-footed baths anchored the corners of the courtyard. Into the one nearest the bench, the women had stowed all of their earthly belongings. The heap was gone entirely, as was the latrine. Zoya had vanished, along with her fleet of high heels. But Vitek remained, lashed tightly to the lime tree.

'Hey, Fatty!' Vitek called. 'Man cannot live on bread alone. For ten roubles I'll gladly explain what that means.'

Tanya studied Vitek. A splintered broom handle and bits of cardboard had been strategically stacked around his shoeless feet. Obviously he'd been thrashing for some time. Sweat and cheap hair dressing ran down the back of his neck and his hands were chafed where they were bound. Quite likely he'd never worked so hard at anything in his whole life. Not far from Vitek stood Good Boris, both his feet stuffed into one of Vitek's dress shoes. Bad Boris wore the other shoe. The twins stood side by side, jumping like pogo sticks. The boy with the hair the colour of a pollution sunset and the girl Anna kept their gazes on Vitek.

'You are tied to the tree,' Tanya observed at last. 'You are in no position to barter.'

Vitek smiled. His bronze skin had taken on a sharp brassy colour. She couldn't be sure whether it was due to the sudden shock of sun or something else more primal, like rage or fear. Vitek opened his mouth.

'Blessed are the poor in spirit. They shall inherit what is left of the earth. Blessed are the ignorant. What they can't know they won't miss. Blessed are...' Vitek yelped and whipped his head to the side. A chunk of concrete smashed against the trunk of the tree. And then came another rock, this time catching Vitek. An angry gash opened above his left eye.

Tanya felt her stomach fold and her face turn pale as a rusk.

'Well, excuse me, but a man will bleed,' Vitek said, maintaining that smile.

'This life,' Big Anna leveled her watery pink eyes on Vitek's, 'what's it for? Tell me the truth now.'

'Tell us what we want to know,' Gleb said, raising a plastic water bottle filled with rock and rusted metal. 'Or else.'

Vitek attempted a laugh. 'Why don't you go and blow up a skip or something?' Vitek pumped his shoulders and tried to work a hand free. 'Or how about this – I've got a pack of herbal cigarettes in my coat pocket. Why don't we go and smoke ourselves silly? It'll be therapeutic.'

'Give us cognac,' Good Boris said, hopping a few metres closer to Vitek.

Bad Boris closed the gap with a single jump. 'Now,' he said. The twins kicked out of the shoes and circled the tree. Their teeth! Definitely longer and sharper now than last week. And was that foam in the corners of Big Anna's mouth?

'Kids.' Vitek smiled weakly and hooked his chin towards Tanya. 'They've got the entrepreneurial spirit. But they're amateurs. They're in way over their heads.' Vitek freed a hand.

And not a moment too soon. Big Anna lobbed another chunk of concrete.

Vitek ducked and the chunk sailed past his head. 'Listen, you little glue-sniffing shits. I taught you everything you know.' And here Vitek yelped, a sound of genuine pain, for a whole fleet of smooth objects and edged, flat and round objects, forks and spoons, ladies' compact mirrors and men's bootjacks, rained down on him.

Tanya opened her umbrella and charged at Big Anna. 'Stop!' Tanya bellowed. And incredibly, the girl froze. Dropped the rock. Took a step backwards.

Big Anna looked at Tanya. Though her eyes were pink, smeared and bleary, there was something open, almost wholesome to them.

'The laws of prosperity permit the daughter to eat her mother,' Big Anna said. It was then that Tanya could see that she was wearing Zoya's most prized out-of-door high heels.

Just then Vitek worked his other hand loose. And it was as if some kind of spell had been broken or temporarily suspended, for the children didn't seem to notice him backing away from the tree and smiling as he disappeared beyond the crumbled archway. Instead, they dropped their arsenal of rocks and circled Tanya, closing her in the ring of their bodies. Behind Tanya the women kept at their soft talk of vegetables, forging some kind of cultural compromise of history and God as understood through their making and consuming of certain soups.

'Look,' Tanya sighed. 'You're all smart kids. Each of you

has a bright future, er, somewhere doing something. Don't you want to go out and do some good – change the world?'

Gleb and the twins tipped their heads. Their eyes clouded, their pupils pinpointing in and out of focus.

'The past outstrips the future. The future consumes the past. All that is left is the present.' Big Anna had her hand on Tanya's umbrella. 'We don't want to change the world. We want to conquer it.'

Tanya shook her head, trying in vain to keep the words from finding her ears. These were not the sayings of a ten-year-old girl.

'All we have is what we can see. What we can take. And only what has been bought with blood has value,' the girl intoned. 'This is why suffering in the New Russia is the truest com-modity.'

Tanya's throat tightened. That their suffering had no better, higher meaning – unthinkable. Unbearable. Even if it were true, she would not say it. Not to this child. 'No,' Tanya shook her head slowly now, with deliberation. 'That's not true.'

'Then prove to me otherwise.' Big Anna let go of the umbrella and rolled up her sleeves. The twins, snuffling and oozing from their eyes and ears, closed in on the flanks.

'I can't. But I know that you are wrong. You have to be wrong,' Tanya said. 'All I have is what I have lived, what I've seen. And of course, my colour and cloud observations,' her voice trailed.

From behind the toppled archway came a horse-like combination of snorts and whinnies. Vitek. Laughing. At her. Tanya had never been so grateful for that laugh. Never so grateful for the way that noise instantly recast the spell.

Big Anna lifted her nose towards the arch. And then she was off, loping in long dog-like strides. Gleb followed, a piece of rusty cable dangling from his belt loops. Only Good and Bad Boris remained.

And Yuri, sitting upright in the far tub, woozy from an afternoon of a fisherman's sweet repose. He hooked a leg over the rim of the bath. Tanya helped him over, steadying him on a patch of solid ground.

Yuri lifted the visor. 'I had a dream,' he said. 'A bomb exploded in the ground. I was thrown clear. I sailed through the air. I flapped my arms and for a moment, I was flying. Until I fell. At which time, I died. The orderly, who looked a lot like Mircha, by the way, told me to take heart because nothing stays dead in Russia. And then I travelled from death to life, one windowpane of light at a time.'

'That was not a dream,' Tanya said. 'All those things really happened to you.' Tanya rested her forehead on his shoulder. Took in the smell of his dream-soaked shirt. 'You sailed through the air. In Grozny. For a brief time, you flew.'

'But I'm not dead.'

'No. You're very much alive.'

Yuri sighed. 'What a relief.' He turned his head first one way and then the other, taking in the open architecture of the courtyard.

'Where's Zoya?'

'Gone. I think.'

'Vitek?'

'Gone.' Tanya dusted the shoulders of his shirt with her fingers. A convoy of army trucks rumbled in the distance.

Yuri cranked his head sideways. He bent at the waist and slowly straightened.

'The ticking?' Tanya ventured.

Yuri grinned. 'Gone.'

Together they sat on the bench and watched Good and Bad Boris, paddling in the mud shallows. The boys scooped at the mud, flinging handfuls of it at each other. And they were laughing as only children do during pure play.

'Have you ever seen anything so beautiful?' Yuri slung his arm around Tanya's shoulders.

She thought of Big Anna, then. She wished that the girl could have seen what they were seeing now: the twins playing, the women sitting together on the bench, the sky unfurling in colours there were no names for, their building sinking. 'No,' Tanya said at last. Over the low and widening horizon they could see that other buildings were sinking, too. The old news building, the former KGB offices, the old pavilion of media and art, the prison, the All-Russia Museum – all of them, large concrete structures the ground could no longer shoulder. Strains of *Swan Lake* floated in the air.

'Look!' Good Boris elbowed Bad Boris.

'Listen!' Bad Boris hopped up and down.

The mud made a gulping sound as if it were drinking down the building, as though it had waited decades for this moment. Yuri and Tanya sat frozen, watching the slow spectacle. The metal heating vent snapped and the TV antenna, angled towards the horizon like the bowsprit of a ship, disappeared metre by metre. And after it went, the mud kept pulling with the same kind of steady patient force that would, some day years from now, push the bones of prophets, convicts and slaves to the surface. But for now there was only wet darkness breathing quietly. A darkness so deep that it could have been the same dark over which God hovered before there was anything. And from that deep came life. Light. Colour. Cloud and sky.

It could happen here too. Russia was just that kind of place. They could start over. In certain hills, Tanya knew, green shoots were already pushing through the soil. And the discovery that there could be something new, something better rising from the earth and that it started with them, with her and Yuri, was itself a cause for something like joy. And that she could even feel joy, that it could come crawling on knuckles and knees, come knocking this way was such an astonishment that Tanya had to surrender her analyzing, lest this feeling, so wholly unfamiliar and foreign, evaporate.

'What will happen next?' Yuri wondered.

Above them the news helicopters ploughed through the strange and shifting sky. With the horizon opened, Tanya imagined she could see cotton, the stuff of her dreams and

Yuri's, could see this visible realm breathing on the horizon, fainting, reviving, then fainting again.

Tanya closed her eyes. 'The inert elements will sublime. Certain stars will bow out. But the universe will keep expanding. Not long from now the sorrel will overtake spring. The wheat and mustard will volunteer along the verge. The fish will bite without even wondering why.'

Yuri pushed open his visor. 'That was very artistic.'

Tanya opened her eyes. 'Thank you.'

'Don't you want to write some of that down?'

'No.' Tanya breathed.

'What then?'

Tanya spread her fingers across the yoke of Yuri's shirt. 'Take off that ridiculous helmet.'

Yuri removed the helmet.

'Now,' Tanya leaned closer. 'Kiss me.'

ACKNOWLEDGMENTS

Endless gratitude to Philip Gwyn Jones, who brought this book into the world and never once doubted. Thanks to Julie Barer and Caspian Dennis for creating safe passage, and special thanks to Willing Davidson for his keen eye and kind heart. Deepest thanks to Jenna Johnson for making the impossible possible.

Grateful thanks to the National Endowment for the Arts, the John Simon Guggenheim Foundation, the Oregon Arts Commission, and Literary Arts, Inc., for awards that supported the writing of these stories.

My enduring thanks to the Luftmenschen for their collective wisdom, and to the Chrysostom Society.

Thanks to my family for their support, patience, and many prayers. Thanks also to Louise T. Reynolds.

Special thanks to Al and Carolyn Akimoff, Nathan and Sheree Johnson, Andrei Zoryn, Dale Tubbs, and Lana Serotsin for help with vital research.